P9-DVO-683

CALGARY PUBLIC LIBRARY

BY

MERVYN J. HUSTON

Tree Frog Press
EDMONTON

Tree Frog Press Limited
would like to express its appreciation
of the assistance granted by
the Film & Literary Arts Branch
of Alberta Culture

Canadian Cataloguing in Publication Data

Huston, Mervyn J., 1912 -
Gophers don't pay taxes

ISBN 0-88967-039-0

I. Title.
PS8515.U87G6 C813'.54 C81-091397-6
PR9199.3.H87G6

© Copyright Mervyn J. Huston, Edmonton 1981

No part of this publication may be reproduced or transmitted in any form or by any means, electronic or mechanical, including photocopy, recording or any information storage and retrieval system now known or to be invented, without permission in writing from the publisher, except by a reviewer who wishes to quote brief passages in connection with a review written for inclusion in a magazine, newspaper or broadcast.

5 4 3

Printed in Canada by Friesen Printers, Manitoba
Cover illustration & chapter illuminations by Norm Chaput

TREE FROG PRESS LIMITED
10144 89 Street
Edmonton, Alberta, Canada, T5H 1P7

This book is dedicated to Megan

TABLE OF CONTENTS

	Introduction	9
1	Blossom	11
2	The Embassy	21
3	No Lady	41
4	Humpty Dumpty	52
5	Wedding Bells	64
6	The Devil And Big John	76
7	Curtain Time	82
8	Bootleg Justice	93
9	Bible Bibble	111
10	Santa Had A Hangover	120
11	The Venetian Affair	131
12	A Hero One Day, A Bum The Next	149
13	The Other Side	160
14	Tea Party	173
15	Golf Is A Four-Letter Word	183
16	The Great American Lover	205
17	Give A Dog A Bad Name	221
18	Poisoned Relations	230
19	Serenade	249
	About The Author	261

INTRODUCTION

BLOSSOM WAS AN UNTIDY, DUSTY VILLAGE in southeastern Alberta just north of the Cypress Hills; the nineteen-thirties were the days of the Great Depression. This was the time of unemployment, relief cheques, riding the rods, soup kitchens, drought and crop failures. Things were tough everywhere, but the farming areas of Alberta and Saskatchewan were particularly hard hit. It was an era that tried men sorely; they rose to the challenge or they went under. So did towns. Blossom met the test in her own unique, slaphappy fashion.

Towns, like people, have personalities of their own. The character of a town might be thought to be simply the sum of the personalities of the people living in it. But the situation is not quite that simple. A few strong or unusual personalities can give a place a flavour which is unique. Geographic and economic factors influence both the type of people who tend to settle in a particular area and the situations to be encountered. The interactions of the people of a community with each other and with their physical, economic and sociologic environment give a place its individuality. Some towns are coöperative, others divided; some are hard-drinking, others sober; some are sporty, others intellectual; some are happy, others morose. Of all the dozens of places I visited in travelling about the prairies, Blossom was my favourite. She showed great courage and vitality in meeting the economic vicissitudes of the day. But also she had a certain irrepressible, barmy charm about her which captivated me completely. The times were tough, but Blossom always wore a jaunty feather in her battered straw hat.

When George Ingraham first came to the town of Blossom in the Dirty Thirties to open a law office, he had a difficult time getting established. Not only did he have to contend with the depressed economic situation of the era, but with the tightly-knit community itself and its suspicions of strangers in general and lawyers in particular. He was also faced with the necessity of finding his proper place in the complex social hierarchy which characterizes small towns. In order to appreciate the problems facing George, it is necessary to know something about the times and the town and its people.

Chapter One

BLOSSOM

STRANGE AND SURPRISING THINGS tended to happen to Blossom. Plans seldom worked out the way they were supposed to. When disaster ensued, Blossom's sense of humour came through – she had a good laugh at her own expense and carried right on. However, more often than not, when plans went awry the results were better than the plans had called for. For example, when the citizens pooled their meagre finances to drill a well, no water was found but a supply of natural gas was discovered which provided the town with much-needed cheap fuel. The thick gumbo, which was roundly cursed every spring because it mired vehicles to the axles, turned out to be excellent for making bricks. As a result of this clay and the cheap fuel, Blossom was able to develop a small, but economically viable brick factory which comprised the town's only industry. Fred Peters, at one time, suggested Blossom's name be changed to Serendipity. Jeb Wilson, the local bootlegger, in describing the town's penchant for the fortuitous, quoted a western aphorism: "Blossom could fall down a privy and come up smelling roses."

My own involvement with Blossom at this time was occasioned by my peregrinations as a travelling salesman for a farm implement company. I didn't make many sales and most of those I did make were on credit which later evaporated. Much of my trade was in spare parts which were purchased in forlorn hopes of keeping decrepit machinery operating in some fashion. Since I covered all of southern Alberta and Saskatchewan in my battered old Star, Blossom was central to my district so I was able to spend a good deal of time there. I usually stayed at the Palaza Hotel, the town's only hostelry.

The hotel came by its unusual name, I was told, by an interesting mischance. Many years earlier, an itinerant painter had run up a substantial bar bill which he undertook to pay off by painting a sign for the hotel. He was apparently no great whiz as a speller, or was still under the influence of his indebtedness, because the sign came out Palaza. The hotel was stuck with the sign; the owner decided "what the hell" and went along with it. Palaza it remained.

An interesting feature of the hotel was its double-decker backhouse. There was no inside plumbing, of course, and since the hotel was two storeys high, a catwalk had been built to the upper level of the biffy. This was considered the ultimate in gracious living, because the roomers on the second floor didn't have to go downstairs to go to the bathroom. The structure had an ingenious architectural arrangement to permit the use of the upper facility without hazard to those on the lower level, although it was a disquieting experience to be below when someone was upstairs.

The reception room of the hotel served as a social centre for a regular group of the town's loafers. In the winter they sat around the huge potbellied stove, arguing, dozing and playing endless games of cribbage. In the warm weather they carried their chairs outside on the plank sidewalk in the shade of the wooden balcony which ran the length of the hotel. Here they were able to chat with passers-by and ogle the occasional woman who passed that way. During the summer the dowagers of the town avoided this part of the street if at all possible; they cringed at the murmured comment and snigger which followed their passing. The younger wenches flounced by with the gratifying assurance that they were being appreciated.

Another informal social centre was the pool hall where the young bucks hung out. They slouched there on the rickety chairs in endless hours of boredom, boasting about, or planning, amorous pursuits. They played pool when they had the money, which wasn't often. They were expert players, however, and woe betide any visitor who got suckered into a game with these local sharks. On Saturday nights when the farm boys came to town, the place was a hive of activity. The proprietor doubled as the town barber and was known as Pete the Barber – no one seemed to know his proper name. He played for the house on occasion and was an expert hustler in his own right.

One striking architectural feature of Blossom was the railway station, which was huge and remarkably well-appointed for the size of the town. It seemed an extraordinary facility to accommodate the one or two passengers a week who got on or off the train and to transmit the tiny bag of daily mail. The whole town turned out each day at the station to watch the six o'clock train go through. This was one of the dramatic events of the day. The train would come majestically into the station with the bell ringing, the whistle tooting, the brakes clashing and the steam chuffing and huffing. Oh, it was grand. The engineer always smiled graciously down at us from the cab with a regal wave of a gauntletted hand. The train gradually jerked to a stop with a great clanking of couplings and swishing of steam; the engine panted and huffed impatiently to be off again; Jerry Rusk, the postmaster, handed over his skimpy bag of mail; the conductor strutted importantly about, looked at his watch before hollering "All aboard" at the appropriate second; the engine leaped back into noisy life; and it was all over for another day.

But in the meantime, through the windows of the carriages, we had caught a fleeting glimpse of another milieu – a transitory contact with the big, wide, exciting world outside. The passengers gazing aloofly down from the Pullman coaches seemed creatures from another planet. The dining car, with its white tablecloths, shining crystal, gleaming silver and hovering waiters, represented an opulence which was a dream world out of the Arabian Nights. After this evanescent glimpse of sophisticated living we trudged back to our mundane affairs refreshed in the knowledge that not all life was harsh and niggardly. Maybe someday we also would participate in such lavish living. Maybe. Someday. When the Depression was over.

A less happy pastime associated with the railway was counting the number of transients on freight trains. Many of the trains were covered with men, like ants on a candy stick. Jerry Rusk claimed some kind of a record when he tallied over two hundred on one train. These were the jobless – grimy and discouraged, pathetic and forlorn. These were not bums or panhandlers; these were honourable men travelling about the country seeking desperately for work – any kind of work. The hundreds going east passed the hundreds going west. Futile. Tragic.

Sometimes a few men dropped off at Blossom to seek work, but there were no jobs to be had. Half the town was on relief and those who weren't made a living selling things to those who were. People did not go on relief willingly or happily – only when forced by necessity. These were proud and independent people who found relief humiliating and demeaning; but for many it was accept relief or starve.

Blossom took great pride in another remarkable structure which matched the railway depot for incongruous size and splendour. This was the government building which was known to the local inhabitants as The Embassy. This two-storey edifice took up half a block and housed various government offices including a spacious post office, liquor store, telephone exchange, RCMP headquarters, a jail, a courtroom, a customs office, and a posh facility for handing out relief cheques.

Dances and large social gatherings were accommodated in the Elks' Hall which had a kitchen in the basement. Smaller meetings, if of impeccable propriety, could be held in the church hall. The town had two restaurants: one was the Buffalo Grill in the Palaza Hotel, and the other Wong's Cafe operated by Wong Toy, a delightful, affable Chinaman. Sporting facilities consisted of an outdoor skating rink and a ramshackle building which housed two sheets of curling ice. There was also a baseball diamond on the edge of town. This was a dusty field known as Slaughterhouse Park because of an adjacent building where the local butcher prepared his animals. Efforts to impose the more elegant title of Petal Park were unsuccessful. The facilities at the park consisted of a sagging backstop of chicken wire, a few splintery bleachers, and two privies without doors.

There are no secrets in a small town. Everybody in Blossom

knew everyone else's business and discussed it freely. Social gatherings were primarily gossip exchanges because there was little else to talk about. Not all of the gossip was malicious by any means. There is a peculiar introspection to a small community, where the affairs of an individual are of personal interest and concern to everybody. This mutuality of concern had particular emphasis at this time due to the rigours of the Depression when everyone was struggling to survive. People helped one another to the best of their ability. It must be conceded, however, that the gossip exchange perked up when some spicy pecadillo was discovered or imagined.

One of the principal sources of information on local affairs was Mamie Sutherland, the telephone switchboard operator. There was no impropriety in Mamie's dissemination of news – indeed it was expected of her. She was in a position to know what was going on and was happy to keep people informed. The party lines into the country were a particularly rich source of information. Anytime you made a rural call you could hear phones clicking on for miles. A few people resented the lack of privacy but, in general, a trunk line was considered a communications network.

Mamie had one of the most delightful personalities I have ever known. She had a deep-throated, happy laugh which bubbled up from her ample bosom with a *joie de vivre* which was infectious and heartwarming. It was impossible to be sad in Mamie's presence. She was a tall handsome girl in her mid-twenties with a magnificent figure. Everyone loved Mamie. People making a phone call would have a chat with her and exchange gossip before giving her a number to call. Her switchboard was in the corner of the Embassy so she had a good view of the goings and comings of the populace. She served as sort of an informal receptionist for the businessmen of the community. If someone was going to be out of his office for awhile he would tell Mamie where he could be reached; if you couldn't contact someone at his usual phone you could ask Mamie where he was and she would usually be able to tell you he was at the bank, or post office, or pool hall, or whereever; if she didn't know she would phone around to find out. It also followed that if you were going to be doing something you didn't want noised about you'd better keep it from Mamie.

The social life of Blossom was structured on a caste system implemented by competitive cliques. Everybody who amounted to anything in the town was a member of some select group. It was not always obvious what governed the membership in a particular set. Factors which influenced these polarizations were: economic status, ethnic derivation, educational background, drinking habits, religious affiliations, and business interests. Not infrequently however, membership in a particular coterie would override these factors for no apparent reason. There was a strong matriarchal authority in these social circles which may account for the occasional illogicality. In general, the groups formed on the basis of relative compatibility and shared pretensions. The cliques once formed tended to be remarkably stable so there was little transition from one to another. The several cliques coöperated on matters related to the common good under the aegis of the Board of Trade, since the town was not large enough to have a Mayor or Town Council or other formal structure.

One of the major cliques, and the chief competitor to my own group, seemed to be drawn together by shared cussedness and acerbity. It was composed of: Ralph Morsh, the banker, a humourless, sour individual; Syd Hefflewait, who ran a grocery store and was so mean he wouldn't give you a drop of water if it were raining; Jerry Rusk, the dyspeptic postmaster; Mr. Fidge, the school principal, a self-important ass; and others of similar jollity. There wasn't a chuckle in the whole shebang but they seemed to get along tolerably well and were a power in the community.

I first got to know George Ingraham through my gradual acceptance into the clique to which he belonged. I became a member through my friendship with Fred Peters which had developed over many hours of trying to keep my old Star in running order. Fred operated a garage and service station. He was a good mechanic who had a talent for maintaining vehicles and farm machinery in working order on spare parts scavenged from derelicts; his services were therefore much in demand in the area. He was of English background although he had come to Canada as a boy; he had the quiet reserve and dry wit of that race. He was short and slim with a round head and buggy, inquisitive eyes.

Everything about him was neat, from his carefully combed hair and clipped mustache to his well-shined shoes. He even managed to keep clean when doing messy jobs about the garage. His wife, Audrey, was from Belfast. She was a plump, pretty woman with short, straight black hair and a happy nature.

By the time I arrived on the scene in Blossom, George Ingraham was already actively involved in community affairs and, to some extent, integrated into the social scheme of things. He was about thirty years old and a bachelor. He was tall and very thin with an angular, bony face; his thick, black hair formed a marked widow's peak, which, together with his saturnine cast of countenance, gave him a slightly Mephistophelian appearance. In repose his expression was severe and forbidding but this could change in a flash to one of great charm when he smiled. Like all lawyers he loved to talk, although when he was in one of his black moods he could be singularly uncommunicative; when the devil had his tongue he was best left alone. George had received classical musical training in his youth and would occasionally, when in his cups, perform with considerable virtuosity on the piano.

Mamie Sutherland was a member of our select group, partly by reason of her delightful self, but also because she was George's girlfriend. They had been "going together," as the natives put it, for some time in a relaxed sort of fashion but things had never progressed beyond this point despite broad hints and encouragement from all of us. I felt that Mamie was prepared for marriage, but George appeared to be reluctant to take the leap. Mamie, with her cheerful bubbling laugh and great good spirits, added a parameter of joy and fun to our gatherings.

Another regular couple in our tight little group were the Elliotts, Dick and Florence. Dick was manager of the brick factory and drove an Auburn car which put him in a class by himself. He had bristly grey hair and a heavily-lined face. He was slow-spoken, amiable and terribly bullied by his wife. Florence was still beautiful at forty with blond hair, big blue eyes and a peaches-and-cream complexion. She was English, which she never let you forget by repeated references to "home" and all the fine things she had given up to come to Canada; Blossom suffered sadly by comparison with Upswich-on-the-Puddly. She was a bit of a pain, but had a good heart. As befitted a representative from a more enlightened milieu she felt it encumbent upon her to endeavour to bring some aspect of gracious living to this benighted community. As a result she was the acknowledged cultural leader of Blossom and its admired and resented fashion plate.

Mal Morgan and his wife, Hortense, rounded out the regular membership of our little clan. Mal ran the local hardware store although he had done a variety of other things before settling down in Blossom. In contrast to the others in the group, Mal was poorly educated, boisterous and happily coarse. He was a huge man with a round, cheerful face and a shiny bald head. He had one cauliflower ear for which he gave a variety of explanations, including a wrestling match with Strangler Lewis, a kick on the head by a cayuse at a rodeo in Calgary, and a wallop with a chamber pot by an irate madam in Yellowknife. He loved to make naughty remarks to shock the ladies; he was certainly successful insofar as Florence Elliott was concerned, who found his vulgarity repugnant. Mal's wife, Hortense, a wispy little woman with her hair in a bun, thought Mal was wonderful. She giggled at his sallies and invariably said, "Oh Mal, you're just terrible." She came from a farm near Winnipeg. Mal claimed she was so ignorant when he married her, that she thought an Arctic char was an Eskimo cleaning woman. Mamie, of course, was a great foil for Mal's witticisms; she was in a constant state of humourous exuberance when he was around.

One small but formidable clique was a coven of religious females who terrorized the town with good deeds. The locals called them the Vested Virgins, or VV's for short. They served as the community's conscience and were ever alert to live up to their self-appointed responsibility of stamping out pockets of evil, such as children playing marbles on Sunday. They were high on rectitude but low on charity. They were also afflicted with a malaise, which Fred Peters called the Carry Nation syndrome, characterized by eruptions of vague demands for women's rights. Their queen harpy was Mrs. Frobisher, who felt that she alone had a pipeline to God. Her most famous contribution to the folklore of the community resulted from her sudden arrival at the church hall where a group of ladies were playing whist. She gazed around the room sadly and then said, "What a waste of time and the Lord coming." The phrase was much used thereafter with reference to any frivolous undertaking.

There were four churches in the town, although only one, the Presbyterian, operated on a regular basis; Reverend Slye came to town from Swift Current once a month to hold services. Reverend Slye was a kindly, tolerant old gentleman with a craggy face stuck loosely on a scrawny neck. Since the town was primarily Protestant, most of the upper crust, of whatever affiliation, attended the services. Mrs. Frobisher supervised the Sunday school on a weekly basis and managed to inculcate an aversion to religion in most of the youngsters which lasted them all their lives.

Below the cliques of the upper classes there existed in the town an amorphous group of the proletariat who didn't matter in the social scheme of things. What these people did with their lives no one knew or cared particularly. There was also a subculture of outcasts which impinged only occasionally on the aristocracy. The chief representatives of this group were Flossy Macabee, the town prostitute, and Jeb Wilson, a moonshine distiller and bootlegger. Jeb would sometimes get involved with polite society, but Flossy never. For the most part the upper classes pretended such people didn't exist although making use of their unique societal contributions from time to time.

There were a number of citizens who fitted no particular category. These included: Grandma Akerbilt, who had come west in a Red River cart; Angus MacNab, another authentic old-timer who was said to be a hundred years old; Brother John, who was the leader of a religious community a few miles from town; and Miss Peabody, a slightly addled old maid. Also, no listing of the town's personalities would be complete without mention of Roscoe, Jeb Wilson's dog. Roscoe had a mixed ancestry from whom he had inherited all their worst traits of ill temper, uncomeliness and moral turpitude. Some place in his career he had picked up a scar which pulled one eye down and his mouth up. This gave his facial expression a sort of sardonic leer which reflected his attitude rather well. His ears were tattered from innumerable fights which had established him as the undisputed lord of canine society in the district.

This then was the town of Blossom and the people in it who gave the community its unique and delightful personality. And this was the milieu in which George Ingraham finally found his niche, although not without difficulty.

Chapter Two

THE EMBASSY

WHEN GEORGE ARRIVED IN BLOSSOM he did all the things a young professional man is supposed to do in a new environment. For one thing, he joined every organization in sight.

He promptly became a member of the Enthusiasts, the community's only service club, which met every Monday for lunch at the Palaza Hotel. When his musical ability was discovered, he took over playing the piano for the singsong which was an inevitable part of each meeting. News of George's musical ability was promptly conveyed to the wives of the members, so it was not long before he was approached by Reverend Slye to play the old footpump organ for church services. Up until that time, the organ had been played by Miss Peabody whose weak old legs had great difficulty in forcing enough air into the instrument to keep it functioning; the sound tended to disappear when she was concentrating on a difficult passage. Furthermore, she only knew about six hymns which the congregation were mighty sick of singing. Miss Peabody relinquished the post with considerable relief – a relief which was shared by the congregation.

George also joined the Board of Trade which brought him into the mainstream of the business affairs of the community. His legal training and administrative ability soon led to his appointment to some of the key committees; he tended to get the stinky jobs or those at which others had failed. He accepted this cheerfully as part of the process of integration into the business life of the town. It was one of these jobs, the chairmanship of the Post Office Committee, which gained him initial acceptance by his associates.

The work of this committee finally got Blossom's rather tangled geography straightened out, although the process stirred up quite a ruckus on the international scene. With Blossom's usual flair for the serendipitous she managed to come out of the exercise with a substantial bonus.

The ambiguity of Blossom's geographic whereabouts arose from the fact that the town was located very close to the Alberta-Saskatchewan border. When the railroad was first built across the prairies, the station and post office were located on the Saskatchewan side of the border. However, in the strange and unpredictable way of prairie villages, growth took place to the west on the Alberta side, so that eventually the whole town was located in Alberta with the only buildings remaining in Saskatchewan being the station, the post office, two grain elevators and a few abandoned shacks. Therefore, although the town was entirely in Alberta, all maps, railway timetables and other records showed it to be in Saskatchewan; all incoming mail was addressed to Blossom, Saskatchewan.

Blossom didn't really care whether it was in Alberta or Saskatchewan, but what annoyed the citizens was that the station and post office were now about a half-mile from the centre of town. Going that distance for deliveries or mail was bad enough in the summer, but in the winter at thirty degrees below zero with the wind blowing, the trip was a curse. Efforts to get these facilities moved into town came to naught. The railroad hinted strongly that if they were pressed on the matter the station would be closed. The citizens were bloody annoyed about the whole thing and wrote vigorous letters of protest to various governmental departments, all of which were ignored or fobbed off. During the Depression, governments were very reluctant to do anything that had any chance of costing them money. One year, to prove a point, the citizens of Blossom voted in both the Alberta and Saskatchewan provincial elections. Since that poll voted solidly against the incumbent governments, both of which were returned to power, Blossom did not endear herself to either capital.

At the first meeting of the Board of Trade which George attended, the whole problem was again discussed with considerable heat. After a couple of hours of useless breast-thumping, somebody got the bright idea of appointing George the chairman of a committee to investigate the matter. This proposal was enthusiastically endorsed by everybody with a deep sigh of relief. The other members of the committee were Fred Peters, Mal Morgan and Ralph Morsh, the banker. George didn't have the faintest idea what he was getting into but he accepted with alacrity, since he was rather flattered at being named chairman of such an important committee right off the bat.

The committee held a number of meetings during which most of the time was spent bringing George up to date on the background of the situation. George was dismayed at the difficulty of the problem to which they had been assigned since he didn't want to fail at the very first job the community had given him to do. One important bonus to George from these early meetings was the close personal relationship he established with Fred Peters and Mal Morgan. Despite, or because of, their marked differences of personality – Fred's quiet reserve, Mal's ebullient coarseness and George's cynical pragmatism – they got along very well indeed. Thus began a close friendship which lasted all their lives. Ralph Morsh was another kettle of fish. He was a sour individual completely lacking a sense of humour who regarded life with petulant acerbity. As Mal said, Ralph was as out of place in any group of jolly fellows as a condom in a collection plate.

George and his committee discussed and discarded a number of ideas on strategy. They decided that writing any more letters of protest would be a waste of time; a delegation to the government would get the same old run-around; an appeal to their member of parliament at either the provincial or federal level would lack any political attraction; pressure on the railroad might be counterproductive and anyhow they had nothing to use for pressure. They felt they needed some new dramatic approach which would get through the wall of governmental indifference. Finally George, in consultation with Fred and Mal, came up with the rather elaborate scenario which rocked the ramparts of empire. The three of them kept their plans from Ralph as they were sure he wouldn't approve of their tactics.

The scheme which they cooked up was as follows: they appointed themselves the Committee for an Independent Blossom and set out to prepare a brief for submission to both the Canadian and British governments asserting the policital independence of the State of Blossom. They did a substantial amount of background reading with George handling the legal research and Fred the historical studies. Then they got together and concocted an impressive document quoting legal precedents, constitutional authority and historical references in support of their proposition. When it was completed they mailed off copies to both governments and sat back to await results.

George told me the subsequent developments one night in our favourite hangout in the back of Wong Toy's restaurant. The events had transpired some two years before my first trip to Blossom.

The rest of this account is in George's words.

There was sufficient legal basis to the brief to lend at least a quasi validity to the proposition (explained George). The Indians of this area have never signed a peace treaty with the Canadian government. Thus, theoretically, the land from Blossom south to the American border still belongs to them. Our brief stated that our committee, representing the white settlers of the area, was about to enter into negotiations with the Indians to establish an independent conclave. The matter of the legal aspects of the aboriginal rights of the native peoples is far from clear at the present time and will eventually be a major problem to the Canadian government.

It was necessary to make the submission to both the British and Canadian governments since the authority for Canadian jurisdiction arises from the British North America Act. We timed the arrival of our submissions so that they were received in London and Ottawa on the same day. Our brief implied that we were prepared to consider remaining under the British crown if mutually satisfactory terms could be arranged, but the point was left somewhat moot. Within the British framework we mentioned precedents such as Hong Kong, Aden, Singapore and Tonga, but we rejected crown colony status. On the world-wide scale we made reference to Danzig, Monaco, Liechtenstein and Luxembourg. We suggested the possibility of an appeal to the League of Nations; and to give them the collywobbles properly, we hinted at the possibility of a treaty with the United States.

When they got our brief, the British Cabinet met in emergency session; so did the Canadian Cabinet. Westminster cabled Ottawa to find out what was going on. Ottawa replied that they didn't know, but were looking into the matter. The Prime Ministers of both countries phoned me as Chairman of our Committee. I reiterated our stand with a few embellishments. The British Cabinet went back into session, checked the map and dispatched a destroyer carrying a squad of marines to Hudson Bay, apparently planning to sail up the Saskatchewan River. When the Canadian government was informed of this action, they cabled back telling them to keep their goddamned boat at home – probably in more diplomatic language than that. The boat later got stuck in an ice floe in Hudson Strait, so that problem resolved itself. Cables continued to zip back and forth across the Atlantic – some of considerable sourness.

The Canadian Prime Minister phoned me again requesting that I take no action until he could send an emissary to discuss the matter with me. I agreed to do so with a certain degree of assumed reluctance. While he didn't come right out and mention Riel by name, he did refer darkly to the sad and tragic history of Western insurrections. I commented that such extremes seemed to be the only way that the West could attract Ottawa's attention. I assured him that at the present time our approach was a peaceful and legal one. He seemed relieved. There is no doubt, however, that throughout our later discussions, the spectre of Riel hovered over the negotiating table.

The PM dispatched his emissary in a military aircraft which landed at Calgary. The trip continued in a hired limousine which broke down five miles west of Blossom. The last leg of the trip was made in a Bennett Buggy, which seemed singularly apropos.

Thus, Mr. Fenwick Dickens, Plenipotentiary Extraordinary, arrived unannounced in Blossom, tired, dishevelled, disgruntled and dusty. He reported immediately to my office. I got him ensconced in the Palaza Hotel where he did what he could to refresh and restore himself – principally with a bottle of Scotch I gathered. In an hour he returned to my office where I had assembled the Committee for an Independent Blossom. Mal, Fred and I had still not fully informed Ralph Morsh what was going on in case he objected to our procedures and scuppered the negotiations. His uncertainties about our manoeuverings led to some problems in our discussions with Mr. Dickens.

Mr. Dickens had been chosen for the mission with Ottawa's usual skill. He was an authority on international fisheries who had spent several years at the legation of Bolivia; he had never before been west of Toronto. Furthermore, he was the type of Englishman who was guaranteed to turn off a Westerner at the drop of his first broad "a." He was pompous, superior and self-important. He had a round, fat, florid face, watery-blue eyes, and thin blond hair carefully combed to hide a pink bald crown. His haberdashery was right out of the handbook for aspiring diplomats – bowler hat, black suit and a white waistcoat into which was tucked his old school tie. He looked as out of place in Blossom as a Hottentot.

After I introduced him to the other members of the Committee we sat around in my tiny office exchanging banalities. Then apparently Mr. Dickens decided to take the lead and straighten out us colonials right off the bat. He leaned back in his chair, fixed me with a condescending look and said, "Harrumph, now what is all this bloody nonsense about a proclamation of an independent Blossom? It just won't do, you know."

"Then why are you here?" I asked.

"To tell you so."

I rose from my desk and said coldly, "Then this interview is at an end, Mr. Dickens. We shall proceed with our plans forthwith. Good day to you, sir."

"No, no, I say," he cried in alarm. "Let's not be hasty, what. Let's have a bit of a chat. Do sit down, my good fellow. Yes, let's have a chat." He mopped his red face with a dusty handkerchief.

"Shall I throw him out, George?" asked Mal hopefully.

"No, not yet," I answered. "I promised the Prime Minister to hear what this, ah, fellow has to say. But if he is beginning from an entrenched and rigid position, he has said his piece and there is no point to further discussions. Is that the situation, Mr. Dickens?

Speak up. I'll give you three minutes. We are busy men." I remained standing.

Mr. Dickens mopped his face again with his handkerchief. He was completely flustered; he could see his whole career with the diplomatic corps going down the drain. His bumptious, overbearing manner had evaporated. "Oh, I say, I do seem to have gotten things off to a bad start, haven't I? Off on the wrong foot and all that."

"Yes, you have," I nodded frostily.

"Frightfully sorry, old man. Do sit down like a good chap. There, there, now. Let's continue our discussions in a friendly and co-operative fashion. I'm sure we can, er, um, work things out in a sensible manner, what?"

I sat down stiffly on the edge of my chair, placing my elbows on the desk. "Very well, proceed."

"There, now, that's better. Yes, let us proceed by all means. Harrumph. After all," he continued with an arch look, "it would not be to the advantage of you gentlemen to terminate our negotiations so summarily."

"What do you mean?" I asked.

"Well, hum, if I may speak bluntly. The government is most appreciative of your excellent brief and the many useful things you have drawn to our attention. We would not want to see your efforts go unrewarded. No indeed. We would be happy to provide recompense for your work, I am sure."

"Explain yourself."

He got a crafty look in his eye. "We are all men of the world, are we not, and we know that there are various ways of doing things, what? I am sure that I could arrange for, oh say, a thousand dollars for each of you, hmm?" He gave us each a knowing look.

We stared at him in appalled amazement. Fred had his mouth open like a netted trout. Ralph Morsh recovered first. "Do I understand, sir," he demanded in an incredulous voice, "that you are offering us each a thousand-dollar bribe to drop the matter?"

"There's no need to be quite so blunt, Mr. – er, ah, ahem. What I am saying is –"

Mal rose slowly from his chair to stand menacingly over Mr.

Dickens; he flexed his huge hands. "Have you got the gall to sit there, you bastard, and offer us a chicken feed bribe? Have you? Is that what you are saying?"

Mr. Dickens looked in alarm at Mal's huge size. Things were not working out at all the way they were supposed to. I gather the procedure he was using had been standard practice in the diplomatic negotiations he had previously handled.

"Well, two thousand then," he bleated. Mal glared. "Three thousand and not a farthing more."

"You can throw him out now, Mal," I said quietly. Mr. Dickens spun out of his chair to place it between him and Mal. He retreated towards the wall dragging the chair along in front of him. His usually ruddy face had turned a yellow colour. "No. No," he shouted. "No violence, please! This is unseemly. This is outrageous. I am a governmental envoy. I have diplomatic immunity. You can't do this. It's not done." He continued to babble as Mal advanced. "But I apologize. I was wrong. I apologize. I withdraw the proposal. I was wrong."

"Hold it, Mal," I said. Mal stopped but continued to scowl. "Tell me, Mr. Dickens," I asked, "did the Prime Minister approve this bribery attempt?"

"No, no, certainly not. It was my idea. It was approved by my immediate superior, that is all. But I was wrong. I apologize. It has always worked before when I was in South America. But you are men of honour. I can see that. I underestimated you. I apologize."

"Very well," I said. "Let him be for the moment, Mal. Maybe he has learned a lesson." Mal backed up slowly to his seat but continued to glower. Mr. Dickens breathed a sigh of relief. "I need a drink," he quavered. He certainly did; his hands were shaking and his face was the colour of putty. A hero he was not.

"I'll see what I can do," I said, rummaging in my desk. Mr. Dickens returned cautiously to his chair but kept a wary eye on Mal. Fred and Ralph stared at him in frigid dislike. I found a half-bottle of Jeb Wilson's home-brew and some glasses. I poured Mr. Dickens half a glassful and a smaller portion for each of the rest of us. "Treat it with respect," I cautioned, "it's a powerful brew. Cheers."

"Pip, pip," he responded somewhat incongruously. He tossed off the fiery liquid without turning a hair. "Whew, I needed that, I must say." He dabbed at his mouth with his handkerchief and set the glass on my desk. He gradually regained his composure; some colour returned to his cheeks and his hands stopped trembling. He took a deep breath and began again to babble apologies.

I cut him off sharply. "You made a mistake; don't dwell on it. We now understand each other, so possibly we can continue in a rational manner. I'm surprised to hear you say the PM knew nothing about your proposed *modus operandi* here."

"You shouldn't be. Heads of state never know anything. All they are interested in is remaining in power. Yes, quite. Knowledge is embarrassing. That's why they have large staffs – to keep information from getting to them. They have no interest in the nitty and the gritty – only results. You see, ah, the nitty can get pretty gritty at times and they don't want to know about it; if they don't know, they can't be held responsible. Caesar's wife and all that, what?" He paused and passed a hand over his face. "I say, do you think I could have just another little touch of that, er, ah, delightful beverage?"

I poured him another dollop of Jeb's moonshine, which he drank appreciatively. He leaned back somewhat more relaxed. "Ah, yes. You see, in the diplomatic corps you find that internal diplomacy is more sensitive than external diplomacy. The important decision is how much to tell your superior – you don't want to embarrass him with facts – and so on up the, ah, ladder. By the time information reaches the top, it is so filtered there is nothing left. See?" He spread out his hands, palms up.

"Ah, yes, thank you," I responded. "That explains some things I have often wondered about. But now to continue. Have your read the brief?"

"Yes, yes. Of course. A splendid brief! A jolly good brief, I must say. Well reasoned. Excellent," he stated enthusiastically.

"Then you accept the proposition?"

"No, I'm afraid not." Then he added hastily, "While I might myself, I'm afraid my superior finds it unacceptable. At the moment, at any rate. Might we go through the document?"

"Certainly," I agreed. We got out our copies of the brief and for the next hour discussed the issues covered in it. Mr. Dickens gradually regained his aplomb and his pompous manner – Jeb's home-brew undoubtedly helped. While he may have been a whiz on fisheries jurisprudence he had practically no knowledge of Canadian or international law so I was able to bamboozle him completely in these areas, which was a big help.

After we had gone through the brief in detail, our discussions ranged in more general terms. The objective of our Committee was to keep Mr. Dickens off balance and confused, yet persuaded of the seriousness of our intention and the validity of our proposition. After the hornet's nest we had stirred up, we were loath to come right out and admit that all we were trying to do was get our railway station and post office moved a half-mile. We had gotten ourselves so far committed to our proposition that we couldn't see how we could back down gracefully. The sledge hammer was in danger of crushing the walnut. Also I found that we were beginning to convince ourselves of the validity of our arguments. In a way we were caught up in our own intrigue. I confess, also, that in our discussion with him we were so challenged by his absurd Wodehouse façade that we took some pleasure in pulling his leg. This caused difficulties with Ralph who is completely devoid of humour.

At one point in our discussion Mr. Dickens asked me what form of government we had in mind if we were granted autonomy. I answered that we hadn't really decided, but a republic seemed the most obvious.

"Why don't we go for something more glamourous?" asked Mal. "How about a kingdom? The Kingdom of Blossom. Ain't that got a good sound to it?"

"Yes, it does," agreed Fred, with a flicker of the eyebrow in my direction. "George might be elected king. King George the First of Blossom. Sounds good." He frowned thoughtfully. "Might be confusing. Too many King Georges around."

"One advantage of a kingdom would be that we could sell knighthoods and make a lot of money," suggested Mal. "That would be in the finest English tradition, wouldn't it, Mr. Dickens?"

Mr. Dickens looked shocked. "Certainly not," he huffed.

"Utter rot. My father was a peer, you know." He straightened his waistcoat. Mal scratched his nose. "On second thought, I don't think we ought to sell knighthoods. I'm a democratic sort of guy and I think we ought to bestow a knighthood free on everybody in Blossom. Every Blossomite would be a Sir Somebody or Other. It would add a nice touch of class to the place. And every dame would be a Dame So and So. Wonderful." He looked very pleased with the idea. "But maybe we could sell higher titles like duke, count, baron or, uh, churl."

"Fair enough," said Fred. "I'll nominate you Churl of the Realm forthwith."

"Thank you," said Mal. "What other forms of glamourous government are there if we decide we don't want a kingdom?"

"How about a duchy?" suggested Fred. "We could appoint Flossy Macabee our first duchess. She has many of the attributes of the great duchesses of history." Mr. Dickens had no way of knowing that Flossy was the town prostitute.

Ralph, of course, took the proposal seriously. "She'd be singularly inappropriate," he said stiffly. "She –"

Mal interrupted hastily. "If we decide on a sultanate, I'd be happy to offer my services," he said hopefully.

"Surely you would want to carry on the, um, fine British tradition of democratic government," said Mr. Dickens severely. He launched into a long discourse on the virtues of democracy in general and the British variety in particular.

Fred, allowing his English accent to become more noticeable, agreed that we would prefer to remain under the British crown if at all possible, as had been stated in the brief. However, he emphasized that this would depend on suitable arrangements being made. "We would have to be completely autonomous," stated Fred. "No crown colony status for us – we don't want to be told how to do things by some damfool Englishman. No offence intended, Mr. Dickens. However, I am sure we would be prepared to accept partnership in the British Commonwealth on the same basis as Canada. We would, of course, control our internal affairs and foreign policy. We will have our own army and navy and be free to enter into pacts with foreign powers. Don't be alarmed, Mr. Dickens," he added as he noticed Mr. Dickens' startled reaction to this statement. "We would be prepared to enter into a non-aggression pact with Canada."

"Jeb Wilson would be a good general for our national army," suggested Mal. "He's a good shot with a rifle when he's sober. Roscoe could be his second in command." Mr. Dickens, of course, didn't know that Roscoe was Jeb's dog.

Ralph looked puzzled at this reference to Roscoe but let it pass. "I really don't think we need a navy," he observed. "After all, the only water around here is the Blossom River and it's not very big."

"All self-respecting countries got to have a navy," stated Mal flatly. "Maybe we could get Chief Buffalo Tail to sign over his six war canoes to the state. That would about counterbalance the Canadian naval power."

"Then you haven't discussed this matter of naval power and, er, ah, the whole proposition with the Indians yet?" asked Mr. Dickens shrewdly.

"No," I admitted. "We are planning to explore and consolidate our other relationships first."

"Aha," smiled Mr. Dickens. "Then what makes you think the Indians will go along with you? Why would they do business with you instead of with the Canadian government?"

"For a very good reason," stated Fred. "They have been dealing with the Canadian government since Confederation and it has been a disaster for them. They couldn't help but do better with us. Furthermore," continued Fred, warming to the subject, "we would offer them a full and equal partnership in the new state; we would thereby give them back their identity and their dignity. We will provide a true bicultural political and social environment, bringing the best of both traditions to a new way of life.

"They will leap at the opportunity, believe me. We shall have two official languages, Cree and English. We shall –"

"But the white people don't speak Cree," interrupted Ralph.

"They will in time," affirmed Fred. "Although the Indians are a minority, they would be one of two equal founding nations.

It is mandatory under such circumstances of equality that a true bilingual milieu be provided so that the minority can communicate in their chosen language at all times. Both languages must be used in our courts and civil service, and both races must be involved in the administration thereof."

"But they don't understand these things," complained Ralph.

"That doesn't matter," answered Fred. "A founding minority group must be recruited into such operations whether they know what's going on or not. It is more important that they be involved, and be seen to be involved, than that they make any useful contribution. It's the only democratic way to do things. Furthermore, it is obvious that everybody must be forced to learn to speak Cree. Crash courses can be provided for this purpose. All our schools must undertake instruction in both languages. The next generation will be completely bilingual and therefore integrated. We shall learn to love each other. In the past this minority group has been inhibited in its development by being unable to communicate with the rest of us. Now, they will be able to tell us exactly what they think of us in terms we can understand. This will foster brotherhood. All our publications, official documents, road signs and grocery labels must be in both languages. With Cree the primary listing, of course – we must make them feel wanted."

"How many citizens would you have in your new state?" asked Mr. Dickens. "That would have an influence on the viability of the proposition for independence."

Mal pulled at his lower lip. "About a million and a half," he suggested. We all looked startled. "That includes gophers," admitted Mal. "Gophers are people, too," he added defensively.

"Gophers don't pay taxes," snorted Ralph.

"True," admitted Mal. "But they don't go on relief either."

"Harrumph," interjected Mr. Dickens. "If we might disregard the gopher, er hum, populace for the moment, could I ask what proportion of your citizenry would be Indian? Would it be over half?"

"Yes," I admitted.

"Aha," said Mr. Dickens. "I thought so. On my trip through the area my impression was that the proportion of Indians to, er, cowboys was about ten to one. Returning to the language matter, I would point out that, whereas Mr. Peters kept referring to the Indians as a minority, this would not obtain in your new state. Therefore, in a democratic form of government the Indians could legislate Cree as the official language. Then where would you be?"

"No group," stated Fred, "on this continent of English-speaking people and with English being the universal means of communication would be stupid enough to deliberately sink themselves in a well of silence."

"Don't be too sure," said Mr. Dickens solemnly.

"Piffle," said Fred.

"Furthermore," continued Mr. Dickens, "with a voting majority the Indians could render your position otherwise untenable and force you to leave."

"But that would be economic suicide," objected Ralph.

"Maybe they would rather return to living in sod shanties and eating, er, pomegranates and get rid of you. But if you continue to live in Canada, then the Indians remain a minority and the problem disappears." Mr. Dickens sat back in obvious satisfaction at having made a good point.

"Anyhow," grumbled Ralph, "I don't see why we should give the Indians an equal voice in our government. After all, they were defeated on the field of battle."

"There's some doubt about that," said Fred. "It is apparent now that the Indians actually won but weren't aware of it. They were sold down the river by their politicians."

"One must be generous to the vanquished, what?" intoned Mr. Dickens. "British fair play and all that, you know."

"One thing I've always observed about the application of British fair play is that the British always come out on top," growled Mal. Mr. Dickens looked pained.

"Another thing that bothers me about giving the Indians a say in our government," complained Ralph, "is that they are Catholics."

"So what?" asked Mal in surprise.

"Catholics don't seem to get along with other people," said

Ralph. "It makes them ornery. I think the problem is that the Pope isn't an Englishman, you know – he's an Eye-talian."

"Cheer up, Ralph," said Fred. "God is an Englishman."

"Anyhow, Ralph," said Mal soothingly, "when we establish the State of Blossom, the Catholics can set up their own Pope right here. An Indian Pope would be a dandy idea. It might be a bit of a surprise to God for awhile, I admit. But God is versatile; He'd take off His skullcap, stick a feather in His hair and switch back to being Manitou."

"We could sell indulgences in the best ecclesiastical tradition." suggested Fred, "and make a little money."

"Good heavens," cried Mr. Dickens in alarm. "Surely you're not thinking of making Catholicism the state religion. I would strongly recommend a strict separation of church and state."

"You misunderstand me," said Fred. "We would have no state church. There would be complete freedom of religion, which means that the government assumes no responsibility for the religious idiocies of its citizens or the intolerant horrors perpetrated on one another in the name of Christianity."

"I am relieved," sighed Mr. Dickens.

"I'm still a bit concerned about the economic viability of our new state," fussed Ralph, gnawing on his knuckle.

"We couldn't be in any worse bloody economic shape than we are now," said Mal, "thanks to the Canadian government. There's lots of things we can do once we're independent. We can nationalize anything that makes money and leave everything else to free enterprise."

"That sounds like socialism," said Ralph in a horrified voice.

"Why not?" said Mal. "We're halfway there already since half the people are on relief now. We'll just put everybody on relief and then we'll all be working for the state. Only we'll call it something different, like maybe unemployment insurance."

"What have we got now that makes money?" demanded Ralph.

"Well, the brick factory for one. It makes money. Not much, I admit, but some. And we can start new industries too."

"Like what?" asked Ralph skeptically.

"How about nationalizing Jeb Wilson's bootleg operation? That's sure a going concern."

"We'd have to find his still first," observed Fred.

"We could appeal to Jeb's patriotism," said Mal. "I'm sure a fine upright citizen such as Jeb would be happy to turn over his operation for the national good and welfare."

"Like hell he would," snorted Ralph.

"For a price," added Fred. "The new state could legitimize his operation and make him a respectable member of the community. It's been done in our neighbouring country of Canada. Some of Canada's most revered citizens are former bootleggers. We could make Jeb head of the national distillation franchise with a monopoly on hooch."

"That might work," conceded Ralph. "And then we could tax hell out of it."

"No," said Mal. "I don't think we should have taxes on anything. No liquor tax, no income tax, no tax on a bloody thing. Taxes are a pain in the ass. One sure way to make our new regime popular with everybody would be to eliminate taxes. People would come from all over the place to drink cheap booze and deposit their money here to avoid taxes. We would have secret numbered bank accounts to avoid governmental snooping. We would become the tax haven of the world. Ocean-going freighters could be registered in Blossom at a modest fee. They – "

"But you are two thousand miles from the ocean," objected Mr. Dickens.

"That don't matter," answered Mal grandly. "We could declare the Blossom River an international waterway; the fact that no boat could get to it wouldn't matter a damn. Blossom can be an international free port where people can come from all over the world to buy and sell stuff tax-free. I can see it all clearly." He spread his arms wide. "Blossom will be a world renowned international trading centre."

Ralph was dubious. "I'm not at all sure my head office would countenance such an arrangement."

"Who would need them?" asked Fred. "Blossom would have its own national bank." Then he added slyly, "Undoubtedly with you as its president, Ralph."

This opened up a whole new vista to Ralph. He stared at the wall with his mouth open. You could almost see the wheels turning around. He was visualizing himself representing a national bank in the financial capitals of the world – London, New York, Toronto, Paris. He was the new Rothschild; he was the respected and feared financial wizard of the international money marts. He swallowed and returned to the present – although with a new aura of authority about him.

"What would we use for money?" he asked.

"Print it, of course," answered Mal. "Like every other country does. Alberta is already issuing phoney money and getting away with it. But ours would be better – it would be legitimate. You know, I'd suggest we use some unit other than the dollar to avoid confusion. How about wampum?"

Ralph was delighted with the idea. His dusty little banker's brain was all atwitter. "Excellent idea! Excellent. We certainly would not want our currency confused with that of other countries. Wampum, good. But I do think we ought to retain the decimal system – there are so many advantages. Yes. One wampum could be pegged to be equal to a dollar; the dollar could be one hundred, ah, say, beads. Yes, one hundred beads to the wampum. Hmm. What would be the plural of wampum? I presume wampa. Yes, one wampum, two wampa. Good." He lapsed into happy thoughts of financial wheeling and dealing.

"What would you do for a police force?" asked Mr. Dickens abruptly.

"One mountie handles the whole district now so that's no problem," answered Fred. "We could name Corporal Rankin as Police Commissioner and let him carry on."

"In summer, when the tourists flock in here for our tax-free booze we could get Corporal Rankin to perform the ceremony of changing of the guard," suggested Mal. "In front of the presidential palace. That's always a popular tourist attraction."

"How can you have a changing of the guard when you only have one guard?" asked Fred.

Mal scratched his chin. "You have a point. I'll cogitate on it."

"What presidential palace?" queried a puzzled Ralph.

"The one we'll build, of course," answered Mal. "Maybe it'll be a tepee."

"How about your courts?" asked Mr. Dickens. "An independent judiciary is an, um, ah, vital bulwark of the democratic state."

"George is our only lawyer so he would have to be the whole judicial shebang," said Mal.

"You would be in good hands, I am sure," beamed Mr. Dickens. He became conspiratorial. "Actually the fewer lawyers you have around the better off you will be – no offence intended, Mr. Ingraham."

"No argument there," said Mal.

"There are many fascinating and important matters to be worked out in establishing a new state," I commented. "As you can see, Mr. Dickens, we have not yet come to grips with many of the details of governmental structure but it is exciting to let one's imagination range widely and freely in considering alternatives."

"I confess I find myself caught up in the excitement," said Mr. Dickens, "but I must reiterate my stand that the proposition is basically unsound and inimical to the best interest of yourselves and of Canada as a whole."

"What are some of the other details we'll have to consider?" asked Mal who was thoroughly enjoying himself.

"Oh, things like the form of the legislative assembly, methods of elections, a national flag, a coat of arms, a national anthem, uniforms for the army – "

"Breechclouts," said Mal.

"In the winter?" asked Fred.

"Fur-lined." Mal waved his hand in dismissal.

"Since we're letting our imaginations soar," said Fred, "for a coat of arms how about a gopher couchant or maybe rampant on a field of cactus."

"We've got to work in a rattlesnake somewhere," said Mal. "How about a gopher and a rattlesnake shaking hands? Then we've got to have a Latin motto – something aggressive and belligerent in the best tradition of peaceful nations. How do you say 'Up your Kilt' in Latin?"

I felt the boys were getting a bit carried away which might

give Mr. Dickens the impression we were not serious so I decided I'd better try to wind things up. "Ahem, well gentlemen," I interrupted, "there are many details to be worked out which can be left till later." I turned to Mr. Dickens. "I think we should return to the basic issue before us. Now sir, are there any additional comments you would care to make or any further questions you wish to put to us?"

"Harrumph. Thank you. I must say that there are many, ah, hum, aspects of your proposition which are intriguing, to say the least. Possibly not realistic but, um, I would say, fascinating. There is one question I have been intending to ask and that is: what precipitated the actions which led to your, er, submission. That is sometimes very significant in political, ah, um, movements. What triggered the unrest?"

I replied lightly, "Oh, a relatively minor matter, as is often the case in national upheavals. Blossom wanted the railway depot moved into the town. Also the post office." I explained the problem to him.

He was all of a sudden the wily negotiator. Maybe he wasn't as dumb as he appeared – it is very easy to underestimate Englishmen because of their marshmallow façade. "I'm quite sure those matters could be accommodated relatively easily," he stated. "Do you think doing so would, um, defuse the unrest of the, um, natives? At least for the time being?"

I shrugged. "It would certainly help," I admitted cautiously. "It would at least demonstrate that Ottawa is aware of the problems of Blossom and is prepared to be sympathetic and helpful."

"Is there anything else that you might suggest which would serve as a token of the government's high esteem for the State of Blossom – er, ah, I mean, the town of Blossom?"

I frowned thoughtfully. He was sounding so co-operative I felt the time was propitious to push our luck a little further. "Yes," I replied. "I would suggest an adequate governmental building to accommodate various administrative agencies. If we go ahead with our plans for independence, the building could become the Canadian Embassy. Possibly you will be returning here, sir, as Canadian Ambassador to the State of Blossom in the not too distant future."

The prospect did not seem to fill him with any great joy. "Ah, yes. Thank you. But that would be an honour to which I would scarcely have the, um, temerity to aspire. Harrumph. Be that as it may, can I have the assurance of this committee that you will take no further action until these, ah, tokens of appreciation, affection and high regard, have been, ah, implemented? I give you my solemn promise, and I have been given authority to make such a commitment, that your post office and railway station will be moved into the town and that a substantial government building will be constructed. Do I have your agreement on these terms?"

I did not want to appear to be too eager. I gazed around solemnly at the members of the Committee for an Independent Blossom. Mal winked at me; Fred cocked an eyebrow; Ralph furrowed his brow judiciously as befitted the Dustbowl Rothschild.

"Gentlemen," I said, "this is an historic moment. Are you prepared to accept Mr. Dickens' proposal made on behalf of the Government of Canada?"

There was a dramatic pause; Mr. Dickens held his breath. The three members of the Committee sat in deep thought for what seemed an hour. Fred ran his thumb back and forth, back and forth across his mustache. Mal rubbed his bald head, then tugged at his lower lip; he shook his head slowly, then nodded solemnly only to change sadly back to a negative reaction. Ralph scowled at the floor, obviously weighing the attractions of being an international financial tycoon. The silence dragged on. Mr. Dickens let out a shuddering breath.

Finally, Mal said, "Agreed."

Fred said, "Agreed."

Ralph said, "Agreed."

Mr. Dickens said, "Jolly good show."

Chapter Three

NO LADY

URING THE DEPRESSION, people in small towns such as Blossom had no money to spend on expensive entertainment. They were therefore thrown on their own resources to make their own fun – and great good fun it was – with low-cost activities such as picnics, barn dances, sports, working-bees, house parties and so forth. The necessary social lubricant was supplied economically by Jeb Wilson's moonshine operation.

The twenty-fourth of May holiday in Blossom was a fine example of good fun at low cost. I had been told that the festivities would include a picnic, sporting contests and a dance which would go on to the wee small hours. Since I thoroughly enjoyed such affairs, I arranged my itinerary to arrive in town on the twenty-third.

I drove up in my old Star to the Palaza Hotel; the evening was warm and balmy which augured well for good weather the next day. The usual row of loafers was sitting along the wooden sidewalk with their chairs tipped back against the hotel, digesting their dinners and picking their teeth. I greeted each one as I walked past them into the hotel. I checked into my room and then walked up the street to Fred Peters' garage where I found Fred applying another patch to an already well-patched inner tube.

"Hi Fred," I greeted him as I squatted down on my haunches at his side.

"Hi pal," answered Fred, giving me a quick glance. "Welcome to the big city." He was, as usual, immaculately dressed, which always surprised me in view of his messy occupation.

"Will it bother your concentration with this complex technical operation if I watch?" I asked.

"To quote that old philosopher and pundit, Jeb Wilson, 'I concentrate real good; my only problem is I ain't got much to concentrate with.' "

"That'll do for both of you."

"You in town for the big goings-on tomorrow?"

"Yep. What's on the programme?"

"Oh, some of the usual. Big dance at night in the Elks' Hall, with music by the Cypress Hills Hillbillies; picnic and races for the kids in the afternoon; ball game with Dazzle in the evening."

"I can bring you greetings from the great metropolis of Dazzle – I have just come from there," I said. "There will be a large delegation down for the festivities." The neighbouring town of Dazzle always supported the twenty-fourth of May celebration in Blossom making it almost a joint project; Blossom returned the compliment for Dazzle's Labour Day Stampede.

"Glad to hear it," responded Fred. He placed the inner tube in a bucket of water and swore vigorously at the telltale line of bubbles which came to the surface. "There are some innovations this year I should tell you about. For the last month we have been running a Blossom Queen contest – you got one vote for each dollar's worth of stuff you purchased in a local store. Bessie Hefflewait won it for the obvious reason that her father runs our leading emporium. I voted for Flossy Macabee but she lost out. We were going to run a liars' contest but when I entered your name everyone else withdrew."

"Thanks, pal."

"Anytime." Fred waved his hand. "There's another new exciting event in the arrangements this year. Florence Elliott is President of the Ladies Auxiliary and she has talked the committee into holding a parade in the morning. The theme is to be an historical one with a salute to the early pioneers who settled the area. She's even sweet-talked Chief Buffalo Tail and his band of Indians into turning out in full regalia. There'll be a marching band and prizes for floats; the kids will compete for best-decorated bicycle, best-dressed dog, and so on. All the merchants have put a few bucks in the kitty for prizes. All except old Syd Hefflewait who wouldn't donate a nickle. He's tight as a bull's arse in fly time."

Fred finished patching the tube, then started stuffing it in the tire. "The big highlight is to be the unveiling of a cairn down by the station in honor of the pioneers who founded our noble town. I have it on good authority that the cairn is made of petrified buffalo chips. Some of the old-timers from the district are to be honoured and will be on the platform. I understand that Florence is to give the address of tribute and then break a bottle of champagne over the head of the nearest old-timer – or some such."

"Sounds exciting."

"Yeah. I think it'll be a good show. Should draw a lot of people into town, which is the object of the exercise – at least in part, I hasten to add."

"Have you got a float in the parade?"

"Of course. It won't win any prizes, I'm afraid. I have the old truck fitted out to look like a fort. Come around to the back and see it."

The truck was surrounded with logs to represent a stockade with turrets and gunholes. Some arrows were impaled in the wood. A large sign on the radiator proclaimed Peters Motors.

"Very good,'" I said. "Historical as all get out. I didn't know Peters Motors had been around that long."

"Foof to you! Some of the kids from the high school are going to ride in it; some inside with rifles, and others wahooing along beside dressed as Indians. Want to go to the parade with Audrey and me? I'm not involved in the organization of it, thank goodness."

"Sure. I'd like to very much."

"Fine. The parade starts at nine, so meet us here a few minutes before that. The parade goes right along this street."

"Good. I'll be here."

Next morning I sauntered over from the Palaza Hotel a little before nine to join Audrey and Fred. It was a pleasant sunny day; the streets were lined with happy, expectant people. The whole of

Blossom had turned out, and many families had come from farms in the district and from neighbouring towns, with a particularly large representation from Dazzle. Children pushed forward to the edges of the sidewalks; the older folks stood patiently behind them. Some had brought boxes to sit on. There was an air of excitement in the crowd which only a parade can engender. The children were practically bouncing, and kept running out in the street to see if the parade was coming. They were summoned back by warning cries from their mothers. I exchanged greetings with many of the folks as I went along.

I found Audrey at the garage and asked where Fred was. "He's taken the truck down to the schoolyard where they're assembling the parade. He's in a big tailspin. One whole side of the float fell off, and they have to stick it together again."

Audrey looked charming in a blue gingham dress which set off her plump figure admirably. She was much amused at Fred's predicament. "I hope it doesn't fall off again during the parade, or Fred will have conniptions," she laughed.

Mal and Hortense Morgan, accompanied by Mamie Sutherland, joined us. Mal's round, fat face wore a cheerful grin beneath a large straw hat. He exchanged ribald comments with the men near us. I looked around for George Ingraham.

"Where's George?" I asked Mamie, who was looking beautiful with her long auburn hair piled high on her head.

She chuckled. "He's Master of Ceremonies so he's down at the station thrashing around with last-minute arrangements. Really, he's in such a swither I don't think his feet are touching the ground. You'd think he was convening the League of Nations."

"That doesn't sound like George – he always seems so poised and sure of himself."

"It's a pose. He can get pretty excited." She giggled and blushed at my knowing look. "Part of the strain is brought on by his having to be nice to Cyril Thorndyke who is head of the Dazzle delegation." She laughed. Cyril was the lawyer from Dazzle; he and George heartily detested each other, as is common amongst lawyers.

"I haven't seen the Elliotts," I said, glancing around the crowd near us.

"No, they won't be here," said Mamie. "Florence is giving one of the speeches so she's full of the jitters too. Dick, like a proper husband, is holding her hand and trying to calm her down."

"Yeah," I nodded. "Fred mentioned that Florence was on the programme but I thought she might be able to mingle with the proletariat beforehand."

"There'd be no time."

By nine-thirty the parade had still not appeared; the mothers were having an increasingly difficult time controlling the youngsters. Fred came panting up. "That place is a madhouse down there. I don't know if they'll ever get it sorted out. There's kids and horses and dogs and floats milling around and everybody hollering different orders. It's a shemozzle."

"Have you got Fort Ticonderoga stuck together again?" I asked.

"I hope so," Fred answered, mopping his forehead.

Suddenly a cry went up from the crowd. "Here they come!"

The children all ran out into the street to screams of protest from their mothers. Down the street we could see some movement and hear the sounds of a band. The children clapped their hands and jumped up and down.

At the head of the parade on a beautiful, skittish horse appeared Corporal Rankin of the RCMP carrying a Union Jack. Behind him came the Elks' band in ill-fitting blue and white uniforms. The band had an unusual instrumentation: three sousaphones, one alto horn, two trumpets and one clarinet, plus a bass drum and two kettle drums. The emphasis on the bass horns meant that the *oompah* had a great deal more *oom* than *pah*. Fred said it sounded like a man with a wooden leg going upstairs. As the band progressed down the street the crowd cheered and clapped; when they got opposite us we joined in the applause. I found a rising excitement in me. I have always been a great sucker for a marching band – even one with an overemphasis on the *oom*. The two trumpet players were red in the face, giving "Colonel Bogey" everything they had. I was surprised to see that one of the trumpeters was Jerry Rusk, the postmaster. I hadn't known he was a musician, and I still have some doubts about it. The clarinet tweedled away in the upper register and appeared to be playing a different number entirely.

Behind the band came the float bearing Bessie Hefflewait, the Blossom Queen, sitting on an elevated rickety gold throne. She wore a gold cardboard crown on her head, and was dressed in what appeared to be a white nightgown. Her ladies-in-waiting stood around her similarly dressed, but wearing silver crowns. It was obvious that the Blossom Queen had not been chosen for her beauty. Bessie was a skinny kid with frizzy blond hair, and buckteeth which had earned her the nickname Gopher.

A large sign on the side of the float proclaimed Blossom, Flower of the Prairies. The girls waved to the bystanders; everyone cheered and waved back. The float lurched along, with the throne teetering back and forth. Bessie looked a little apprehensive. Fred shouted in my ear, "Uneasy rides the head that wears a crown."

Behind the queen came a series of floats on trucks or Bennett Buggies, all bearing signs extolling the virtues of some business concern. All the participants wore numbered placards to identify them for judging purposes. A Red River cart went squeaking by and there was even a covered wagon pulled along by a team of oxen. Fred's fort was a big success; the cowboys inside fired cap pistols at the Indians whooping alongside. The floats were interspersed with children on horseback dressed as frontiersmen or cowboys or Indians. As always happens, many of the horses disgraced themselves, making a hazard for those behind. There must have been forty or fifty decorated bicycles festooned with streamers and with coloured paper woven through the spokes. One youngster, dressed as Barney Google, led an old white horse with a sheet over him lettered Spark Plug. A small child in blackface rode on the horse and waved at the crowd. The bystanders cheered and clapped for the presentations which appealed to them, or for their own progeny.

A group of dressed-up dogs appeared, each one led by a grinning child, many in costumes matching those of their dogs. Some of the dogs were dressed as clowns, some as prospectors, pirates, and comic strip characters. There were Maggie and Jiggs, two Andy Gumps and a Moon Mullins. Each dog wore a hat of some kind, which tended to slip around under the dog's chin, necessitating frequent adjustments. The dogs didn't appear very happy about it all, and some had to be dragged along.

The crowd *oohed* and *aahed*. As they got opposite us, Jeb Wilson's dog, Roscoe, walked stiff-legged and bristling out into the street. He made straight for a collie dressed in a clown outfit. That dog of Jeb's must be the most ubiquitous troublemaker the canine world has ever produced. I think he was miffed because he had not been invited to participate in the parade as would have been expected by the town's canine social leader. I had no great love for Roscoe, and I hoped that the collie would clean his clock. But it was not to be. Roscoe lit into the collie who was hampered by a hat under his chin and pants on his hind legs. Roscoe was getting much the better of it when the other dogs, disregarding their finery, pitched into the battle. Pandemonium ensued. The children screamed and tried to drag their dogs away. Jeb Wilson ran out to try to grab Roscoe. A number of other men joined the mêlée, kicking and cursing. Four or five other dogs appeared from behind the onlookers as if they had been waiting for Roscoe's cue to join battle with their pampered brethren.

It was a dandy row. Fred Peters ran into the garage and came out with a bucket of dirty water. He threw the water at the dogs, missing them completely but nearly drowning Jeb Wilson. Fred said later that it was the first bath the old coot had had in twenty years. After a great deal of kicking and shouting, the men finally succeeded in separating the combatants and chasing the interlopers off. Jeb took a big kick at Roscoe as he went by, missed him completely and fell flat on his back in a pile of horse manure. Everyone cheered.

None of the dogs were seriously injured, but the costumes were a shambles. The only one to escape unscathed was an old basset hound in a gingham apron and sunbonnet, who had watched the fracas with sorrowful, disdainful eyes. Some of the children were crying and were soothed by friends in the crowd. After bystanders had made hasty repairs to the tattered costumes, the disorganized cortège continued on its way.

The rest of the parade went by, including the little band of Indians in full regalia. Then came Jock Timchuk, playing "Scotland the Brave" on his pipes. His mother had been a Macdonald; it was easy to figure out who was the dominant personality in that household. The two baseball teams filed by, with the local boys getting a big hand and the team from Dazzle receiving a lot of good-natured razzing. Clowns pranced back and forth through the procession eliciting screams of delight from the children. The last group in the parade was the Blossom Volunteer Fire Brigade, which consisted of a hose reel pulled along by a pickup truck, with the volunteers, in fireman hats, tramping along behind it.

As the Fire Brigade went by, the spectators fell in behind to follow the parade down to the railway station where the formal ceremonies were to take place. Gradually a large crowd assembled in the wide street in front of the depot. An elevated stage, decorated with red, white and blue bunting, had been erected on the edge of the station platform.

On the stage sat George Ingraham, Reverend Slye, Florence Elliott, Grandma Akerbilt and Angus MacNab; also, representing the town of Dazzle, Cyril Thorndyke and Bob O'Neill. Grandma Akerbilt and Angus MacNab were authentic old-timers. Grandma certainly looked the part, with her poke bonnet and grey, ankle-length, homespun dress. Angus was a spry old bird, skinny as a wheat straw, who certainly didn't look his hundred years. He lived with his granddaughter and her husband on a farm near the town. Although he had a tendency to drop off to sleep, he was intellectually acute and loved to talk about the early days in the West.

George, who had been elected President of the Board of Trade after his successful performance as Chairman of its Post Office Committee, acted as Master of Ceremonies. He opened the programme by calling on the band to play "O Canada." This was apparently a surprise to the band, so there was a slight pause while they found the music. By the sound of things I suspected they didn't all find the same piece. After one false start they managed to get through it with the crowd singing lustily along with them. George then called on Reverend Slye for the invocation. Reverend Slye's craggy old face beamed at the crowd with a benignity which was sincere and unaffected. The public-address system squeaked and whistled but we could hear reasonably well.

There was a bit of a wait while the Awards Committee

brought up the list of winners for the various categories in the parade. George read off the identifying numbers of the recipients who then came forward to receive their prizes from Reverend Slye. It was apparent that an effort had been made to recognize as many Dazzle entries as possible. There were interminable delays while winners were located and sent forward. Each recipient received a vigorous round of applause. Some little people who didn't win a prize burst into tears and were comforted, or bribed, by their families. Fred won an award for his float and was inordinately proud of the achievement. When he brought back his prize I asked him what it was. "Five gallons of gas from my competitor down the street," he laughed, showing me the chit.

When the prizes had been distributed, George gave a short address explaining that the final item on the programme would be the unveiling of a cairn to pay tribute to the pioneers who had settled the West and had established the town of Blossom. He congratulated the various members of the committee whose hard work and unselfish effort had brought the project to fruition.

He then introduced Florence Elliott to give the dedication address. Florence was looking very pretty in a brand new hat; her big blue eyes sparkled with excitement and nervous tension. She came to the microphone carrying her prepared speech in a fluttery hand. She spoke slowly and well, her clipped English accent giving clarity to her words. Her talk was somewhat flowery, but probably appropriate for the occasion. She dwelt on the courage and vision of the pioneers whose energy, devotion, and dedication had brought them west to subdue a vast wilderness and to extend across the continent from sea to sea our great heritage, traditions, and culture. She continued: "And when these weary pioneers came to this verdant bend in the river, they recognized that here could be developed an oasis on the parched plain to soothe their tired spirits and rest their weary limbs. And so they called it Blossom."

"Blether," said old Angus MacNab clearly. "That ain't right at all."

Florence was thrown for a loss. She paused, then turned to Angus. "Am I not right, Mr. MacNab?"

"No, you ain't right at all. Blossom were named for a woman by the name of Blossom," said Angus firmly.

"Oh, I didn't know. There wasn't anything in the library at all. I –"

"Should've asked me. I'd've told yer," sniffed Angus.

"Well, uh. Isn't that marvellous to know that our fair city is named for one of the pioneer ladies who had the courage and devotion to, ah, accompany her husband on the trek to the west." I thought Florence was recovering rather well. "We should be, ah, grateful –"

"That ain't right neither," interrupted Angus again.

At this point Florence gave up. "It would appear, Mr. Chairman," she said, turning to George, "that my, er, research has been inadequate. I think we should seize the opportunity to have a real old-timer like Mr. MacNab tell us the true story about Blossom's founding." With that she groped her way back to her chair in something of a swither.

The crowd was enjoying this contretemps thoroughly. Cries of "Let's hear from Angus" and "You tell 'em, Angus" arose on all sides.

George was up a stump; he really had no alternative but to comply. He returned to the microphone and spoke to Angus. "Why, yes. A splendid idea. Mr. MacNab, would you be so kind as to come forward and tell us about the founding of Blossom."

"Why sure," said Angus. He rose slowly to his feet and tottered toward George. George reached out and held his arm. I thought to myself, "Holy smoke, they'll never get him stopped."

"What do yers want to know?" asked Angus in his deep husky voice.

"Tell us about the lady for whom Blossom is named," said George.

"Wall, in the first place," said Angus with a deep chuckle, "she weren't no lady. She were a hooer." He chuckled again. "For a long time she were the only hooer west of the Lakes, and she done real good. Boys from as far away as Fort Whoop-up would say, 'Let's go see Blossom,' and that's how the town got its name. She were brought west by a trader named Garble, and he lost her in a poker game to a guy named . . . let me see."

"Mr. MacNab," interrupted George hastily, "I am sure –"

"Blinker," said Angus. "Yes, Blinker. That were his name.

Soapy Blinker. And he got scalped by an Indian, and Blossom went into business for herself. Done real good and went back to Toronto and married a duke, or something –"

"Mr. MacNab," George tried again.

"I never knew her," continued Angus. "She were before my time, and that's a hell of a long time ago. I heard tell she were a very fine figger of a woman. Real handsome. You got a statue of her under them sheets over there? Should be real good if you have." The crowd gave him a rousing ovation.

I'm sure my disappointment was later shared by everyone present when the sheet came off the memorial to disclose a pile of rocks and not a statue of Blossom – that fine figger of a woman – even if she weren't no lady.

Chapter Four

HUMPTY DUMPTY

A SPORTS DAY IN BLOSSOM has it all over the Olympics for excitement, rivalry, colour and drama. After the parade and cairn dedication ceremonies in the morning, the twenty-fourth of May celebrations continued in the afternoon with a picnic and sporting events. The affair was held in the pasture of Roschuk's farm about two miles from town. This was a fine place for such a gathering because there was a flat field for the races with a small stream flowing through it which was lined with trees to provide shade and shelter for the picknickers.

By twelve o'clock the dusty road to Roschuk's farm was a stream of cars, trucks, Bennett Buggies and wagons. When they arrived at the pasture, they spread out along the creek, each family staking out an area for themselves by setting out blankets, food boxes and other paraphernalia. In many instances, several families joined together in a communal compound. The early arrivals got the choice spots under the trees, leaving the exposed areas for others. The cows had been banished to a neighbouring barnyard where they bawled their protestations. Members of the Enthusiasts, the local service club, set up a refreshment stand where they sold ice-cream cones and cups of watery punch for five cents. The area gradually filled up to take on the appearance of the bivouac of an invading army.

All was noise and confusion; children ran screaming back and forth to visit with friends. I never could understand why children can't communicate with each other at something other than the tops of their voices – but then they wouldn't be children. They screeched, "The twenty-fourth of May is the Queen's birthday, and if you don't give us a holiday we'll all run away" over and over again. They leaped back and forth across the stream or forded it on slippery stones. Some inevitably fell in and had to be dried out. Mothers set out food for a noonday snack – the big picnic would come later. Each family appeared to have enough provisions for the entire assembly. Children would dash back to home base to grab a sandwich and then rush off again. The men gathered in groups under the trees, where they squatted on their heels to discuss farming, business and politics while they passed a surreptitious bottle of moonshine back and forth. Mothers gossiped and shrieked at their children. Another thing I don't understand about children is why they are expected to mind their mothers in public when they are not trained to do so at home.

I went to the picnic with Fred and Audrey Peters and their three children; Audrey insisted there was plenty of food to include me in their party. We were one of the early arrivals so were able to select a good spot near the creek. The Morgans came along right behind us and we were shortly joined by the Elliott family who brought Mamie Sutherland and George Ingraham with them. We all congratulated Audrey and George on their fine performances, although, truth to tell, they had both been completely upstaged by old Angus MacNab and his startling disclosures.

After the noon hiatus, a bell rang to call the assembly together for the races. The crowd gradually gathered at the spot designated for this purpose. The place was a pandemonium. The athletic events were under the inept direction of Mr. Fidge, the school principal, who went around all afternoon in a state of irritation and exasperation because nobody paid him the attention he thought he deserved. I was assigned the responsibility of holding one end of the finishing string with a chap from Dazzle holding the other end; Mal was a starter; George was one of the judges. The races were organized according to age and sex although in some events both sexes competed. It took a long time to get the contestants sorted out and lined up for each event. Then, at a shouted "Go" from Mal, the runners started off pell-mell to the shouts and screams of the crowd.

I was particularly intrigued by some of the races which, so far, have not been accepted for the Olympics, such as the three-legged race, the sack race, running backwards, and the egg race. The egg race ended up in a contretemps in which I got involved.

In this race, the contestant runs with an egg held in a spoon which he must get intact across the finish line. At the shouted "Go," a swarm of youngsters of both sexes started up the field with their eggs balanced precariously in their spoons. Some contestants ran rapidly, trusting to luck to keep the egg on the spoon, while others ran more slowly, taking greater care to keep the egg from falling. The race was run with real eggs so very soon the field was awash with broken eggs to the accompaniment of cries of despair from the unlucky ones. A red-headed youngster from Blossom, named Joey Fordick, was well in the lead but just before he reached the finish line he dropped his egg. The egg didn't break so he scooped it up to charge over the line the winner. A lad from Dazzle was second.

My colleague from Dazzle immediately entered a protest. He demanded an examination of the winner's egg which surprisingly had not broken when dropped.

A crowd promptly assembled. The egg in question was retrieved from Joey and cracked open with great ceremony and solemnity. It was found to be hard-boiled; Joey affected great surprise. The Dazzle official demanded that the win be disallowed; Blossomites objected. The argument became general with everybody putting in their two cents' worth. Mr. Fidge was appealed to, but he just dithered. George Ingraham got in the act with some solemn pronouncements. When the Dazzle people saw that Blossom had retained legal counsel, they sent for Cyril Thorndyke, the lawyer from Dazzle. Cyril was short, fat and sweaty with an arrogant mien which didn't quite come off. George stared coldly down his long nose at Cyril from his six foot, two inches' height. The two lawyers fenced with the elaborately polite invective which lawyers tend to use on one another. It was apparent that no solution was going to be reached in this way. Mr. Fidge had a brain wave and suggest that an outsider be chosen to adjudicate the dispute. He pointed at me. I certainly didn't want to get involved in the controversy and did my best to get out of it. However, the loud encouragement of the disputants around me eventually persuaded me reluctantly to act.

I drew Cyril and George to one side, shooing the bystanders away. George, assuming his best courtroom manner, stated frigidly, "There is nothing to establish that an impropriety has been committed by my client. There is no documentation extant which stipulates that the egg in an egg race must be raw. The win stands *ad vitam aut culpam.*

"Certainly there is no written documentation," protested Cyril. "I would point out to you, my learned friend, that British Common Law is not written either, but is not rendered null and void thereby. We must draw on the *lex non scripta* governing the code of egg-racing. The force of custom assumes the strength of law. It has been traditional for many years that egg-racing is undertaken in this part of the country with raw eggs. The tradition therefore takes on legal status. *Consuetudo pro lege servatur.* The use of a hard-boiled egg provides the participant who does so with an unfair advantage which is therefore illicit and *ultra vires.*"

"It is unfair to the defendant," proclaimed George, "that he be penalized for his initiative in using a boiled egg, which I submit is not proscribed under the terms of the contest. *Audaces fortuna juvat.* Furthermore, there is no proof in evidençe to establish that the egg he dropped would have shattered if it had not been hard-boiled."

"Nonsense," stated Cyril. "All other eggs dropped from that height were fractured. Irrevocably."

"I suppose you would quote the case of *Humpty Dumpty* versus *All the King's Men* in support of your latter point," sneered George. "The evidence is nonconclusive."

"I shall reserve on the point," said Cyril. "The fact remains that the defendant was using an illegal piece of equipment which disqualified him from the contest whether or not the infraction worked to his advantage. *In maleficiis voluntas spectatur non exitus.*"

"Piffle," said George. "It has not been established that the equipment was indeed illegal. *Quod lex non vetat permittit.*

There is therefore no proper basis for your argument, which is irrelevant and immaterial." George turned to me. "My distinguished colleague has made reference to *jus commune.* The effectiveness of common law rests on precedents. I have not heard him quote any such references. I would be interested to hear him do so."

"I haven't heard you quote any either," retorted Cyril.

"The onus is on the prosecution," stated George, sententiously. "*Actori incumbit onus probandi.* The defendant is presumed innocent until proven guilty."

"Quite," said Cyril. "My friend is stating the obvious about the irrelevant to obfuscate his weakness about the pertinent. *Ignoratio elenchi.* We are debating a point of law here. My learned colleague has suggested I quote precedents. All precedents are set by decisions on new cases such as the one we are now considering. Therefore a heavy responsibility rests upon our distinguished jurist here," he bowed to me, "since his decision will have an impact on egg-racing for all time to come."

"I have every faith in the good judgment of our adjudicator," said George, with a meaningful look into my eyes.

"So have I," affirmed Cyril. Sweat ran down his forehead to drop off his nose. He wiped it away with the back of his hand. "There have been very few cases related to egg-and-spoon-racing which have reached our courts, as far as I know. We must, therefore, extrapolate from related situations, placing due emphasis on simple equity. We must begin *ab ovo.*" Cyril gave a harsh laugh. "How very apt, come to think of it."

Cyril took a soggy handkerchief from his pocket and mopped his face. He gazed over my shoulder in deep concentration. "Hmm, we must draw on races or athletic events of basic and traditional import. A race that leaps to mind of such classical quality is that between the hare and the tortoise. Does the situation have relevance?" Cyril frowned in concentration. "Yes, I think it does. This was a contest where honesty and perserverance triumphed over –"

"*Crambe repetita,*" interrupted George. "Anyhow that whole case is highly suspect. Not even a rabbit would go to sleep in the middle of a race unless he had been drugged. There is a strong inferential suspicion of malfeasance on the part of the tortoise. If that rabbit had received advice from competent legal counsel it is most likely that an appeal would have been sustained."

"What a sad and cynical evaluation of our noble profession," sighed Cyril. "If truth is to prevail –"

"*Quae Erebe vẹra*?" snapped George.

"Quite," said Cyril. "But let us leave that case, which I still submit affirms that virtue is rewarded. I would refer you to the case where Marcus Augustus Secundus was found using loaded dice in a game of chance to determine who would be proconsul of Sicily. He was forthwith taken out, drawn and quartered."

"What has that to do with the subject under discussion?" demanded George.

"Both cases involve a contest in which improper equipment was used," asserted Cyril.

"Nonsense," snorted George. "And if you are suggesting that young Fordick be drawn and quartered, Counsellor, I would submit you are being a mite harsh. However, if you are going to go that far afield I would refer you to the case of *David* versus *Goliath*, which is much more germane to the issue. In this contest David used a device, viz., a sling, which heretofore had not been used in combat. He employed the same ingenuity as the defendant in this case and was not penalized for his resourcefulness for doing so."

"Goliath was scarcely in a position to protest," objected Cyril.

"True," agreed George. "But you will note that the Philistines accepted the verdict and decamped without quibble."

"Irrelevant," huffed Cyril. "*Brutum fulmen*."

"It would appear, Your Honour," said George, bowing to me, "that my esteemed colleague has been unsuccessful in quoting any precedents which support his position. May I be permitted to present some classical cases which support mine?" I nodded politely. George turned back to a sweating Cyril. "I would refer you, Counsellor, to the case of the Golden Apples. You will recall, sir, that this case dealt with a foot race between Atalanta and

Hippomenes wherein if the latter won he was to be awarded the hand of Atalanta, but if he lost, his life was forfeit. He was given three golden apples by Aphrodite which he tossed on the ground in front of Atalanta during the course of the race. Atalanta stopped to pick these up and thereby lost the race. The important point here is that the race was not ruled 'no contest' because of the unorthodox and imaginative methods employed by Hippomenes. Indeed, he was acclaimed for his initiative and cleverness and was awarded Atalanta for his bride."

"They came to a bad end, as I recall," said Cyril. "A romance based on deceit is doomed."

"Piffle," said George. "All romance is based on deceit. But let me refer you now to another race in which matrimony was involved. Pelops won the hand of Hippodamia on the basis of beating her father in a chariot race despite strong evidence that Hippodamia had bribed her father's charioteer. The results were not contested." Cyril began to object, but George held up a peremptory hand. "Permit me to continue, Counsellor, *cum bona venia*. Similarly in another famous case, Messala did not protest the outcome of that race despite certain irregularities of conduct undertaken by Ben Hur. And my distinguished friend, surely you must accept the validity and high repute of the *Lex Romana*."

"The *lex* was lax," stated Cyril. "Anyhow, in that case both contestants displayed regrettably unsportsmanlike behaviour, whether or not their actions were legal. Messala could scarcely protest an irregularity which he himself initiated. The plaintiff in the present case could scarcely complain if his egg had also been hard-boiled."

"How do you know it wasn't?" demanded George.

"Certainly it wasn't," cried Cyril.

"You are assuming a fact not in evidence, sir."

"We shall get the egg and examine it then."

"That is not possible. There is now no way of identifying the egg with certainty since it has been outside the jurisdiction of this court of enquiry. But by making the suggestion you have conceded the cogency of my position.

"In the name of good sportsmanship, I would suggest that you withdraw your protest," said George haughtily.

"On the same basis, I would recommend that you concede the case and race," answered Cyril.

They glared at one another. This seemed like an appropriate time for me to intervene. "Gentlemen, I have listened to your presentations," I said solemnly, "and I am prepared now to render my decision. You have both presented telling and cogent arguments which are a credit to your erudition and ingenuity – I congratulate you both. However, I am impressed by the following points: egg racing has customarily and traditionally been undertaken in this area using raw eggs; the use of a boiled egg gives a contestant an unfair advantage; raw eggs make the race more exciting. I therefore rule in favour of the prosecution; the previous winner is disqualified; the race has been won by the lad from Dazzle."

"A wise and proper decision, sir," cried Cyril, seizing me by the hand. "Future generations will have occasion to recall your name with gratitude, for, by this decision, you have restored the art of egg racing, which was dangerously in jeopardy, to its preëminent position in the sporting world. I do congratulate you on your sound and courageous finding, sir. *Haec olim meminisse juvabit*."

I nodded graciously. "*Illegitimis non carborundum*," I said solemnly.

"Quite, quite," cried Cyril bouncing off to spread the glad tidings. George didn't speak to me for the rest of the day.

My decision was received with great joy by the Dazzle followers, but with scorn and derision by Blossomites. Dazzle accepted my judgment as an impersonal vindication of the validity of their case, whereas Blossom saw it as a dereliction of responsibility on my part and a reflection on my honour, integrity and acumen. Ah, the loneliness of the Bench!

As the afternoon progressed it became apparent that a ding-dong battle was shaping up between the two towns. Each event was scored on a point system of three, two and one for first, second and third standing; an aggregate score for each town was tallied on a blackboard set on a wobbly tripod. After each competition, the new totals were recorded before an attentive audience, the new figure being greeted with cheers or boos depending on loyalties. When the contests came down to the last two events,

Blossom was four points behind. The remaining events were the tug of war and the baseball game; by prior agreement the tug of war counted five points and the baseball game ten.

A long, thick rope was brought from a truck and stretched out on the ground for the tug of war. Each team consisted of ten men; the contest was to be two out of three pulls. The teams lined up along the rope, digging holes with their heels to get purchase for pulling. The contestants had been well chosen – heavy, powerful fellows with muscles toughened by hard physical work. Mal Morgan was our anchor man where his size and strength could be used to the best advantage. He looked puny, however, compared to the anchor man for Dazzle, who must have weighed three hundred pounds. Fred Peters said if the fellow just sat down there was no way he could be budged. After a good deal of jockeying back and forth, the starter hollered "Go" and the teams tugged and strained to screams of encouragement from the crowd. Muscles strained; cords stood out on necks; faces got red and then purple. Mal looked as if he would pop a blood vessel.

Gradually the Dazzle team inched backward until the handkerchief on the rope was pulled over the prescribed line for a win. On the second pull Blossom managed a win by starting the pull before the other team got set. There was a great deal of bickering about this, but finally the win was allowed. The final and deciding pull was a contest of heroic proportions. The outcome continued in doubt for several minutes, the rope inching one way and then the other. The crowd screamed itself hoarse.

Finally Mal's feet slipped from under him knocking the next man's feet from under him, and so on down the line like duckpins. The Blossom team was hauled ignominiously across the line on the seats of their pants. Great jubilation for the Dazzle supporters; chagrin for Blossom.

Blossom was now nine points behind on the aggregate, but could stave off defeat with a win in the baseball game. While the other events had been in progress, the baseball players had been warming up and preparing the diamond. A makeshift backstop of chicken wire had been constructed to protect the spectators from wild pitches. The infield was cleared of debris, but the outfield still had some hazards left behind by the previous tenants of the pasture; an outfielder, therefore, in running for a fly ball had to keep one eye on the ball and one on his footing.

I was very surprised to see that George was a member of the team. I had no idea that he could, or would, play baseball. He joined us at the edge of the diamond after changing to his uniform in the car. He looked ridiculous. The shirt fit reasonably well but the pants had obviously been made for someone of quite different proportions. The legs of the pants were barely long enough on his shanks to tuck into the top of the socks below his knees, while the waist and back would have accommodated someone of Mal's size; the seat hung down like a knapsack.

"You could carry a watermelon in the ass of them pants," said Mal with a loud guffaw.

Mamie giggled, looking at George's long, skinny legs. "You look like a grasshopper," she chuckled.

"One with a caboose," roared Mal.

George was not amused. His face took on the frigid look it did when he was annoyed. He stomped off without a word. As he walked away, part of the problem with the pants became apparent; the belt loops at the back were broken producing a gap so that the waist hung outward. He kept tucking the pant top up under his belt at the back, but every time he bent over, it came loose again. I hoped George would play well in order to redeem his prestige with the locals which had plummeted when he lost the egg-and-spoon debate.

The umpire, an import from Medicine Hat to assure impartiality, summoned the captains of the teams to home plate. Blossom lost the toss, so had to bat first.

Baseball in small towns is much more exciting than in the professional leagues where the proficiency of the players leaves very little to chance. But in a rural game nothing is predictable; a fly ball has about a fifty-fifty chance of being dropped; a throw to a base is as apt to be wide as not; the batters swing at nearly anything pitched to them, which is fortunate because the pitchers have a great deal of trouble getting the ball over the plate. These uncertainties provide an excitement not engendered by more efficient operations. Any hit precipitates a chain reaction of thrilling, counterbalancing errors. Games therefore tend to be high-scoring; pitchers' duels are unheard of.

This game between Blossom and Dazzle ran true to form. The usual series of sparkling disasters brought Dazzle to bat in the last of the ninth inning behind by three runs with the score at fourteen to eleven. A lead of three runs was not considered by Blossom to be a safe margin by any means.

George was no great whiz as a baseball player, but he seemed to me to be no more inept than most of his teammates. He played shortstop which was a strange assignment for someone of his lanky size. He had scored two runs, once getting on by a walk and once reaching first when a wild pitch flipped the saggy seat of his pants. The latter decision elicited a violent protest from the Dazzle pitcher, but the umpire remained firm.

The bottom half of the ninth started off very well for Blossom. Surprisingly enough, the pitcher struck out the first two batters. Then things started to fall apart. He walked the next batter and hit the following one on the shin, putting runners on first and second. The next batter hit a pop fly into short left field. George at shortstop and the second baseman, both shouting "I've got it," collided disastrously and dropped the ball. George finally grabbed up the ball and threw it six feet over the catcher's head. The two runners scored and the batter ended up at second base. Loud cheers from Dazzle; loud moans from Blossom. The next batter got a walk. Dazzle was now only one run behind with the tying run on second and the winning run on first. The situation was very serious indeed; the crowd was in an uproar.

At this critical juncture in the game, the catcher walked slowly out to the mound to discuss the situation with the pitcher; they were joined there by Bill Foot, the manager. The three of them conferred for several minutes to much shouted advice from the spectators. Finally, the manager clapped the pitcher on the back and walked solemnly back to the sidelines. The catcher returned to the plate, put on his mask and squatted behind the batter. I found myself with my hands clenched, saying over and over again "One to go. Put him out. One to go. Put him out." The umpire called for play. The pitcher scowled for a long time at the batter; then he went into his windup; the crowd hushed; he delivered the ball.

CRACK! The sound of a solid hit. Disaster. The crowd roared. The ball streaked for George at shortstop, hit him on the head, bounced up in the air and ran down his back into his pants via the gaping flap at his belt. The runners were dashing for home. The crowd was screaming. The infield, including a dazed George, were running around shouting "Where's the ball?" George finally became aware of something bobbing around in the seat of his pants. He reached in, fished out the ball and held it triumphantly aloft. The batter was out. The game was over. Blossom had won! Bedlam! George was hoisted on the shoulders of his teammates and carried jubilantly off the field.

The Olympics should be so exciting.

Chapter Five

WEDDING BELLS

UDY ELLIOTT AND BILL ROSCHUK announced to their families that they were going to get married. The two families had a fit. "You're too young," they objected. "It's the middle of the Depression. Where are you going to live? How are you going to make ends meet?" All the usual comments by families under like circumstances. Judy and Bill replied, "We are in love, we are eighteen and we will get along just fine." The two families sighed and accepted the inevitable. Once they got used to the idea, they entered into the arrangements with joy and enthusiasm.

Judy was the daughter of my good friends Florence and Dick Elliott, and Bill was the son of the biggest farmer in the district, Theodore Roschuk. Judy was the prettiest girl in town, with wavy blond hair, impish blue eyes and a pert little nose. Bill was a strapping big lad, well over six feet tall, with a shock of black hair and an amiable, slow grin. Delightful youngsters, both of them.

A wedding in Blossom was always a big social event; in this case it would be particularly noteworthy because of the prominence of the two families in the community. The whole town participated in the preparations. Nobody had any money to speak of, so it was a matter of make do and share what they had. The bridesmaids were appointed and immediately began remodelling their best dresses. Grandma Akerbilt came over to the Elliott's house with an offer of her wedding dress which had come west in a Red River cart. Grandma Akerbilt wasn't Judy's real grandmother, nor anybody else's as far as I know, but she was a kindly old lady everybody in town called Grandma. Her offer of the dress was gratefully accepted; alterations and fittings were promptly begun. Arrangements were made with Reverend Slye to come from Swift Current to perform the ceremony; George Ingraham agreed to play the organ; and Mamie Sutherland was delighted to be asked to sing.

While these activities were going on in the Elliott household, Bill's parents were busy too. Mr. Roschuk began remodelling an old bunkhouse on his farm about a half-mile from his own house. Neighbours came from the town and from miles around for a working bee. They cleaned the house out completely and put new tar paper on the walls and roof. A new privy appeared, set a sensible distance away – far enough not to be a nuisance yet close enough for convenience at thirty degrees below zero. Rooms were partitioned and shelves and cupboards built. A chicken run was set up and someone contributed a few chickens. A root cellar was dug under the house; Jerry Rusk left a sack of potatoes in it. Fred Peters contributed the frame and wheels for a Bennett Buggy, and Wesley Ward provided a big fourposter bed. My contribution was a slightly-used water pump which I wrote off my inventory as defunct.

Then the ladies descended on the place with mops and brushes to give it a thorough scrubbing. Curtains and pots and pans and other household effects soon put in their appearance. Grandma Akerbilt, who was fond of Judy, provided an eiderdown mattress. Hand-hooked rugs graced the floors; jars of preserves and pickles lined the shelves.

By the day before the wedding, the place looked real shipshape – not exactly the Taj Mahal, but very cosy and homey. It was a remarkable example of the good will and coöperation of a generous community in a time of crisis.

I arranged to go to the wedding with Fred and Audrey Peters. On the morning of the big day I drove around in my old flivver to pick them up. I thought we were in plenty of time, but when we arrived, the church was nearly filled so we ended up near the front.

The whole town was there, and folks from miles around, all looking very dressed up as only country people can, with their tanned faces and white foreheads.

The church filled up rapidly and extra chairs were brought from the church hall. Mr. and Mrs. Roschuk appeared and were escorted to their places. It was easy to see where Bill got his large size; both his mother and father were over six feet tall and must have weighed four hundred and fifty pounds between them. The diminutive usher beside Mrs. Roschuk looked like a tugboat bringing in an ocean liner. Mr. Roschuk strode behind them with a dignified and solemn mien. The pew creaked as they seated themselves.

Florence Elliott, Judy's mother, arrived and was escorted to her seat. She wore a pink lace dress, matching hat, and a tremulous smile. She was an older and plumper version of Judy, blond and lovely, with large blue eyes and an air of English gentility.

A feeling of expectation gripped the assembly. The door from the vestry opened and the best man entered, followed by Bill and Reverend Slye. They took their places at the front of the church. Bill was dressed in his best blue suit, which was a bit short in the arms and legs. He towered over his best man. Bill seemed to be almost in shock. His face was very white and his eyes had a slight glaze to them. The muscles along his jaw were bunched and knotted. The boys faced Reverend Slye, who beamed benignly upon the congregation. His neck stuck out of his clerical collar like an asparagus shoot to support a lined and kindly face. Fred Peters always felt that Slye's name was an unfortunate one for a minister. I suppose it gave him a problem to which he had become reconciled long ago.

Then we had a rather long wait. George Ingraham was noodling around on the organ, and peering at the back of the church. Finally he launched into *Lohengrin*; everyone stood up and gazed expectantly at the door. But George had apparently got his signals crossed. After a few moments the door opened and Miss Peabody stuck her head in. She looked startled when she found everyone staring at her, and she popped back out of sight. Miss Peabody was a most unlikely substitute for the bride. She was an old maid who, Fred claimed, was a camp follower left over from the Riel Rebellion. In a few minutes she reappeared and scuttled to a chair at the side of the church. George was starting *Lohengrin* for a second time when one of the ushers finally smartened up and looked outside; he shook his head at George. George gave up on the wedding march and branched off into something else. The crowd gradually seated itself, with shrugs of interrogation and disappointment.

The usher kept a watch at the door and finally gave George the high sign; George struck up *Lohengrin* again. Most of the crowd stood up, but a few remained seated with a wait-and-see attitude, having lost faith in George at the organ. But it was for real this time.

The three bridesmaids started down the aisle one at a time with slow, trembly steps and fixed, happy smiles. Then came little four-year-old Peggy Smith as flower girl – as cute as a chipmunk on a pine branch. Then Judy, on her proud father's arm. The ladies all rustled and *oohed* and *aahed* quietly. It is always said that the bride is beautiful, but Judy was really a knockout. Her big blue eyes and flushed cheeks made her face sort of gleam against the background of misty white veil. Grandma Akerbilt's dress of heavy creamy satin fitted her to a tee. She was so lovely that I felt a lump in my throat and a bit of moisture in my eyes. Judy and her father progressed slowly to the front of the church.

At this point things started to come unstuck.

As they turned at the front of the church and Judy moved in front of her father, he stepped on the train of her gown. When she moved forward, the train pulled off. Fortunately, the train was not an integral part of the dress so it just detached from her shoulder and she was not exposed. The top of the train did, however, get caught in the veil and pulled it off. Judy let out a squeal and grabbed for the veil, but too late. Her father picked up the train and tried to stick it back on, but didn't know how. Judy retrieved the veil and, with the aid of a bridesmaid, got it back on her head at a somewhat rakish angle. They abandoned the train, and her father was left somewhat forlornly holding it.

Little Peggy Smith, the flower girl, was supposed to join her mother in the third row, but she was enjoying things so much that she proceeded up the steps behind Reverend Slye to a spot where she could see better. Her mother waved at her to come, but she just shook her head. When her mother resorted to threatening gestures, Peggy stuck her tongue out, and stayed. Mrs. Smith gave up and Peggy remained at her vantage point.

Judy and Bill exchanged gentle smiles, then faced the minister. Reverend Slye beamed happily upon them and began the time-honoured and beautiful ceremony. However, there must have been some flowers in the bride's bouquet to which Reverend Slye was violently allergic. Some people can sneeze with a short little "chew," while others wind up with a preliminary series of "yeh, yeh, yehs," and then practically lift the roof. Reverend Slye unfortunately was one of the latter.

The first sneeze apparently caught him unawares. He got as far as "Dearly beloved, we are gathered here –" when he let out a great, juicy "WHARF," which blew the bride's headdress off. At least, that's what it looked like. Actually, an unexpected forty-kilowatt sneeze in the face from two feet away is a little disconcerting; Judy jumped back and the already precarious headdress went sailing. A bridesmaid picked it up and put it back on. Reverend Slye said, "Excuse me," and started over again. This time he got only as far as, "Dearly beloved –" when he went into a great "Yak, yak, yak, vroom, SHRASH –" Judy was ready for him this time and held onto her headdress.

Reverend Slye said "Excuse me" again and turned his back, reaching frantically for a handkerchief, which apparently he didn't have. He wiped his nose surreptitiously on a corner of his gown, and after a few moments turned back to the bride and groom. "Beerly belubbed – we are rar-rar-rar-rar, eep–eep–SWISHSS –" At this point he saw a handkerchief in the breast pocket of the best man and made a frantic grab for it. He missed, and nearly blew the poor boy's head off.

The lad staggered back a few steps, but returned manfully to hand his handkerchief to the minister. Reverend Slye pushed the prayer book into the best man's hands while he turned his back and blew his nose with a stentorian blast. He had two more whopping big sneezes, which doubled him up so hard that he hit his head a wallop on the choir stall. This left him slightly dazed. He staggered back into a stand holding a large vase of lilacs. He whirled in time to catch the vase before it fell. He walked along bent over almost double, with the vase in both hands, crying, "Yuk, yuk, yuk, yea, ya, yo –" George nipped over from the organ and as the Reverend ended up with a great "WHEEE –" George grabbed the vase from him and returned it to its pedestal. George handed Reverend Slye a handkerchief, which he snatched and had a couple of vigorous blows. He had apparently identified the cause of his difficulty, for he returned to the bride and groom and said desperately, "Throw those bloody flowers out!" He probably intended it as a whisper, but it came out on the wings of a sneeze, which gave it a force he didn't intend. His words carried loud and clear, ending in a great sneeze.

The best man got the message. He collected the girls' bouquets and placed them on the floor at the side of the church. As he passed me, I handed him my handkerchief, and so did Fred. The boy gave them to Reverend Slye, who was stomping and wharfing like an Indian chief on the warpath.

At this point our attention was diverted from Reverend Slye's problems. Peggy Smith had remained on the steps at the front of the church to watch the proceedings. Earlier she had been the centre of attention, but she had been upstaged completely by Reverend Slye's remarkable performance. The excitement had become too much for Peggy. A frantic call of "Mummy" drew our attention to her. She was bent over, desperately holding onto her knees and crying. An ever-widening puddle on the rug revealed the reason for her distress. Mrs. Smith assessed the situation immediately, and charged out of her pew to rescue Peggy. Unfortunately, she tripped over her husband's feet, and did a belly-flopper in the aisle. Her hat rolled under a pew; her handbag flew open, distributing debris over a wide area. She ignored this, scrambled to her feet, exclaimed "Stupid oaf" at her husband, and bustled up the aisle to whisk Peggy out a side door.

In the meantime, Reverend Slye had gotten himself more or less under control. The offending flowers had been removed, and he was prepared to give it another whirl. Apparently his plan was to rush the thing through as fast as possible. But, alas, his fondest hopes were doomed.

With two handkerchiefs held in front of his face, which muffled not only his sneezes and sniffing but also the words, he began rushing through the ceremony. It came out a bit like this: "Bearlybelowedwearegathered, snif, here in the eee–shee–eep–YIPE, sightofGodandintheface of dis com . . . compa – ARFLE company . . . bazoo, bazoo, bazoo, WHARF . . . tojointogether this shish – shish sheeeeeRARK inholymatrimonygalu, galu, GALOOF whidhisanorible, snif, estate, ya, ya, ya, YORK, instooted gow, gow, kee, kee KRIST . . . "

It was probably only coincidence that the groom fainted at that point where the minister asks if any man knows any reason why the couple should not be wed, speak up or forever hold his peace, but that's when it did happen. Bill had been standing throughout the ceremony as stiff as a frozen stump. But at this point he spun halfway around so that he was partially facing the congregation; his eyes went up and he just collapsed on the floor – all six feet of him. You always hear stories about the groom fainting, but this time it really happened.

There was mass consternation and a great hubbub. Everyone stood up; those at the back stood on the pews to see what was going on. Judy screamed and burst into tears. The bridesmaids rallied around to comfort her, and burst into tears also, to keep her company. Judy's mother felt she was going to faint too, for awhile, but she thought better of it. Reverend Slye asked plaintively, "Wod hobbened?" and went off in a series of foot-stomping sneezes, a total loss. Those in the front pews grouped around Bill, offering advice and solicitude. Miss Peabody whispered in my ear, "Who shot him?" Maybe Fred was right about her. Somebody hollered, "Give him air," and the crowd moved back a half-inch. George Ingraham pushed through the crowd with a glass of water he had obtained from somewhere. He loosened Bill's tie and poured the water over Bill's face. After a few minutes Bill's eyes began focussing and he tried to get up. George held him down and said, "Take it easy, Bill. You fainted, that's all."

Finally they got Bill up and sitting on the front pew with his head between his knees. Bill kept muttering, "I'm okay. I'm okay."

The best man said to George, "What he needs is a real good slug of hooch."

"By God, you're right," said George. He got up on a pew and called out, "Has anybody here got a bottle of whisky?" He stared straight at Jeb Wilson.

At this announcement all eyes of the congregation followed George's gaze to focus on Jeb. He looked startled and uneasy, and touched himself on the chest with a sort of a "Who me?" attitude. The eyes continued to stare at him. Jeb jumped up and ran outside to his old Essex, to return promptly with a beer bottle securely sealed with a cork. Jeb's home-brew was famous in the district for medicinal and other purposes. Roscoe, his dog, followed Jeb back into the church and sat quietly under a pew.

George tipped up Bill's head and poured some of Jeb's raw moonshine liquor into his mouth. Bill sputtered, coughed, and shook his head. After a few minutes George made Bill have another good pull at the bottle. The colour started coming back into his cheeks, but he was still pretty groggy.

George told Reverend Slye, who was by now relatively free of the sneezes, that they should not take a chance on getting Bill back on his feet, but to continue the ceremony with Bill sitting down. Reverend Slye agreed, and this was the way it was done. George gave the bottle of whisky to the best man, who stuck it in his hip pocket.

The good reverend raced through the ceremony in record time. Bill was still pretty woozy; when it came to the point where he was to respond, the best man nudged him and told him to say "I do." Bill wasn't clearheaded enough to understand, but Reverend Slye heard the "I do" and hurried on. When it came time to put the ring on Judy's finger, Bill couldn't do it. The best man gave it to her and she put it on herself. These two facts led to some discussion later as to whom Judy had really married – Bill or the best man. But Bill went on the honeymoon, so I guess that settles that.

When Reverend Slye had zipped and sniffed his way through

the ceremony, the bridal party retired to the vestry to sign the register, the best man and an usher supporting Bill and directing his wobbly steps. After they had tottered off behind the scenes, there was an outburst of subdued whispering which soon subsided when Mamie Sutherland got up and walked to the front of the church. She had been asked by the bride to sing "Because."

I'd heard Mamie sing before, and while she didn't have much of a voice, she made up for the lack of quality by plenty of volume. She used a very wide vibrato, so if she got anywhere near a note she was apt to get part of it.

After waiting a moment for silence, she bowed in a gracious way to George Ingraham who had returned to the organ. George played a short introduction. Mamie took a huge breath, increasing her already ample upper proportions by a good four inches, and launched off in a completely different key. I guess maybe the earlier confusion had shaken her up some. Both Mamie and George looked shattered, but carried on heroically. George tried changing keys to find where Mamie was, but I guess she was singing in the cracks that day. Anyhow, every time George changed key, Mamie did too. It was a very interesting chase, and they never did get together.

When she came to her first high note, she sailed up to it at full throttle, and went right out of sight. She had gotten herself into a key where that note was just not available to her. She stood there with her mouth wide open, straining every muscle, but not a sound coming out.

At this point Mamie showed the quality she was made of. She closed her mouth and said quietly, "I'm sorry, we seem to have begun in the wrong key."

She turned to George at the organ and said politely, "Shall we try it again, Mr. Ingraham. And let's do it in the key we rehearsed, shall we?" I could see George's face from where I sat; he mouthed a comment at Mamie that was rather inappropriate for the surroundings, if not for the situation. He played the introduction over again, and held Mamie's cue note until she found it after a few trial glissandos. Away they went, more or less together, and we all breathed more easily.

When she came again to that first high note everyone in the

church was leaning forward, tense and apprehensive, but really pulling for her. She took a big breath and swooped up to it, with everyone in the audience straining with her; and she sailed right on past it. With her wide vibrato, it didn't matter too much. Mamie looked real pleased with herself, and everyone settled back with a sigh of relief.

However, that high note was too much for Jeb Wilson's dog, Roscoe. He let out a piercing howl. That note had hit some responsive chord in his head and he just had to join in. From there to the end of the number, Mamie and Roscoe sang a duet. I don't have a very good ear for music, but I rather felt that Roscoe was doing a better job of it than Mamie. Mamie tried to drown him out. Roscoe was enough of a ham that he wasn't going to permit it, so he just upped his volume too. Jeb was down on his knees trying to catch the dog, and muttering things you don't expect to hear at a wedding. Mamie and Roscoe finished the song with a rousing finale. On that high note at the end, both Mamie and Roscoe gave it all they had, and it was a wowser.

When the number was finished the congregation did something I've never seen at a wedding before or since – they burst into rousing, spontaneous applause. I don't know if they were clapping for Mamie or Roscoe, or both. Mamie bowed graciously and took her seat. Roscoe didn't get a chance to take a bow; Jeb finally caught him and threw him out the door. I felt that this was rather shabby treatment for a star performer.

Bill was looking more like his old self, when the bridal party reappeared some minutes later, so I presume he had had a couple of good belts of Jeb's brew. The bridal party was all smiles. George Ingraham broke into a march on the organ, and everyone rose, beaming happily.

The reception in the church hall was something of an anticlimax – and no wonder. But even here a few minor hitches developed. Judy's uncle Arthur had been chosen to give the toast to the bride because he was considered to be quite a wit. He went on for a good twenty minutes, and some of his stories would have brought a blush to the cheeks of a threshing gang. He'd forgotten the groom's name completely, and referred to him as "what's-his-name." Bill retrieved the situation somewhat with his speech of reply, which was simply, "Thank you all very much. I guess it was a terrific wedding. I don't remember much of it." And then he just grinned.

The wedding cake was cut with proper ceremony and bits of it were passed out to "sleep on." The bride and groom wandered about the room receiving felicitations and hugs and kisses from their friends. They looked so happy it made you want to cry.

While I was standing in the crowd with a glass of cheerless punch in my hand, George appeared at my elbow. "Ah," I said, "here is the hero of the hour. You certainly saved the day with that bottle of Jeb's moonshine. Without that nip I don't think the groom would have made it. How did you know Jeb would have a bottle available?"

"An educated guess," said George with a grin.

I looked around. "Where's Mamie?"

"She's in tears somewhere, and refuses to speak to me. For some reason or other she blames me for the whole fiasco of her solo."

"Was that you howling? I thought it was Roscoe."

"Women," said George with feeling.

"Since weddings are very much on our minds today," I said, "why don't you solace her by proposing marriage?"

"Approached with your usual subtlety," growled George. "Anyhow, after today's performance, your timing is bad."

"I've arranged with Judy to throw her bouquet to Miss Peabody. I think she has her eye on you so you're a gone goose anyhow. Better settle for Mamie."

"I am unworthy."

"How true. How very true."

After what seemed an interminable length of time, the bride and groom disappeared for a brief period, to return in their going-away clothes. There was much milling about, good-byes, kissing and a few happy tears. The best man had retrieved the flowers from the church for the ceremony of throwing the bride's bouquet. Judy stood on the steps, closed her eyes, and threw the bouquet over her shoulder, not to Miss Peabody, but right into Reverend Slye's smiling face. He doubled up and went stomping off in a series of head-shattering sneezes.

Judy and Bill, liberally sprinkled with rice and confetti, got into her father's old Auburn car, decorated with Just Married signs and the inevitable cluster of tin cans, to take off for their honeymoon at Waterton Lakes. Reverend Slye returned to the steps and called out, "God be with you and good-bye – yi, yi, yi, whurra, whurra, SHARUSHAFISH!"

Chapter Six

THE DEVIL AND BIG JOHN

TO QUOTE ANOTHER WESTERN APHORISM of Jeb Wilson's: "If the dog hadn't stopped to have a crap, he'd have caught the rabbit." If I hadn't got the hives, if I hadn't told George about it, if he hadn't mentioned Mrs. Forsythe – various "ifs" without which I never would have learned about Big John's epic struggle with the Devil.

Now to explain the series of "ifs." I came down one morning from my room at the Palaza Hotel to have breakfast at Wong Toy's restaurant where I joined George Ingraham who was having bacon and eggs in a back booth. We chatted about this, that and the other thing while Wong prepared my breakfast. I was kept very busy scratching myself.

"What's the matter?" asked George. "Have you forgotten the old adage, 'No use standing on the seat, Blossom crabs jump thirty feet'?"

"No, I haven't forgotten that venerable bit of graffiti. But I seem to have come down with the hives. It's funny, because I've never had hives before." I showed George the red welts on my wrists and ankles.

George laughed. "You've run into some Cypress Hills coyotes."

"What do you mean?" I asked in alarm. "Not crabs, for heaven's sake?"

"No. Bedbugs. Where did you stay last night?"

"The Palaza, of course."

"Yeah," said George offhandedly. "It happens there every once in a while. You'd better check out till they get the place cleared up. Tell the room clerk about it when you leave."

"But where could I go?" I asked. "The Palaza is the only hotel in town."

George spread some jam on a piece of toast. "Have you ever met Mrs. Forsythe?"

"No. Who is she?"

"She's a widow who lives on the outskirts of town. She takes in roomers occasionally to make a few dollars. I stayed there for a time when I first came here – before I got my present digs. Tell her I sent you; she'll probably put you up. You'll find it very comfy." George got a strange, warm reminiscent look in his eye.

"George," I said sternly. "You're holding back something. Tell me more about Mrs. Forsythe."

George sighed. "Was I so transparent? Very well, but I'll have to swear you to secrecy since two, no, three reputations are at stake. However, I've never found you a gossipmonger so I guess I can trust you."

I held up my hand. "I swear on one of Wong Toy's T-bone steaks, which I hold more dear than anything else in life."

"Do you know Big John?"

"What's Big John got to do with it?"

"Quite a bit. Do you know him?"

"No, not really. I've seen him around town in a long brown cassock from time to time, that's about all."

"Then I'll start off with a preamble about Big John before I get back to Mrs. Forsythe. Here's the story."

Big John is the spiritual leader (began George) of a religious order called the Brothers of Peace, who operate a large farm about five miles west of here. As far as I know they have no affiliation with any other order or with any church. There are about fifteen of the brothers who run the farm on a communal basis. They live a harsh, ascetic life; they sleep in a barracks on pallets and eat in a common dining hall; work begins at dawn and continues until sunset with periodic breaks for prayer and meditation. I visit the brothers occasionally and am always received with warm and kindly hospitality. I admire them greatly for their sincerity and simplicity.

Their community is practically self-contained. They raise their own vegetables, grind their own grain and even weave the cloth for their habits. In the summer they wear straw hats which they make out of wheat straw; in the winter they wear knitted toques. I have little knowledge about their religious beliefs beyond the fact that they are pledged to celibacy, poverty, and not shaving. In this part of the country at this particular time there's no great trick to remaining dedicated to poverty – it's a way of life for everyone.

The members of the order are known by adopted names, such as Brother Luke, Brother Mark, and so forth. Brother John, their leader, as you have observed, is a huge man who must be six feet, six inches tall. His hard vigorous life has made him tremendously strong; he can handle a bale of hay as if it were a matchbox. He's the only brother who comes to town, which he does in order to pick up the few supplies they cannot provide for themselves. In view of his huge size the people of Blossom call him Big John.

Now, back to Mrs. Forsythe. When I first came to Blossom to set up my practice, I stayed at the Palaza Hotel, of course. I was looking for less expensive accommodation and someone suggested I try Mrs. Forsythe's. I went out to her house and she agreed to take me in. She's a handsome, buxom woman in her early forties who wears her hair wrapped around her head in braids. She showed me my room which was upstairs and immaculate; it contained a sagging double bed covered by a fluffy comforter. I told her I was uncertain what day I would be ready to move in but she said it didn't matter – just to come in and go up to my room if she wasn't around. Doors are never locked in Blossom.

I finished moving my stuff into my office that day, sooner than I expected, so I checked out of the Palaza and about midnight went out to Mrs. Forsythe's. I tiptoed up to my room and fell into bed completely exhausted.

I don't think I had been asleep long when I was awakened by voices in the next room. The walls were paper-thin so it was easy to hear the conversation. One voice was practically bellowing anyhow, and the other, a female voice, was answering quietly in monosyllables. I don't know how long this had been going on, but when I became aware of things, the male voice was proclaiming loudly, "I know you for what you are. You are the instrument of Satan. I know who you are. You are Jezebel! You are Jezebel! You are the Devil himself come to tempt me – come to taunt me – come to make a mockery of me. But I shall prevail. I shall resist you. With God's help I shall prevail and you shall not triumph. No, you shall not triumph. I shall wrestle with you, Satan, who represents the evil within me and I shall prevail. You are not what you seem – so soft – so seductive – I know that. You are Jezebel, perfidious wife to Ahab."

The woman's voice said quietly, matter-of-factly, "Okay, if that's what you say – I'm Jezebel."

The man's voice continued. "And here is your devil's due. Here are your filthy shekels – your greedy offering to obscene Baal, tribute to carnal Mammon. I fling them at you and I defy you to do your worst. I shall prevail. With God's help I shall triumph."

The woman's voice said, "Thank you," which seemed uncalled for under the circumstances.

"Now tempt me. You instrument of the Devil. I defy you, Satan. I shall be firm. Display your blandishments of seduction and lust, and I shall spurn them."

"Okay, big boy."

"Ah yes, Satan, you have the beautiful instruments of seduction – so beautiful, yet so wicked, so vile, so contemptible. I behold and I gaze and I turn my back in disgust. I defy you because I am firm in the Lord. He will give me strength."

I was sitting up in bed listening to this fantastic dialogue and wondering if I were dreaming the whole thing. There was a quiet tap at the door and Mrs. Forsythe – clothed in a silk dressing gown – her long hair hanging down her back – slipped into my room with her finger to her lips. She tiptoed over to the bed and sat on the edge. She leaned over and whispered, "Shh, be quiet."

I whispered back, "What the hell is going on next door?"

"I thought I'd better come and explain," she answered in a hushed voice. "It's Big John. He's come to wrestle with the Devil.

I didn't think you were coming until tomorrow or later when I allowed him to come in."

"There's two people in there. Who's representing the Devil?"

"Flossy Macabee."

"Oho," I cried.

Big John in the next room was tramping up and down, quoting scriptures at the top of his voice and defying the Devil in the form of Flossy Macabee.

"The Brothers of Peace," whispered Mrs. Forsythe, "are sworn to – to – you know, not to have anything to do with women. And it gets pretty hard." She giggled. "I mean it doesn't come easy. They are tempted, and Big John fights the temptation this way."

"Why do you permit him to come here?"

"I didn't know what I was getting involved in. Big John came to me and asked if he could have a room here to wrestle with the Devil. I have a great admiration for the Brothers and for Big John, and I thought he was going to come here to pray or something, so I said all right. I had no idea he was going to bring Flossy Macabee here."

"Why do you permit it to continue?"

"Well, I'm sort of afraid of him – he's so big and impressive and I admire him so much. He is a fine man and maybe this helps him. Anyhow," she giggled, "it's sort of, er – interesting."

"How long has this been going on?"

"A little over a year. He appears at the door late at night every two or three months or so and if I don't have others in the house I allow him to bring Flossy in. Since my house is so far out of the main part of town I have no close neighbours and no one knows. There's no place else he could take her; he can't go to her house 'cause people watch it."

We sat quietly and listened to Big John fulminating in the next room. "The Lord brought down the fiery fury of his wrath on Sodom and Gomorrah because their people had given themselves up to the lusts of flesh. And verily he visits his wrath upon the sinners of today and throughout all time who follow in the path of Sodom and Gomorrah – upon those who permit the depravity and bestiality of the animal in man to overrule and conquer his purity of soul. And he is lost. Then he is lost, lost, lost. The trumpets of Joshua were never as puissant as the strumpets of Babylon or the harlots of Herod."

Flossy's voice could be heard, "Hurry up with the sermon, big boy. I have another date."

"Another assignation on behalf of your master, the Devil," roared Big John. "To lure another soul to destruction. To smother and burn another soul in the brimstone of perdition. The gate to Hades carries a blood-red sign upon its portals and it reads, Woman.

"The Devil is portrayed as a man with horns and a tail, but this is not so. The Devil is a woman – soft, voluptuous and seductive. Her mouth is a snare, her body a trap. She has a body of wicked beauty, a form of wanton entrapment for the unwary. Just as I see before me. But I am aware of the dangers. I am strong in my resolve. I am a rock, unmoved by these enticements. See, I can touch the very lure of damnation and remain unmoved. See, I can . . ."

His voice broke off in almost a scream. A sudden silence fell. Or rather, his talking ceased, and sounds of a very different nature began emanating from the bedroom next door.

"It sounds to me," I whispered to Mrs. Forsythe, "as if the Devil won the battle this time."

"Of course," she smiled.

"Is that what you expected?"

"Certainly," she whispered. "Big John loses the battle every time. He doesn't have a chance. But he tries so hard. Maybe someday he'll make it. But I doubt it."

Mrs. Forsythe smiled into my eyes. "I'm getting cold," she whispered. "Move over."

I didn't put up anything like the fight Big John did. In fact, I didn't fight at all.

Chapter Seven

CURTAIN TIME

I WAS SURPRISED at the lengths to which George Ingraham would go in his programme of joining organizations with the objective of establishing himself in the good graces of the community. The man was shameless. He was even present the night that Blossom missed the opportunity to become the Parnassus of the West and the avant garde leader of world drama by forty years. I also was present by an accident of timing; it happened in this way.

I bumped into my friend Dick Elliott outside the Palaza Hotel late one afternoon and he invited me home for dinner. I demurred for a decent interval, but was happy to accept. The prospect of dinner alone at Wong Toy's filled me with no great enthusiasm, and I knew Dick's wife, Florence, was an excellent cook. I always have some hesitation in facing a wife unannounced for dinner, and Florence in particular. Although she was pretty and could be charming on occasion, she had that aura of superiority and self-approval so characteristic of the English, and so challenging to non-Sassenachs. She could make you feel mighty uncomfortable in a very polite way.

However, Florence seemed to be sincerely pleased to see me and we had a delightful dinner of prairie chicken. While we were dawdling over our coffee, Florence gave Dick one of those knowing looks that wives use and said, "You haven't forgotten, Richard, about the meeting tonight. You promised to go, you remember."

"Oh, yes indeed dear, certainly not," replied Dick somewhat ambiguously.

Florence turned to me. "We are intending to start a Little

Theatre group and we are having our first meeting tonight. I don't suppose you would care to go."

I glanced at Dick. He nodded his head slightly so I replied, "Why yes, thank you, it sounds very interesting." I had an evening to kill and night life in Blossom was practically nonexistent.

"Well fine," said Florence without much enthusiasm. "The meeting is at eight o'clock at the Elks' Hall."

While Florence was doing the dishes, Dick filled me in on the planned Little Theatre organization. Florence, as the acknowledged cultural leader of the community, was always planning flower shows, musical soirées, study groups and so on. If Blossom was to have a Little Theatre, Florence would undoubtedly be the guiding light. Dick had little stomach for these cultural activities, but he went along with them to keep Florence happy. Indeed, should the truth be told, he didn't have much choice if he didn't want to have his finger in a woodpecker's nest around home. He usually acted as treasurer and general troubleshooter for all Florence's projects.

"This last brainstorm of Florence's is the worst one yet," growled Dick. "She actually wants me to act. I wouldn't get up in front of an audience for all the delight in Turkey. However, I'll be so lousy they'll keep me backstage or in the ticket booth or something. I thought if I brought you home for dinner maybe I could get out of going tonight, but I could see that wasn't going to work."

"Oho, I'm not very flattered."

"Oho, to you too. Don't be so sensitive. We're always glad to have you for dinner as you very well know. Anyhow, I thought if I have to go I'd like to have you along for moral support."

"I'll nominate you to play Hamlet."

"You nominate me for anything and you'll have trouble walking with a pitchfork up your arse, my fine feathered friend."

"What got Florence on this drama kick?"

"Some character named Anthony Plum blew into town on a freight and started hanging around the church library talking literature and drama. Some idiot sicked him onto Florence, and the upshot of it all is this plan to form a theatre group. Plum has had quite a bit of experience in acting, he says, and is even going to write and direct the play for them to do. Florence thinks he is a genius. I think he's a nut. Jeb Wilson summed him up pretty well when he said he sure wouldn't recommend Plum for breeding stock. I wish to hell he'd fallen off that freight train somewhere else."

Dick always complained bitterly about Florence's pet projects, but he ended up going along with them. I tried to kid him about the thrill and challenge of treading the boards, but he wasn't amused. A few minutes before eight Florence came in all prettied up and with the tense, brittle manner she always affected when she was in an organizational state. We piled into Dick's old Auburn and wheeled around to the Elks' Hall. Dick and I turned on the lights and set a dozen or so chairs around in a circle, with a card table for Florence as the chairman. Florence fussed and directed and moved everything we set up to some other place, and then back again.

At a few minutes after eight the fledgling thespians began to arrive. Some of them I knew and some I didn't. Laughing cheerfully, Mamie Sutherland strolled in with George Ingraham who was looking rather sardonic about the venture. One surprise was the appearance of big, fat Mal Morgan, who seemed as likely a candidate for the Muse as a bale of hay. "My wife made me come," he whispered sheepishly. There were several housewives, two schoolteachers – one male and one female – and a half-dozen giggling teenagers. All in all, Florence had about fifteen people, which was a very good turnout, I thought.

Anthony Plum, the artist in residence, arrived late as befitted his position. I took an immediate scunner to him. He was slight and willowy, with long, greasy, brown hair and a skimpy beard on his chin, called locally a "billy goat." He wore a dirty ascot scarf with a T-shirt, khaki pants and tennis shoes. He was about twenty-eight years old. He had deep-set baggy eyes and a surprisingly resonant, powerful voice. His manner was arty and, at first, rather diffident. Later, when he felt in command of the situation, he assumed a posture that was theatrical and commanding. Although I could detect no evidence of charisma, his magnificent voice made him impressive. His fingernails were filthy.

Florence Elliott introduced him around. He bowed to each

of the ladies and said "Charmed." He shook hands languidly with the men, and I had to make a conscious effort to keep from wiping my hand on my coat afterwards.

Florence fussed around getting everyone seated, with herself and Plum at the card table. Dick, Mal Morgan and I took chairs as far away as possible. Florence called the meeting to order and explained that the purpose of the evening was to form the Blossom Little Theatre Association. She called for nominations for offices and she was elected president; a schoolteacher named Miss Phibbs, secretary; Dick, treasurer; and Mal, much to his dismay, vice-president.

Florence then gave a pretty discourse on the importance of Culture in a community, with emphasis on the performing arts and drama in particular. She was flushed and happy and tended to repeat everything she said several times.

"Now I am sure," she continued, "that many of us have not had much experience with drama, acting, the stage and all that. So we are fortunate indeed that the winds of chance, yes, the fortunate winds of chance, have brought to our little community a world-renowned actor, director and writer in the person of Mr. Anthony Plum." She bowed to him and he affected a modest *moue*. "Yes, we are fortunate indeed. Mr. Plum has had great experience in the theatre in the East, in England, Paris, New York, and oh, just everywhere. I have had a number of exciting talks with Mr. Plum, and I have been most impressed with his knowledge, and, and, his enthusiasm. He is convinced we can have a very successful theatre in Blossom. He has agreed to give us the benefit of his wonderful experience and act as our director and producer. Aren't we lucky?" Everyone smiled and nodded their heads dutifully.

Florence continued happily. "Mr. Plum has even agreed to give us the benefit of his ability as a playwright and will allow us to produce one of his original plays which he is adapting especially for us. It's all so exciting, isn't it?" Everyone looked properly excited. "And now I shall ask Mr. Plum to outline for us what he has in mind. He tells me he does not have the play in final form, but can give us a general synopsis of the plot and motivation and – and – all that. Mr. Plum, if you please."

Plum rose gracefully and stood for several moments gazing at us. "Madame Chairman," he began in his rich voice, bowing to Florence, "may I commend you for your vision and energy in undertaking the inauguration of an organization to foster the development of the performing arts in your fair city." Eyebrows went up around the room. "We may well, in the years ahead, look back upon this evening as an historic milestone in the cultural life, not only of this community, but of the entire country. Who knows when one tosses a pebble in a limpid and virginal pool on what faraway shores the ripples may lap. It is the courageous cultural leaders of the community, such as yourself, Madame, and your associates here gathered," he made a graceful sweeping gesture to include us all, "who must have the vision to woo the gentle muses and lure them down from misty Olympus to mingle awhile with their humble subjects." Florence wiggled deliciously.

"Your Chairman was most gracious and generous in her introductory remarks with reference to my humble gifts. It is true I have devoted my life to the theatre and have had the privilege of participating in presentations in many a distant milieu. This varied experience as performer, director and writer and my talents, such as they are, I humbly and freely, yea gratefully place at your disposal. If I can be of service in furthering your laudable objectives in bringing a rich, cultural experience to this charming community, I shall be richly repaid."

Mal whispered in my ear, "He has a firm command of malarkey, don't he?"

"Honey wouldn't melt," I whispered back. Florence frowned in our direction. The women were all gazing at Plum with expectant, fatuous smiles and the men with skeptical reservations.

"Your charming Chairman," continued Plum, "has indicated that we are suggesting that for our first offering we present a play which I am writing. She has asked that I outline this to you. You must realize that the play is not in final form, and I shall be able to present an adumbration only. I should warn you that the play will be a departure from the contemporary, mundane, stereotyped format, but I am sure you fine people assembled here will have the courage and the imagination to launch into the unknown and to establish a new parameter of theatrical experience.

"The foundation of the play will rest right here in the rich, verdant soil of your countryside. We shall portray the necessary and coöperative interplay of man, nature, water, machinery and the elements in wresting from the reluctant soil the fruits of the harvest. From this basic concept we shall launch widely into the broader spheres of man's interaction with both his internal and external environment."

"Isn't this exciting?" breathed Florence, fluttering her eyelashes at us.

"There will be a general ferment of protest throughout," continued Plum, now getting into high gear.

"Protest against what?" asked George Ingraham. Mamie gave him a dirty look.

"Everything," answered Plum. "Unemployment, soup kitchens, government, the church, war, the entrenched power of the greedy privileged, man himself, man's inhumanity to man, sex, the restrictive and stultifying mores that society inflicts upon its own freedom – all those factors which grind down, distort, degrade, corrupt, dehumanize, cripple and deform the free soul of man. Each man must have freedom of spirit in order to work out his own individual destiny. His psychic expression must not be inhibited nor restricted by man-made stupidities and sanctimonious and hypocritical affectations. This is our protest and this is our theme.

"Now with this motivation established, let us look at the evolution of the concept in the dramatic vehicle. As I indicated, we shall open with the bucolic motif using a farm milieu. The heroine, if you like, the Earth Goddess, the Spirit of Fecundity will make the first appearance. I would suggest Miss Sutherland for the part."

"Who me?" said Mamie with obvious pleasure and a glance at the younger girls present.

"Yes. Now the Spirit of Fecundity enters bare-breasted and with a sheaf of wheat around her waist. She –"

"Hey," squeaked Mamie, "what's that bare-breasted bit?"

"Now Mamie, don't be a prude," said Florence firmly.

"Okay, then you be the Spirit of Whatever."

"Certainly not," said Florence in alarm.

"But Miss Sutherland, you are so magnificently endowed for the part," urged Plum with an appreciative glance at her sumptuous figure.

"Sure, Mamie," grinned George Ingraham, "you would be a sensation."

"Not bloody likely," said Mamie vehemently, "and you keep out of this, George Ingraham. If you think I'm going to romp around on the stage with nothing on but a sheaf of wheat, you've got another think coming."

"Prig," grinned George, happily. Mamie glared at him.

"You would be accompanied by the other ladies dressed in diaphanous costume," explained Plum with a glance at the young girls. "They will be the spirits and nymphs of fertility. Their costumes will be brutally torn from them in a voluptuous dance with the Earth Demons." The girls looked appalled and the men delighted. "We can work out the costuming later, Miss Sutherland. The Earth Goddess dances a seductive and provocative dance directed at the water pump. The water pump represents Poseidon, the Spirit of Water. The earth must have water in order to realize its potential of fecundity."

"If Miss Sutherland is the heroine, who is the hero?" asked George. "The pump?" He was obviously enjoying himself.

"No, a tractor. This represents the mechanical monsters that man has tamed and mobilized in his service."

"Romantic as all get-out," said George. "Lends itself to some touching love scenes."

"Symbolically, yes," asserted Plum. "Now if I could be permitted to continue without further niggling interruptions –" George didn't look at all crushed.

"Before proceeding further," continued Plum, "I should explain that this is total, absolute theatre. In the past the audience has played a passive, indeed negative or even antagonistic role. But in this presentation the audience is part of the play – they are participants completely caught up in the action – phagocytosed, engulfed, integrated. They will be involved in the theme – agonizing, protesting, contorting, along with the actors. There will be no chairs. The audience will stand or sit or lie and move and mill around – in short, participate. They will be given placards of protest; they are the lines at the soup kitchens; they are the beaten and frustrated masses screaming their hate and revolt."

"I think this guy's nutty as a fruitcake," whispered Mal in my ear.

"And vice versa," I murmured.

"This is total theatre – a total sensuous experience," continued Plum. "We shall assault and assail all the senses from every side – sight, sound, touch, taste, smell. We shall direct flickering and flashing lights into their eyes from above and below with changing colour patterns of kaleidoscopic and prismatic surrealism. We shall flash pictures upon the ceiling and walls of scenes relating to the theme – huddles of unemployed workmen, riots, starving children, war mutilations, depraved scenes of man's bestiality and brutality."

George held up his hand. "Could I make a suggestion here, Mr. Plum?"

Plum was annoyed at being interrupted in full oratorical flight. He glowered at George. "Yes, Mr. Ingraham, what is it?"

"While all this exciting action is going on, how about having three or four chaps playing cricket?"

Plum stared at George in amazement. "Playing cricket? That would be silly."

"Oh, sorry," said George. "We wouldn't want anything silly in this play of course. I just thought –" He hunched his shoulders and held his hands out palms up. "Ouch!" shouted George, grabbing his foot.

"What's the matter, George?" asked Florence.

"Mamie just stomped on my toes," said George, massaging his shoe cautiously.

All eyes turned to Mamie. A slow flush spread from her neck up to her face. "Really, George!" she said in exasperation. Then she started to chuckle, which ended in a full, rich laugh in which everyone joined.

"Carry on, Mr. Plum," said George, with a wave of his hand.

Plum turned his back on the audience with his hand to his forehead. "Now where was I?" He stood for a moment collecting his thoughts before slowly turning around to face the group. "Yes, I was saying that all the senses will be invoked in the development of our theme. The ears of the audience will be assaulted and overwhelmed. Phonographs about the hall will contribute appropriate music which will rise and fall in keeping with the level of action being depicted." He paused in deep thought, staring at George.

"You know, Mr. Ingraham, on second thought, your suggestion about introducing the theme of cricket is a good one. This group, in its preoccupation with a trivial and frivolous activity, epitomizes that decadent segment of society which has lost touch with the serious realities of modern life. Yes, yes, a good thought. A stroke of genius, Mr. Ingraham."

"I have my moments," said George, with a self-deprecatory gesture. Mamie smothered a giggle in her handkerchief.

"I shall return to the matter of cricket later," said Plum, "but in the meantime let me continue my outline of how we shall recruit the various senses. The sense of touch will be aroused. The audience will be able to feel the actors, for they will be enmeshed and entangled with them. The concupiscence of the audience will be aroused and they will be lured into participation. For example, in the scene depicting Man's rise from the primordial ooze, the actors and actresses will be slithering and crawling over and about one another and communicating by speaking in tongues. The younger and more attractive members of the audience will be enticed into this primitive vat of fecundity by sibilant, seductive whispers, fondlings and titillating cajolery.

"We shall call upon the olfactory sense by throwing into the fans appropriate aromas. For example, when the scene is one of voluptuous seduction, exotic and erotic perfumes will be used.

"In summary, we shall recruit and commandeer all the senses so that the audience will be totally involved and whirled, as it were, into the maelstrom of the action."

I am sure that Plum as an actor never had a more attentive audience. I glanced around the circle and saw nothing but staring eyes and open mouths. Only George Ingraham seemed to have retained some detachment as evidenced by an amused and quizzical expression. Florence was completely transfixed. Plum was firmly in command. His rich, deep voice rolled out at us with persuasive intensity. He emphasized his points with dramatic and effective gestures. He was a ham, but a good one.

"Now, after the opening scene which we may anticpate will have successfully secured the audience's attention," he glanced at Mamie who started visibly, "we shall proceed to develop the theme. I should explain that there is not a plot in the traditional manner, but rather the evolution of an ambivalent experience. There will be a magnificent and delicious ambiguity so that each may derive from and relate to the play according to his needs, his frustrations, his cultural resources and his psychic aberrations. Beauty is in the eye of the beholder, but so also is lust, greed, sadism, masochism, pride, and so forth. Each person will find in the play what his nature permits."

"Besides," interjected George, "the ambiguity removes the responsibility from the author to make any sense."

"By no means," contradicted Plum, glancing superciliously at George. "It is a simple matter to present a specific entity of an idea which anyone can understand, but most difficult to formulate a montage which challenges and probes the imagination and psychic depths of every beholder differently." He turned away from George.

"The action will take place in several parts of the stage and auditorium at the same time. Reality and fantasy will be mixed. The audience must decide what is real and what is a phantasmagoric product of delusion or hope or libidinous dreams. Similarly, time will be inextricably scrambled so that the past, present and future will appear concurrently. Sex in the play will go beyond Freud. There will be a strong homosexual theme throughout."

"Homoss –" quavered Florence.

"Why?" asked George.

"To add piquancy. And furthermore," stated Plum somewhat belligerently, "it is one of the major misunderstood and victimized facets of the realities of human relationships. It is the wave of the future in drama. Heterosexuality will become passé except in its more aberrant forms."

"Good heavens," gulped Florence.

"The principal protagonist in the play is Man who represents Everyman. He is the soul in torment striving to find himself and to rise above his atavistic nature. He is followed about by Despair, a player with his face a death mask; every time Man begins to arise from the depths, then Despair beats him into submission.

"Man's only claim to specialness in the animal kingdom is his power of reason – his wisdom. He will worship at the foot of Minerva, the Goddess of Wisdom. But Minerva will be plied with liquor by Bacchus and seduced by him. This leaves Man without wisdom and he descends to bestiality and depravity. The play then portrays what Man is like without wisdom which gives us the license to present many exciting scenes. We shall use the argot of Everyman, the harvester, the prostitute, the bum riding the rods – the four-letter words with impact which are usually eschewed in polite drama, such as –"

"Never mind," interrupted Mal, "we get the picture."

"Very well," said Plum disdainfully. "Insofar as words are concerned, for a change of pace, the dialogue of the second act will consist entirely of the repetition of the same four-letter word over and over again. Since there seems to be some reticence here at the moment in specificity, I am referring to a common Anglo-Saxon word for 'ordure.' The communication between the actors will be entirely by means of this one word with various inflections and emphases. This will demonstrate man's boredom, withdrawal, dissociation, isolation and loneliness – the sickness unto death."

"Easy dialogue to memorize," murmured George.

Plum ignored him. "And now we come to the orgy scenes where we present man's depravity and debauchery when bereft of the tenuous restraints of Wisdom." Plum paused and licked his lips. Everyone leaned forward.

"Madame Chairman," shouted Mal Morgan in my ear so unexpectedly I nearly fell off my chair. "Madame Chairman," he repeated. Mal had some difficulty in getting attention, but finally succeeded. "Madame Chairman, I feel Blossom is not quite ready for Mr. Plum's, er, ah, delightful play. I move that the Blossom Little Theatre present *Charley's Aunt* as its first production."

"Second," said Mamie Sutherland.

"All in favour?" said Florence.

"Aye," said everyone.

And that's how Blossom missed the opportunity to leap forty years ahead in the dramatic arts.

Chapter Eight

BOOTLEG JUSTICE

BLOSSOM WAS UP IN ARMS. The whole social structure of the town was threatened; the comfortable, accepted functioning of society was in jeopardy; the established order of the community was faced with dislocation. Jeb Wilson had been arrested for bootlegging. Disaster!

The nodes, neurons and synapses of the town's efficient communication network flashed the news throughout the community. The pool hall, the bank, the post office and other gathering places buzzed with speculation about this surprising and alarming development. Everyone knew, of course, that Jeb was a bootlegger since he'd been supplying the whole town with his particular brand of moonshine for years. Few people during the Dirty Thirties could afford liquor-store prices, so Jeb's poteen brew, which he provided at a very low cost, was considered an essential community service. The Mounties had always, heretofore, used a sensible reticence in ignoring Jeb's operation. As Mal Morgan stated, "They've always turned a deaf eye to Jeb up till now. What the hell's got into them all of a sudden to screw things up for the whole district?"

The story gradually got pieced together during the coffee hour at Wong Toy's restaurant, the principal gossip exchange of the male population. As might have been expected, Mrs. Frobisher, leader of the Vested Virgins, was at the bottom of the imbroglio. Her husband, Harry, had gotten involved in a poker game with some of his cronies in a back room of the Palaza Hotel and had arrived home at three in the morning minus fifteen dollars and boiled as a goat. Mrs. Frobisher was furious; she blamed everybody involved, except her dear Harry, for his fall from grace. It didn't take her long to get the information out of him that the booze had been supplied by Jeb Wilson and that this was part of a large-scale operation.

The next day, full of pious wrath, she and several of the VV's descended on Corporal Rankin to demand that he take immediate steps to eliminate this vicious threat to the morals of the community. Rankin expressed great surprise and chagrin that such a wicked and illegal activity could have been going on right under his nose; he thanked the ladies for so courageously doing their civic duty by making this matter known to him. The hapless Rankin, faced with a formal complaint, had little choice but to take action. He communicated the information to his superiors, who sent a plainclothes man to Blossom to conduct the investigation. Rankin insisted that an outsider be brought in, claiming that he was too well-known to the defendant to be able to make a purchase of the illegal booze. Actually this was nonsense, because Corporal Rankin not infrequently bought liquor from Jeb, always paying the full price and thereby maintaining the integrity of the RCMP.

When the whole story became known to the coffee klatsch at Wong Toy's, the reputation of the RCMP for good sense and fair play was restored. Not much blame was attached to Harry Frobisher as it was recognized that the poor bastard was completely dominated by his formidable spouse. However, coals of malediction were heaped on the head of Madame Twitchnose, as they called Mrs. Frobisher.

It evolved that the charge was not to be a simple one of bootlegging, which would come under provicial jurisdiction, but rather the more serious charge of operating an illegal still, which came under federal law. Cyril Thorndyke had been appointed prosecutor and made this decision, no doubt prodded by Mrs. Frobisher. The object was to do more than just slap a trivial fine for bootlegging on Jeb – it was to put him out of business entirely.

Jeb appointed George Ingraham as his legal counsel. Both George and Jeb were recipients of a great deal of sympathy and well-meant advice which they accepted gracefully without comment. Until the case came to trial, the town continued to simmer; the popularity of Mrs. Frobisher and the VV's, never high at the best of times, reached a new low.

The case was heard at the next sitting of the circuit court when Judge Broome made one of his periodic visits to the town. Judge Broome, known as Old Flint Face, was a distinguished member of the bench with a high reputation for legal erudition and sound judgment. He prided himself on being a Westerner and was not much concerned about protocol or procedures as long as the interests of justice were served. When he had been on the northern circuit he had held court in igloos, bunkhouses, planes and bars and under all sorts of bizarre circumstances. He was a man of unquestioned integrity and, while he could be severe when the occasion demanded it, he had a deep understanding and sympathy for the confused underdogs who blundered into trouble with the law. His unorthodox procedures were the despair of his more conservative associates; but none of his decisions in the north had ever been reversed, although some of the stuffed shirts in Ottawa had huffed and puffed about some of them. He rather enjoyed his controversial reputation.

The courtroom of the Embassy was packed for the trial. Mrs. Frobisher and a group of the Vested Virgins took over the front row seats since nobody had the temerity to challenge them for this vantage point. They sat haughty and frigid, basting themselves in the sweet juice of moral rectitude. Their mouths were pinched like a section of oboe players trying to hit a high note. The room rustled with sibilant whispers and nervous shufflings. The assembly was excited by the impending real life drama, while at the same time subdued by the austere surroundings of the courtroom and the nebulous, but formidable majesty of the law. The sympathy of the audience for the defendant was, as usual, diluted by the happy realization that it was somebody else involved and not them – thank God.

George Ingraham sat nonchalantly conversing with his client. Jeb's red, splotched face and bleary eyes did not make him a very prepossessing defendant – he was scarcely the picture of outraged innocence. The betting was ten-to-one that George wouldn't dare to put Jeb on the stand. George looked handsome and elegant in the black gown which accentuated the Mephistophelean impression of his long thin face and marked widow's peak. Cyril Thorndyke, the prosecutor, in sharp contrast, was short, fat and sweaty; in moments of crisis he oozed like a sponge. Cyril was George's bête noire, the lawyer from Dazzle, who had been brought in by the court to act for the crown; George acted in a similar capacity when the court met at Dazzle.

The Clerk of the Court called the session to order; everyone rose while Judge Broome took his place. It was easy to see how the judge had gotten his nickname of Old Flint Face. He was completely bald, with a long, bony, cadaverous face and a prognathous jaw like a block of granite. His expression, which was cold and hard, never changed. However, it was known that his left eyebrow went up when he was amused and down when annoyed. Lawyers had learned to watch this indicator very closely.

George entered a plea of not guilty and requested trial by jury. Cyril Thorndyke objected to the case being heard by a jury since he was well aware that practically the entire population of Blossom was on Jeb's side; he hinted darkly at the difficulty of obtaining an unbiased and unprejudiced panel of jurors. George pointed out that since the case came under federal statute, trial by jury was an available option. The lawyers bickered for several minutes until Judge Broome intervened to rule in George's favour.

There was no difficulty in selecting the jury of six people since practically the whole town was in attendance. Neither lawyer issued any challenges; Cyril on the basis apparently that it didn't much matter who was chosen. Everyone felt that George committed a strategic error when he permitted Mrs. Jensen to be selected, as she was a well-known member of the VV's. Mrs. Frobisher and her côterie smiled with grim satisfaction when Mrs. Jensen's name was called. Mrs. Jensen was a thin little lady with bright blue eyes and a flat straw hat set squarely on the top of her head. She was the only female member appointed. Mal Morgan was also named to the jury and was elected foreman, which must have given George some satisfaction.

When the jury had taken its place, Cyril rose to make his

opening remarks. He was sweating profusely, which necessitated frequent moppings of his forehead.

"Ladies and gentlemen of the jury," he declared pompously, "I would explain that the accused, Mr. Jeb Wilson, is charged under Section 176 of the Excise Act with the operation of an illegal still in that he undertook the distillation of spirits without having a license to permit him to do so. He is also charged under Section 181 of the same Act with the offense of the sale of unlawfully manufactured spirits.

"We shall establish these matters beyond peradventure of doubt by means of the testimony of an officer of the Royal Canadian Mounted Police, and two pieces of physical evidence – the still itself and a bottle of the product of that still." Cyril pointed dramatically at a homemade still sitting on the Clerk's table with an unlabelled bottle beside it. All eyes turned to examine these exhibits – some with disgust, most with admiration.

After waiting a few moments for effect, Cyril continued, "I must emphasize to you members of the jury that you must consider the evidence to be placed before you and make your decision divorced of sympathy or personal bias. You must not let sympathy for the accused, nor friendship based on long association, nor lack of agreement with the law as it now stands, influence your judgment. You must –"

George leaped to his feet to interrupt, addressing himself to the judge but looking out the corner of his eye at the jury. "Surely, your Lordship," said George with great gravity, "my learned friend is not questioning the integrity of this distinguished group of worthy citizens. Surely he is not suggesting for a moment that this fine jury of noble and upright men and women, in whom, I might add, I myself have the greatest faith and confidence, would do anything but approach their responsibilities with honesty and propriety."

Cyril was thrown somewhat off-stride. "Oh no, certainly not. I just want them to do their duty."

"Surely my learned friend –" began George again.

Judge Broome intervened. "That will be enough. I am sure the members of the jury understand their duties and will discharge them with probity." He turned to Cyril. "Please proceed, Counsellor."

"Yes, your Lordship." Cyril turned to the jury. "As I was saying, ladies and gentlemen of the jury, when I was so rudely and improperly interrupted by my learned friend –"

"Get on with it," growled the judge.

"Very well," sighed Cyril. "I call Corporal Rupp to the stand."

Corporal Rupp, a handsome, clean-cut young man in formal RCMP uniform, came forward and was sworn in by the Clerk. After his name and position had been established, Cyril asked him to recount the events which had transpired on the day of August 17th, relative to the considerations before the court.

"Yes sir," said Rupp, speaking slowly and carefully. "I had been keeping the accused, Mr. Wilson, under surveillance for several days hoping he would lead me to his still since nobody seemed to know where –"

George rose to his feet. "I must object, your Lordship, to these speculations."

"Sustained," growled the judge.

"Just confine yourself, Corporal Rupp, if you please, to what you did," directed Cyril.

"Yes sir," said Rupp. "On August 17th at 2:15pm, I followed Mr. Wilson's car at a safe distance to a point approximately fifteen miles north of town where he stopped at an abandoned barn in a coulee. I stopped my car some distance away, behind some trees. The accused got out of his car, but he had apparently become suspicious because he returned –"

Cyril held up his hand. "Report only what you did and observed, please."

"Sorry. Mr. Wilson looked back in my direction, returned to his car, and continued along the road past the barn. After waiting for his car to disappear, I entered the barn."

"And what did you find there?"

"A homemade still."

"That still there?" asked Cyril pointing to the still on the table.

"Yes sir."

"Let this item be listed as Exhibit A for the prosecution, if you please," directed Cyril. When this had been done Cyril continued. "Now, Corporal Rupp, what else did you do on August 17th with reference to the matters before us?"

"On the night of August 17th, I went to Mr. Wilson's shack."

"You are referring to the home of Mr. Jeb Wilson, the accused?"

"Yes sir."

"And what did you do there?"

"I asked him for a bottle of whisky, paid him two dollars for it and received the bottle into my possession."

After the bottle had been identified and entered into evidence, Cyril made a mocking bow to George and said, "Your witness, Counsellor."

George rose slowly to his full height, hooked his thumbs into the lapels of his gown and stared levelly at Corporal Rupp for several moments. "Now Corporal, you said you kept Mr. Wilson under surveillance for several days. Did you follow him around?"

"No sir. I was watching his car because, uh – I kept his car under surveillance really."

"So when you said you kept Mr. Wilson under surveillance you were in error. You kept his car under surveillance."

"Well, uh, yes."

"You should be more accurate in your evidence, Corporal. So when Mr. Wilson left in his car you followed him."

"Yes sir."

"You followed him some fifteen miles north of town to what you referred to as an abandoned barn in a coulee?"

"Yes sir."

"As I understand your evidence, Mr. Wilson got out of the car, looked back in your direction, and then drove on."

"That is correct."

"He did not go into the barn?"

"No sir."

"Does Mr. Wilson own that barn, or the property on which it stands?"

"I don't know."

"Well, I can tell you that he does not. Later you entered the barn and confiscated a still. Was the still in operation?"

"No sir."

"So possibly the still had been abandoned there by persons unknown."

"No sir. The still was in working order. There is a small spring in that coulee, the waters of which had been piped into the barn to provide a cooling device for the distillation. It is an excellent arrangement for an illegal still."

"Was there any liquor present?"

"No sir."

"Was there any evidence, fingerprints or any other factor, which connected Mr. Wilson with that still?"

"Well, he drove right there and stopped, so –"

"Just answer my question."

"No tangible evidence. No sir."

"So, for all you know, that still might belong to anybody?"

"All the indications are that the still belonged to Mr. Wilson."

"But there was no tangible evidence, as you put it, that connected Mr. Wilson to that still."

"Well, uh, no sir. But –"

"Thank you." George turned to the judge. "M'lord, I request dismissal of this charge on the grounds that there is no evidence connecting the defendant unequivocally with that still. As required under Section 176, evidence has not been adduced that he distilled any spirits or had a still in his possession or in a place or premises owned or controlled by him."

Cyril leaped to his feet. "I must object, m'lord. Mr. Wilson drove directly to that barn and was scared off by the presence of Corporal Rupp. He obviously knew there was a still there, and it is a fair and reasonable assumption that it belonged to him. Furthermore, this evidence proves that he had access to a still, and later in the day sold a bottle of illegal whisky of a kind produced by such a still, to Corporal Rupp. These two pieces of evidence are incontrovertible establishment of illegal manufacture of spirits."

"The alleged sale of a bottle of illegally distilled whisky," said George, "is covered under Section 181, to which I shall give my attention in due course, but is not pertinent to Section 176, which deals with the operation of a still."

"I disagree, with respect," retorted Cyril. "The bottle of contraband whisky is germane to the issue because it proves illegal manufacture. The two pieces of evidence, the bottle and the still, are complementary. Moonshine whisky droppeth not like the gentle rain from heaven, you know."

"More's the pity," sighed George. The audience chuckled and Judge Broome's left eyebrow elevated slightly.

Cyril ignored this sally and continued. "The sale of contraband spirits is covered under Section 181 of the Excise Act." Cyril picked up a document in front of him. "I shall read the pertinent passage: 'Every person who sells or offers for sale, or who purchases, or has in his possession any spirits unlawfully manufactured or imported, whether the owner thereof or not, without lawful excuse, the proof of which shall be on the person accused, is guilty of an indictable offence.' End of quotation." Cyril tossed the document back on the table and seated himself with an air of smug satisfaction.

"With respect, m'lord," said George, "my worthy colleague is out of order. My request is for dismissal of the charge under Section 176. I shall deal with the matters covered under Section 181 in due course, as I have already indicated."

"The request for dismissal under Section 176 is denied, at this time," said the judge.

"Very well, m'lord," said George without apparent perturbation. He returned his attention to Corporal Rupp. "Now Corporal, when you went to the home of Mr. Wilson on the night of August 17th, how were you dressed? As you are now?"

"No sir. I was not in uniform."

"Rather a sneaky procedure, wasn't it?"

"Those were my instructions. He would hardly sell a bottle of hooch to an officer in uniform."

Mal Morgan, in the jury box, whispered to Cicero Pinkles at his side, "He's done it lots of times."

Judge Broome looked at him sharply. "What was that comment?"

"Nothing, your Worship, sir. Sorry," said Mal hastily.

"When you went to Mr. Wilson's house, Constable Rupp," continued George, "were you invited inside?"

"No sir, I waited at the door, outside."

"What did you ask for?"

"A bottle of whisky."

"Were those your exact words to Mr. Wilson?"

Constable Rupp hesitated. "No, not my exact words. I asked him for a bottle of Panther Piss. Those were my instructions," he added defensively, as a snigger rippled through the audience.

"You didn't ask for a bottle of whisky?" asked George in assumed surprise.

"No sir. Not in so many words. I understand that Mr. Wilson's whisky is known locally by the term I used."

"Never mind what you understand. You didn't ask for whisky?"

"No sir."

"You asked for a bottle of Panther Piss?"

"Yes sir."

"Then for all you know, the bottle may contain what you asked for – the urinary product of a large carnivorous feline?"

"It doesn't seem very likely."

"I didn't ask for your opinion. Just answer my question."

"I don't know what the bottle contains. I presume –"

"Thank you. That will be all for the moment."

Judge Broome leaned forward. His left eyebrow was elevated noticeably. "Do I understand that Counsel for the Defense is alleging that the bottle does indeed contain the, er, urinary product of a large carnivorous feline?"

"I am pointing out, Your Lordship, that the witness did not ask for whisky, or for liquor, and may indeed have gotten what he asked for."

"Your Lordship, I must object to the line of enquiry entered into by my learned colleague," protested Cyril heatedly. "He is desperate and grasping at straws. There isn't a panther within a thousand miles of the town of Blossom. Mr. Wilson's, ah, beverage is infamous in this district under the rather apt sobriquet used by the witness. We could have the bottle sent up to Regina for assay, but my learned friend must realize that he would only be postponing the inevitable."

"That's what you should have done in the first place," observed Judge Broome coldly.

"With respect, Your Lordship, I submit that it was not, and is not, necessary. Alcoholic beverages are known by various names throughout the world. It is appropriate to use the term, vernacular or otherwise, indigenous to a particular locale. The term recently used in this court, unfortunately vulgar though it may be, and I have the greatest reluctance to use it myself, has a specific and designative meaning for a particular potion peculiar to this district. Moreover, the term is uniquely applied, not in a generic sense, but to the particular potion sold by the defendant. In Blossom when you say – and you will pardon me Your Lordship – Panther Piss, you mean Jeb Wilson's brand of moonshine, not the, ah, carnivorous discharge of a urinary feline. I mean, not the felonious charge of a – I mean to say, in Blossom, Panther Piss isn't literally the panth from a pisser."

The crowd guffawed and Judge Broome banged his gavel. His expression hadn't changed, but his left eyebrow was riding high. In a complete dither, Cyril mopped his red face.

George smiled sardonically, obviously enjoying Cyril's discomfiture. "My learned friend is indulging in some pretty fancy polemics and is somewhat entangled in the convolutions of his own arguments. He is also extrapolating his undoubted erudition in the field of alcoholic beverages into the hazardous realms of sociology and semantics. I would observe that the bottle is not labelled whisky, nor indeed is it labelled at all. I would also point out that the witness has admitted that he did not ask for whisky and does not know whether he received liquor or not.

"I therefore respectfully request, m'lord, that the charge against my client under Section 181 be dismissed on the grounds that the prosecution has not shown that the bottle entered in evidence does in fact contain alcohol."

"I must object strongly to this proposal, m'lord," said Cyril vehemently. He pointed at the exhibit. "That bottle contains whisky just as sure as shooting. That's what was asked for –

under a vernacular parlance to be sure – and that's what was received. It may be that we have been remiss in not having a laboratory report available, but frankly, m'lord, this is such an open-and-shut case we had not even anticipated a plea of not guilty."

George looked shocked. "I must object to the use of the term 'an open-and-shut case,' Your Lordship. Such a comment is prejudicial to the defendant. No case should be tried in advance and every accused is innocent until proven guilty."

"The comment was ill-advised," said the judge looking at Cyril.

"I withdraw the remark, m'lord," said Cyril apologetically, "but it did seem, an, er, um, straightforward proposition. We had not anticipated the devious manoeuvering undertaken by the defense."

"The prosecutor is attacking me to cover up his own deficiencies," said George. "There is nothing devious about requesting that a charge be dismissed on the basis of lack of evidence. And I so request."

"I must oppose the request most strongly, m'lord," said Cyril.

"I am not prepared to accept the proposition that the charge be dismissed," said Judge Broome, "but it may be necessary to postpone this case until the prosecution has prepared itself properly – as it should have done originally."

"May I make a statement, Your Lordship?" asked Cyril.

"You may," nodded the judge.

"My interest here, m'lord, is to save the time, energy and expense of this court. What possible utility can be served by postponing the inevitable? Why delay the outcome of this case when my learned friend must recognize what the verdict will be. He knows there is liquor in that bottle. I know it. Everyone in this room knows it. The jury knows it. If the members of the jury could smell and taste the contents of that bottle they would be certain of it. I ask my esteemed friend what advantage can possibly accrue to his client by delaying this court needlessly in its proper function?"

"I also am interested in saving the time of this court," said the judge harshly. "I would like to see this case disposed of promptly, if possible – provided of course we may be assured that justice is achieved. We have taken some considerable time in preliminary matters, and have selected a jury. It would be unfortunate if this time were to be needlessly wasted. If there is indeed liquor in that bottle and the defense knows there is, I would wonder at the necessity for a delay. Do I take it, Counsellor," he addressed his remarks to George, "that you are not prepared to so stipulate?"

"No sir," said George. "I note with regret Your Lordship has not seen fit to rule that the charge be dismissed. However, as I also am interested in saving the valuable time of this court, I am prepared to accept the suggestion of my learned friend as a means of expediting our deliberations."

"What suggestion?" asked Cyril, suddenly wary.

"Why, you said if the jury could sample the contents of the bottle they could determine whether or not it contains liquor. I am prepared to accept your proposition and to abide by the jury's decision on the matter."

"Well now, just a minute," said Cyril hastily. "That wasn't exactly what I meant."

"It's what you said and I have accepted your proposal. Are you not prepared to stand by your own statements?"

"Well yes, of course I am." Cyril took out a handkerchief and mopped his neck. "Yes, I would be prepared to accept their judgment if I could be sure they would be honest. I know damn well there's liquor in that bottle."

"I must object, m'lord," declaimed George. "My learned friend is once again impugning the integrity of this group of dedicated citizens who –"

"The Counsel for the Defense will stop making florid speeches to woo the jury," interrupted Judge Broome. "This is an interesting proposition. Do I understand that you are both prepared to allow the jury to determine by taste whether or not the liquid in the bottle is liquor or not? And are you both prepared to abide by that decision? There can be no wiggling out later."

"I am," said George firmly.

Cyril mopped his face again. "I shall put my faith in the integrity of the jurors." He glanced apprehensively at the jury. "Yes, I am."

"This is a very intriguing suggestion," said Judge Broome, stroking his jaw with a bony finger. The proposition obviously appealed to his penchant for the unorthodox. "It is accepted practice that the members of a jury may look at, touch, examine and smell, physical evidence to ascertain its nature. I would see no reason why another of the senses, that of taste, might not be recruited when appropriate. The identification proposed here would involve the olfactory and the tactile senses, as well as that of taste. Such a test would require the approval of legal counsel, which has been given, and that of the members of the jury." He turned to the jury. "Is the jury prepared to accept this proposal?"

Mal Morgan spoke first. "Yes sir, Your Excellency," he said with a happy grin.

As the judge's eye moved along the row, each juror in turn replied with a "Yes sir," until he came to Mrs. Jensen. There was a long pause; every eye in the room was upon her. She glanced over at Mrs. Frobisher who nodded slowly with pursed lips, implying that there are some distasteful things one has to force oneself to do for the good of the Cause. Mrs. Jensen looked at the judge and said quietly, "Yes sir." The courtroom let out a sigh of relief.

"Then I am prepared to approve the proposition," ruled the judge. "The Clerk will pass the bottle to the jury."

The Clerk picked up the bottle and then somewhat uncertainly held it to the judge. "Do you wish to, er, ah, sample the evidence, sir?"

"No thank you," answered Judge Broome politely. "I shall place my reliance, as agreed, upon the educated palates of the jury."

The Clerk pulled the cork out of the bottle and handed it to Mal Morgan. Mal sniffed the bottle solemnly before taking a long drag at it. He smacked his lips judiciously, holding his head to one side. He held up the bottle in a salute to Jeb. "A good batch, Jeb."

"Thanks, Mal," said Jeb. George gave him a sharp elbow in the ribs.

Mal handed the bottle to Cicero Pinkles, the juror next to him. Cicero rubbed the top of the bottle with his sleeve and raised it to his lips. Apparently Cicero was unfamiliar with the fiery quality of Jeb's brew. He took a large mouthful, strangled, gasped and blew spray across the room. Mal beat him on the back.

"Take it more cautious-like," advised Mal. "That stuff's got a kick like a randy cayuse."

Cicero finally stopped coughing, straightened up, took a couple of deep breaths, and then carefully a deep swallow. "Lovely stuff. Lovely," stated Cicero solemnly. He passed the bottle to Harry Rolf, the juror beside him. "Watch it," he warned. "It's dynamite."

"I know," said Harry. "Jeb's stuff's a skull-popper."

The bottle passed along the line of jurors, with each one taking an appreciative pull at it until it came to Mrs. Jensen. She accepted the bottle hesitantly and with repugnance. She glanced at Mrs. Frobisher, who again gave a solemn nod. Whereupon, Mrs. Jensen tipped up the bottle and guzzled off a good two ounces without batting an eye. She wiped her mouth with the back of her hand and passed the bottle to the Clerk.

As the Clerk passed in front of the jury to return the bottle to the exhibit table, Mal reached out a hand for it. "I'm not quite sure about that there stuff," said Mal. "I would like to, ahem, refresh my recollections." He took a long pull and handed the bottle to Cicero beside him. The bottle continued along the line of jurors as before until it reached Mrs. Jensen. She tipped it up and drained it dry. The Clerk returned the empty bottle to the table.

"Now ladies and gentlemen," said Judge Broome directing his attention to the jury, "may I have your considered opinion. Is the liquid contained in the bottle indeed liquor as alleged by the prosecution?"

"Just one moment, Your Lordship," interrupted George, "with all due respect, may I draw your attention to the fact that the case for the prosecution has disappeared. The evidence has evaporated. The bottle has been inadvertently emptied so that there is now no evidence on which to substantiate a charge."

"Now just a minute yourself, my fine feathered, I mean, my distinguished friend," cried Cyril leaping to his feet. "We agreed that the decision as to the nature of the liquid in the bottle would be made by the members of the jury. They have now sampled the contents and must render their decision – and it must be an honest decision." He glared at the jury.

"They may be able to report what was in the bottle, it is true, but you cannot proceed because you now have no evidence to support your case."

"This is shenanigans, pure and simple," shouted Cyril, his jowls bouncing. "The Defense has deliberately contrived this cheap and transparent trick. This is chicanery of the grossest sort."

"It was your proposal. And I accepted it," interposed George quietly.

"It wasn't my proposal that they drink up the entire evidence," objected Cyril furiously. "Anyhow, it doesn't matter. We agreed to abide by the judgment of the jury as to the nature of the contents of that bottle. They are certainly in a position to render that judgment and I demand that it be given. And that you abide by it. If they will be honest, there is only one answer they can give."

"Their judgment is no longer pertinent," maintained George. "It is possibly unfortunate that in their thirst for knowledge the members of the jury have been overly conscientious in the discharge of their duty. I repeat, the bottle is now empty and there is no evidence."

"This is skulduggery," shouted Cyril. "You have contrived to interfere with evidence – a very serious offence. I shall report this matter to the law society. I shall appeal the case."

"How can you appeal a case when you have no evidence on which to base it?"

"I shall appeal on – on – procedural grounds."

"You are letting your ill-temper interfere with your judgment, Counsellor. I would point out: (a) that you can't initiate an appeal without evidence, and (b) the procedure used was proposed and approved by you, yourself. I only agreed to it. With some reluctance, I might add."

"I was hornswoggled into it," shouted Cyril, shaking his head and spraying the surrounding area with sweat. "Anyhow, I didn't propose that they drink up the whole bloody bottle. Thirst for knowledge indeed!"

George elevated his eyebrows disdainfully and turned to the judge. "In view of the circumstances which have developed, I renew my petition, m'lord, that the case be dismissed for lack of evidence."

"I must object most strongly, m'lord," shouted Cyril. "I insist that the jury be required to report on whether or not that bottle contained liquor. But even without that decision, there is sufficient evidence on the basis of the confiscated still to warrant a verdict of guilty under Section 176. And I note that Your Lordship has already ruled that the charge under that section not be withdrawn."

"When I made my initial request for dismissal of the case under Section 176, his Lordship's ruling was denial *at that time*," said George, emphasizing the last three words. "The situation has changed, and I therefore have renewed my petition for dismissal. The case for the prosecution under Section 176 is now untenable. Your evidence included both the still and the bottle of – er – whatever. You, yourself, referred to them as complementary. It is quite obvious that you considered that the evidence of the still by itself was weak and needed the bolstering of the alleged product of that still. One of the props of your thesis has been knocked out from under you, so the whole issue collapses. With regard to Section 181, the sale of contraband spirits, that evidence has now disappeared."

While the lawyers continued to wrangle, it became apparent that the beverage consumed by the jurors, whatever its nature, was beginning to have an effect. Mal Morgan was gazing happily at the court, a beatific grin wreathing his round, flushed face. Cicero Pinkles had developed an extreme case of the hiccups. With each hiccup, Cicero and Harry Rolf next to him, unsuccessfully tried to smother guffaws behind their hands. Mrs. Jensen, her hat askew, had developed an uncontrollable tendency to giggle. What was amusing her were the glowers being levelled at her by Mrs. Frobisher and the other VV's. She finally rose unsteadily to her feet, thumbed her nose at Mrs. Frobisher and gave her a loud, juicy raspberry. The crowd cheered.

This byplay attracted Cyril's attention. He looked at the jury and assessed the situation immediately. "My learned friend is yattering about evidence," he cried, pointing dramatically at the jury. "There is the evidence. The jury are all as tight as lords – I mean ticks, m'lord. If that doesn't prove that the bottle contained whisky, I don't know what would."

Judge Broome switched his attention to the jury in considerable alarm. Cicero Pinkles hiccupped loudly and he and Harry Rolf guffawed uncontrollably. Mrs. Jensen, her little hat raffishly over one ear, stood up and blew him a kiss. The judge didn't mind unorthodox procedures, but this was a bit much.

He turned hastily to the two lawyers. "I have listened carefully to your arguments, gentlemen, and while there are possibly certain indications that the bottle did indeed contain an intoxicating liquid, the fact remains that there is now no physical evidence on which to proceed under Section 181. I also find that under Section 176, ownership of the still by the defendant has not been unequivocally demonstrated. The case is dismissed." He banged down his gavel. Then he beckoned George over to him. When George approached the bench, the judge leaned down and hissed, "George, for God's sake get that bunch of drunks out of here."

"Yes, m'lord," said George with a smile.

The judge beat a hasty retreat.

As soon as Judge Broome left the courtroom, all hell broke loose. Well-wishers from the audience crowded around Jeb and George, cheering and patting them on the back. The members of the jury staggered over to participate. Mal Morgan did a happy tap dance. Cicero hiccupped loudly and he and Harry collapsed in each other's arms laughing uproariously. Mrs. Frobisher tried to drag Mrs. Jensen away but she broke free, ran over to Jeb, threw her arms around his neck and kissed him soundly.

The crowd finally hoisted Jeb on their shoulders to loud cheers and carried him in triumph from the room.

Chapter Nine

BIBLE BIBBLE

HE NEWS THAT FLOSSY MACABEE had got religion hit Blossom like a bombshell. The word was around that Flossy would give a soul-cleansing testimonial on Friday night at the Reverend Bible Bibble's prayer meeting. If there's one thing guaranteed to blow a small town wide open, it's the local prostitute telling all she knows. It looked as if half the male population was planning to leave town.

I got the story from George Ingraham. George was buying cigars at the desk of the Palaza Hotel as I was checking in late one evening. We greeted each other as usual; then George looked at me speculatively.

"Hmm, maybe you're just the person I'm looking for. Can you meet me at Wong Toy's restaurant after you check in?"

"Sure," I replied.

I found George later in a back booth at Wong Toy's. After Wong had brought us mugs of coffee, George gave me a crooked grin and said, "I've just come from a visit with Flossy. A professional visit."

"Her profession, or yours?"

"An obvious rejoinder. Mine."

"What's the matter, is Flossy in trouble with the law?"

"Not any more than usual. It's more complicated than that. Let me give you some background. A few days ago, the Reverend

Bibble blew into town, and set up his tent in Slaughterhouse Park. He calls himself Bible Bibble. Maybe you've heard of him."

"No, I haven't. Who is he?"

"He's one of these itinerant hoot-and-holler revivalists who turn up from time to time. They've become quite a common phenomenon since the onset of the Depression. Bibble travels with his wife and two scraggly, teenaged children – a boy and a girl – in an old Ford, with a beat-up truck to carry the tent and folding chairs. He's been holding save-your-soul meetings every night, and some in the daytime. You can hear them praying and carrying on if you come within a block of the place. He plays a trumpet, the two kids blow horns of some kind, and his wife pounds the bass drum. They hold meetings on street corners and then parade off to the tent when they have collected enough spectators. He's been getting a small play from the religiously motivated and from others who go along for the free show."

"Must be pretty slim pickings."

"You'd be surprised. They make pork-and-beans money which isn't bad these days; then every once in a while they run into a grateful redeemed sinner who antes up big. I've got nothing against these fellows, if they're sincere. I figure a person's religion is his own damn business. But there's something about this set-up that isn't quite kosher."

"A strange objection. But where does Flossy come in on all this?"

"Somehow or other Bibble has gotten to Flossy and made her see the light. She repenteth and is saved, hallelujah and all that. She's seen the error of her ways and will henceforth lead a pure and sinless life. I just don't believe it."

"Why not? It happens."

"Yeah, I know, Magdalene and all that. But not Flossy. She's hard as nails and happy in her work. It's a common fallacy to believe that courtesans want to be something else. They're doing what they're doing because it suits them. When I saw Flossy tonight she didn't seem awfully repentant. She tossed in a few perfunctory hallelujahs, but her eyes were sharp and wary. And why wait five days for her testimonial?"

"What's a testimonial?"

"That's when she stands up in front of the congregation and makes, if you will pardon the expression, a clean breast of things – states names, places, events, and so forth."

"Did you say 'state names?' "

"Yes. Now you see the dilemma. Think about that for awhile."

"Great Scott!" I thought about it. "Wow! She'd set the town on its ear."

"Yes indeed," said George. "I see you get the picture. Flossy could blow this town to smithereens. As a result, a group of, er, disinterested, civic-minded citizens has banded together in sort of vigilante group to plan strategy to circumvent this catastrophe. I have been brought in as legal counsel."

"Not a concerned participant?"

"It is unseemly to impugn the motives of legal counsel. The Committee has had several meetings, the last one earlier this evening. I shall not tell you the names of the Committee, as this is privileged information – but you would be surprised. I shall refer to the individuals as Citizen A, Citizen B, and so forth. We have discussed a number of stratagems. Citizen A suggested Bibble be run out of town, but there is no legal excuse, and force would be self-defeating. Citizen B said that putting Flossy out of business was eliminating an essential public utility like water or light. This approach is not apt to influence Bibble significantly. Citizen C asked if Flossy couldn't get saved without her shooting her mouth off. This was a reasonable possibility, so I was directed to approach Bibble with this enquiry.

"As a result I went to see Bibble this morning at his tent. He is an unctuous, slovenly slob who spouts eccelesiastical platitudes at the tinkle of a tambourine. He enquired into the state of my soul and when I said it was beyond redemption since I was a lawyer, he surprisingly seemed to agree. At least he didn't pursue the matter."

"Not surprising at all."

"He verified Flossy's conversion. On the subject of reticence in her testimonial he was adamant. It appears that in order for her to be saved she must make a complete disclosure of her sinful past. When I suggested this might cause unfortunate embarrassment to others, he said, 'Well and good. They should come forward and be shriven as well.'

"I continued to press the point without any success; I reported to the Committee this evening."

"What was the Committee's reaction?"

"They weren't very happy about it, to put it mildly. A further counsel of war was held. Citizen A suggested that if Flossy was hellbent on being saved, we should sic another preacher on her with a better sense of reticence. However, none are available, and time is too short. Citizen B asked about libel laws, but libel does not exist until it has been uttered, and the harm we are trying to avoid would have been done. Anyhow, the libel would not apply to Bibble, but to Flossy. We had no idea what Flossy's true position was in the imbroglio; and since she seemed the weakest link in the chain, I was directed to have a talk with her this evening; and frankly, if all else failed, I was to see if I couldn't buy her off.

"When I went to see Flossy, I felt my arrival was not unexpected. Also, throughout our discussions there was no doubt she had been carefully coached. My plea, based on civic loyalty, elicited only a short comment couched in terms you might not expect a penitent to use. My more pragmatic approach of how she was going to earn a living in the future was answered with the undebatable 'The Lord will provide.' It is very awkward to be in a position of trying to persuade someone who has gotten saved to get themselves unsaved. You feel as if you are wearing horns and a tail. I didn't get far on that track, and it was treated with the contempt it deserved."

"I would have thought you admirably suited for the part," I observed.

"Possibly, but it's still awkward," grinned George. "When I asked Flossy about the necessity for being specific in her testimonial she said she must follow the directions of Reverend Bibble. She even went so far as to mention some people and events she felt she would be constrained to include, and I shuddered. I raised the question of a payoff with some circumlocution, but Flossy got the message right away. She got a greedy look in her handsome eyes – she does have nice eyes – but she turned me down flat. So that's where we stand at the moment."

"It doesn't look encouraging." I thought for a moment. "Tell me," I asked, "how did the information about Flossy's upcoming disclosures become known?"

"Partly from Bibble. She is a cause célèbre. But largely from Jeb Wilson. He's been running around telling everybody. As you probably know, Flossy is the principal retail outlet for Jeb's moonshine whisky. If she goes out of business, it will seriously cripple his operation. He and Flossy are bosom companions. Anyhow, anything she would say about Jeb won't damage his reputation. He doesn't have any reputation to damage."

"Yes, but my point is this: was Jeb told to spread the rumour?"

"I see your point. I'll look into it tomorrow."

"What else are you going to do?"

"I want to get some information on Bibble."

"Can you check up on him through his church or through others, such as Reverend Slye?"

"I think not. I enquired about his affiliations in my discussions with him and I gather he is an independent operator without connections with any recognized church and undoubtedly self-ordained. No, I need another approach, and that's where you come in."

"What can I do?"

"Are you going out of town tomorrow?"

"Yes, down the Ajax line, but I'll be back tomorrow night."

"Good. I want information on Bibble. I can't leave town tomorrow as I have some appointments and I can't phone through the exchange for reasons that are, er, personal as well as civic." George's girlfriend, Mamie Sutherland, was the local telephone operator. "So I would like you to phone from some other town and find out Bibble's itinerary. You travel all over the prairies and know someone you could call in various towns, don't you?"

"Yes."

"Good. Find the route Bibble has been following and, in particular, try to find a town where something odd happened while Bibble was there. Some place where he left suddenly or some kind of rhubarb developed. I'm not quite sure what."

"Okay, I'll do my best. I should have no trouble in finding the towns where Bibble has been, but the other part will be difficult – it's so nebulous."

I spent the next day on the road calling on farmers and implement dealers, but I found time to make the phone calls for George. I returned to Blossom in the evening and located him in a booth at Wong Toy's. I handed him a slip of paper. "Secret Agent XY5 reporting in, sir," I said and saluted. "Here is the list of towns Bibble has graced with his presence. I did my phoning from Dazzle, which incidentally he has not visited. Before I forget, you owe me eleven dollars and thirty-eight cents for phone calls."

"I'll make a note of it," said George, taking out a pad. "It will come out of Committee expenses."

"Apparently Bibble has been following a route west from Winnipeg. Once I got a line on him, it wasn't too difficult. He couldn't travel far in that bucket of bolts he drives. See, here are Bonnyford, Prince, Forville and Apollo."

George studied the list. "Did you get a hint of any kind of dustup that Bibble was involved in?"

"Yes, I think so. At Arrowville, in Manitoba, my informant said that some kind of a fuss developed over Bibble's activities. He had no idea what the problem was, but Bibble left town suddenly. Arrowville is a lot bigger than Blossom, and the grapevine isn't as efficient."

"Aha," said George, elated. "That sounds like what we're looking for. I'll have to go there to check it out. Arrowville would be too far to drive. Is it on the main line?"

"Yes."

"Good. Let's see. Today is Tuesday, and Flossy isn't slated to perform until Friday. I can catch the six-fifteen tomorrow morning and be in Arrowville sometime in the afternoon. I'll stay there overnight and get back here Thursday evening. Should work out just fine."

"You're putting a lot of chips on one card. My informant was very vague about what the difficulty with Bibble was all about. I don't want to give you a bum steer."

"It's the best we've got. And I'm reasonably hopeful it will serve. I really just need to appraise Bibble's *bona fides* so as to know how to deal with him."

George and I sat a long time over our coffee cups at Wong Toy's, discussing the situation. George was much more optimistic than I was about what he might find at Arrowville which would be useful. He was sure that if Bibble was pulling some kind of a fast one, he would have done so before and he was certain that Bibble was a crook. He said the Committee was getting pretty frantic.

I had to leave Blossom the next morning for a swing through southern Alberta to cover my accounts there. I didn't get back to Blossom until late Friday afternoon, and drove an extra two hundred miles to make it. I'd have driven three times that far not to miss Flossy's performance that evening. I experienced a great letdown when I drove by Slaughterhouse Park and couldn't see Bibble's tent. I rushed around to Wong Toy's, and found George in his favourite back booth just about to devour a large steak.

"Hey, what happened to Bibble?" I asked, slipping into the seat across from him. "I don't see his tent."

"Bibble has flown the coop. The town is saved," said George in great good humour. "And I am the knight in shining burlap. And for you, Secret Agent XY5, I am prepared, for your splendid service to the cause, to buy you one of Wong Toy's best steak dinners. Wong Toy," called George, "one of your very best steaks with all the trimmings for Agent XY5 here."

"Okay, Mr. Ingraham," answered Wong with a cheerful wave. "One Wong Toy special coming right up. You must be pretty flush today. Throwin' money around like crazy."

"My, you *are* in a good mood," I said to George. "You bet I'll have a steak on you. Medium rare, Wong. Now, hurry up and tell me what happened with Bibble? Did your trip to Arrowville pay off?"

"It sure did. Better than I dared to hope. Here's what happened. I got to Arrowville and looked up a colleague of mine and hit the jackpot right off. It took me a little while to get the story out of him, because he was one of the not-so-disinterested participants. Anyhow, Bibble used exactly the same tactics as here. He made a deal with the local demimondaine to threaten to tell everything she knew in a testimonial. He saw to it that the news got spread around well. Incidentally, your idea about Jeb being told to broadcast the rumour here was correct, although he was not privy to the plot. Bibble let the tension build up for several days, just as he did here, and then when those threatened with disclosure were really frantic, he made a deal with them to call it off. Made a real killing on it, including a substantial contribution from my associate. The whole setup was a straightforward blackmail operation, with the interesting religious switch that made it difficult to pin down. The payoff was accepted as a contribution to the missionary fund. Bibble was supposed to split fifty-fifty with the girl, but he skipped out. She raised blue blazes, but there was nothing much she could do about it. Anyhow, that's where he made his biggest mistake and gave me the lever I needed.

"When I got back Thursday evening I called on Flossy and persuaded her to come with me for an interview with Bibble. She was pretty leery about it, but I talked her into it by assuring her it was in her own best interest. When I got the two of them together I recounted what I had learned in Arrowville. Bibble denied everything, of course, but I told him I had been there and got the information firsthand. He resorted to bluster and protestations of injured innocence. He even had the effrontery to accuse me of blackmail – which was true, of course. The bit about double-crossing his partner came through loud and clear to Flossy, and once I got the two of them at each other's throats it was all over but the shouting. And there was plenty of that. I told Bibble if he wasn't out of town by morning I would take action here and get in touch with the girl in Arrowville. This was largely bluff, because I didn't want to take any action. I also said I would look into his past record, and I could tell I scored on that point by the frightened look in his eye.

"I slapped Flossy on the fanny and told her to go home and behave herself – and choose her companions with more care in the future. Bibble was packed and gone inside of an hour. And so, my friend, the town has been saved from disaster; a lot of the pillars of the community are unpacking their bags tonight. Interestingly enough – although not surprisingly, I suppose – this little caper has done more to ingratiate me with the community than all the creditable, legitimate and brilliant ventures of my tenure in the town."

"Well, congratulations, George! You handled it very well. Bibble certainly met his match in Blossom. You might say that Bible Bibble bobbled."

"Please," said George, looking pained. "No whimsy."

Wong brought my steak; it looked beautiful.

"Who says that crime doesn't pay?" I asked, rubbing my hands together. "What say, Wong?"

"Confucius say crime pay very good, fo' lawyer," answered Wong with a cheerful grin.

Chapter Ten

SANTA HAD A HANGOVER

ONE OF THE IMPORTANT EVENTS of the year for the youngsters in a small town is the Christmas concert. In Blossom this was always held in the Elks' Hall on the evening of the last day of school before the vacation. After the concert, in which all the classes in the school participated, came the highlight of the evening, the arrival of Santa Claus and the presentation of gifts for the children of the town from beneath the huge Christmas tree.

Weeks of work went into the preparations. The junior classes made tiny lanterns, stars and miles of paper chains and cranberry strings to decorate the tree. Every day saw rehearsals of plays, skits and pantomimes. Each child had to be worked into the show somewhere, even if it was just as an angel in the background or a shepherd on the hillside. There was great competition for the leading parts. Traumatic disappointments and displays of temperament were frequent both by students and by their mothers. Parents were recruited to provide costumes and props. Not infrequently, parts were assigned on the basis of a coöperative or aggressive mother, rather than on ability or aptitude. As the day of the concert approached, the level of excitement increased; the teachers developed a harassed and frantic look about them. During the last week, rehearsals were transferred to the Elks' Hall, and there was a steady stream of little people to and from the school. Piles of decorations, props and lumber were carted by parents. In the evenings fathers turned up with hammers and saws to build mangers, huts, scaffolds, and so forth. The Enthusiasts service club brought the Christmas tree and anchored it securely in place. Then the children began its decoration.

It was traditional in Blossom that the Grade Four class be assigned to the supervision of the tree, including the arrangements for the presents. This was a big job. There had to be a suitable present for each student in the school and for any preschool child who was going to attend. The presents had to be purchased or scrounged from the local merchants; then they had to be sorted, allocated to appropriate students, wrapped and clearly marked so that Santa would call out the right name. For two weeks prior to Christmas, Grade Four did practically nothing but fuss with presents while Miss Phibbs, the room teacher, went gradually "around the bend," to quote her own words. The class was divided into committees: one for procurement, one for allocation, one for wrapping and one for decoration of the tree. Superimposed over these committees was a small Supervisory Committee which theoretically coördinated and directed all activities. None of the committees agreed on anything, and the class was in a constant rhubarb.

The chairman of the Supervisory Committee was Nancy Peters. She was the daughter of my good friends Fred and Audrey, and it was from them I got most of the background information about what went on. Nancy was an intelligent, self-assured youngster of nine, with big, black eyes and a bony, thin face that would later be beautiful. She was also willful, bossy, and aggressive, which fitted her admirably for her job. She gradually took over the Christmas tree arrangements and ran it as a one-man show, much to the relief of Miss Phibbs. As Nancy said to her parents, someone had to straighten out the shambles they were in, and she was obviously the only one who could do it.

The other members of Nancy's committee were Sherry North and Joey Fordick. Sherry was a plump little girl with stringy, blond hair, and Joey had red hair, freckles and jug ears. Sherry and Joey were vigorous personalities in their own right, but no match for Nancy's strong will. At a meeting of the Committee it was decided that since the person who was chosen Santa Claus played such an important part in the success of the program, the choice should be in the hands of the Committee. This recommendation was carried by Miss Phibbs to the Principal, Mr. Fidge, a skinny, humourless man with a wart on his Adam's apple. Mr.

Fidge had played the part of Santa Claus the previous year and expected to be asked to do so again. He therefore readily agreed to the proposal. The Committee thereupon informed Miss Phibbs that their choice for Santa Claus was Mr. Jeb Wilson.

When the news of this reached Mr. Fidge, he nearly had a fit. "My God," he shouted at Miss Phibbs, "why of all people do they want Jeb Wilson, the town lush? He's a disreputable old bum who hasn't drawn a sober breath in twenty years. It would be a travesty – a, a disaster!"

Miss Phibbs agreed completely and fluttered her hands helplessly. Nancy and her committee were brought to the Principal's office, where Fidge did his best to persuade them of the inappropriateness of their choice without coming right out and saying why. Nancy remained adamant. Sherry and Joey fidgeted, but backed her decision. Nancy pointed out that the Principal had promised that the Committee would have the choice, and he couldn't go back on his word. Mr. Fidge, after considerable hemming and hawing, said that he himself would be prepared to act as Santa Claus. Nancy thanked him politely, but said their choice was Jeb Wilson. Mr. Fidge finally said they would have to choose someone else and dismissed them.

Nancy returned to the classroom and called a meeting of the entire class. Miss Phibbs was politely asked to leave the room. Nancy explained what had happened, putting considerable emphasis on the fact that the Principal had broken his word. The class was outraged at this evidence of adult perfidy. After a good deal of angry discussion and a certain degree of bullying by Nancy, the class voted unanimously in support of Jeb as Santa Claus. This decision was conveyed to Mr. Fidge and he promptly convened a meeting of the teachers. Although the other teachers didn't say so, they felt the Principal had gotten himself into the mess and he could darn well get himself out. The meeting went round and round the mulberry bush. It was finally decided that since Nancy was obviously the key to the situation, overtures should be made to her parents to try to dissuade her from forcing the issue.

That evening at dinner Nancy was not surprised to have the matter raised by her parents. They pointed out as gently as they could that Jeb was something of an old reprobate and, thus, scarcely a person to fill the part of the patron saint of Christmas. They also said he would almost certainly not accept and even if he did, would probably get sloshed and not turn up. Nancy stuck to her guns and her parents shrugged and dropped the subject. They had had experience in the past in trying to dissuade Nancy from a course of action once she had made up her mind. Anyhow, they felt there was some validity to the students' position and they should be allowed to work it out themselves.

Actually the choice of Jeb for Santa Claus by the students was not dictated by perversity or mischievousness. Jeb was very popular with the students, although they were well aware of his drinking and bad reputation. You can't fool children; they knew that Jeb was sincerely fond of them. They recognized a gentleness and a kindness in him that was not put on. He made bows and arrows and slingshots for them, and helped them to make a toboggan run down the riverbank. They all called him by his first name. The younger children enjoyed his stories. Their parents had been alarmed about what kind of stories he told them, until they found out that the tales were mostly about two characters named Charlie Chipmunk and Goofy Gopher. When drunk, he kept well away from the children and wouldn't even speak to them. At such times they left him alone. The children saw Jeb as a kindly old man, and therefore well suited to be Santa Claus. There was undoubtedly some degree of bravado and protest in their sponsorship of Jeb, because they knew very well that he was *persona non grata* in the adult world of the town. By this time, of course, an issue had been established and a principle was at stake.

The next morning, discussion between Nancy and Miss Phibbs indicated that neither the Principal nor Nancy's Committee had changed position. Nancy called another meeting of the entire class; the upshot of this was the issuance of an ultimatum to the Principal that if he did not live up to his word to permit the students to choose their own Santa Claus, the class would boycott the concert and persuade the other students to do likewise. Mr. Fidge capitulated.

That evening the Committee, comprising Nancy, Sherry and Joey, called at Jeb's shack. Jeb was in his usual state of limited insobriety. He courteously invited them to come in out of the cold and drew up chairs around the old cookstove. Roscoe growled and withdrew under a bunk in the corner. The children looked around the neat and compact room in some surprise.

"Now what brings this delightful delegation of young people out to see me on such a cold night?" asked Jeb.

"We want you for Santa Claus," blurted Sherry.

"You what?"

"We want you to be our Santa Claus at the school concert," explained Nancy. "Will you, Jeb?"

"Moses on a cayuse," gasped Jeb. "Me play Santa Claus? You've lost your marbles."

"All the kids want you," urged Joey.

"Will you, Jeb?" asked Nancy eagerly.

"Good heavens, no! It wouldn't be fitten. Me as Santa Claus! Great balls of fire and little fishes."

"Aw, Jeb," pleaded Sherry.

"No. No. No. Why me, of all people?"

"You've got a nice red nose and you're the right shape and most important of all, you like kids and they like you. Mr. Fidge doesn't really like us," explained Nancy. "He just pretends."

"What does Mr. Fidge say?" asked Jeb. "Does he know you're asking me to be Santa Claus?"

"Yes," said Nancy.

"Does he agree with the idea?"

"He does now," said Nancy. "He didn't at first."

"What made him change his mind?"

Nancy somewhat reluctantly explained what had been going on at the school. "So you see," she concluded, "we have his approval."

Jeb squirmed unhappily. He desperately wanted a drink, but heroically set the idea aside. "Look, Nancy," he explained, "I'm afraid Mr. Fidge is right. I sure appreciate the honour you kids are paying me, but it just wouldn't be right. There are things you young people don't understand about – about – things. I'm not exactly a – a –"

"Oh, we know all about that," interrupted Nancy. "We know you drink a lot and aren't respectable at all and everyone thinks you are a no-good bum, but we don't care. Really we don't."

Jeb was somewhat taken aback by Nancy's bluntness. "Well, uh, you see it wouldn't hardly be right for a no-good bum to play Santa Claus, would it?"

"But you're not," wailed Nancy. "People just think you are. You have a kind heart, and that's the important thing."

"Thank you, thank you, my dear," said Jeb, deeply touched. "I appreciate your comments and I hope I am worthy. But –"

"We don't care if you are a no-good bum," said Joey firmly. "We want you for Santa Claus anyhow." Diplomacy was not exactly Joey's long suit.

"If you won't do it, then you are siding with the teachers against the kids and that's not fair," said Sherry. "You've always been a friend of the kids before."

Jeb mopped his forehead with a red bandanna handkerchief. He was in a terrible position. He was very appreciative of the honour that was being offered him, but he recognized the impossibility of accepting. He felt he had to let the children down gently somehow without hurting their feelings. He had a bright thought. "Anyhow," he pointed out, "I couldn't do it. I've never been a Santa Claus, and I wouldn't know what to do."

"Oh, we would teach you all of that," said Nancy brightly. "The school will provide the costume and you could make a real beard of horsehair or something. Last year Mr. Fidge wore a complete mask, and it was horrible. With his face I suppose it was a good idea, but the mask scared the little kids all to pieces. But we'll tell you exactly what you have to do and say. Don't worry about that."

"No, it wouldn't work," argued Jeb. "And what would your parents think of me as Santa Claus? They'd pop their poopers."

The arguments continued back and forth. When it finally became clear that Jeb was digging his heels in, Nancy burst into tears. Sherry, taking her cue from Nancy, also began to cry. "You're letting all the kids down," she wailed. Jeb was aghast. The sight of two weeping females was a new experience to him and more than he could stand. He was completely unnerved. He stood on one foot and then the other, making vague soothing noises and patting the girls on the shoulder. They just wept harder. Finally, in desperation he cried, "All right, all right, I'll do it. Just stop crying." The tears shut off with remarkable promptness. "Oh, you will, Jeb? You will? Oh, marvellous," cried Nancy. Jeb looked at her suspiciously. She threw her arms around his neck and hugged him warmly. He was committed.

Jeb was completely shattered. He tottered back to his chair. "Can I have a drink?" he asked plaintively.

"No, you can't," said Nancy fiercely. "We've got things to talk about, and that's one of them. You've got to stop drinking right now and until after the concert."

"Aw, Nancy, you don't know what you're asking. Just one little drink. The concert's a week away," Jeb pleaded pathetically.

"No," said Nancy firmly. Jeb was now completely under her dominance, and she knew it. "No drinks until after the concert. We can't have a Santa Claus breathing liquor into the faces of the little kids, can we? Also, the teachers expect you to turn up plastered, and we've just got to show them." Nancy's intense little face was firm with resolve.

"But a whole week," protested Jeb.

"You've got to go in training. It'll take you that long to dry out." She stood up and faced Jeb. "Now repeat after me," she demanded. " 'I promise not to take a drink until after the concert, cross my heart and hope to die.' Then spit over your left shoulder."

"Aw, Nancy," complained Jeb. "Have a heart."

"Maybe one little drink wouldn't hurt," suggested Joey sympathetically.

"No," said Nancy. She stared fixedly into Jeb's eyes. His eyes fell away. "Now repeat after me." She led him through the pledge phrase by phrase, with Jeb saying the words in a hoarse croak. "Now spit over your left shoulder." Jeb did as he was told. "Good, that's taken care of," said Nancy sitting down with a deep sigh. "Now another thing," she leaned forward, "before the concert you're to have a big bath and get all cleaned up. We can't have Santa Claus smelling like an old mukluk, can we?" She glanced around the room. "You can come over to my house for a bath."

"No, no," gasped Jeb. "I'll manage."

"Good," said Nancy standing up. "Then everything is taken care of. We'll go now, but we'll come back later in the week to coach you on the things you'll need to know. Thank you for everything." She kissed him on the cheek. Sherry did the same and Joey shook hands with him. Then they left.

That night Jeb took all his liquor over to Flossy Macabee's and told her she was on no account to let him have any until after the concert. Jeb was going to give it a real try.

News that Jeb was to be Santa Claus at the Christmas concert spread around the town like wildfire. Most of the parents were highly amused. The betting was ten-to-one that he wouldn't show up, and a hundred-to-one that if he did he'd be loaded to the gills. It promised to be an exciting concert. A few of the parents were appalled and phoned the Principal. Mr. Fidge told them sententiously that Christmas was a children's affair and that Mr. Wilson had been their choice; the matter was out of his hands. He thereby established his lack of responsibility for the fiasco he anticipated.

The day of the concert was clear and cold. Although the performance was not to begin until 7:30pm, little people and mothers and teachers began arriving at the hall by 5:30. The mothers carried pieces of costume and shepherd's crooks and spears and what-not in their arms. All disappeared into the basement of the hall. By six o'clock the place was a pandemonium. Costumes were fitted on, adjusted and readjusted. Small boys wrestled and chased each other about. Mothers scolded, coaxed, and cajoled. Teachers tried to organize the children into classes to no avail. The Virgin Mary clobbered a classmate over the head with a Roman spear. Halos would not stay in place and had to be propped up. Balthazar's turban did duty as a football until rescued. Joseph's beard refused to say on. The angels' wings proved to be structurally unsound and had to be redesigned. The supply of safety pins ran out. The noise was deafening. Older children rehearsed lines in the corners of the room, and couldn't remember a thing. A parade of youngsters lined up at the one toilet. One little boy couldn't wait and wet his pants. A little angel was sick down the front of her robe. The excitement of a Broadway opening is nothing compared to the preamble of a Blossom Christmas concert.

Upstairs, the crowd gradually assembled; many hearty Christmas greetings and good wishes were shouted back and forth. The audience consisted principally of parents, grandparents, younger brothers and sisters and other relatives. The hall was jammed by 7:30. The curtain on the stage was in a constant state of agitation. Small faces peeked out, to be hauled back and replaced by others. The beautiful Christmas tree towered to the ceiling at the right of the stage with a great pile of presents beneath.

Finally the lights in the hall went off, and a subdued hush fell over the crowd. The curtain swung back to disclose the Grade Eight class. Or rather, half the curtain slid back. The other side stuck, and Mr. Fidge had to come out and pull it along. Miss Ure hit a chord on the piano and the class sang a spirited, but ragged rendition of "Jingle Bells" complete with jingling sleigh bells. The curtains closed to loud applause. There was then an interminable wait while much movement, whispering and hammering could be heard from the stage. The curtains finally opened (they had been fixed in the meantime) to reveal the scene of the Nativity. Everyone *oohed* and *aahed*. The Wise Men brought their gifts and the shepherds, following a star on the end of a fishing pole, arrived to pay their tributes. The Virgin Mary looked beautiful, serene and pure, and you would never have guessed that she had recently walloped a Roman general over the head with his own spear. Midway through the scene, Joseph's beard fell off. A group of angels in the background sang "Away in a Manger" more sweetly than real angels could possibly have done. The whole scene was delightful, and as lovely a tribute to the Holy Infant as could be imagined.

The next item on the programme was a piano solo, "The Avalanche," by Cedric Peebles. This was followed by a recitation by a little girl who forgot her lines, and in spite of loud and repeated prompting, gave up and ran off the stage in tears. And so it went – songs, recitations, skits – some well done, some badly, but all heartwarming.

From time to time during the performance, Mr. Fidge read telegrams indicating that Santa had been sighted on his way from the North Pole. These announcements were received with great excitement by the young fry and with knowing smiles by the older children. After the first announcement Fred Peters whispered to his wife, "Santa was last seen in a beer parlour in Yellowknife." His wife gave him an elbow in the ribs.

The final number of the evening brought the entire cast on the stage to sing Christmas carols in which everyone joined. When this was over, Mr. Fidge came on stage and said loudly, "The last telegram I received indicated that Santa was very near. In fact, I hear him at the door right now." He looked hopefully at the back of the hall and everyone craned their necks in that direction. Mr. Fidge said more loudly, "I hear Santa at the door right now." There was a long pause and Mr. Fidge looked rather sick. "I hear Santa at the door right now," he shouted desperately. "I think I did." There was another long pause. Suddenly the door banged open and Santa bounded in. The whole hall breathed a long sigh of relief.

And what a magnificent Santa he was! His nose was as red as a cherry and his clear blue eyes sparkled beneath shaggy white brows. A great flowing beard reached down to his chest and his bright red jacket was suitably plump. On his back he carried a huge bag of presents. He *Ho! Ho! Hoed!* his way up to the front of the hall, calling out Christmas greetings to everyone and patting the children on the head. He was escorted to his throne at the side of the tree by a beaming Nancy and Sherry. There he presided with all the aplomb and good will of a true spirit of Christmas. He called out the children's names prompted by Nancy, and presented the gifts with a few appropriate kindly words for each child. There was no doubt about it: Jeb was cold sober and in complete command of the situation. "I wouldn't have believed it," whispered Fred Peters to his wife. "It's a miracle." The other parents were also whispering in amazement. Mr. Fidge beamed proudly as if it were his own idea.

When the last present had been given out, Santa made his way through the throng speaking to each child as he went along until he got to the door. Then with a cheery, "Merry Christmas to you all, and to all a good night," he was gone. Everyone cheered and clapped and called out their Merry Christmases. Jeb had been a thundering success.

Later, as the adults were standing about the hall having coffee and the children were playing with their presents, Jeb returned as instructed by Nancy. He had changed to a suit and even wore a tie. He looked clean and fit. Nancy met him at the door and led him proudly about the room introducing him to parents. She presented him as if he were her own creation – which indeed he was. Everyone shook his hand warmly and congratulated him on his stellar performance. Jeb just grinned happily and said he had enjoyed himself thoroughly.

I wish I could report that Jeb was a changed man from that day on and never touched another drop, but it was not to be. In going about the hall, Nancy and Jeb came finally to Mrs. Frobisher. She was the self-appointed religious arbiter of the town and was obsessed with saving souls. She had a long thin nose and a mouth as uncompromising as the Ten Commandments.

"I am very pleased to see, Mr. Wilson," she said stiffly, "that you have seen the previous error of your ways and have resolved to be a better man. I congratulate you, but warn you not to let the demon drink ever again get you in its vile clutches. I will gladly help you to continue upon your road to salvation."

"Well, thank you very much, ma'am," mumbled Jeb, backing away. "But I wouldn't want to put you to no bother." He looked frantically about.

"Excuse us, Mrs. Frobisher," interrupted Nancy. "We must go along now."

But Mrs. Frobisher smelled a soul to be saved and she was not to be denied. She pursued Jeb through the crowd telling him she and her ladies' Bible group would call on him to pray with him. Jeb continued to back away. Finally Nancy, nearly in tears, stepped between them and stamped her foot. "You leave him alone," she shouted. "You leave him alone. You're a mean old thing."

"Well, I never," gasped Mrs. Frobisher, glaring at Nancy. "I'll speak to your mother, young lady."

Jeb took advantage of the opportunity to escape. He hurried through the crowd and out the door.

That night Jeb went on a bat which even for him was something of a wowser. Nancy wept for him; but Mrs. Frobisher didn't.

Chapter Eleven

THE VENETIAN AFFAIR

HE CITIZENS OF BLOSSOM were not particularly litigious which made it difficult for George Ingraham to establish a reputation for competency to deal with lawsuits and other such legal pleasantries. His first big opportunity came with the case later known as the 'Venetian Affair.' The possibility of him emerging from this challenge as a shining legal light looked very dicey indeed. He filled me in on the background of the case one evening in our usual booth at the back of Wong Toy's restaurant. Mal Morgan, who was of course familiar with the situation, was also present.

"The story has its beginnings back many years ago," said George, stroking his long nose pensively. "When the railroad was built through the West, the government provided land grants for right-of-way but also quite large blocks of property for development, with all mineral and other rights thereto. About ten years ago, Harry Frobisher bought a tract of land just east of the town from the railway. He had inherited a little money from his father who had made a bundle rumrunning in Saskatchewan – a point which Mrs. F. would like everyone to forget. Harry was planning to farm the land, but gave up on that idea when he got a chance to move into town to operate an elevator. The land wasn't much good for farming anyway.

"About five years ago, the town wanted to drill a well for water and Harry's land looked like a good place; there was also a vague idea of building a park in the area. A group of citizens, including Mal here, formed a little company and put enough money into the pot to buy the land at a price not much above what Harry had paid. Harry was tired of paying taxes on useless property and was happy to get rid of it. He also made a big thing of being a generous citizen of the community, although he would not let the town put down a trial hole for water before buying the property."

"Harry ain't a bad guy," interjected Mal. "But that wife of his is a dragon on wheels."

"Anyhow," continued George, "when the town drilled for water they didn't find any, but instead ran into a large deposit of natural gas. This was thought to be a disaster at the time, but turned out later to be a godsend – Blossom's typical serendipity. Dick Elliott was smart enough to realize that by combining cheap fuel from the gas with the natural clay of the area it might be possible to establish a brick factory. After looking into the technical feasibility and economic potential of the proposition, he formed the Blossom Brick Company which took over ownership of the property by giving stock in the new company to the land owners. The project got off on a shoestring budget with a loan from the bank and just about everybody in town investing a few dollars. The company is obviously very much community-oriented with so many of the citizens having a vested interest in its success. The Board of Directors is composed of townspeople. You're one, aren't you, Mal?"

"Yeah," nodded Mal. "Without pay, I might add. Any money we get we plough back into the business."

"The company is very important to the town, since it is the only primary industry we have and provides a fair number of pay cheques. Furthermore, because of the community-orientation of the Board, the company has expanded its service by providing gas to the town for heating, and electricity from a small gas-powered generator – both at very reasonable rates. As a result Blossom probably has the lowest energy costs in Canada. The company is now involved in developing a water-pumping system. Dick Elliott deserves a great deal of credit for bringing the company along so well in these difficult times."

"It sounds like a wonderful symbiotic relationship between

the company and the town," I commented. "What's the problem?"

"So far, so good," agreed George with a nod of his head. "But now the plot thickens. The railroad owned the oil and mineral rights to the land which were transferred when Harry bought the property. "But," George held up a finger, "these rights were not included when Harry sold the property. This happened more by accident than by design apparently because Harry didn't even know about it until recently. There was either some very clever legal work done here or some very sloppy work. Since Cyril Thorndyke, my esteemed colleague from Dazzle, handled the transfer for Harry, I have my opinion."

"Is there no honour?" I asked, smiting my forehead with the palm of my hand.

George ignored me. "Certainly the legal work done for the Blossom Brick Company by some knothead in Calgary was shamefully inadequate, because, of course, the BBC thought they owned the rights to the gas."

"Were you involved in any of this?" I asked.

George shook his head. "No. This all transpired before I came to Blossom."

"What happened to alert Harry to the situation?"

"Some engineers of the Great Prairie Oil Company have been in town looking over the oil prospects in the area. On the premise that where there is natural gas there is apt to be oil, they want to drill an exploratory well. Their lawyers looked into the ownership of the oil rights and discovered the situation I have described to you. They approached Harry to make a deal with him for drilling privileges. Harry, of course, was delighted with the proposition because all of a sudden he sees himself as an oil millionaire and his wife envisages her pumpkin being transposed into a golden carriage. But the oil company is reluctant to sign anything until the situation is clarified with the BBC which owns the land. So Harry hotfooted over to break the glad tidings to Dick Elliott. Dick was horrified, to say the least, and has retained me as his legal counsel. Harry brought in Cyril Thorndyke, and the four of us have held several fruitless meetings trying to work something out."

"Surely, that shouldn't be too difficult," I said. "It would seem to be to your mutual advantage to coöperate. Discovery of oil would be a tremendous boon to the town, to the district, and oh, everybody."

"Sure," agreed George. "Except that we've never seen any sign of oil in all the time we've been pumping gas, so it's an iffy proposition at best. However, you still apparently don't appre-iate the gravity of the situation. All the BBC owns are the surface rights. Since Harry owns the petroleum rights, he can sue the brick company for all the natural gas it and the town have used in the last four years; furthermore, he can set rates in the future. He can therefore bankrupt the BBC overnight if he wants to or be able to take it over at his own price."

"Good God," I exclaimed. "You are in a mess."

"That's for sure," growled Mal. "Harry's got us by the short hairs, and he's tugging hard."

"It is in our interest, of course," continued George, "to make some kind of an agreement which won't ruin us. We've tried to buy the petroleum rights from Harry but he's got sugarplums dancing in his head and is demanding an impossible figure. He responded, through Cyril Thorndyke, with an offer to buy the property from us, but at a niggardly sum and with conditions which would leave us at his mercy. About the time we think we may have worked out something reasonable, he goes back home to that welterweight he's got in the kitchen and comes back to the next meeting with his backbone all restarched."

"You won't get no help from Mrs. Twitchnose, I can tell you that," said Mal. "The whole town is in an uproar over the situation and the Frobishers' popularity has hit a new low. They couldn't care less. Unpopularity rolls off Harry's back like butter off a dog's whack."

"Our problem is obviously that we are dealing from weakness and Harry from strength," said George. "We've really got nothing to bargain with except nuisance value. Harry, on Cyril's advice, finally threatened to go ahead and sign up with the oil company. We responded by taking out an injunction to prevent him from doing so until our rights are protected. But I confess it's just a delaying tactic. I don't see at the moment how we can prevent him from doing so, nor taking over control of the gas supply. There is to be a hearing in front of Judge Broome when he comes to town next week."

"There's one good thing about all this, George," I said. "If you can come out of it not too badly, you'll be established in your profession hereabouts for all time to come."

"Thanks a lot," said George, turning his mouth down at the corners. "Because the opposite also obtains. If Harry would give us the gas rights or sell them at a reasonable figure, we'd say go ahead and drill for oil and good luck. But Cyril won't let him make any concessions, and of course Harry has to report back to his wife who is so mean she wouldn't give you a grain of sand if she owned the Sahara." George grimaced unhappily.

"Yeah," I conceded. "You can expect Harry, or rather, Mrs. Harry to demand her pound of flesh, but possibly –"

Suddenly George gave a start and stared blankly over my shoulder with his mouth open. He sat stiffly for several seconds, then rose and walked as if in a trace across the restaurant and out the door.

"What's wrong with George?" I asked Mal in amazement. "Did I say something to offend him?"

"Naw, I don't think so," replied Mal. "George is like that sometimes. He can be with you and then all of a sudden he drops a shutter and withdraws into a world of his own. Maybe he got some kind of an idea about this bloody case."

"It would be a wonderful thing for George if he could pull off something here. Do you think he has a chance?"

Mal scratched his chin. "I don't see how," he said slowly. "He doesn't have a snowball's hope in hell."

During the week preceding the court hearing, the town was in a dither. The gossip exchanges dealt in nothing else. Everyone was well aware of the seriousness of the situation: the hazard to the brick company which provided the only viable industry in the community; the possibility of suit to recover back gas charges; the probability of increased cost of utilities in the future; the humiliation of being under the virtual control of Mrs. Frobisher who was thoroughly detested by practically everyone anyhow. It was well recognized that Mrs. Frobisher, and not Harry, was the force to be reckoned with. Any advantage which might accrue to the discovery of oil was dismissed as too uncertain and indirect. Methods of dealing with the situation were discussed and discarded. Gradually a deep gloom settled over the town.

The courtroom of the Embassy was filled to overflowing for the hearings. I attended with Mal Morgan and Fred Peters. Mrs. Frobisher and some of her VV friends pushed forward to the front row of the spectators' area.

"Mrs. Twitchnose is here to see Harry don't sell the farm," whispered Mal in my ear. He also pointed out two well-dressed men he said were representatives of the Great Prairie Oil Company.

George Ingraham and Dick Elliott occupied one table in front of the bench while Cyril Thorndyke and Harry Frobisher sat at another. George, looking rather elegant in his black gown, sat with his long legs extended under the table. His manner was one of bored detachment. Dick Elliott, beside him, looked worried and tense, his heavily-lined face set in immobility. Cyril, trying to match George in elegance was hampered by his short, fat stature and untidy appearance. He was, however, quite obviously happy and relaxed, feeling no doubt that he had the upper hand in the case. He chatted cheerfully with Harry Frobisher, nudging him from time to time in amiable discourse. Harry was a mousy little individual in an ill-fitting grey suit and an unfortunate purple tie. He was plainly ill-at-ease and fidgetted uncomfortably at Cyril's comments.

Judge Broome, Old Flint-Face to the locals, presided over the hearings with his usual stony composure. His face rarely changed expression, but his icy blue eyes never missed a trick.

The first part of the hearings was very dull, consisting principally of a presentation and verification of a gallimaufry of documents. Both Dick Elliott and Harry Frobisher gave evidence as to the circumstances of the transfers. Dick spoke in short, terse sentences in response to questions from George. He indicated that when he purchased the property on behalf of the Blossom Brick Company, he had been given to understand that all rights were included. Cyril didn't bother to question him.

Harry Frobisher was a poor witness. He fidgetted and dithered and seemed reluctant to admit anything in case he made a mistake. He shot frequent glances at Mrs. Frobisher who was staring at him with fixed intensity.

"Now, Mr. Frobisher," said George, "when you bought the property from the railroad you were aware that the oil and mineral rights were included?"

Harry cracked his knuckles and recrossed his legs. He looked at Cyril who nodded slightly. "Yes," mumbled Harry.

"And when you sold the property you understood that the rights were transferred?"

"No," said Harry promptly.

"Is that so?" said George affecting surprise. "Is that what your legal counsel has directed you to say?"

Cyril leaped to his feet. "I must object, m'lord."

"Sustained," said Judge Broome coldly.

"Is it not true that you were not aware that the mineral rights had not been transferred until recently?" asked George staring into Harry's eyes.

Harry swallowed. "Not very recently."

"How recently?"

"Some time ago."

"Weeks? Months? Days?"

"I guess weeks."

"But after you had sold the property? Remember you are under oath."

Harry looked very unhappy. "I guess so."

"You guess so," said George severely. "Don't you know?"

"I don't remember just when."

"But after you sold the property?"

"I guess so," admitted Harry reluctantly.

"So when you sold the property you understood and intended that the oil rights be included?"

Harry looked helplessly at Cyril. "M'lord," said Cyril getting to his feet, "I would submit that it is irrelevant whether or not the oil rights were withheld unintentionally or deliberately. The fact is that they were not transferred."

"But, m'lord," said George, "Mr. Frobisher has admitted that it was his intention to include the oil rights in the sale. I would submit that this was a simple oversight which should now be corrected. Mr. Elliott has testified that it was his understanding that the oil rights had been transferred; Mr. Frobisher intended that they be transferred. The honourable thing would be for Mr. Frobisher to complete now the transaction according to the understanding of the contracting parties."

"Nonsense," snapped Cyril, adding belately, "with respect."

Judge Broome placed his elbows on the desk and made a steeple of his fingers. "A written contract cannot be changed except by mutual consent of the contracting parties," he said in a grating voice. "I gather from the pithy expostulation of Mr. Thorndyke that he is not prepared to agree to the change proposed by Mr. Ingraham." He glanced at Cyril who nodded. "Mr. Thorndyke is correct in stating that it is irrelevant whether the petroleum rights were reserved by inadvertence or not. This court must therefore concern itself only with the written documentation before it."

"Very well, m'lord," said George.

I could not tell from George's manner whether this ruling was a severe blow to his case or not. If this were the only string to his bow, then apparently he had lost the contest. The manner of presentation of the two lawyers was in sharp contrast. George affected a rather theatrical style of unruffled urbanity. He hooked his thumbs in his gown and paced back and forth behind the table with his head held at an arrogant angle. His manner so accentuated his Mephistophelian appearance that I wouldn't have been surprised if he had burst into "Le Veau d'Or" at any moment. Cyril, on the other hand, stood behind his table going up and down on his toes while nervously shuffling the papers in front of him.

Judge Broome leaned forward. "I have no objection to the contestants in this hearing using this court as a forum in which to work out an agreement. But tell me, gentlemen, have efforts not been made to settle this matter out of court by some mutually beneficial financial arrangement?"

"Yes, m'lord," said George promptly. "In the interests of harmony and in a spirit of coadjuvancy we have made a generous offer, but have been stultified by the obdurate acquisitiveness of my learned friend and his client. It may be that they have taken an extreme stand for negotiating purposes. We think that they are pursuing this matter to the last hour of act and then will make a generous arrangement. Is that so?" George turned to Cyril with elevated eyebrows.

"M'lord," said Cyril. "We have made every effort to accommodate our friends on the other side of this room, but have been met with absurd and outlandish demands. Therefore, with regret, we find we must stand upon our legal rights."

"The Blossom Brick Company is owned by the citizens of this town and is of vital importance to the welfare of the whole community," said George. "Are your motives not questionable?"

"Motivation is not the question! We demand that a decision be reached here and now." Cyril tilted his head back in a parody of George's manner.

"We are prepared to pay again an amount equal to the sum of the original purchase," said George. "I offer it to you here in open court."

"Negative," said Cyril loftily.

"Then twice the sum."

"Same response," said Cyril shaking his head.

"Then be fair. Take thrice the money. That is my last offer."

Cyril hesitated. "Let me consult with my client, m'lord," he said to Judge Broome, who nodded stiffly. Cyril took his seat beside Harry Frobisher and whispered in his ear. Harry bit his lower lip in obvious uncertainty. He turned and glanced at Mrs. Frobisher who was staring fixedly at him. She shook her head sternly. Harry turned back to Cyril and said a few words to him. They continued their discussion for a few minutes. Cyril then rose to his feet and faced the judge.

"We are not prepared to accept the offer, m'lord," he said disdainfully. "Let the discussions continue."

"Very well," said George without any evidence of disappointment. "Then we are prepared to concede the point that the oil and mineral rights reside with Mr. Frobisher."

"My learned friend is being generous in accepting the apodictic," said Cyril sarcastically.

George, hooking his thumbs in the lapels of his gown, made a turn up and back behind the table. Then he whirled upon Cyril.

"But that does not mean that he owns the gas," he declared forcefully.

"Of course he does," shouted Cyril, suddenly alarmed. "You have conceded that Mr. Frobisher owns the oil rights which certainly embraces gas."

"Is gas oil?" asked George softly with a smile. Judge Broome looked at George speculatively; his left eyebrow was slightly elevated.

"Certainly it is," affirmed Cyril. "I mean – just a minute." He pawed through his papers in considerable perturbation, beads of sweat suddenly appearing on his forehead. "Yes, here it is." He held up a document. "My client owns what are described as petroleum rights, not oil rights, which obviously includes gas." He breathed a sigh of relief and swabbed his neck with his handkerchief. "Yes, that does it."

"With respect, no, it doesn't," said George flatly. "The term 'petroleum' does not embrace natural gas. Oil may be considered to be a type of petroleum, but not gas. Oil and natural gas are very different things both chemically and physically."

"Nonsense," shouted Cyril. "What shenanigans are you trying to pull here? Gas is a form of oil – or I should say, a type of petroleum – and is certainly included in a definition of petroleum rights."

"May I be heard on this matter, m'lord?" asked George, turning to Judge Broome who was following the discussion with keen interest.

"By all means," he stated.

"The rights held by Mr. Frobisher are described in the document before you as, 'all coal, petroleum and valuable stone on or under the said land.' I presume that not even my esteemed friend would maintain that natural gas is coal or valuable stone, so we must direct our attention to the interpretation of the word 'petroleum' as used in the original sale agreement."

"Everyone knows that the word 'petroleum' includes gas," interrupted Cyril.

"No, they don't," stated George. "But I am indebted to my learned friend for introducing the point I wish to make. The generally understood meaning of the word 'petroleum' is that it refers to oil. Possibly the term would be considered to include gasoline which is often abbreviated to gas, or, as the English say, petrol. But that sort of gas is prepared from petroleum and is a very different thing from natural gas which is what we are concerned with here. I would submit then, m'lord, that in common parlance the term 'petroleum' does not embrace natural gas."

"I shall reserve on the rather bizarre point my friend is trying to make with regard to common parlance," said Cyril scathingly, "which I suggest is irrelevant anyhow. Certainly, in a technical sense gas is included in the term 'petroleum,' and I would submit that it is in such a sense that this controversy must be resolved – not some nonsense about common parlance." Cyril paused uncertainly, then his face lit up happily. "I am informed by people knowledgeable in the field that natural gas is frequently dissolved in oil in nature. My friend has already conceded that we control the oil rights. Surely he would not try to maintain that something dissolved in that oil is not part and parcel of that oil." Cyril beamed in triumph. Judge Broome's cold eyes turned to George.

"Yes, I would," George asserted. "If salt is dissolved in water it does not become water. The salt remains a separate chemical entity. When you use the term 'water' you do not include 'salt' in the technical definition." George emphasized the word 'technical.'

"Ah yes," said Cyril, "but if a person owns water rights, he owns the salts, the gases and whatever, which are contained in the water."

"But that does not imply that he owns the gases above nor the salts nearby the water," said George. "For example, there is oxygen in the air above a lake. Surely you would not suggest that if a person owned the water rights to that lake he could enjoin that others not breathe that air and utilize the oxygen, or indeed the water vapour, contained therein."

"I can turn your argument back on you," asserted Cyril. "Surely you would not suggest that a person who owns the water rights must extract the oxygen from the water before he could use it."

"Possibly, if someone else owned the oxygen rights. However, this argument would suggest, m'lord," said George turning to the judge, "that it may become necessary to distinguish between dissolved gas and free gas."

"I am pleased that my friend has conceded my point," said Cyril with an exaggerated bow.

"I have not conceded the point at all," replied George. "I am simply pointing out that this may be one of the options open to m'lord in the resolution of this case."

"I would comment that your analogy between gas and oil vis-a-vis oxygen and water does not hold water." Cyril paused, realizing that he had made a blunder. The audience sniggered quietly. "I mean water and oxygen are very different things, whereas gas and oil are chemically similar, and therefore both are covered by the term 'petroleum.' "

"You could make as good a case that oxygen is water because the latter is chemically H_2O," objected George.

"You have bankrupted your own position," said Cyril with a smile.

"I see it otherwise." George turned to the bench. "I would like now, m'lord, to return to the aspect of the definition of the term 'petroleum' to which I made reference earlier.

"As Your Honour is well aware, although my learned friend has apparently forgotten, there are certain basic rules or principles governing the interpretation of contracts. One of the cardinal principles governing the interpretation of contracts is that there must be assigned to each word in the contract its plain, ordinary meaning. All contracts must be construed according to the primary and natural meaning of the language in which the contracting parties have chosen to express the terms of their mutual agreement; and if a party to a contract contends that a term has a different meaning to its plain, ordinary, or, in other words, vernacular meaning, the burden of proof is on him to show that it should be interpreted as he suggests. I would submit, m'lord, that my esteemed friend has not been able to provide such proof. It is our contention that the vernacular meaning of the word 'petroleum' does not include natural gas." George wrapped his gown around himself with a theatrical gesture and took his seat.

Cyril mopped his forehead and neck with his handkerchief.

His earlier manner of superiority and condescension had disappeared. "M'lord," he began with a hoarse voice. He cleared his throat and started over again. "M'lord, I would submit that the vernacular meaning of the term 'petroleum' does indeed embrace natural gas. However, it is our position that the vernacular is irrelevant to the matter at issue before us and is a red herring introduced by my learned colleague to confuse the situation. It is our contention that the decision as to who owns the gas rights must be based on the technical significance of the terms involved and the technical relationship of gas and oil. It is my understanding that my learned friend has not seriously challenged the fact that, in a technical sense, gas is included in the terminology of the word 'petroleum.' "

George began to rise, but Judge Broome held up his hand. "It is past the hour of the noon recess," he said glancing at the clock. "We shall adjourn until two o'clock."

During the noon break, the principals in the hearings lunched in private, apparently planning strategy for the afternoon session. The rest of us meandered along the street in little groups discussing the case. There was some alleviation of the earlier gloom, but not even the most optimistic gave George much of a chance of winning.

Mal, Fred and I had lunch in Wong Toy's restaurant. "Well, what do you think, Mal?" I asked.

"I don't know," muttered Mal glumly. "It don't look too good to me. Do you think George will get anywhere with that vernacular stuff?"

"It's about all he had to hang his hat on, I guess," said Fred.

"It's as difficult for a layman to assess a legal battle as a landlubber to tell who's winning a yacht race," I observed. "There's so much tacking back and forth and manoeuvering around that you can't tell who's ahead. I don't know if George is getting anywhere or not. What do you say, Fred?"

Fred scratched his chin. "He seems to have got Cyril worried at any rate. If that's any indication."

"That don't mean nothing," said Mal. "Cyril gets in a sweat making up his mind to go to the biffy."

We continued to discuss the case rather gloomily until it was time to return to the Embassy.

The courtroom was again packed with spectators. Nothing particularly new was introduced by either side for the first hour or so. Both lawyers reiterated their stand of the morning, with George emphasizing that the decision on the ownership of the gas rights must be based on the vernacular meaning of the term 'petroleum,' and Cyril insisting that the matter must be resolved on technical grounds. Cyril had apparently looked up some chemical information during the noon hour and launched off on a confused dissertation on the nature of natural gas which he claimed showed that gas was chemically closely related to oil. George said the information proved just the opposite and anyhow was irrelevant. They continued to wrangle interminably.

Finally, in complete exasperation, Cyril stated, "My learned friend is just being obstructionistic. He is trying to parlay the nuisance value of his fatuous contention that gas is not covered under the term 'petroleum' into a good deal for his client. The court should not permit itself to be manipulated into participation in such devious manoeuvering."

"If the gas rights are just a nuisance, why doesn't my friend concede our contention, and we can resolve the case forthwith?" asked George, spreading his hands out palms up.

"I cannot concede a point which would be inimicable to my client's best interests on the grounds of expediency," answered Cyril sententiously. "The nuisance value relates to the fact that my friend is trying to block the search for oil, which, if found, would be of inestimable value to this community and, indeed, to the country at large. The search for oil is inevitable in any event. My friend has generously conceded that the oil rights belong to my client, since he had no alternative. We shall, therefore, proceed with the search for oil regardless of the decision on the gas rights. However, I would submit that we have presented an unimpeachable case which establishes that the gas rights are encompassed in the technical term 'petroleum.' I would suggest, m'lord, that you proceed with the decision on the matter. We are prepared to rest."

"Just a minute, if you please, m'lord," said George. "My friend has stated that his client will go ahead with the search for oil regardless of the decision on the gas rights. I submit that the gas belongs to my client, and I am confident that the decision will be in our favour. Therefore, if in the search for oil one bubble of gas escapes," George paused dramatically, "there will have been an infringement upon the rights of my client." George levelled a finger at Cyril. "You will be beholden to us."

"But, but," stuttered Cyril aghast, "you can't obtain oil without some gas escaping."

"Exactly," affirmed George, nodding his head solemnly.

Cyril stood with his mouth open for a moment before pulling himself together. "That would be preposterous," he blurted. "It is inconceivable that a worthy business enterprise could be thwarted by such a trivial consideration. This proposition of my learned friend, which I do not for a moment accept, only emphasizes, m'lord, the importance of the recognition that gas and oil are intimately associated and cannot be separately distinguished. My friend has inadvertently provided me with the final topper to my argument. Gas and oil are part and parcel of the same package and both are covered under the term 'petroleum.' " Cyril sat down and mopped his forehead.

Judge Broome leaned forward. "Have you anything further to add, Mr. Thorndyke?"

"No, m'lord."

"Mr. Ingraham?"

"I am content, m'lord."

"Very well," said Judge Broome. "I am prepared to render my decision." He swung his swivel chair sideways and gazed thoughtfully at the wall for a good half-minute. The initial sibilance of whispering in the room died down to be replaced by an expectant hush. Time seemed to stand still. The judge was something of a ham and was well aware of the dramatic impact of the delay. Finally, he turned back to face the room and fixed his cold blue eyes first on Cyril, then on George.

"The basic element in this case," be began in his dry, harsh voice, "is really very simple – is gas oil? Or more specifically, is natural gas to be included in the term 'petroleum?' There is no doubt that the petroleum rights reside with Mr. Frobisher. I have already rejected the contention by Mr. Ingraham that since the rights to 'all coal, petroleum and valuable stone on or under the said land' were not included in the transfer of the property to the Blossom Brick Company by inadvertence, therefore, they should now be transferred. It does not matter whether the rights were withheld by design or by accident; the fact remains that they were withheld. I reconfirm my ruling in this respect. The bond must stand." He shot a sharp look at George who smiled slightly.

"Mr. Ingraham has questioned the motivation of Mr. Frobisher in pressing this matter to the last hour of act, and that his deeds are questionable. Mr. Thorndyke's response was essentially, 'My deeds upon my head, I crave the law.' This is a valid attitude; the matter of motivation is irrelevant.

"Mr. Thorndyke rejected the proposition that he waive the gas rights on the grounds of expediency, saying essentially that he could not condone a little wrong to facilitate a great right. In view of Mr. Ingraham's later submission concerning the effect which ownership of the gas rights might have on oil exploration, Mr. Thorndyke was wise to have avoided this potential contretemps." Cyril beamed happily at this compliment from the judge. "Mr. Thorndyke also rejected the offer, made here in open court, of up to thrice the original cost of the property, as was within his province to do. He said he stands for judgment, and he shall have it."

Judge Broome paused and ran a thumb down his long, bony jaw. "The Blossom Brick Company owns all rights to the property except those specifically withheld," he continued slowly. "I shall turn my attention now to the matter of free gas and gas dissolved in the oil. There is no question that oil is covered in the term 'petroleum.' Mr. Thorndyke has made the case that gas dissolved in the oil is part and parcel of that oil. Mr. Ingraham has suggested that it may be necessary to distinguish between free gas and dissolved gas. I accept that proposition. It would be irrational to maintain that rights to the oil would not embrace dissolved materials. I therefore find that the term 'petroleum' includes dissolved natural gas." Cyril smiled broadly and heaved a sigh of relief. Judge Broome frowned in his direction and added, "It does not necessarily follow that free gas is likewise included." Cyril's face straightened out abruptly.

"In enquiring into the status of free gas, very different parameters of consideration must be taken into account. Mr. Thorndyke maintains that, technically, natural gas is included in the term 'petroleum.' Mr. Ingraham maintains that the word 'petroleum' must be interpreted according to the vernacular understanding of the term. On the technical side, natural gas is not a gaseous form of oil. Mr. Thorndyke has suggested that natural gas is chemically related to oil. However, all organic compounds have some atoms in common. There is some relevance to the analogy proposed by Mr. Ingraham between water and oxygen on the one side and oil and natural gas on the other. Free oxygen over the water is not included in water rights, although they have a common atom. However, the technical considerations may be set aside.

"Mr. Ingraham is correct in stating that in a contract there must be assigned to each word its ordinary meaning, and if a contestant claims otherwise, the onus of proof is upon him to so show. Mr. Thorndyke has not done so.

"I therefore find that the term 'petroleum' does not embrace free natural gas. The rights to the free natural gas under the said property are owned by the Blossom Brick Company. It follows, as Mr. Ingraham has stated, that, if, in the search for or removal of oil from the said property, free gas is allowed to escape, there has been an infringement of the rights of the owners. This hearing is concluded."

Judge Broome banged his gavel and rose. As he turned to leave he beckoned George to approach. His face was impassive, but his left eyebrow was noticeably elevated. He leaned forward to George and said in a quiet voice, "A Daniel has come to judgment."

"Thank you, O wise and upright judge," murmured George.

As sort of a postscript to the story, I should mention that the decision in this case went through a number of appeals which were financed by the Great Prairie Oil Company. The case ultimately ended up in the Judicial Committee of the Privy Council in England, where Judge Broome's decision was upheld. Later, the oil company made a financial arrangement with the Blossom Brick Company to drill for oil. None was found. However, the funds from this transaction put the BBC on its feet financially. The BBC therefore continued to flourish and to provide the town with an inexpensive supply of heat, water and electricity. Needless to say, George Ingraham was the hero of Blossom and firmly established as a legal wizard.

Chapter Twelve

A HERO ONE DAY, A BUM THE NEXT

ON MY WAY INTO BLOSSOM, I stopped at Fred Peters' garage to fill up with gas. Fred came out and said, "Hey, did you hear about the bank holdup last week?"

"Yeah, I know. A belt held up a pair of pants."

"No, this was the real McCoy. Guns and everything. Didn't you read about it? It was in the papers."

"No. I've been on the road for a week. The only paper I've seen was the *Balzac Bugle.* The lead story was an oat-judging contest. But what happened? Did they get away with anything?"

"No. And Jeb Wilson and Roscoe are the big heroes. Also George Ingraham."

"You mean Roscoe is a hero and I have to change my mind about that miserable flea-bitten pooch?"

"Yep. We're going to rename Main Street Roscoe Avenue. At least we were last week. After last night we're not so sure. Roscoe reverted to type. Come on in and I'll tell you all about it. I was a bit player in the drama myself."

I hurriedly parked my car and joined Fred in his cluttered office. A bank holdup in the sleepy town of Blossom would be the talk of the place for years.

"What happened?" I demanded. "Did anybody get hurt?"

"No, thanks largely to Roscoe. And I missed my chance to be a hero – twice due to stupidity and once due to ignorance, on account of I don't speak Latin."

"The stupidity and ignorance I can believe, but what does Latin have to do with it?"

"Just about everything."

"Come on. Come on. What happened?"

"All in good time," said Fred, holding up his hand. Fred prided himself on his talents as a raconteur and he wasn't going to be rushed into doing less than an artistic job on such an important story. "I should have twigged that something was up when Jeb came in Monday night with his old Essex and said, 'Fill 'er up.' He never has enough dough for that. And he has this tough-looking bozo in the front seat with him. Then when he paid me with a five-dollar bill and said, 'Keep the change,' I should have smartened up instead of fainting."

"Don't tell me they were planning to use Jeb's old junk heap for a getaway car?"

"It isn't as crazy as it sounds. If they had driven up to the bank in a big limousine and left the motor running, everyone would have known something was up; also the car and licence could have been identified later. So they parked their big car about twenty miles south of here, behind an old barn. They were going to get there in Jeb's old Essex. The gang was made up of four American thugs; they planned to get back across the border just as quickly as possible. We aren't far from the border, as you know."

"How did they think they would get through immigration? The authorities at the border could have been alerted by phone."

"That's where Jeb came into it. He has a secret route across the border he has been using for years for rumrunning. The holdup men came across by that route at night and would have returned the same way. Once they got into the States they would just have disappeared. There would be no description of the car or of them coming or going."

"You mean that Jeb was in on it?"

"No, not really. These guys had got a line on Jeb through some of his rumrunning contacts in the States. He thought the whole deal was a bootlegging operation until they got here and he found out it was a bank stickup. Jeb has no compunction about breaking certain laws – particularly the stupid ones involving liquor, just like the rest of us – but a bank heist was too rich for his blood. He didn't like the hazard and didn't want any part of it. However, he had to play along or the thugs would have had to shoot him because he knew too much and could identify them. They promised him a share of the loot and said they would take him back with them. There were two things wrong with this from Jeb's point of view. He didn't want to leave Blossom and, more important, he had a suspicion, and a valid one, that they would knock him off for security reasons once they got away. No, the whole deal had nothing to recommend it to Jeb. They obviously didn't trust him because they didn't let him out of their sight once they arrived; Jeb, therefore, had no chance to tip anybody off. He did his best, but I flubbed it.

"The gang stayed overnight in Jeb's shack and spent most of the time reviewing their plans. They knew a lot about the town and the setup at the bank. They checked this all out with Jeb. They had chosen that particular day for the operation because they knew Corporal Rankin would be out of town on his weekly tour around the district. American thugs have no desire to tangle with the Mounties. At about one in the morning, an old customer of Jeb's turned up for a bottle of hooch. Jeb completed the transaction at the door with four guns pointing at his back. When they finally went to sleep they tied Jeb in his bunk, which didn't improve his peace of mind any. He didn't sleep much, and tried to figure some way out of his dilemma. He came up with the couple of forlorn hopes which he used."

"What were they?" I demanded.

"We're coming to it," said Fred. "Be patient. In the morning, after a shot of Jeb's moonshine to give them courage, they piled into the old Essex and arrived at the bank on schedule, a little after ten. Three of them went into the bank, and one stayed in the front seat with a gun in Jeb's ribs in case he got any bright ideas about resigning from the group. As instructed, Jeb left the motor running.

"They had no great difficulty in the bank. There's only a staff of three; the manager, the teller and the stenographer. The teller, that fat poop with the buggy eyes named Frank Jal, was no problem. He promptly fainted and was tied up and gagged. They also tied and gagged Frieda, the stenographer, and Rick Sisk, the only customer in the place. One guy remained at the door and tied up two other people who came in. The vault hadn't been opened yet, so they made the manager, Ralph Morsh, open it. He stalled around as long as possible, but finally had to do so. Then they tied him up. Incidentally, you may have noticed that you can't see into the bank very well unless you go right up to the door. The people tied up were placed on the floor behind the counter and weren't visible anyhow. The whole operation was very professional.

"While they were inside, I walked by the bank on my way back from the post office. Roscoe was sitting on the sidewalk by the car with his tongue hanging out. I didn't pat him because he doesn't like me, and anyhow he usually smells something fierce."

"He doesn't like anybody," I interjected.

"Please," said Fred, "you are talking about a hero. I said good morning to Jeb and he replied something I didn't understand. His eyes were more than usually bloodshot and his florid, jowly face under the dirty Stetson was red as a beet. I thought to myself that Jeb must have had a tough night. He winked at me, so I winked back. 'What are you doing, Jeb,' I asked. 'Planning to rob the bank?' He replied, 'That's right, Mr. Rankin, that's just what I'm a-doing,' and sat up straight suddenly. That was due to a prod in the ribs with the gun. Now Jeb knows my name as well as his own, and Rankin is the name of the RCMP officer, but did I get the message? No. I'm stupid." Fred smote his forehead with his palm.

"Ah, don't feel badly," I urged. "It was pretty subtle. I'd have missed it too."

"That's damned small consolation, pal, but thanks for trying. Anyhow, I thought to myself that Jeb had finally really blew his cork, so I just waved and went on.

"I met George Ingraham up the street and we exchanged greetings. When George walked by the car he said 'Good morning,' and Jeb replied wth the same phrase he had used on me. George just nodded and went on to his office."

"What was the phrase? What did Jeb say?"

"I know it now. It's Latin. Let me see if I can get it straight. He said, '*Morituri te salutamus.*' "

"What does it mean?"

"It's the salutation that was used by the gladiators in ancient Rome before they fought. It means, 'We who are about to die salute thee.' When George got to his office he was mulling over this phrase and he suddenly remembered what it meant. So he says. I think he looked it up. Anyhow, he put two and two together and got a million. That phrase plus the car at the bank with the motor running and that goon in the front seat with Jeb all fitted together. He grabbed the phone and hollered, 'Holdup at the bank, Mamie! Phone everybody to come and bring guns.'

"I had just walked into the garage when my phone rang and Mamie practically screamed the message at me. I grabbed my old Remington and a handful of shells and started off down the street hellbent for election. You do funny things in an emergency that you can't account for afterwards. The garage is only two-and-a-half blocks from the bank, but I'm not as young as I used to be. At the end of the first block I was puffing like a steam engine in heat, wondering why in blazes I hadn't taken the car. I slowed up some. Mal Morgan came panting up carrying a double-barrelled shotgun. Three others joined us toting guns of various kinds. When we passed the restaurant, Wong Toy ran out in his white apron with a meat cleaver in one hand and a potato masher in the other. What the hell he thought he was going to do with them I'll never know, but give him A-plus for guts. I could hear a couple more coming behind us. We were too pooped to exchange comments.

"We were, of course, running along the street at right angles to the street the bank is on. When we got to the intersection we rounded the corner and kept right on going down the middle of the street. This obviously, in retrospect, was a pretty stupid thing to do. George Ingraham later referred to us as magnificent fools. Fools we were for sure, but magnificent I *hae my doots*. We just weren't thinking, that's all. Our advance must have been the craziest charge since The Light Brigade. I could see Jeb's car facing us down the block, with Jeb and the goon in the front seat.

Then I noticed George Ingraham standing in a doorway to our right with an appalled look on his face. He roared at us, 'Go back, you idiots. Take cover. Take cover.' We suddenly realized the vulnerability of our situation. Mal Morgan hollered, 'Hit the dust,' and threw himself on the ground on his stomach. I followed suit and most of the others did also. Two of them scuttled for doorways. Wong didn't get the idea, and kept on going. Fortunately he was behind us, and as he went by, Mal grabbed him by the ankle. Wong went arse over teakettle and lost his meat cleaver but kept his potato masher – so he was still armed. George hollered again, 'Don't shoot or you'll hit Jeb. Don't shoot.'

"Jeb said the sight of us suddenly bursting around that corner, throwing ourselves flat on our bellies and then Wong doing a somersault down the middle of the road was the funniest sight since the Keystone Cops. I can believe it. The goon beside him couldn't believe his eyes. He sat paralyzed for about ten seconds. Then he jabbed his gun into Jeb's ribs and yelled, 'Turn around and beat it.' Jeb pulled out the choke and stalled the motor. The goon jumped out and ran behind the car. He sighted along the mudguard with his revolver and took a shot at us. I'll swear that bullet zinged right by my ear. Each one of the other boys swears it went by his ear, but pay them no attention. George hollered again not to shoot. It was frustrating. Jeb was right smack in our line of fire. Wong was talking vehemently in Cantonese and Mal was cursing in old-fashioned Anglo-Saxon. I was hugging the ground and wishing I was a gopher.

"A truck came slewing around the corner and nearly ran over us. I glanced over my shoulder and saw it skid to a stop right behind us. Jerry Rusk had been picking up boys along the way and about five or six of them jumped off and took up positions behind and under the truck.

"By this time the thug was taking careful aim for his second shot; right at the middle of my forehead, I was convinced. Jeb hollered, 'Get him Roscoe,' and the dog practically crawled up the guy's back. The shot went wide and the goon dropped the gun trying to fight off Roscoe. From that moment on, Roscoe became my favourite dog, and I'll tolerate no unkind remarks about him in the future. Jeb opened the door of the Essex, fell out and rolled underneath. The goon started to run down the street pursued by Roscoe. Someone hollered 'Fire,' and we let go a salvo that sounded like the opening barrage of the battle of the Somme. It was a long distance for shotguns, which was what most of the boys had, but they sure added mightily to the din. We shattered the window of the bank and the two stores on each side of it, knocked out the windshield and one headlight of the Essex, and gave it a flat tire. Just as we fired, Roscoe got the guy by the leg; the two of them rolled over and over down the street in a heap. The goon was screaming, 'I surrender. I surrender. Call off your dog.' Jeb calls out, 'Roscoe, guard; guard,' and Roscoe lets go and stands over the guy with his fangs bared hopefully. The guy just lay there afraid to move a muscle.

"The three guys in the bank come charging out with their guns drawn and the sacks of money in their hands. George hollers to us to hold our fire. These characters were staring at enough artillery to put down the Riel Rebellion. I counted up later, and by this time there were fifteen guns – and a potato masher. And that opening fusillade must have impressed them plenty. George hollers at them that they are covered and to throw down their guns. They look the situation over quickly, including their pal on his back with Roscoe sitting on his chest, and decide wisely that it's hopeless. They throw their guns out into the street and hold up their hands. The battle was over.

"George tells us to cover him and he walks slowly over, picks up the guns, and makes the goons lean against the wall with their feet out and their hands up while he frisks them. Then we all come bustling up and there is a great yackety-yak. Jeb calls off Roscoe, and he leaves his charge very reluctantly, all growls and bristles. Rope was brought from the hardware store and the would-be bank robbers were securely tied up. They were a surprised and sorry-looking sight. Someone went into the bank and untied the prisoners there.

"People continued to arrive with guns for the next half hour, until someone thought to go and tell Mamie at the switchboard that the emergency was over. Even Grandma Akerbilt turned up toting a muzzleloading rifle as tall as she is. And she was mad as hell that the fighting was all over.

"So when Corporal Rankin got into town – Mamie had gotten in touch with him at Dazzle – we proudly turned the prisoners over to him. When he heard our story, he held his head in horror. I guess it wasn't a very polished performance, but it sure worked."

"One thing really puzzles me, Fred," I mused, "How come an old rubby-dub like Jeb knew that Latin phrase he used to tip off George?"

"God only knows. He just grins and says he picked it up somewhere. George thinks maybe Jeb isn't such an uneducated, ignorant bum as he appears. That's probably the answer, 'cause nobody knows anything about his background, and he isn't telling. Jeb was lucky that George came along, because as a lawyer he is about the only person in town who would understand it. I sure as hell didn't and I blew that tip on being called Rankin. What a dope."

"So Jeb and Roscoe are heroes?"

"Yep. Up until last night anyhow."

"What happened last night?"

"The bank gave a big banquet in the Elks' Hall to honour all the vigilantes who were involved in the capture of the bandits. Since just about everybody in town was involved, Blossom had gathered in all its beauty and its chivalry. The hall was packed with heroes all telling their stories over again for the umpteenth time. The bank had sent out their western supervisor from Winnipeg, a guy named Spindle, to handle the affair and to present cheques of five hundred bucks to Jeb and to George Ingraham, who were rightly considered to be the key men in the success of the operation. That's more cash than Jeb's seen in his entire life before. It'll keep him in beans and bacon for years, if he doesn't blow it the first week. Those hoods are probably wanted in the States too, and it may be that Jeb and George will get some more dough later when the investigation is completed. Sheesh, I sure wish to hell I'd spent more of my time as a kid on Latin and less on Kelly pool.

"Ah, but now is not the time to bemoan my misspent youth," Fred sighed deeply. "To continue. It really was a delightful affair. The Ladies Aid catered the thing and put on a bang-up turkey dinner with all the trimmings. Mr. Spindle, the supervisor, was a real pleasant guy for a banker, and shook hands with everybody and made them welcome. He had the gift of the gab and handled the emcee job just fine. The room was arranged with small tables around the main part of the hall and the head table up on the stage with all the principals at it. There was Jeb and George, of course, and Mamie Sutherland for phoning out the alarm; and the local bank staff, although they sure as hell had done nothing noteworthy during the holdup; and Corporal Rankin, Mal Morgan, and Grandma Akerbilt, looking like she'd just stepped out of a covered wagon with her hair up in that tight topknot she wears; I was there as prize idiot, along with other assorted luminaries."

"Was Roscoe there?" I asked.

"He sure was. After a certain amount of preliminary difficulties, I might add. It was planned that Roscoe was to be one of the most highly honoured heroes, but they had a little trouble in getting the idea across to him. When Jeb went to the hall he took Roscoe with him as instructed, but Roscoe wouldn't go inside. The dog had never before been accepted by polite society, and he couldn't believe he was really wanted. He thought it was a trick of some kind. Jeb finally had to get a length of rope which he tied around Roscoe's neck and pulled him along to the head table where he tied him to a leg. Roscoe was highly suspicious about the whole deal. The role of hero was a new one to him, and he was having trouble adjusting to it. Furthermore, he has a deeply ingrained and well-justified suspicion of humans. He wasn't going to swallow all this sudden 'Nice Roscoe' malarkey right off the bat from people who up to now had given him nothing but abuse. He just looked at them with that cynical leer he has, and reserved judgment. I guess his suspicions were at least partly laid to rest when he was given a huge plate of turkey bones to gnaw on. He then curled up at Jeb's feet. As a matter of fact, Jeb Wilson sitting beside a banker looked more out of place than Roscoe did.

"When dinner was over, Mr. Spindle got on his feet and spoke eloquently and glowingly about the bank's and society's great appreciation for the contribution of the citizenry of the entire community in corralling the evildoers who would undermine the etceteras and so forth. He had a tendency to equate the welfare of society with that of the bank, but he was picking up the tab for the dinner so no one was critical. He paid tribute to the cool courage of the bank staff in their moment of crisis but didn't overdo it, which was just as well; they were cool all right – frozen stiff. He waxed almost poetic in depicting Mamie Sutherland staying loyally at her post of responsibility and sounding the tocsin or blowing it or whatever you do with a tocsin. In a surprise move, unexpected by everyone including Mamie, he presented her with a cheque for a hundred dollars for her loyal service to society – for 'society' read 'bank.' Everyone was delighted. Mamie was flustered, but recovered long enough to accept the cheque with thanks and her usual cheerful laugh.

"When Spindle came to Jeb and George, he pulled out all the stops. He gave a great rooty-toot about their daring, valour, cleverness, selflessness, courage, perspicwhatever and so forth. In fact, he ascribed to them every virtue except chastity – which he didn't mention, come to think of it. An oversight, no doubt. He made good mileage out of the gladiator bit, referring to Jeb and George as modern warriors against the forces of evil. Jeb looked kind of sheepish about all the hogwash and flattery 'cause all he'd been trying to do was save his own bloody neck. Spindle's chapter on Man's Best Friend would have brought a blush to Roscoe's chops too, if he had understood a word of it. All in all, Spindle did a fine job and he got a big hand.

"Mr. Spindle then presented a cheque to George, who was seated on his right. George is, of course, something of a ham and enjoys the limelight despite his assumed cynicism. He made a graceful speech of acceptance paying tribute to the others involved in the affair and to Jeb in particular. George also got a big hand.

"Then it was Jeb's turn. As Mr. Spindle stepped to the left to hand the cheque to Jeb he trod squarely on Roscoe's knackers. This treatment just verified what Roscoe had suspected all along – that he was being set up for a dirty play of some kind. Roscoe let out one great howl of outrage and pain and lit off for the door by the shortest route, forgetting he was tied to the table leg. He went off the stage and through the tables like his tail feathers were on fire.

"Now you must have eaten some time or other at the Elks' Hall, and you know those are not real tables they use, but boards supported on trestles. Well, Roscoe was tied to the main prop of the head table, so when his eighty or so pounds hit the end of that rope, out went the prop. And down came the entire head table with a crash. Dishes, cutlery and everything went flying in all directions. Roscoe's rope jerked loose from the trestle and he just kept a-going. When he went through that door he must have been logging sixty miles an hour, and as far as I know he hasn't stopped yet.

"So that's why Roscoe was a hero yesterday and is a bum today. But I don't think people are being quite fair about it all. Look at it from Roscoe's point of view. How would you feel if you had been invited to a banquet as an honoured guest and then the host had tromped on your knackers? Furthermore, it provided a smashing finale to a delightful evening. Roscoe's still a hero in my books."

Chapter Thirteen

THE OTHER SIDE

I WAS USUALLY PROUD of the citizens of Blossom. On the whole they were kind, generous and tolerant, but sometimes they could be harsh and unsympathetic to those who did not subscribe to their standards of conduct. Since I had a background similar to the majority, I shared their prejudices and biases, so rarely was I aware that there might be two sides to the coin.

The people of the area were hard-working, thrifty and self-sufficient. During the Depression these qualities were essential for survival and were taken for granted. They retained a good deal of the Puritan ethic of hard work, but some of the intolerances too. They were invariably honest in their dealings with one another although they had little compunction about diddling outsiders. They were fiercely loyal to their friends; their word was their bond; and they paid their bills when they could.

The people I mingled with lived by a relatively high code of social conduct. Infidelity within this social group was practically unknown, due in part to the moral standards but also, and possibly more importantly, to the impossibility of getting away with any hanky-panky for any length of time in such a closed environment. Any philandering took place outside of the normal social milieu. Divorce was unheard of. Suspicion of homosexuality was dealt with summarily. When certain ugly rumours started to circulate about the night clerk at the hotel, he was visited by four citizens who escourted him to a westbound freight. That was the end of that.

The sexual mores of the young people of the community were

no different, I suppose, from that of any other time or place. They devoted a great deal of thought and energy to such matters, but, as Mal Morgan put it, that's been going on since time immoral. The Depression had an inhibiting effect on romance because few young people could see the financial feasibility of marrying and raising a family. Many of the brightest and more adventuresome boys left town riding the rods to seek their fortunes elsewhere; this avenue of escape was not available to girls. Thus, many bright and attractive girls ended up marrying some rather second-rate fellows because they were all that was available.

The youngsters of Blossom had developed a language all their own relating to sex which, as far as I know, was unique to that locale. I learned about this from Pete the Barber one night in the pool hall after listening to a completely incomprehensible exchange between some of the local boys. Girls have been called all sorts of things over the years, including dames, flappers, dolls, shebas, broads and floozies. In Blossom they were called minnows. According to Pete, this initial terminology had produced a whole series of words relating to fish. A fellow didn't go out with a girl, he went fishing; he used various kinds of lures, baits and hooks; once he had her on the line he played her gently into the landing net. Girls were various kinds of fish: rainbow trout – beautiful; cut throat – uncoöperative; Dolly Varden – sporty; suckers – stupid; brown trout – Indian girls; and so forth. A father was the game warden; a mother was a pike. There were various double entendres relating to poles, rods, flies, licenses and gaffs. All in all, it was a complicated and imaginative argot which enabled the young people to talk freely in front of adults without them having a clue what was going on.

Indians came to town frequently for shopping and to sell or barter baskets and other handicrafts, but they had no impact on the community. They were treated with remote kindness but like creatures from another world – which indeed, in a way, they were. People of mixed blood were called "half-breeds" or "breeds," and were automatically assigned a secondary status. They lived in a sort of limbo between the two cultures but related more to the Indian side than the white, since they had little social contact with the latter. As far as the whites were concerned, mixed-bloods were indistinguishable from Indians unless they were at least three-quarters white. The whites had low expectations for the mixed-bloods which tended to be a self-fulfilling prophecy. Bereft of meaningful business or social outlets, they drank too much and got into trouble with the law. When this happened the whites shrugged with an attitude of "what can you expect from a breed." Most of them were Catholic and had large families which exacerbated the problem of their social environment. The children of mixed parentage did as well in school as the whites but usually dropped out early because of different family expectations and pressures.

The mixed-bloods were considered by the whites to have lax moral standards, which probably meant only that they were less circumspect. The local boys considered that Indian and mixed-blood girls were fair game and easy pickings. Such fleeting liaisons as developed were almost invariably disastrous for the girls who were abandoned if they sought marriage or became pregnant. The mixed-blood community never rejected any of its members, male or female, regardless of what troubles they got into; this attitude was considered by the whites as evidence of moral turpitude. The mixed-bloods never challenged white supremacy, feeling they had no hope of redress.

Both Indians and mixed-bloods had a well-earned reputation for unreliability in employment; if they took a job they stayed until the first payday, at which time they took off until they had drunk up their pay cheques. There is something to be said for this charming, pragmatic attitude toward money but it was very annoying to employers. They were considered bad financial risks so were seldom granted credit for any purpose; credit was known by the delightful term of "jawbone" since it implied you had talked your way into it. Mixed-bloods were seldom entrepreneurs and when they were, they didn't hire their own kind.

All eastern Europeans in the community were conveniently grouped together under the terminology of "hunkies." Most of them worked on the railroad and were well-behaved, solid citizens.

Each small town has its own hierarchical structure. Blossom was dominated by British Protestants – the group which later became known as WASPS. This was a fairly common situation on the prairies at that time, but was by no means invariable. One town I visited had a large Scandinavian population which was dominated by the Norwegians who accepted the Swedes with reservations, tolerated the Danes and ignored everybody else. Farther north some communities had a French majority where the situation was reversed and the WASPS became a petulant minority – WASPS do not take kindly to a secondary status.

Since Blossom was predominantly Protestant, the few Catholic families were thrown together socially although they had little else in common. There was no open animosity between the two religious groups; they just kept apart. Mixed marriages were unknown; any teenager who showed an interest in a girl from the other camp got straightened out in no uncertain terms. I only saw the situation from one side, but it is possible that the Catholics were equally bigoted.

Everyone in the community seemed to know where they belonged and accepted the situation. There was little possibility for upward mobility, so social climbing was rare. The various cliques, however, were fiercely competitive in social affectations. When a new family came to town they very soon found where they belonged. If there was any doubt in the newcomer's mind, the community sorted it out for them rather quickly. A check-off list would be: white or breed; west European or hunky; Protestant or Catholic; on relief or working; professional or working class (a professional was anyone who did not do manual labour); educated or ignorant (educated meant beyond grade eight); churchgoing or wicked. Other social indicators included: white, khaki or blue shirt; suit and vest or windbreaker; tie or open neck shirt; Stetson, straw or fedora hat; white or bandanna handkerchief; use of toothpicks in public; use of printed calling cards; whether or not they smelled of smoke or knew how to play bridge. Once the new family was established in the social pecking order, they stayed there.

The rigid social structure of the town sometimes had strange loopholes. For a time there resided in Blossom a young Englishman named Robert Dobey who managed to bridge the extremes of the social hierarchy. He was an unprepossessing individual with a weak chin, shifty eyes, buck teeth and a slight stutter. He never did anything useful in the community and existed on a remittance from home. He ran up bills at all the shops and condescendingly borrowed money from anybody foolish enough to lend it to him. He drank like a fish and hung out most of the time with Flossy Macabee and her gang of roustabouts. It was generally conceded that he was an utter rotter. However, his family background was considered excellent and his manners were impeccable, so he was accepted in all the best homes; mothers with nubile daughters invited him to dinner. It was surprising, in view of the self-righteous standards of the community, that one night he would be on a drunken binge with Flossy and her gang and the next night he would be playing whist sedately at the Rusks. He left Blossom suddenly, owing money to everybody in town, after some kind of a dustup with a section hand at Flossy's.

From the point of view of the majority group, everything was neat and properly structured in the town so there was no reason to question the comfortable established order. However, a situation arose which made me feel that maybe everything wasn't quite so right and jolly after all.

I was returning to the Palaza Hotel late one night when I was accosted by a girl on the street. This sort of thing was unheard of in Blossom so it took me a couple of minutes to realize that she was propositioning me. In the darkness I could make out only that she was blond and small with deep-set eyes in a thin face. She seemed very young.

"Take me to your room and I will give youse a good time," she said with a grotesque effort at seductiveness.

"No, no," I said brusquely, starting to push past her.

"Only two dollars, mister," she whispered fiercely, clutching my arm. I shook myself free and continued along the street. "One dollar?" her voice followed me.

Something in the desperation of her voice stopped me. I returned slowly to the still figure in the dark; I approached closely enough to stare down into a pair of haggard blue eyes. "Are you broke?" I asked abruptly.

"Yes."

"Are you hungry?"

"Yes, of course."

"When did you eat last?"

"Couple of days ago."

"Haven't you any place to go? Don't you know any people here?"

"I know some people. They won't help me."

I wondered what to do with her. I didn't like to just abandon her on the street, but on the other hand I didn't really want to get involved. I felt sure she was telling me the truth and not peddling me a sob story; the least I could do was buy her a meal. The problem was that at such a late hour both restaurants would be closed. However, I knew that Wong Toy slept in the back of his place.

"What's your name?" I asked the girl.

"Jenny," she answered.

"Okay, Jenny, come with me. We'll get you something to eat. Then you can be on your way."

"Whereabouts?"

"Wong Toy's."

"He'll be closed up."

"We'll get him out of bed."

I took her by a skinny elbow to escort her down the street to Wong's front door. I banged on the door until Wong appeared in his slippers, stuffing a shirt into his pants. He turned on a light and came to the door, peering out at us. "Whatsa malla?" he demanded sleepily.

"Emergency, Wong." I explained. "This young lady hasn't eaten for a couple of days and I want to buy her some bacon and eggs."

Wong opened the door a crack. "Hello, Wong," said the girl.

"Hello, Jenny," answered Wong. "Long time no see. You hungry?"

"Yes," said Jenny.

Wong paused for a moment looking speculatively into my eyes, "Okay, come in." He opened the door for us to enter. I asked him to cook up half a dozen scrambled eggs, some bacon and a big pile of toast. As he shuffled off to the kitchen, Jenny and I sat down in a booth at the back. This gave me a chance to study her more closely.

She was even younger than I had thought – not more than

sixteen or seventeen – and was terribly thin. She was not particularly pretty and, I suspected, not very bright. Unkempt, pale blond hair hung limply around a gaunt, bony face with sunken blue eyes. She had made a pathetic attempt at glamour with a slash of smeared lipstick. She wore a soiled pink sweater over a disheveled flowered dress. She was dirty – her hands, her face, and her clothes. Her manner was one of great weariness – almost like that of a sleepwalker. She slumped in a pitiful heap across the booth from me, avoiding my eyes, but well aware that I was studying her.

"How old are you, Jenny?" I asked.

She started visibly at my voice. "Eighteen."

"How old really?"

She sighed deeply, "Seventeen."

"Ever done any hustling before?"

She shook her head, "I didn't know what else to do."

"Now, tell me about yourself."

"What is there to tell?" She made a gesture of despair with both hands.

"I gather you come from Blossom since you know Wong."

"Yes, I went to school here."

"Tell me about it."

During the next half hour, while she demolished the bacon and eggs, she gave me a summary of her history. Her tired, flat, unemotional voice presented the story with a stark impact which a more dramatic presentation would have lacked.

Jenny's family name was Zarda; she had been raised on a farm near Blossom in a strict Protestant home. She had met Johnny Sweetgrass at a rodeo in Dazzle. Johnny, who was a handsome part-Indian boy of nineteen, had been the star of the show. To Jenny he was soul-stirring in his black Stetson, buckskin jacket and silver belt buckle. Johnny had been attracted by her blond prettiness, and intrigued by the fact that a white girl would take an interest in him. He later came around to the Zarda farm where her father threatened to shoot him if he ever came back. I have no doubt her father meant it. Jenny and Johnny met occasionally in Blossom and finally ran off to Calgary where they were married by a priest.

Jenny had never been anyplace bigger than Blossom before, so she found the city exciting and romantic. They were ecstatically in love. But then, all too soon, the realities of life brought them down to earth with a vengeance. Neither of them could get jobs; they ran out of money and returned to Johnny's reservation. Johnny tried to get a job on the ranches and farms in the district, but nobody would hire an Indian even if there was an opening. They returned to Calgary where things were no better than before. Johnny started to drink heavily and beat Jenny up from time to time. He finally jumped a freight for Vancouver. For a while, she was taken in by an unemployed lumberjack who treated her with great kindness, but then he too took off without notice.

In desperation she had hitchhiked her way back to her father's farm. He had shut the door on her. She walked to Blossom where our paths had crossed.

When she had finished her story she stared dazedly at her empty plate. "You're tired," I said. "Do you know where Mrs. Forsythe's rooming house is?" She nodded. "Now, here is some money." I gave her most of my cash, about six dollars. "Go to Mrs. Forsythe, she'll put you up. Come back here tomorrow about three o'clock and I'll see if I can work out some way to help you."

"Okay," she said, accepting the money lethargically.

Wong unlocked the door and she trudged away into the dark. When I went to pay Wong for the meal he said, "On the house," and refused the money.

The next morning I met Mal Morgan, George Ingraham, Fred Peters and Dick Elliott, as usual for coffee at Wong Toy's. I started to tell them about Jenny, but they knew her whole history – as I should have realized. They verified the early part of her story, although they didn't see Johnny's role as romantic or blameless as Jenny had painted it. I was appalled at the offhand manner with which they accepted the situation.

"You didn't take her to your room, did you?" asked George.

"No, of course not. I brought her here to Wong's to buy her a meal," I answered sharply. "She was hungry."

George held up a hand. "I enquire as a lawyer, not as a moralist."

"She's jailbait," said Mal. "Keep away, boy."

"I have no interest in her sexually," I said stiffly.

"Then what *is* your interest?" asked Dick.

"I'm just trying to help her."

"Like how?"

"I don't know, I thought maybe you guys could advise me."

"My advice is to leave her alone. She's poison," said Mal.

"But how can you turn your back on a fellow human being in such a mess?" I demanded heatedly.

"Look, Sir Galahad, don't tilt at windmills, if I may indulge in an anachronism," said George. "Jenny broke two of the major taboos of the community: she married an Indian and she married a Catholic. Either one would have been a social disaster; the combination puts her beyond the pale."

"But that's wrong," I shouted.

George shrugged, "Of course it's wrong. But that's the way it is."

We continued to discuss the problem without coming up with anything helpful. When they got up to leave, Fred said, "What are you going to do?"

"I don't know. I promised her I'd help," I answered.

"Get out of town," said Mal.

"I guess I'll approach some of the ladies to see if they'll help her," I commented vaguely.

"Best of British luck to you," said George, patting me on the shoulder.

When they had left I sat for several minutes mulling over what to do. The reaction of my friends had left me discouraged and disgruntled. In those days there were no effective social agencies to help individuals in difficulties; governmental resources had been overwhelmed by unemployment and other problems of the Depression. I decided finally to approach Mrs. Frobisher. I had always found her harsh and stern, but she was a pillar of the church so I hoped she might rise to a crisis. I didn't see how she could refuse. I drove out to her home.

Mrs. Frobisher was surprised to see me, but received me politely. She led me into a gloomy parlour which smelled faintly of moth balls. When I mentioned Jenny's name she knew the whole story. "She was a member of my Sunday school class for years," she stated. "I did my best for her, but she was always a silly and irresponsible child. I was afraid she would come to a bad end. I am not surprised." Her nose twitched.

"But it's not fair," I objected. "Can't you do something to help her?"

"I don't see what I could possibly do."

"Could you speak to her father?"

She looked down her nose at me. "Her father has made his decision. I would not think of interfering."

"Couldn't you take her in, give her a home?"

She looked horrified. "Certainly not. She is now a Catholic," she stated firmly. "Let her look to her own church."

I continued to urge her to come up with some kind of help, but I was up against a brick wall. Finally she asked, "And what is your interest in Jenny, may I enquire?" When I said I was only trying to help a person in difficulties she said, "Indeed," with a strong implication of disbelief.

I drove away from Mrs. Frobisher's feeling depressed and, I confess, somewhat alarmed. On impulse I stopped at Flossy Macabee's place. At least, I thought to myself, I'm covering the two extremes in the community.

Flossy met me at the door with an affectation of great surprise. "What's a member of the elite doing at my door at this time of the day?" she demanded loudly, her handsome dark eyes challenging me sardonically. "Usually your group waits till after dark. Come in, come in." She led me into a dim room filled with overstuffed furniture. "Want a drink?" she asked.

I declined and explained succinctly about Jenny's difficulties.

"What the hell do you think I can do about it? Give her a job?" she demanded.

"I don't think there's anything you can do," I admitted. "I suppose really I just came here to get your advice. You know this town pretty darn well, so what do you think I should try to do for the girl?"

"Get her out of town. There's no place for her here. The

local hypocrites would slit her throat. And if you think I'm going to help, you're crazy. The idea that girls like me have a heart of gold is just so much bull. However, I don't need amateur competition around, so I'll contribute a few bucks towards her bus fare. By the way, what's your interest in the kid?"

My explanation was greeted with scorn and disbelief. I left shortly afterwards.

"Come back anytime, big boy," she grinned, "after dark."

I next drove around to see my good friend, Audrey Peters, who was as warm-hearted and gentle a person as I have ever known. I found she was also a realist. Surprisingly enough, her advice was essentially the same as Flossy's. "There's no way she can return to this community and not be an outcast," she stated. "She will have to make a place for herself somewhere else, preferably in a much larger town."

"But there's something wrong," I objected, "when two fine young people who are in love can't get married and be accepted."

"I agree," she nodded, "but that's the way it is. Things would be tough enough under any circumstances, but now with the Depression everything's so much worse. If couples could get along financially they could manage, but now it's almost impossible."

"Couldn't you talk her father into taking her back?"

She shook her head. "I know him. He's the stuff witch-burners are made of. When he says he disowns her, he really means it – literally. There's no way." She shook her head again. "Tell me, why are you so interested in the girl?"

"I'm just trying to be helpful."

She looked into my eyes. "I believe you. But most others won't." She sighed, "For your own sake you've just got to get out of this thing."

I drove back to Wong Toy's to keep my appointment with Jenny, discouraged and troubled. What was I going to say to her? Also, I am ashamed to confess, I was regretting my own involvement in the situation and wishing I could get out of it somehow. I went to a back booth and Wong brought me a cup of coffee.

"Any luck?" he asked.

I shook my head. "Why don't you give her a job as a waitress, Wong? She could do that just fine."

"Can't afford," said Wong. Then he went on to add, showing he had a much better appreciation of the local situation than I did, "If I hire her, people here know her, not like, not come to my place." He paused and stared at the wall for a moment. "I got a cousin in Calgary, who owns big restaurant. He give her a job if I ask him."

"Hey, would you do that?" I cried. "That would be wonderful."

"Will do," said Wong, "I write note." He went off to the kitchen to return after a few minutes with a piece of paper on which were some Chinese hieroglyphics. "Give this to Jenny," he said. "Tell her to take it to Sunshine Cafe in Calgary."

"Wong," I said fervently, "you are a lifesaver. I could kiss you."

"No thanks," said Wong hastily.

When Jenny turned up a few minutes later looking cleaner and less haggard than the night before, I excitedly told her the good news. She was less than enthusiastic. "Okay," she said dully, with a shrug. "It's better than nothing." Completely deflated by her reaction, I gaped at her. "How'll I get to Calgary?" she added petulantly.

"I'll get you the money," I promised. "Have a cup of coffee and wait here till I get back." I dashed off and scrounged enough money from my friends to buy her a bus ticket to Calgary with a few dollars left over. I returned and presented the ticket and the money to her. "There you are Jenny, a ticket to a whole new way of life."

"Yeah," said Jenny.

"The next bus leaves in half an hour. Have you got a suitcase?"

"I ain't got nothin'."

I walked with her to the bus depot and stood around until the bus arrived, trying to make conversation. She answered me in churlish monosyllables. When the bus arrived, she boarded it without saying goodbye or uttering a word of thanks.

I walked slowly back to Wong Toy's with mixed emotions. Again I felt a sense of shame that my principal reaction was one of relief at having got out of a sticky situation; any sense of satisfaction over having done a good deed was overwhelmed by this selfish attitude. I was not very proud of myself over the whole affair. Nor of my friends in Blossom.

I heard later that Jenny got as far as Medicine Hat, turned in the rest of her ticket and shacked up with a worker on the road gang there. Oh well, I shrugged, what can you expect from a hunky minnow who marries a Catholic half-breed?

Chapter Fourteen

TEA PARTY

MY FIRST EXPERIENCE with a Blossom tea party was not exactly a thundering success. I didn't, however, drop my cup or drink from my saucer or commit any quite so obvious gaucheries.

Dick Elliott, acting under instructions from Florence, asked a number of us to come back to their place for tea and a sandwich after morning church service. I went to church with Fred and Audrey Peters and enjoyed the service thoroughly. Reverend Slye, looking in the pulpit more than ever as if he had wandered out of a Dickens novel, gave a fine sermon on doing God's work by helping one another. Mamie Sutherland, accompanied by George Ingraham at the organ, sang a simple hymn during the offering and gave one of her better performances. George was having a bit of trouble with the old foot-pump organ because one of the keys got stuck and throughout all the hymns this one note continued to growl, providing a remotely bagpipish effect which was rather intriguing. The simplicity of the service, the unadorned little church and the presence of kindly people made me feel as if God were actually in attendance – a feeling I never get in a city church. The only other times I have felt God's hand on my shoulder have been in the open, by the side of a mountain lake or viewing a dell of wild flowers in a hushed forest. Somehow or other, I felt that God and I were on rather good terms that day despite my many sins, and I sang the old hymns happily in my cracked baritone.

After the service we stood around outside talking with friends while Reverend Slye exchanged greetings with members of the congregation at the door of the church. The men told him they sure hoped his prayer for a good harvest would be answered. The ladies twittered pleasantries and asked after Mrs. Slye, whose ill health prevented her from accompanying her husband except on rare occasions. The Reverend's recounting of his wife's latest symptoms elicited much sympathetic clucking and many kindly suggestions for treatment ranging from tansy tea to Minard's liniment. The congregation gradually dispersed in various directions, chatting along the way. The people from out of town got in their flivvers or wagons, which had been left at the back of the church, and set off for their homes. Since it was a beautiful sunshiny day, our little coterie walked the few blocks to the Elliott's home.

The Elliotts lived in a large ramshackle house set back from the street behind a parched lawn. A few spindly flowers grew along the wooden sidewalk leading up to the veranda. Florence Elliott was a rather untidy housekeeper. The large living room was cluttered with furniture and bric-a-brac. A gilt-framed picture of her grandfather in naval uniform glowered down from above the fireplace. Every chair and couch had crocheted antimacassars on the backs and arms which tended to fall off anytime you got near them; I saw one later dangling from a button on Mal Morgan's coat sleeve.

We trouped into the house and got distributed around the living room. As well as the Peters, Reverend Slye and myself, there were present: Mamie Sutherland, George Ingraham, Grandma Akerbilt, the Morgans, the Frobishers, the Morshes, and the Rusks – more than enough to crowd the scant areas between the furniture. The ladies seated themselves while the men stood awkwardly about trying to look poised and at ease. George lit the fire, which had been laid by Dick before church, in the fireplace. George then leaned nonchalantly back against the mantlepiece. I was left standing like a boob in the middle of the floor wondering what to do with my hands. Reverend Slye was warmly congratulated on his fine sermon and Mamie was complimented on her singing; both accepted the accolades gracefully. I gathered that noon was an unusually early time for a tea party and Florence was commended for her social daring in initiating this charming after-church gathering. We stood about interminably, discussing the weather, the crops and the latest idiocies of government in stilted, trite phrases. We agreed over and over again that the weather was fine, the chances for a good crop were poor, and the possibility of governmental sanity nil.

Dick had dashed off to the kitchen to poke up the coal fire on which kettles of water had been left simmering. Audrey Peters joined Florence in the kitchen to prepare the tea and organize the goodies. The dining room opened off the living room through a wide archway hung with heavy velvet drapes held back by tasselated cords. The dining room table had been spread with a snowy linen tablecloth on which rested the teacups and other paraphernalia associated with the tea rites. I had long since run out of things to talk about when Dick finally appeared from the kitchen carrying a huge silver samovar, with Florence fussing along beside him issuing unnecessary instructions and warnings. With something of a flourish Dick set the samovar at the head of the table facing the living room. Everyone admired the hideous, ornate receptacle which Florence explained was a sterling silver memento of her ancestral home in Essex given to her by her grandmother. She glanced fleetingly, but significantly, at the picture of the glum naval officer over the mantlepiece. Audrey wheeled in a mahogany tea wagon with a squeaky wheel, which was laden with plates of sandwiches and some things which Florence called sweets, but were actually tarts.

Florence then approached Grandma Akerbilt to ask if she would be so kind as to pour. I thought it was something of a dirty trick to ask the oldest lady in the room to do such a menial job. However, in view of the way the invitation was politely issued and graciously accepted I gathered that this was considered to be a great honour. Florence ceremoniously escorted Grandma to the urn where she presided with all the dignity and graciousness of a grand duchess. Florence then asked Audrey, Mamie and Mrs. Rusk if they would act as servers – a lesser honour I assumed. We could all very easily have gone out to get our tea from Grandma, but that was not proper protocol apparently. Orders were taken for tea by the servers; then the cups were carried one at a time to the appropriate person. Mrs. Rusk asked me if I would have my tea white or clear. I had been watching carefully and had observed that white meant a revolting mixture of about half tea and half hot milk, so I asked for clear. This was presented to me in due course by Mrs. Rusk with sort of a half curtsy. I accepted the cup with an urbane bow which nearly shoved Fred Peters, who was behind me, over a side table. I made a note not to bow again without checking first. When everyone had received tea, the servers passed plates of the tiniest sandwiches I had ever seen and from which the crusts – the best part – had been cut. The sandwiches were all within easy reach, but apparently you were not supposed to take one unless it was proffered by a server.

This was my first experience with a stand-up English type tea party, so I found I had a lot to learn. I kept a wary eye on the more experienced members present so I wouldn't commit a *faux pas* of some kind. In particular I surreptitiously watched Reverend Slye who was obviously an old hand at this type of charade and performed with great skill. The tea was served in tiny cups which held about a gill of tea. The cups, which were exclaimed over by the ladies, were Spode and were so fragile you could see through them. I was scared to death I would crush one in my hand or pull the handle off. The procedure, I observed, was to hold the cup and saucer in your left hand leaving your right hand free for other activities. You received a spoon, whether you needed it or not, which invariably got in the way of the cup when you returned the cup to the saucer. I slipped my spoon into my coat pocket to have one less thing to worry about, where I found it when I reached home that night.

Before a server gave you a sandwich she handed you a tiny serviette for which there was absolutely no utility that I could determine. Since there is no way you can eat a sandwich with the serviette in the same hand without also eating the serviette, it is held by the little finger of your left hand under the teacup. The sandwiches were so small you could dispose of them easily at a gulp, but that is not the way it was done. You nibbled off a piece, set it carefully on the edge of the saucer so that it wouldn't fall off and then had a sip of tea. This was repeated over and over again while you tried to carry on a scintillating conversation with others similarly encumbered. The difficulties of conversation were enhanced by the fact that some of the ladies remained seated, so in order to talk to them you had to lean over without pouring tea in their laps or sticking your fanny out to jostle someone behind you. I now realized why George, the canny rascal, had staked out a spot by the fireplace; he set his cup on the mantle and was impregnable from the rear. I felt he was not quite playing the game.

In my careful observation of the veterans in the tea game, I noted that all the ladies and most of the men had their little fingers elegantly extended when they lifted their cups. Even Jerry Rusk, who always clutched his coffee mug in both hands when he hunched over the counter at Wong Toy's, had his little finger sticking out so far you could hang your hat on it. Some aficionados elevated one finger, some two and some three. Ralph Morsh, who used three, appeared to be thumbing his nose at you when he lifted his cup. I shrugged my shoulders and thought "when in Rome, eat spaghetti." I extended my own pinky, experimenting with various styles – one finger, two and three, straight out, curled and half curled. I decided that one finger, half curled, added the proper degree of elegance without ostentation. I became aware that George Ingraham was watching me sardonically, so I sheepishly tucked my finger back in. George grinned at me.

The movements in the crowded room were haphazard, but as stylized as a gavotte. The peregrinations of the servers kept the place in continuous turmoil, motivating a frequent reconstitution of conversational groups. The server would appear at your elbow, say politely, "Excuse me," whereupon you carefully reconnoitred on all sides, did a cautious semipirouette to let her past and thereby joined a different group. In view of the limited space for groupings, one such change not infrequently initiated a chain reaction around the entire room. For some reason I was unable to determine, the movement always went in a counterclockwise direction.

On one of these periodic reshuffles I ended up beside Mal Morgan. In view of his huge size I would have expected him to have difficulty in these tight manoeuverings, but I had noticed him in action and he displayed a grace and nimbleness of foot worthy of a prima ballerina. The teacup in his huge hand looked like a thimble in a catcher's mitt. He growled in my ear, "These sandwiches are so damned small I keep biting the ends of my fingers. It takes two of them to make a swallow."

"Noblesse oblige," I answered.

"Yeah, they taste okay," he nodded. "But everything's so ruddy, ruddy English I expect at anytime to be invited out for a chukker of cricket."

"Tallyho," I said, waving my teacup.

"Keep your pecker up, mate," he grinned and sidled off.

The overriding aura of the tea party mystique, I decided, was an exaggerated elegance of manners. Everybody was being so polite it was unbelievable. There was none of the rough, slightly ribald banter usually characteristic of Western chitchat. The effect was one of complete artificiality. You smiled inanely over the top of your teacup and simpered banalities at others performing in a similar fashion. Everyone entered into the playacting. Even Mamie's exuberance was muted and Mal's usual vulgarity was under strict control. There was no gossip as such. When the names of people not in attendance came up they were commented on with a kindliness which was astounding. Even Mrs. Frobisher's well-honed stiletto was sheathed in a scabbard of charity for the moment, and I actually heard her say something pleasant about a neighbour I knew she detested. The whole performance was a beautiful exercise in insincerity, which may well account for the English skill at international diplomacy.

I got temporarily shunted off into a cul-de-sac behind a small table bearing an ornate vase with a broken handle, which gave me an opportunity to muse on the paradox of the virtue of dishonesty. All social intercourse is facilitated by a sensible reticence with the truth. It seemed to me, this thesis was being carried to extremes in the genteel pantomime before me. I decided that maybe there was some merit in subjecting one's veneer of civilization to the pressures of a contrived decorum. Furthermore, the experience carried with it certain surprising bonuses. When two dogs meet, if one wags his tail the other probably will also. When I had been exuding specious charm on Mrs. Rusk, whom I had always written off as a total loss, I found she responded with a warmth in her lovely contralto voice which surprised me; I found her quite delightful. One has a tendency to judge people to some extent by their spouses and since her husband Jerry was a sour, humourless individual, I had assumed she was also. A mistake. I gave up on shallow philosophy and rejoined the circle.

There is something about a cup of tea which brings out the English in the English, so I was not surprised to note that the accents of those with an Anglo background became progressively more marked. The effect tends to be self-potentiating. One Englishman may speak fairly normally (like a Canadian, that is), but if you get two or more of them together the broad a's get broader and broader. Fred Peters, who had been in this country for forty years, began to sound like an Oxford don. Florence, of course, was setting the pace with her version of Essex public-school elocution. Even the rest of us tended to pick it up and spoke a mannered sort of synthetic language which protocol seemed to demand. I am rather easily led as far as accents are concerned, so when I found myself replying to a comment with a clipped "Quite so," I felt I had better get ahold of myself before my Scottish-Irish ancestors flipped in their graves.

I had been managing so well with the teacup ritual that I got careless. I was chatting with Audrey Peters and Mrs. Frobisher at the time. I bit into a lemon tart topped with whipped cream. The accursed thing flipped up, deposited the whipped cream on my upper lip and the end of my nose, then collapsed in my hand. There I was standing helpless, with a teacup in one hand, a crumbled tart in the other, and a great blob of whipped cream on the end of my nose. Audrey, whose sense of propriety was fighting a losing battle with her sense of humour, was choking on a laugh. Even Mrs. Frobisher was regarding me with amazement and going, "Arf, arf, arf," which I gather for her was a manifestation of merriment. I gazed down in horror at the blob on my nose. In sort of a reflex action I blew at it, which was a mistake. A gob of cream landed in Mrs. Frobisher's right eye, which neatly disposed of her. Served her darn well right, I thought viciously. But to add to my own predicament, I had blown some cream up my nose, which threatened to bring on a sneeze. And when I sneeze, I really let fly – so a total disaster was in the making. The tears started to run down my face. "What do I do now?" I bleated at Audrey.

Audrey, smothering her laughter, said, "Don't cry, follow me," and led me through the mob with many an "Excuse, please" out to the kitchen. Decorum did not permit sniggers, but my streaming eyes and cream-festooned nose certainly elicited some highly amused glances. When we went through the swinging door to the kitchen, Audrey set down her cup and grabbed mine just as I let fly a sneeze which sprayed whipped cream all over the room. Audrey started to laugh.

"What's so darned funny?" I demanded, searching frantically for my handkerchief.

"That gob of cream on the end of your nose," she hooted, pointing at my nose. "It's priceless."

By this time, with disaster averted, I was able to see the humour of the situation and I started to laugh too. Then the two of us leaned against the sink, doubled up with hilarity.

At this point, Mrs. Frobisher pushed through the door with her right eye closed; she obviously had come out for repairs also. When Audrey and I saw her we went off into fresh gales of laughter. Mrs. Frobisher looked rather startled at first, then joined us with her husky "Arf, arf, arf." The three of us laughed like idiots. I'd never cared much for Mrs. Frobisher before, but after this episode I had something of a liking for the old trout.

When the three of us had quieted down, and Mrs. Frobisher and I had completed our repairs, Audrey said to me, "Now, come on. We've got to go back and join the others. Just pretend nothing happened. I'll get you another cup of tea."

"Never in a million years," I shouted.

"Oh, come on now," said Audrey. "You've got to try it again. Don't you think so, Mrs. Frobisher?"

"Yes, I do," she answered firmly. "My father always used to say if you got bucked off a cayuse, the thing to do is get right back in the saddle before you lose your nerve."

"Well, I'd rather ride a bucking cayuse than have another cup of tea," I stated firmly.

"Oh, foof," said Audrey. "It's not all that bad. Just avoid tarts in the future."

"I'll return to face the music, but I won't take a chance on another cup of tea," I said with finality.

The three of us adjusted our faces to the typical sweet grimace appropriate for a tea party and entered the dining room. Here we landed in the middle of a different type of social contretemps.

The tea from the samovar was delivered into the cups from a small spigot at the bottom. When the first cups had been returned for refills, the spigot refused to deliver; Grandma Akerbilt had summoned Florence to correct the difficulty. She was fiddling with the tap as we walked in, but no tea was forthcoming. She lifted the top off the samovar to peek in and found there was plenty of tea remaining. Puzzled, she reached in with a spoon and lifted out a wet dollar bill. She let out a little scream, and in front of our horrified gaze she fished out four more soggy bills. "Good heavens!" she cried. "I wondered where I had hidden that money." Everybody looked unhappily into their teacups with puckered lips. I noted with minor satisfaction that the money was dollar bills and not pound notes, so they weren't something left over from her grandmother's day. After a few moments of paralyzed silence, Mal Morgan let out a great guffaw and said, "Well, I'm very fond of money, but it's the first time I've ever had tea made with it."

"Mint tea," suggested George.

Mamie joined Mal with her infectious laugh and the others gradually joined in, deciding that the best thing to do was to treat the matter lightly.

Florence was in a great flap and full of apologies. The cups were collected and, along with the samovar and the sodden money, were whisked off to the kitchen. Florence explained over and over again that she had passed just gallons and gallons of boiling water through the samovar that morning so the bills were very clean really. The ladies, making sympathetic sounds, helped wash the cups and prepare a new batch of tea.

While this was going on, various people contributed stories about misplaced money. Jerry Rusk told about finding a twenty-five cent bill, known as a shin-plaster, in a bowl of porridge in a restaurant in Medicine Hat and had a great argument with the proprietor about whether or not he could keep it. Mrs. Rusk said she had hidden some money one time and couldn't remember where, but found it eventually in a pickle jar in the icebox. Someone made the obvious comment about cold cash. Mal recounted a tale of finding a diamond ring in a rainbow trout's stomach, but it turned out to be glass. Reverend Slye said he once found a token in the collection plate which entitled him to a free drink at Red's Bar in Polson, Montana.

The new tea finally arrived and was served from a homely brown-betty teapot. None of us really wanted any, but we all had a cup for Florence's sake. Audrey shoved a cup in my hand and said fiercely, "Now you drink it. Get back on that cayuse." I grinned at her.

"It don't taste near as good as the first cup," said Mal, smacking his lips judiciously. Florence giggled uncertainly. Everyone was trying to think of something to talk about to tide over an awkward pause. George Ingraham launched into a detailed explanation of how that particular note on the organ had gotten stuck. I was desperately trying to think of something appropriate to say to Mrs. Morsh, the banker's wife, when a flash of movement in the upper part of the front window caught my eye. It was a beautiful little hummingbird hovering outside the window to peer in at us. I cried, "Hey, look at that," and pointed at the window. As everyone turned to look, the hummingbird zipped away. I began explaining to Mrs. Morsh what I had seen when I became aware that the others were glancing at me rather oddly. Bits of conversation erupted suddenly and everyone turned away from the window.

I glanced out the window. There on the middle of the lawn in full view of the room, Jeb Wilson's dog Roscoe was having a merry go at the little spaniel bitch from across the street.

No sir, my first Blossom tea party was not exactly a thundering success.

Chapter Fifteen

GOLF IS A FOUR-LETTER WORD

ALL OF A SUDDEN, Blossom went bonkers over golf. This led to whole new parameters of fun, sport, rivalry and social discord which eventually saw Mal Morgan haled into court on a charge of disorderly conduct and blasphemy.

The golf bug was brought into town by a chap named Jock MacIntosh who arrived in Blossom to open an insurance office. Jock was a wiry little Scot of about fifty, with grizzled sandy hair and faded freckles scattered over a cheerful, puckish face. Jock, as an Aberdonian, came from a milieu of golfing enthusiasts and had actually once met the great Vardon, of which he was inordinately proud. In conversation with George Ingraham, Jock bemoaned the fact that there was no golf course within three hundred miles, which to him meant he was that distance from civilization.

"Well, let's build one," said George.

"You're daft," said a startled Jock, looking out at the barren hills.

"By no means," replied George. "Why not? It wouldn't be St. Andrews, but it would be a start. After all, the first links were built on wasteland along the sea."

"Aye," nodded Jock slowly, " 'Twould be better than naught."

The upshot of this conversation was the formation of the Blossom Golf and Country Club with George as its president and Jock its guiding light. Membership fees were five dollars plus an informal understanding to do some work on the construction of the course. Half the town promptly joined. George obtained permission for the use of some crown land along the river and work began immediately. Jock laid out the course after walking back and forth for hours over the terrain. He insisted on a full eighteen holes right off the bat because otherwise, he said, it wouldn't be a proper course at all. As Jock planned the course, it zigzagged up one side of the stream over gullies and along side hills before crossing the river with a challenging shot from the top of a bluff and then returned down the other side of the river. Jock was increasingly enthusiastic as the links began to take shape in his mind. George organized the work parties which set to with a will. Picks and shovels and farm machinery pulled by horses cleared the fairways of sagebrush, scrub and bunch grass. It was hard, hot, dusty work but the enthusiastic membership worked like beavers – or maybe gophers would be more apt. Some of the bare hills required little clearing but in some areas, particularly close to the river and around the greens, heavy manual labour was required. Jock had arranged that the holes over gulches would leave the lower terrain intact – but woe betide anyone who shot a ball into them. It was not necessary to build bunkers or sand traps as the course abounded in these natural hazards. The greens were made of sand mixed with heavy oil and rolled flat. When putting on such a surface it was permitted to draw a piece of carpet attached to a broom handle along a path between your ball and the hole.

Within a month the impossible had happened – Blossom had a golf course. And a fine sporty course it was too. True, there wasn't a blade of grass on it and in many places the rough was in better shape than the fairways, but, by golly, it was a golf course and the town was mighty proud of it.

During these preparatory stages, strange and wonderful golfing equipment began appearing from attics and barns, and citizens were frequently seen swinging clubs of ancient lineage in their backyards. After a conference with Jock, Mal Morgan laid in a supply of golf sets comprising a driver, a spoon, a midiron, a mashie, a niblick and a putter, which, along with a canvas bag, sold for twenty-three dollars; he stocked golf balls at twenty-five cents each.

The formal opening of the course was a day of celebration

and jubilation. After a brief ribbon-cutting ceremony on the first tee, George and Jock played the opening round, and were followed by a motley crew of whackers and grunchers. Jock even wore a pair of natty plus fours for the occasion, which was a style of dress few of the membership had ever seen before and elicited a good many humourous comments. Jock's first shot was a good two hundred yards down the fairway to the rousing applause of the spectators. George, who had played some golf previously, took a great whirl at the ball and flubbed it about twenty yards in a cloud of dust and debris. The crowd laughed and cheered and shouted derisive advice. Jock scowled at them, realizing belatedly that the new members had a good deal to learn about the etiquette of the game. Jock, to his chagrin, came in with a ninety-one, and George with a hundred and fourteen. Nobody, other than Jock, broke a hundred. The Blossom golf course was declared formally launched.

During the rest of the summer, the course was in constant use. Between rounds, the members formed work parties to improve the fairways and greens, and began to take umbrage at outsiders who referred to the course as a goat pasture. Some of the golfers began to improve quite dramatically, while others continued to hack and whack in happy abandonment. Jock, as unofficial and unpaid professional, gave lessons to anyone who asked. He spent endless hours with great patience teaching the rudiments of the game to a steady stream of duffers and even managed to inculcate some concept of decorum, such as not shouting during a person's backswing of farting while an opponent was putting. His Scottish composure was sorely tried at times to see the game he loved so wantonly mistreated; but he took great pride in those who showed improvement under his tutelage.

Early in the fall, George and Jock decided it was time to introduce the membership to tournament play. Preliminary rounds were organized, based on medal play, to sort the players into categories for the final competition which was to be a round-robin, knock-out proposition, using hole-by-hole play. The rivalries were viciously keen – you would have thought they were playing the Canadian Open. Jock didn't enter the contest as he would have won hands down.

Mal Morgan and Mr. Fidge, the School Principal, ended up in

the finals of the Championship Flight, which carried with it the dubious title of Club Champion. It was this round which landed Mal into trouble with the law.

Mal had never played golf before this time, but his natural ability and great strength made him a formidable competitor. He used a baseball grip, despite Jock's repeated admonitions, a short backswing, and then slugged the ball a country mile. However, as might be expected in a beginner, he tended to spray his shots wildly. Mr. Fidge, in contrast, played a cautious, conservative game, contenting himself with short, careful shots, never exceeding a hundred and fifty yards, but straight down the middle. Mr. Fidge, a short, skinny man, usually wore a business suit, a collar and tie and a homburg hat while playing; Mal wore a large straw hat, a sweat shirt, jeans and cowboy boots.

The charges of blasphemy and disorderly conduct arising out of this match were laid by Mrs. Frobisher. Efforts by various well-meaning people to dissuade her from this course of action were unsuccessful. Encased in a carapace of rigid sanctitude, she was impervious to gentle persuasion – she was hellbent on teaching Mal Morgan and his ungodly associates a real lesson once and for all. The court had no option but to proceed. The case was heard before Judge Broome, who presided with his usual immutable austerity; Cyril Thorndyke acted for the prosecution and George Ingraham for the defence.

The courtroom of the Embassy was packed for the hearings as was usual in any case of general interest; most of the audience were golfers who were solidly on Mal's side. After brief non-committal opening comments by the two lawyers, they hassled for awhile over the sections of the Criminal Code which were applicable. It appeared that Mal was being charged with vagrancy which seemed odd to us of the laity, since Mal was a well-established businessman and financially secure. However, the lawyers toe-danced around with the posturing ceremonialism characteristic of that ilk until they came to some kind of an agreement on the matter.

After these technical details had been resolved, Cyril Thorndyke called Mrs. Frobisher as his first witness. She strode across the courtroom with a firm, flatfooted gait to take her place in the witness box. Her angular face was fixed in an expression of grim retribution. She was dressed in a long black dress, the collar of which was held up around her scrawny neck by bits of whalebone; she wore black gloves and a dingy, black hat perched on her gray, frizzy hair. Her long nose twitched as she stared out at the largely hostile audience.

"Now, Mrs. Frobisher," began Cyril, after she had identified herself and been sworn in, "would you be so kind as to tell the court in your own words the events which transpired on September thirteenth last which led to the laying of this complaint against Mr. Morgan."

"Certainly, Mr. Thorndyke," said Mrs. Frobisher in her deep, hoarse voice. "September the thirteenth was a Sunday; it was a very hot day. Therefore, instead of meeting in the church, I took my bible-study class for a short walk up the river to a shady nook beneath some trees as we are wont to do when the weather is sultry. We find it conducive in our communication with the Almighty to meet Him in the peace and quiet of a beautiful natural environment which His beneficence has bestowed upon us. A peace which in this instance was disrupted and destroyed by a profane intrusion." Her glance swept with contempt over Mal where he was seated beside George. Mal squirmed uncomfortably.

"How many people comprised your group?" asked Cyril.

"Eight in all. Five young ladies and three of us somewhat more mature."

"What time of the day was this?"

"About 11:30 of a Sunday morning." She emphasized the Sunday.

"This place where you were meeting was separated from the 18th green of the golf course by a narrow copse of trees, was it not?"

"So I understand. And found out to our horror later."

"You did not know when you went there that you were in close proximity to the 18th green?"

"No," she snapped, her jowls quivering.

"Would you continue please with your account of what transpired?"

"We became aware of voices shouting in the distance and

then the voices approached closer until they were just above us on the other side of the trees."

"You could hear the voices very clearly?"

"Unfortunately, yes."

"And what was the tenor of these comments?"

"Mr. Morgan launched off on a profane and sacrilegious dissertation on the location of his golf ball, at the top of his voice. It was simply dreadful the things he said – just appalling. I told the young ladies of our group to cover their ears. Then there was a loud argument between Mr. Morgan and Mr. Fidge about moving the ball – at least Mr. Morgan was loud while Mr. Fidge spoke with quiet firmness. Apparently Mr. Morgan lost the argument for there was quiet for a short time, then a whack which was followed by a roar from Mr. Morgan and a torrent of the most obscene and blasphemous utterances. You could have heard him a mile away. This sequence was repeated several times – a mom-ment of silence, a whack, and a stream of the most outrageous profanity, each time increasing in virulence. Finally, there was a great roar of rage and a bag of golf clubs came sailing over the trees and over our heads to land in the river at our feet."

"Thank you, madam, for the clarity and cogency of your description of this regrettable incident. We all realize the distress and regret which you must feel in taking this action which, in all conscience, you feel compelled to do." Cyril harrumphed gently. Mrs. Frobisher nodded coldly. "Do I understand then, from your comments, madam," continued Cyril, "you and your companions had the peace and tranquility of a lovely Sabbath morning disturbed by the behavior of the defendant?"

"Yes, whereas, before his arrival we had been pursuing our discussions in complete harmony with the Lord and with nature in this lovely grotto, bathed in sunlight and gentle breezes; his shouting and swearing utterly destroyed this sacred communion. That beautiful sylvan dell is forever defiled." She glowered in Mal's direction.

"Did he, in the course of his utterances make derogatory and sacrilegious comments about the Deity and others of the heavenly, er, hierarchy?"

"He certainly did. He blamed all of his troubles on the Lord and called to witness his Son and a remarkable list of saints, taking particular umbrage towards St. Andrew, for some reason or other. He shouted and cursed and swore and heaped maledictions upon the Lord."

"Certain of his comments, then, could be interpreted in no other way than a direct attack upon the Deity?"

"That is correct."

"You may enquire, Counsellor," said Cyril, turning to George with a mocking bow.

George rose slowly and hooked his thumbs in his gown. He did not underestimate Mrs. Frobisher as a witness. He knew her to be highly intelligent, articulate and, above all, encased in the armour of unquestioning self-righteousness.

"Do you play golf, Mrs. Frobisher?" he asked abruptly.

She looked startled. "Certainly not."

"So you know nothing about the procedures of the game nor the tremendous pressure under which a competitive golfer labours?"

"I know nothing about golf beyond the fact that it is a silly game and a waste of time which should be used for the work of the Lord. This brief exposure to the game would lead me to believe it is an instrument of the Devil for it lures man into impiety and sacrilege."

"You have taken exception to Mr. Morgan's comments. Would you please repeat for the court some of these statements."

"Mr. Ingraham," ejaculated Mrs. Frobisher in horror, her jowls shaking.

Cyril leaped to his feet. "M'lord," he shouted. "I must object. It is entirely improper to ask this refined and delicate lady to repeat the obscenities of the accused. Furthermore, it would compound the offence."

"But m'lord," objected George, "how can we know if his comments were as alleged unless we know what was said?"

Judge Broome looked coldly at George. "Objection sustained. It will be sufficient for the witness to indicate the general nature of the utterances of the accused."

"Very well, m'lord," said George with some lack of grace, although I know him well enough to recognize that he was not disconcerted.

"The utterances of the accused were profane, obscene and blasphemous," stated Mrs. Frobisher promptly without being asked.

"But the words were known to you?" asked George. Mrs. Frobisher hesitated. "Otherwise you would not know that they were, as you have described them," explained George.

"Yes," granted Mrs. Frobisher. "I was raised on a farm and I've heard the words before – but never shouted from the housetops with such ferocity and malignity, nor with such squalid, facile and perverted eloquence. Some of his suggestions as to the progenitors of that golf ball and its future fate would shrivel your soul. I have been in church work for forty years and I know blasphemy when I hear it. He repeatedly took the Lord's name in vain."

"Is it not appropriate to call on the Lord in moments of crisis and despair?" asked George.

"Yes," shouted Mrs. Frobisher, "but in an attitude of humility and supplication. Not bellowing like a bull moose in rutting time. The good Lord isn't deaf."

"I have heard ministers of the cloth, when enthused with the fervour and emotion of their calling, raise their voices to a high level," said George, mildly. "Isn't that appropriate?"

"Of course. But they do so with reverence, respect and humility. Not a fulmination of the grossest depravities."

"So it is permissible to raise your voice to attract the attention of the Lord in the church, but not on a golf course?"

"It is ludicrous and a travesty to compare Mr. Morgan's tirade with the humble, sincere and respectful supplications of a clergyman. He –"

"Did you not think Mr. Morgan was sincere?"

"Oh, he was sincere all right. He –"

"Thank you," interrupted George. "Now, Mrs. Frobisher, in the course of Mr. Morgan's swearing did he repeat himself?"

"What do you mean?"

"Did he repeat the same words or phrases over and over again?"

"No. Each outburst was a new and different thesis of evil."

"He showed originality and imagination in his dissertations?"

"Yes, indeed. Each new tirade was a fresh outpouring of a distorted, perverted and perfervid mind. For example, he recited a travesty of the Beatitudes which would rival the Black Mass."

"Did his words flow freely with power and eloquence?"

"Yes, like the flushing of a toilet."

"Would you say that insofar as profanity is concerned, Mr. Morgan's presentation was something of a masterpiece?"

"Yes," hissed Mrs. Frobisher. "A masterpiece of the Devil."

Cyril got to his feet. "I must interpose here, m'lord," he stated. "I have been very patient with counsel for the defence, but I must say I am at a loss to understand the purport of his enquiries. Let us return to square one. We are considering here a case of public disturbance and blasphemy. My friend is going far afield in his questioning."

Judge Broome turned a quizzical look at George. "I have myself wondered at the direction of the inquiry. You have a comment, Mr. Ingraham?"

"Yes, m'lord. Part of the case for the defence is based on freedom of artistic expression. I would submit that profanity in Western Canada is an accepted art form. It is true that most swearing by the vulgar is a monotonous recapitulation of a few basic words. But in its superior forms, the genre can soar to the highest levels of imaginative and inspired rhetoric. While Mrs. Frobisher has understandably found the subject matter repugnant, she has admitted that Mr. Morgan's presentation was a masterpiece; she has conceded that he showed originality, variety and imagination; and that the delivery flowed with smoothness and eloquence. There is no doubt that we have had reported here one of the great declamations which might well rank with those delivered by Macbeth, Hamlet or Lear."

"Oh, m'lord, I must protest," objected Cyril. "My distinguished friend is himself getting carried away with his own eloquence. We are not dealing here with an earth-shattering event, but with inane trivialities involving a golf ball. To raise the names of Macbeth, Hamlet and Lear in such a context is fatuous hyperbole."

"My learned colleague obviously does not play nor understand the game of golf," said George frostily, "and, therefore, does not appreciate the rigours and pressures of the game."

"The simple fact is that the defendant lost his temper and created a disturbance by hollering his head off," stated Cyril flatly.

"My learned friend has missed the point," said George. "Great profanity cannot be delivered *sotto voce*. It must be presented *con fortissimo espressione*. It is unfortunate that this masterpiece was not performed for a more appreciative audience," he added sadly.

Judge Broome's left eyebrow was markedly elevated. "It is a novel defence of profanity that it is an art form. I shall reserve on the matter. Proceed with your enquiries, Counsellor."

"Very well, m'lord," said George. He turned to Mrs. Frobisher who had been following this exchange with ill-concealed fury. "Now, Mrs. Frobisher, it is apparent that Mr. Morgan did not know that you and the other ladies were within earshot. Why did you not make your presence known? He would undoubtedly have desisted."

"There wasn't time nor opportunity. He was on the other side of a row of trees."

"You could have called out."

"I was too dumfounded to think of it. Furthermore, I was ashamed to have it known that we were witnesses to such a disgraceful performance."

"An attitude which you have since modified?"

"Yes. To teach him a lesson."

"Is that not vexatious and mischievous?"

"No," she snapped.

"That is all," concluded George, seating himself with a bow to Mrs. Frobisher.

Cyril next called two elderly women as witnesses, a Mrs. Hefflewart and a Mrs. Snodgrass, who had been members of Mrs. Frobisher's group on this ill-fated morning. The former was stout and belligerant, the latter scrawny and acerbitous. Both verified Mrs. Frobisher's account of what had taken place and both vigorously asserted that they had been scandalized and appalled at Mr. Morgan's language. George didn't question either of them. With these two witnesses, Cyril concluded the case for the prosecution.

George then called Mal Morgan to the stand. Mal had followed the presentation of the evidence against him with amused interest. At times he looked somewhat sheepish, but for the most part he wore a cheerful grin and every now and then chuckled out loud. It was clear that he was not unduly discomfited by the situation.

"Mr. Morgan," said George. "What was the nature of the golf match you were playing on September 13th?"

"It was for the club championship."

"So this was not just an ordinary round of golf?"

"It sure wasn't. It was for the championship of the whole shebang."

"And you had reached this point after a long series of play-offs?"

"Yep. I knocked you out in the semi-semifinals." Mal grinned at George and the audience chuckled.

"Well, that was no great accomplishment," said George with a rueful smile. "However, this was a very important match you were playing?"

"Yep."

"Who was your opponent on this occasion?"

"Cedric Fidge."

"Would you give us some idea of Mr. Fidge's style of play."

"He's a real pain in the ass," said Mal bluntly. "He –"

The judge looked startled. George hastily held up his hand. "Please, Mr. Morgan, you are in a court of law. Kindly moderate your language."

"Sorry," said Mal. "Cedric ain't such a bad guy, but he's slow as the seven year's itch, and just as irritating. He takes longer over every shot than it takes to read a book. He wiggles and waggles and twitches and jerks like he's got St. Vitus dance. Then he knocks it a screaming hundred and twenty-five yards down the fairway. But he's always on the fairway. Me, I knock it twice as far but I'm nearly always in trouble 'cause I shoot crooked. On every putt he does a little ceremony like the mating dance of a hummingbird. The boys in the club call him Fidgety Fidge. One thing I'll say for him, he don't swear none, but he sure talks a lot."

"What does he talk about?"

"Before every shot he tells you what he's going to do, and then afterwards, why it didn't work – he moved his head, or he twisted his left arm or something. Then he swings the way he should have done. He's very generous with advice too. I never played the game before this year, and he played a lot when he was younger, so he gave me advice all the way along the line on just about every shot. It was kind of annoying, to say the least."

"You didn't ask him to desist?"

"Naw. He was really trying to be helpful, I guess, and I didn't want to hurt his feelings. But I wouldn't play with him again just for fun."

"M'lord," interposed Cyril. "I don't understand what is going on here. Mr. Fidge is not on trial and it is singularly inappropriate that he should be maligned in this way when he has no opportunity to defend himself. This line of enquiry is irrelevant and improper."

"M'lord," said George. "The defence will base its case largely on provocation and extenuation, so it is necessary to present the background which led to the episode on the 18th hole. It will also be necessary to cover certain rules and regulations peculiar to this particular course."

"Very well," said the judge, "but it will not be necessary to further delineate Mr. Fidge's golfing *modus operandi* – I get the picture."

"I believe that Your Lordship has a familiarity with the game of golf so it will not be necessary, I presume, to describe basic regulations and protocol." George had had the great good sense to initiate enquiries which disclosed that Judge Broome had been runner-up in the Ontario Amateur when he was a law student at Osgoode Hall and still played a pretty good round.

"I have a working knowledge of the game," said the judge dryly.

George turned back to Mal on the stand. "Mr. Morgan,

what rules apply to play at the Blossom Golf and Country Club?"

"The general rules of golf, I guess. Like anywhere else."

"Yes. And are there certain rules peculiar to that course?"

Mal rubbed his bald head with the flat of his hand. "I don't know how peculiar they are, but since our course is new and the fairways are pretty scruffy, you are allowed to improve your lie on the fairways, but if you get in the rough you have to play her where she sets, or you can move her two club lengths, not closer to the hole, for a penalty of one stroke, like if she goes down a gopher burrow or gets under a sagebrush or something where you can't hit her."

"What was the status of the game between you and Mr. Fidge when you arrived at the 18th tee?"

"We were all tied up. We'd had a ding-dong battle all the way. He'd been dib-dib-dibbing down the middle of the fairway, and I'd been covering half of southern Alberta. So up to that point, it was a saw-off and everything depended on the last hole."

"What happened on the 18th?"

"Just about everything." Mal grinned and scratched his chin. "The first unusual thing was that Fidge sliced his ball off into the rough; the second unusual thing was I got one of my best drives of the day straight down the fairway. As we started to walk along to look for Fidge's ball, with him describing in great detail what he had done to produce that slice, a coyote ran across the the fairway and picked up my ball and headed for the hills."

"A coyote?" asked an incredulous judge.

"Yes, sir," said Mal. "It happens sometimes. Well sir, I took off after that coyote, a-hooting and a-hollering and chased him up a side hill where he dropped the ball and took off. I found the ball chewed up some, and hollered to Fidge could I bring the ball back. He hollered back no, it was the rub o' the green. That's got to be the goddamndest rub o' the green I ever heard of, but I went along with it." The judge apparently decided to overlook this lapse into profanity. "I was up on top of a knoll and the hole was only about three hundred yards away, all down hill, so I took out my spoon and gave her a mighty smite, and that ball just headed for the green like it had eyes. However, the ball had been setting behind a dry cowflop and it wasn't as dry as I thought, 'cause on my follow-through I got myself drenched in cow, er, ah –" Mal reached for an acceptable word, and ended up lamely with 'stuff.' "When I came down off the hill I was somewhat huffy and when Fidge accused me of taking two shots up there I was a bit put out."

"Why did he accuse you of taking two shots?"

"Oh, I forgot to mention. When I denied taking two shots, Fidge said, 'What were you doing, killing a snake?' And I said 'Yes,' because there had been a rattlesnake curled up and a-rattling a few feet from my ball, and I had taken out a club and whacked his head off."

"What club did you use?" asked Judge Broome.

"A mashie," answered Mal. The judge nodded and leaned back. "So I made Fidge climb up that hill and see the snake, and he apologized.

"We went down and found Fidge's ball in the branches of a sagebrush and he took a whack at it and knocked it further into the rough where he had to take a penalty shot because it was unplayable. It's a good thing he don't get in the rough much 'cause he's terrible at it. Me, I spend half my time in the rough, so I'm used to it. Anyhow, Fidge thrashed his way along the rough and finally got on the green in seven strokes. Then we started looking for my ball.

"We finally found it in a deep rocky gully just beyond the green. The goddamned ball had landed on the green – there was a gouge in the sand where it had hit – and then it had skipped across into that effing gully. However, I was setting there in two and Fidge was on in seven, so things didn't look too bad. But that gully was sure full of stones and shrubs and cactus plants and stuff. I asked Fidge for permission to move it out, claiming I could move it two club lengths out of the gully for a one-stroke penalty. He refused, and said I could move the ball two club lengths not nearer the hole from where she was setting for one penalty shot, but that would have put me in a worse position. We argued about it for awhile, but I guess he was right, so –"

"Was there not a marshal or other adjudicator along to whom an appeal could be made?" asked the judge. "In a championship match, I would have thought that would be the case."

"No sir, Your Worship," answered Mal. "We're a new club and we don't have none of them things. Anyhow, as far as breaking rules is concerned, they'd figure we'd keep a pretty sharp eye on each other. Also, Fidge knows the rule book backwards and forwards and quotes from it frequently at the drop of a hat, *ad nauseous*. I'll say for him, however, he's honest as all get-out and is just as mean with himself as he is with an opponent. So when he said what a rule was, I accepted it."

"But is there no special rule in the club regulations to deal with such an exigency?" asked the judge.

"No, sir. Not according to Fidge and he knows them all."

"Another point puzzles me," continued the judge. "Were there no spectators along? In a championship play-off, I would have thought you would have a gallery."

"Naw," grinned Mal. "The game was important to Fidge and me, but nobody else. It seems like once a guy gets knocked out of a tournament, he loses interest. Golfers are only interested in their own game, not somebody else's. You listen to a golfer talking and all he talks about is himself. And nobody listens but that don't matter, he talks anyhow. In my experience, golfers are great talkers, but lousy listeners. Anyhow, Fidge and I decided we didn't want nobody along, so we snuck off early on the QT."

"I see," nodded the judge. "Yes, a certain degree of autolatry is common amongst golfers. Carry on with your account, please."

"Well, I took a whirl at the ball down in that gully with my niblick, and knocked a stone as big as a baseball onto the green, but the ball stayed where it was. I also broke the head off my club and it nearly hit Fidge where he was standing up above me, but he ducked just in time. So I had to use my mashie for my next shot and the ball hopped up to the edge of the green and ran back down again in a worse place than before. On my next shot the ball bounced off several rocks, flew up in the air and landed in the middle of a bunch of cactus plants where it was tied up pretty good. I admit I was in something of a temper by this time. I took a big swing at the ball setting on the cactus plants and got a crotchful of cactus for my trouble. If you don't think a crotchful of cactus ain't a painful situation, then you'd better think again. However, the ball squirted up on the green about ten feet from the hole. I was there in six, and Fidge was lying seven about twelve feet away.

"While I was whaling away at the ball down in the gully, Fidge had been standing up above me, chuckling and chortling and counting my strokes out loud – you know, three, four, five, six."

"You did not attack Mr. Fidge?" asked the judge.

"No, sir."

"Amazing." The judge shook his head in wonderment.

"Fidge had to putt first. He ran that carpet back and forth till I thought he'd wear it out. Then he went into his mating dance of the hummingbird and dithered around taking four or five practice swings with his putter. He stood so long over the ball I thought he'd forgotten what he was there for. Then, by golly, he sunk her.

"So now it was my turn. If I canned that ten-footer, I won the match."

"What happened?" asked the judge, cracking his knuckles.

"I three-putted for a nine, and blew the whole shooting match," said Mal sheepishly.

Judge Broome threw up his hands in horror and fell back into his chair.

"The defence rests," said George.

"Court will take a twenty-minute recess," said Judge Broome, banging his gavel down on his left thumb.

When court reconvened, everyone, including His Lordship, had more or less regained their equanimity. Mal returned to the witness box. Cyril arose and faced him.

"Now, Mr. Morgan," said Cyril, going up and down on his toes, "I have just a few questions to put to you."

"Sure," said Mal affably.

"You have heard the evidence of the three witnesses. Are their statements correct?"

"Just about, I guess. They got the facts right, but their interpretations are subject to interpretation."

"You admit you were swearing and shouting on the 18th green?"

"Wouldn't you if you had a crotchful of cactus barbs?"

"Just answer my question please."

"Yeah, I was sounding off pretty vigorous."

"Sufficient to cause a disturbance?"

"I wouldn't know. They were the ones who said they were disturbed. Hell, I didn't even know they were there. Kinda sneaky, them not letting me know, I figure."

"But you were shouting and swearing?"

"Yeah, I got to admit it."

"And you repeatedly took the Lord's name in vain?"

"I'll say it was in vain."

"You misunderstand me. You made reference to the Lord in a profane and blasphemous manner?"

Mal ran his hand over his head. "I don't rightly know what those words mean, I'm afraid."

Cyril was getting exasperated. "You spoke of the Lord, nay, shouted in a disrespectful and obscene fashion?"

"There ain't no way I'd ever be really disrespectful of the Lord."

"Well, what were the words you used?"

"M'lord, I must object," interposed George hastily. "My learned colleague has insisted that it would be improper for a previous witness to repeat the exact words used by the defendant. What applies to one witness must apply to others."

"Sustained," growled the judge.

"Mr. Morgan," said Cyril. "Is it not true that you were shouting and swearing, and in the course of this tirade you interwove the name of the Lord, of Jesus, and of various saints?"

"Yeah," admitted Mal. "I called upon just about everybody I could think of."

"Thank you. That is all." Cyril sat down, dabbing his forehead with a handkerchief.

The judge turned to George. "Does the defence have any further submissions?"

"No, m'lord."

Mal returned to his place beside George.

"You may summarize for the prosecution, Mr. Thorndyke," said the judge.

Cyril got back on his feet. He shuffled his papers going up and down on his toes a few times. "The summary can be fairly brief, m'lord." He picked up a document. "The pertinent part of the Criminal Code is found in Section 238, and reads as follows: 'every one is a loose, idle or disorderly person or vagrant who (f) causes a disturbance in or near a street, road, highway or public place, by screaming, swearing or singing, or being drunk, or by impeding or incommoding peaceable passengers.' " Cyril placed the paper back on the table. "Three witnesses of impeccable probity have testified that the accused did indeed create a disturbance in a public place by shouting and swearing. The accused has admitted to the fact.

"Offences against religion are covered in Section 198. It has been held that blasphemous libel may be committed in written or spoken words and that a direct attack upon the Deity constitutes such an offence. I can give Your Lordship the references. The three witnesses have testified that the accused did indeed blaspheme against the Deity, and the response of the accused to my questions can only be interpreted as a reluctant admission to the truth of the allegation.

"The suggestion by my esteemed colleague that the offences should be overlooked because profanity is an art form is without legal precedent, is a bunch of balderdash, and should be dismissed out of hand. The matter of extenuation is irrelevant. The accused did create a disturbance in a public place by shouting and swearing, and in the course of that episode was guilty of blasphemous libel." Cyril seated himself, running a handkerchief around his collar.

Judge Broome's eyes turned to George.

"M'lord, the defence also can be quite brief," George began. "In the first place, this complaint should never have been laid; it is clearly vexatious, which is defined as harassing by means of malicious or trivial litigation. Mrs. Frobisher stated she laid the complaint in order to teach Mr. Morgan a lesson, which must be recognized as harassment. Mr. Morgan was not aware that anyone was within earshot of the 18th green; the ladies could readily have relieved themselves of the annoyance by making their presence known. They did not do so. This also is evidence of a vexatious intent.

"I reiterate my contention that in Western Canada great profanity can be an art form. Mrs. Frobisher has admitted that Mr. Morgan's presentation was a masterpiece. It is untenable that self-expression of artistic inspiration be inhibited and stultified by prejudice. This is an infringement of human rights.

"The charge of blasphemy is unproven and should be dismissed forthwith. Your Lordship ruled that the words and expressions used by Mr. Morgan were not to be repeated in court. Without specifics as to his statements to or about the Deity, no basis is established for the charge. Mr. Morgan is a God-fearing, churchgoing member of the community, and it is inconceivable that he would denigrate the good Lord. The basics of profanity are scatology, fornicology and theology. Theology is thus an integral component of profanity, and it is in this sense, and in this sense only, that heavenly participation was invoked. There can be no claim to inflammatory intent, nor action which would lead to a breach of the peace, because, as far as Mr. Morgan knew, Mr. Fidge was the only person within earshot, and he was enjoying himself thoroughly.

"Profanity is an integral and accepted part of golf. Show me the man who has sliced off into deep rough who has contented himself with 'Goodness gracious.' It is true that gentlemanly conduct dictates a seemly reticence in the presence of ladies – when their presence is known." George emphasized the last phrase. "And lady golfers, blessed with the timeless wisdom of their sex, have been known to turn a deaf ear to comments on a golf course, to which, in their drawing rooms, they would take violent exception. Profanity, sir, is as much a part of golf as slicing or hooking and is frequently related thereto. A dubbed drive has initiated the most piteous of profane threnodies which move you to tears – unless he is your opponent. A shank, that most monstrous of all shots, has been known to precipitate some of the great declamations of our time and has imbued a usually inarticulate person with the flowing eloquence and scintillating rhetoric of a Cicero or a Demosthenes. It would be sheer hypocrisy to take punitive action against one exponent of an art which is practised with less subtlety, finesse and skill by so many.

"Consider now the matter of extenuation. You have heard the recounting of a table of difficulties which rival the Labours of

Hercules and the Trials of Job – and even Job cried out unto the Lord. Surely, the irritating behaviour of his opponent, although imposed by ignorance rather than malice, would have abraded the nerve endings of a saint; surely the concatenation of untoward and malignant events on the 18th hole culminated in a disaster which was beyond human endurance; surely, this synergism of tribulations could not do other than precipitate an explosion; surely, these exceptional provocations comprise mitigation and justify exculpation.

"In summary, the defence submits that the charge should be dismissed on the following grounds: the complaint is vexatious; the matter of blasphemous libel is unproven; the defendant was exercising his human rights in an accepted artistic genre; the provocation was insuperable and warrants extenuation." George seated himself with a flourish. The audience clapped and were promptly subdued by the cold stare of the judge and the banging of his gavel.

Judge Broome leaned back and made a steeple with his long fingers. "First, a preamble," he began in his hoarse, gravelly voice. "Golf is diabolically designed to engender frustration, exasperation and despair. A man, when he takes up the game, must counterbalance these perturbatives against the thrills and elation of intermittent successes. He must accept this mix and realize that while he may beat an opponent, he can never beat the course. There are few things more satisfying in life than a shot hit squarely on the sweet spot or a chip-in from the edge of the green. On the other hand, there are few things more devastating than to see a good game disintegrate in the clutches of prehensile gorse. But man must learn to accept vicissitudes with restraint and decorum, no matter what the provocation. However, a man, who in his normal environment is invariably decorous and restrained, may on the golf course become a frothing maniac; a man of unquestioned integrity may be suborned by the game to lie and to cheat; a man usually of impeccable deportment may behave like a scoundrel and a poltroon. Such a metamorphosis is understandable, but not excusable.

"Now as to the particulars of the case. The matter of the motivation in the laying of the complaint is irrelevant. There is no doubt that the complainants were sincerely disturbed and scandalized. I find no evidence of harassment and, therefore, do not interpret the action as vexatious.

"I accept the contention of the defence that blasphemous libel has not been proven. Furthermore, in the matter of blasphemy, the locale of the offence and the intent and motivation of the perpetrator are relevant. I could detect no scurrilous, nor contentious, nor inflammatory intention to bring the Deity into disrepute which could be interpreted as a direct attack; the reference to the Deity was ancillary to a general theme.

"I accept the proposition that, in the West, profanity can be an art form of high aesthetic quality. A great declamation may be initiated by a variety of stimuli, including love, hate, grief, and frustration. Regardless of the stimulus, an oration may be of high artistic merit if presented with imagination, originality and eloquence. From all accounts, the defendant delivered a dissertation of considerable artistic virtuosity. However, as with all forms of self-expression, be it painting, poetry or music, the mode, for acceptance, must be within the bounds of contemporary mores and generally approved standards. Symphonic music played at the wrong time or place could be a breach of the peace. Individual human rights are circumscribed by the broader rights of society in general; an individual cannot trample on the sensitivities and rights of others. An illegal act is not excusable because it is artistically meritorious.

"Next, as to the matter of extenuation. One could not but be moved by the dramatic series of calamaties and provocations to which the defendant was subjected; and one could not but be sympathetic to his distress and consternation. However, that does not justify, in law, his subsequent actions. Insofar as creating a disturbance is concerned, the matter of extenuation is irrelevant. The Act states unequivocally that shouting and swearing in a public place constitutes disorderly conduct. I therefore find the defendant guilty of this offence.

"I have given some thought to the penalty to be imposed. I had considered suspending sentence and binding the defendant to keep the peace. But to enjoin a golfer from swearing would constitute cruel and unusual punishment by placing him in an intolerable situation. Accordingly, I impose upon him a fine of one dollar.

"Now some gratuitous advice. I would suggest that in the future, any Westerner wishing to indulge in traditional, ahem, artistic self-expression assure himself that his audience consists only of those sympathetic to this particular genre. I would also recommend that someone get to Mr. Fidge before we are faced with a homicide case. Court is dismissed." He banged his gavel down, keeping it well away from his left thumb.

As Judge Broome left the room, he paused in the doorway and summoned Mal to him with a crook of the finger.

"How about a game this afternoon?" he whispered to Mal. "I have my clubs with me, and I'd love to play your course."

A broad smile expanded across Mal's surprised face. "I would be delighted, Your Honour," said Mal. "And no swearing, eh?"

"Shit, no," said His Lordship.

Chapter Sixteen

THE GREAT AMERICAN LOVER

NE OF THE MORE BIZARRE PROJECTS George Ingraham got involved in arose during his term as president of the Board of Trade. The situation evolved innocuously enough from a discussion by the Board as to methods to popularize a proposed Frontier Day in Blossom. The proposition was to find some method of attracting Americans (and American money) across the border for the celebration. Since nobody at the meeting had any idea how this was to be accomplished, they took the traditional way out by appointing a committee to study the matter; George, Mal Morgan and Fred Peters were named to the Committee.

The Committee met the next day at their usual haunt in the back booth of Wong Toy's restaurant. I was made a member of the Committee because I happened to be there at the time. After cups of Wong's execrable coffee had been served by our cheerful host, George opened the discussion. "The assignment to the Committee is to come up with some programme which would appeal particularly to our friends from across the border. Frontier Days are traditionally devoted to cowboy activities – bucking horses, bulldogging, chuck wagon racing and so forth – but there's no novelty left in rodeo events that I can think of. Anybody got any bright ideas?"

"How about logrolling?" suggested Mal. "Or axe-throwing?"

"Logrolling on the prairies?" said Fred sceptically.

"Well, then, how about ploughing or stooking or catching

gophers in a butterfly net. We could set up an international contest on something or other. Maybe throwing the bull – Americans are great at that. Hey, how about a cowflop throwing contest – one for accuracy and one for distance?"

"I don't think so," said George with a smile. "This is not a political gathering."

"American westerners fancy themselves as pretty handy with a six-shooter," said Fred. "Maybe we could have a contest to determine the fastest gun in the west."

"That's not a bad idea," nodded George. "Although some idiot would probably shoot his own foot off. However, we could take out insurance, I suppose."

"It's a hell of a good idea," said Mal, "but I'm afraid Laramie already has such a contest."

"Oh, foof," said George in disappointment.

The Committee continued its considerations of a variety of ideas including horseshoe-pitching, hog-calling, cake-baking, a beauty contest, pie-throwing, beer-drinking, square-dancing and lie-telling without finding anything that seemed to fill the bill. I suggested darts but that didn't elicit any support. The four of us sat in glum silence for awhile. Fred signalled Wong for more coffee; Mal rolled a cigarette. "As I understand the object of the exercise," said Mal pontifically, "it is to attract American involvement in our little goings-on. If we go back to fundamentables, what interests Americans is like everybody else – wine, women and song." He lit his cigarette and let it dangle from his lower lip. "One thing wrong with that is, Americans don't drink wine and they can't sing worth a damn, but I never met one yet who didn't think he was God's gift to women."

"Hey, maybe that's the answer," said George, sitting up suddenly. "Suppose we announce we are going to find out who is the greatest American lover of all time."

"You mean have an international contest?" asked Fred.

"No, I don't think so," said George slowly. "Too contentious. If a Canadian won, the Americans would say it was a put-up job. Furthermore, Western Canadian folklore has established H.Q. Snodgrass as the great Canadian lover – who incidentally came originally from Blossom – and we wouldn't want to interfere with that tradition. No, let's keep it strictly American. We can say that as a gesture of international good will we are prepared to act as unbiased adjudicators to serve in this capacity."

"What criteria would you use?" asked Fred dubiously. "I can see certain, ahem, moral objections arising from some components of the community."

"We could put Flossy Macabee on the review committee," suggested Mal enthusiastically.

"No, no," said George impatiently. "That's not what I mean at all. I don't know what the criteria would be at the moment, but they would have to be, er, objective and pristine. Leaving that aside for the nonce, what do you think of the idea?"

"Tremendous," exclaimed Mal, clapping his hands together.

"It would certainly pique the interest of our friends across the border," said Fred cautiously, "but I have some difficulty envisaging the *modus operandi*."

"Later," said George with a wave of the hand. He frowned in concentration for a few moments. "We'd have to get publicity out in the States right away in order to allow time for the submission of nominations. Our Board of Trade is a member of the International Chamber of Trade, with headquarters in Washington, so maybe they'd be prepared to help us in the project. I'll get a letter off to them right away. Hey, I think we're onto something."

"You betcha," said Mal.

George received a prompt answer to his letter expressing interest in the proposition but stating that the matter was being turned over to the Junior Chamber of Trade (JCT) presumably because the topic was thought to fall more within the purview of the younger branch of the organization. Then a few days later George received a response from the JCT office indicating considerable enthusiasm for the project. Apparently the JCT was looking for some kind of a PR undertaking which would get them some publicity and public attention. They invited George to come to Washington at their expense and with a retainer fee. George promptly packed his bag and took off, after consulting briefly with his committee.

George had expected to be gone for a few days or a week at most, but he didn't arrive back in Blossom for nearly three months.

Fred received three short letters from him stating that the organization of the contest was proving to be much more complex than he had anticipated, but without spelling out what the difficulties were. We obtained some information from the newspapers and radio as the repercussions from the project became apparent. We began to wonder if the undertaking would come to fruition in time for our Frontier Day which had initiated the exercise.

When George finally got back to Blossom, he immediately summoned the committee to his office rather than to Wong Toy's, so we knew we were going to be dealing with secret matters. George was looking rather tired and haggard, but was sporting a completely new outfit which we admired extravagantly. Fred, Mal and I were looking forward to his report with considerable excitement.

George slouched his long frame into the chair behind his battered desk covered with three months of dust. He fished a bottle of Jeb's moonshine out of a bottom drawer and set it on the desk. "Ah," he breathed, "back to real whisky." He poured us each a dollop, held up his glass and said, "To the Great American Lover, may his tribe decrease." We lifted our glasses in the toast.

"Okay, okay," said Mal impatiently. "Hurry up and tell us all about it. We're just splitting a gut."

"It's been quite an exercise,'" said George shaking his head. "Unbelievable. I suppose you've followed some of our shenanigans in the press?"

"Bits and pieces," replied Fred. "I gather you stirred up quite a ruckus. But we haven't any idea what went on behind the scenes. Will the denouement be ready for our Frontier Day in three weeks time?"

"Yes," said George. "The announcement will be made in Blossom at that time. You can certainly expect a major influx of Americans into town for the event, including a large contingent of the news media to handle the publicity."

"How were you able to persuade the JCT to have the announcement of such a big event take place in Blossom?" asked Fred.

George grinned slyly. "As soon as I found out how interested they were I took out a copyright on the proposal. However, they were very coöperative in all the arrangements and didn't cavil at the announcement being made in Blossom – indeed, they felt it added a certain panache to the event."

"Come on, come on," urged Mal. "Get on with it."

"Okay," said George. "But first of all, I must swear you to the utmost secrecy in all matters I shall relate to you – including most importantly the name of the winner." He stared around at us; we all held up our glasses in response.

"You know the winner?" I asked impatiently. "Who is he?"

"All in good time," said George. "Yes, I know the name of the winner. Probably."

"What do you mean, probably?" asked Mal.

"You will see in due course," answered George. He settled back in his chair, stretching out his long legs. "I shall be able at the present time to give you only an adumbration of a long and tortuous exercise." He sighed deeply. "Now to begin at the beginning. I was met in Washington by the executive officers of the JCT who treated me with the warmest hospitality throughout my entire stay. They were a grand group of chaps to work with. I found out right away that they were very keen about the whole idea and were tallyho to charge ahead. We got down to cases right away and, in a few days, developed what we thought was a simple, practicable procedure for the contest.

"The *modus operandi* we worked out was as follows: the several state chapters of the JCT would accept nominations; each state would set up a selection committee for that state and would forward to the central office in Washington one name to represent that state; these names would be turned over to a final board of anonymous membership for decision. This looked workable and innocuous. We called a press conference to release the announcement of the contest to determine the Great American Lover.

"The news media took up the proposition with great enthusiasm. During a depression such as we are in at the present time, when the news is invariably sad and grievous, the idea of a frivolous promotion was welcome surcease to the journalists. Furthermore, the public welcomed an exercise which would take their minds off their chronic woes and tribulations. Another factor which you should keep in mind is that the large number of unemployed meant that there was a plethora of people who could devote themselves full time to the subsequent commotion, as we shall see. All in all, the publicity on radio and in the press hit the public like a bombshell.

"Almost immediately some of our errors in judgment became apparent. We had stated that any American, living or dead, would be eligible for nomination. This was our first mistake. It became quickly apparent that just about every American male between the ages of nine and ninety who hasn't backed into a lawn mower figured he was the person we were looking for. There were wholesale resignations from the JCT organization in order to establish eligibility. The central office sent out a hasty bulletin declaring all members of JCT as of the original time of announcement to be disqualified.

"The early publicity gave the unfortunate impression that we were staging a contest to demonstrate qualifications for the award which was interpreted in terms of virility. A high proportion of the male population was prepared to participate in such a competition and each was convinced of his puissance, if provided with an adequate stimulus. Even if they didn't win they figured they'd have a great time losing. Call Girls United of America (a clandestine but powerful organization) offered their services as a patriotic gesture. Line-ups blocks long collected at the state JCT offices. They were inundated by mail and the phone exchanges were jammed. The state JCT executive officers had to go into hiding. All the organized churches were up in arms, with the exception of the Druids and a small sect known as the Natural Church of Total Fulfillment. Clergymen fulminated in their pulpits. Overnight, an association of wives sprang up under the title of Defenders of the Hearthside, and a hundred thousand of them marched on Washington."

"Yeah, we read about that in the papers," said Mal.

"As a result of this, the JCT federal officers fled from Washington and set up headquarters in a secret hide-out many miles away," continued George. "A news release was hastily prepared stating that we were not conducting a virility contest and that nominees would have to rest on established laurels. Wives were urged to nominate their husbands, if they were so inclined. Interestingly enough, throughout the entire procedure, as far as we can determine, no husband was ever nominated by his wife. There is probably some deep sociological significance to this which will bear later study.

"Once our announcement was carried across the nation, the wives got off our backs and things simmered down temporarily. Very soon, however, new problems arose. Fan clubs supporting various movie stars, politicians, radio personalities and so forth quickly formed. These clubs held parades, rallies and picnics and opposing groups fought pitched battles in the streets. The enthusiastic support accorded one incumbent state governor can only be attributed to party loyalty beyond the call of duty.

"A group of unemployed young people on the west coast, operating out of headquarters in a broken-down motel in Santa Barbara called the 'Love Inn,' initiated a campaign to nominate a daffodil as a symbol of love flower-power. This project was soon taken up by others across the country. I understand they got a fair amount of behind-the-scenes support from the Florists Association of America. Daffodils real and artificial blossomed across the country, and this gentle flower took on a significance never envisaged by horticulturists. The flowers were munched as aphrodisiacs and, on the basis that the libido is all in the mind anyhow, it is not surprising that remarkable effects were reported. A number of dubious songs about daffodils appeared on the hit parade. A guitar player in Oakland changed his name legally to Joe Daffodil and cashed in on all the publicity.

"All this turmoil resulted in the police in several cities being completely overwhelmed, and the state guard had to be called out.

"I joined a further council of war with the JCT officers in hiding. We were tempted to call the whole thing off, but felt we did not dare to do so at this stage of the operation. The principal current problems seemed to be caused by the activities of the living contestants and their supporters. We had considerable reluctance to change the rules in the middle of the game, but after many hours of deliberation we came up with the solution to confine eligibility to people not now living. This decision was made known in a national publicity release which raised great howls of protest from various hopefuls and their supporters. We did, however, get substantial support from clergymen, police chiefs, historians and the older politicians. One surprising development was the announcement by one candidate from Georgia that, for the honour of the South, if he were nominated he would shoot himself to make himself eligible. Another hasty release from our headquarters put a stop to that nonsense.

"Instructions were released directing that nominations in writing with supporting documentation were to be filed at the various state JCT offices. Things kind of quieted down for a couple of days and we breathed a sigh of relief. We were premature. Various pressure groups began to develop, based principally on ethnic grounds. Each group felt it a matter of racial pride that the state champion must belong to their ethnic division. This all started humourously but very promptly became serious, and rivalries built up into first-class rows. Conflicting parades and rallies erupted into street fights. The Italians clashed with the Poles in Chicago; the Swedes battled with the Finns in Minnesota; and the Irish took on all comers in New York. In the larger states, the ethnic rivalries were complicated by geographic factors. The unions, fraternal societies and even the churches got in the act by supporting candidates from their particular organizations. These various loyalties meant that just about everyone in the country got involved in the controversy one way or another. Such a high proportion of the population was involved in demonstrations and the general foofaraw that the whole country was in a turmoil.

"The President of the United States was finally forced to declare a state of national emergency. He mobilized the National Guard and recalled the Seventh Fleet. A direct phone line was set up between our secret heardquarters and the White House, so that thereafter we were in close touch with top-level advisors. I must admit that we were not in particular favour with the White House and were urged to wrap the thing up as quickly as possible.

"At this stage the League of Nations got involved indirectly during a conference under its aegis which had been called to discus worldwide oats cultivation. The representative from Bongovia in the course of his address made a snide reference to the current turmoil in America as being a tempest in a teapot. He said that the selection of a great lover in the United States was an exercise in futility since in this area of accomplishment the Americans were nowhere anyhow on the international scene. This was vigorously refuted by the American representative. The French delegate added coals to the fire by stating in a superior manner that it was universally recognized that in the area being discussed France was unequivocally supreme. Spain said a great lover required the stimulus of beautiful women and only Spain had these in abundance. Representatives popped up all over the house to refute this. Russia said love was a bourgeois superstition anyhow, and a decadent, reactionary, capitalistic plot. Canada asked to return to a discussion of oats. Argentina claimed that South Americans were the only really great lovers. This was vigorously supported by Bolivia and Brazil. The representative from Rangoola stated rather cryptically that the term 'underdeveloped' with reference to nations applied only to economics. Greece pointed out that Aphrodite, the Goddess of Love, was a Greek. Iran said she was stolen from ancient Persia. The Italian delegate said it was well known that the Goddess of Love was Venus who was Roman and launched off on a panegyric on the ardour of Italian men. He promptly got told by the Moroccan representative that any nation which thought the ultimate in amorous manifestation was a buttock pinch was a race of idiots. The Italian rejoined with a note of sympathy for a country whose women were so homely they were required to wear veils. The Albanian representative made a slighting reference to Cleopatra and got punched in the nose by the Egyptian ambassador. The British delegate stepped between them and got clobbered by both of them. Fights broke out all over the place. The Secretary beat on the table with his shoe and finally called the guard. The meeting was adjourned for two weeks to allow tempers to cool off." George paused and with a sigh added, "I have abandoned, at least temporarily, my plan to determine the greatest international lover of all time, for reasons which may occur to you.

"To return to the United States. The federal troops gradually restored order throughout the country and state JCT offices were placed under strong Marine guard. The offices were deluged with submissions which ranged all the way from Joe Splutt, a friendly garbage man in Yonkers, up to and including a bishop. The JCT officials announced long and loud that they would not themselves be making the selections – that this would be done in secret by independent, anonymous committees. The mountains of documents in each JCT state office were organized and catalogued by an army of volunteers in a remarkably short period of time. These files were then turned over to the state selection committees.

"These committees had been set up in great secrecy and spirited off to their hidden meeting places. One group met in the basement of a clandestine brewery; one in the national mint; one in the canasta lounge of a federal prison; and one in a crematorium. These committees were each faced with the formidable job of examining literally thousands of nominations. One of the first problems they ran into, which they referred to our headquarters, was the terms of reference or criteria of performance to be applied in their selection. We had thought this would be fairly obvious, but it isn't when you come to think of it. We struggled with this problem for some time and then decided not to get our finger in that particular gearbox. We told them to use any criterion they thought appropriate. This led to some difficulties later in the finals in trying to compare oranges and bananas.

"The White House was on our necks to wind up the programme, so we had to keep bugging the state committees although we were well aware of their awesome difficulties. A couple of the committees got hopelessly deadlocked so we had to send someone from headquarters to get them unjammed. Finally, after many delays and frustrations all the state decisions were completed and we were ready to proceed to the finals.

"The one name and supporting documents from each state was sent in an armoured car under Army escort to the secret site selected for the meeting of the finals committee. I can now tell you that the place selected was the basement of Fort Knox. The members of the Committee had been chosen in great secrecy and were brought to the meeting room at the night by the FBI. I must not even now disclose the membership of this committee, as I am sworn to secrecy on the matter. Suffice it to say that they were men of great and unquestioned rectitude. I hasten to add that I was not a member of the Committee, but was accorded observer privileges.

"The first meeting of the Committee was a dramatic and exciting event. The pouches of documents were brought in under heavy guard and signed for. All personnel other than the Committee and myself then withdrew, and we were faced with our challenging task.

"The chairman, a senior member of the judiciary, made a short opening speech emphasizing the heavy responsibility and high trust placed upon those assembled. He noted we were witnessing and participating in history in the making because their choice would establish a national folk hero to take his place with Paul Bunyan, Johnny Appleseed and Buffalo Bill; also, in another venue, to rank with Don Juan, Casanova and Henry the Eighth. (His knowledge of English history is a bit defective.) He urged the Committee, in the national interest, to apply itself with diligence and integrity and divorced from parochial partisanship or personal bias. The tension in the room was electric.

"Finally, we got to the exciting moment of opening the pouches and our first view of the names of the candidates, one of whom was slated for immortality. I must pay high tribute to the dedicated and meticulous thoroughness of the Committee members. Every submission with its voluminous supporting documentation was given the most exhaustive and detailed study. The pros and cons of each nominee were discussed and debated with vigour and not infrequently with acrimonious intensity. The chairman kept a firm hand and directed the discussions into definitive and productive channels. The meetings went on for three full days with only brief periods out for food and sleep. Gradually, names were eliminated and the focus narrowed down to the finalists.

"I shall not try to give a full account by any means of our discussions and decisions, but I shall comment only on a few of our considerations and difficulties. The principal problem faced was comparing oranges and bananas, as I mentioned earlier due to variations in criteria of merit.

"The candidacy from Maine was based upon a marriage lasting seventy-eight years. This was eliminated on the basis that it was probably not love, but inertia. Alaska claimed that anyone who could persuade a girl to pitch woo in a snowbank at forty below zero just had to be the greatest. Nevada sent in the name of a man who had spent seven million dollars on prostitutes in five years. The Committee felt that while folk heroes needn't be expected to be lily-white this was going a bit far. Utah proposed a man who had been married to eighteen women at the same time and had produced one hundred and three children. This was rejected on the basis that it sounded more like animal husbandry than love. Wyoming missed the point somehow and nominated a pedigreed Hereford bull. New Mexico suggested a Herman Gonzalez who had shot his wife's seven lovers as evidence of his affection and had been hanged for his devotion. California proposed a man who had been married twenty-three times and divorced twenty-two times. The Committee was impressed with the twenty-three marriages, but distressed by the twenty-two divorces.

"Texas took a somewhat anatomical tack. The Committee was much impressed, not to say staggered, by the documentary evidence presented, but felt that in the final analysis, the biggest is not necessarily the best. Michigan recorded the exploits of a man who had sweet-talked over five million dollars out of rich widows. This was certainly evidence of great charm, but the ethical aspects of the case bothered the Committee somewhat. Tennessee nominated a lad who had become a father at the age of seven. The Committee was concerned about the authenticity of the claim and one of the members quoted an old proverb that 'maternity is a matter of fact; paternity is always a matter of opinion.' Furthermore, it was felt that such a youthful winner might make the world unsafe for baby-sitters.

"By debate, analysis and elimination, we finally zeroed in on the nominee from Montana, a man by the name of Horace Quilby Snort. He was a mule skinner and a roustabout who had operated in Montana during the 1860s. He was obviously a man of great charm and romantic accomplishments. He travelled about a good deal, and each new area he visited promptly welcomed him with open arms, figuratively and literally. Even at a time of virile men he was a standout. He had an entrée into all the best salons and tepees. The ladies found him delightful company and his appeal overwhelming. As a result, it would not be long before he would be run out of town by a group of irate husbands, often festooned with tar and feathers. Indeed, his progress across Montana could be traced by a trail of feathers. Once he was almost hanged from a pine tree, but was released when the ladies of the district toting rifles turned up en masse at the ceremony. His name has come down to modern times in that the expression 'to have a snort' has a special significance in Montana not found elsewhere in the country.

"But what impressed the Committee most was the verifiable authenticity of his accomplishments. Mr. Snort had certain physical characteristics which were apparently carried on a dominant gene and therefore transmitted to his progeny. These characteristics of physiognomy which were readily identifiable, included unique eyes and a nose that slanted slightly to the right. An anthropologist at the University of Babb had become interested in this phenomenon some time previously and had undertaken a research project to determine the incidence of these characteristics in the general population. His findings disclosed the fact that fully two-thirds of the people of Montana who could trace their lineage back to the time of Mr. Snort had these determinable characteristics. Snort's other qualities of exuberance, virility and humour were also undoubtedly transmitted, and account for the great charm and ebullience so characteristic of Montanans. The scientifically proven evidence of Mr. Snort's ubiquity and puissance complemented the folk tales and other information about him and finally led the Committee to select him over the formidable array of other contenders.

"The runner-up was the nominee from Idaho, a Herman Quentin Sarcee, but his credentials were less well-documented.

"So that, gentlemen," concluded George, leaning back and downing the remains of his drink, "is the story of the Great American Lover."

"Where does that there 'probably' that you dropped earlier on come into the picture?" asked Mal. "It looks all signed, sealed and delivered."

"In this way," said George. "I have a grave unease about the decision of the Committee. All during the discussion of Mr. Snort by the Committee I was plagued by a vague feeling of *déjà vu*. This was fortified by an analysis of Snort's amorous *modus operandi*, by his initials H.Q.S., by his physical characteristics and by a coincidence of timing. As a result, I wrote to Fred here recently, in strict confidence, to do some historical research for me. Would you care to report on your findings please, Fred?"

"Certainly," said Fred, taking a sheaf of papers out of a brief case. "In view of the shortness of time, my historical investigations are by no means complete, but I think sufficient for our purposes. I have dug into a lot of records here and have also gained a good deal of information from oldtimers, particularly Angus MacNab and Grandma Akerbilt. I also made quick trips to Butte and to Boise. Here is the story I have put together.

"H.Q. Snodgrass was born and raised in Blossom, Northwest Territories, date uncertain and parentage dubious. In his early teens he ran away with a school teacher named Miss Phoebe Fish and disappeared from Blossom for several years. My records show that he surfaced briefly in a mining camp near Fort William, but I have no further information about his activities until he reappeared in Blossom, without Phoebe. He apparently settled down to a conservative life of bootlegging and cattle rustling, and prospered as a respected member of the community. However, his lubricious talents asserted themselves and an irate husband swore out a warrant for his arrest. Mr. Snodgrass escaped from a bedroom window and fled across the border, hotly pursued by the North West Mounted Police. There is no doubt from my findings in Montana that he changed his name there, for obvious reasons, to Horace Quilby Snort."

"Aha," said George. "Just what I suspected. It is like his humour to take a sobriquet of Snort."

"You have heard from George," continued Fred, "the catalogue of his, I guess you would say, triumphant tour across Montana to Idaho, where he changed his name to Herman Quentin Sarcee."

"Again," nodded George, "what I suspected. So Montana

and Idaho were both nominating the same person, which lends credence to his final selection.

"He apparently dallied long enough in Idaho to establish his libidinous reputation there before going to British Columbia where he was attracted by the discovery of gold at Barkerville. It was during this time on the Cariboo Road out of Ashcroft that he made the reputation which has earned him the folklore recognition as Canada's Greatest Lover. So there you have it – there is no doubt that Snodgrass, Snort and Sarcee are one and the same person."

"What a man," breathed Mal enviously.

"Therein lies my dilemma," continued George. "Should I tell my American colleagues that the Great American Lover, named after so much trouble and tumult, is really a Canadian? We certainly don't want to go through the whole complex, turmoil-ridden, contentious procedure again. To withdraw the name of Mr. Snort at this stage would cast grave doubt on the integrity and competence of the Selection Committee and jeopardize the reputation of the Junior Chamber of Trade. On the other hand, the establishment of the greatest American folk hero of all time is not a floccinaucity. What do you think I should do?"

"I have been giving some thought to the matter ever since I received your letter," said Fred. "I feel that you have a responsibility to the JCT to keep quiet. After all, the matter of citizenship during that era was somewhat loose. Furthermore, the accomplishments of Mr. Snort did take place in the United States, and that, I feel is the crucial element."

"I agree with Fred," I said. "You have a wonderful opportunity to keep quiet – a situation which you have invariably blown in the past. Establish a precedent for yourself – keep quiet."

"Sure," said Mal. "Keep your big lip buttoned, George." Mal laughed. "Anyhow, I kind of enjoy the situation."

"Very well," said George with a sigh. "I think you're right and your advice fits my inclination. But if it ever gets out, we'll all be hung from the highest tree available, and there won't be a posse of lovely ladies toting guns to come to our rescue."

The rest is now history. The name of Horace Quilby Snort was announced by the president of the Junior Chamber of Trade as the Great American Lover at the biggest Blossom Frontier Day of its history. The town was inundated with Americans, including JCT officials and a large contingent of reporters. The news was promptly flashed across the world by wire, radio and press.

The proclamation was received with mixed reactions, as was expected. Fortunately, the JCT had the prescience to require a commitment in advance by all states to accept the final decision as binding. All of them did so, but with some lack of grace in a few instances. Boston complained that Mr. Snort was lacking in breeding, which seemed a singularly inappropriate comment in view of his history. The Lone Star Ladies Guild was quoted as saying that Snort might qualify in the north, but if he'd come south it would be sending a boy to do a man's job. Arizona claimed that they had evidence that Snort had been born and raised in that state. The Virgin Islands complained bitterly that their candidate had been under an impossible disadvantage.

Montana was delighted, of course, and declared a state holiday to celebrate the first annual Snort Day during which marriage vows were considered temporarily suspended. This turned out to be a Dionysian potlatch of epic proportions which attracted people from far and wide to share in the goodies. Mr. Snort would have been delighted at the maintenance of the noble tradition which he had fathered.

Our committee had one final meeting on the subject in George's office during which we indulged in a good deal of self-congratulation. "Next week, I've been invited to attend the unveiling of an erection in honour of Horace Quilby Snort at the city of Snortville, formerly called Helena." George paused. "Maybe I should rephrase that to the unveiling of a memorial to Mr. Snort." He grinned and Mal guffawed. George poured us each a dram of Jeb's moonshine. He held up his glass. "Let us write finis to this happy episode and toast Horace Quilby Snort, the Great American Lover – and Blossom's favourite son."

Chapter Seventeen

GIVE A DOG A BAD NAME

I WAS WALKING ALONG THE STREET with George Ingraham one afternoon on our way back from the post office when I saw Roscoe, Jeb Wilson's dog, padding along the street towards us. He had the intense seriousness of purpose of a dog on a mission – he was up to no good, I'd be bound. His ugly face had that cynical leer, accentuated by the scar on one side of his face, which reflected his attitude to life rather well. Roscoe had never been really unfriendly to me; for the most part he just ignored me completely, as he did everyone else except Jeb. Any overtures I had made to him had been repulsed with haughty disdain. He gave the impression that he felt superior to mere humans and just couldn't be bothered with them. His unpleasant personality and unsightly appearance endeared him to no one.

"Here comes that wretched dog of Jeb's," I said to George. "Of all the revolting, misbegotten examples of the animal kingdom, Roscoe has to be in a class by himself."

George just smiled.

As the dog reached us, George said quietly, "Hello, Roscoe." At the sound of George's voice Roscoe stopped abruptly, sniffed at George's pant leg and then wagged his entire back end. George squatted down and began rubbing the dog's ears while talking to him softly. Roscoe snuffled happily and licked George's hand. I was dumfounded. I'd never before seen Roscoe greet anyone other than Jeb with anything but surly hostility. George continued talking to the dog for a few moments before rising with a final affectionate pat. Roscoe sniffled amiably before proceeding up the street.

"George, I'm amazed," I said. "How on earth did you establish a friendly relationship with that benighted mutt?"

"It's quite a story," replied George. "Come along with me to my office, and I'll tell you about it."

We walked along the street to Morgan's Hardware shop over which George had his business office with a small apartment attached where he lived. We climbed the wooden stairs to his office which was lined with shelves of law books and filing cabinets. His desk was piled high with a clutter of books, files and papers, some of which had overflowed onto the floor. He seated himself behind the desk and waved me to a chair.

"Now tell me about Roscoe," I demanded.

George picked up a pipe from the debris on his desk and slowly filled it from a leather canister of tobacco. "It's quite a story, as I said," began George. "Some of what I shall tell you is semi-confidential, so I shall have to rely on your circumspection." He cocked an eyebrow at me.

I nodded.

"Very well," said George. "This is the way it all happened."

One day recently (said George) I was driving through the Cypress Hills on my way back to Blossom when I saw ahead of me on the road an animal going through some strange antics. I thought at first it was a jack rabbit sporting about and then decided it was a coyote having a fit. As I got closer I saw it was Roscoe. He would spin around and around, and then turn a back somersault. He kept this up until I approached and stopped the car. I thought he must be having a distemper attack or had gotten into Jeb's moonshine. He came panting up to the side of the car and started barking at me.

"What's the matter, Roscoe?" I asked. He continued to bark excitedly. The only thing I could think of was that Jeb had been hit by a car and knocked into the ditch or was sleeping off a binge behind a sagebrush somewhere. Since Roscoe didn't appear to be rabid or out of his senses, I got out of the car and searched up and down the ditches on both sides of the road. No sign of Jeb. Roscoe kept barking at me and then running off to the left of the road, looking back over his shoulder. It was a classic display of a dog trying to get you to follow him. He kept repeating the performance as I searched in the ditches.

I was reluctant to follow the dog on some harebrained venture as I wanted to get back to town, but Roscoe's performance certainly seemed to indicate that something must be amiss with Jeb, since Jeb is the only person Roscoe gives a damn about. I reluctantly decided to follow him. When I got back in the car to pull it off to the side of the road, Roscoe nearly crawled in after me, barking wildly. "Okay, okay, Roscoe," I said. "I'm coming. Keep your shirt on."

Roscoe led me off through the brush up the side of a hill at a pace I couldn't possibly match. It was tough going through tangled underbrush and over deadfalls. Roscoe would run ahead, wait for me to catch up and then start off again. By the time we got to the top of the first hill, I was pooped and sat down on a log to recover. Roscoe returned to me and barked and tugged at my pant leg. "Okay Roscoe, I get the message. Just give me a minute to catch my breath. I've only got two legs, you know." I tried to pat him on the head, but he would have none of it. When I had recovered my breath we set off again. We went down the other side of the hill and across a little valley through a most appalling crisscross of deadfall. I fell and skinned my shin and swore mightily with what wind I had left. Roscoe headed straight up the next hog's-back. Wherever we were going we were sure taking the most direct route. Roscoe became more tolerant of my frequent pauses and just waited with his tongue lolling out until I got on my feet again. Then off he went with me puffing along behind. I began to be afraid I would get lost and not be able to find my way back, so I took frequent checks on direction. The direct route being followed by Roscoe without concession to trails or easy ways facilitated this.

When we came to the top of the third hill after I don't know how many miles, I could see down into quite a large valley. I had never been there before, but I recognized it from descriptions I have heard. It is volcanic terrain called Valley of the Many Smokes by the Indians because of the numerous spurts of natural steam which come out of the ground. Roscoe led me along the south slope of the valley nearly its entire length. As we went along I could see puffs of steam emanating from fissures in the rocks. One of the small streams we crossed felt quite hot to the hand, and didn't provide me with the refreshing drink I desperately needed.

Roscoe was getting increasingly excited and more impatient with my slow progress, so I realized we were getting near the end of our trek. He went around a small outcropping and down into a steep chasm. At the outlet of the chasm, I could see Jeb's old Essex behind a clump of willows. "Goddamn it, Roscoe," I shouted, "there's a road into this place. I could shoot you." I followed him down into the chasm and up a steaming brook to the head of the stream where it emerged from the mouth of a cave. Roscoe waited until he saw me approaching and then entered the cave, looking back over his shoulder.

I have always been deathly afraid of caves ever since I read *Tom Sawyer* as a boy, but there was no turning back now. After the bright sunlight outside, the cave was black as pitch. I felt my way along the walls, avoiding the hot, little stream as well as I could; the air was hot and humid. After about twenty feet, the tunnel turned a bend and the darkness began to lighten. Shortly thereafter, I emerged into a large high-ceilinged cavern. The place was full of steam which issued from fissures in the floor to spiral upwards and escape through an aperture in the roof. It was through this hole that a dim light filtered down to illuminate the room. It was a weird and eerie place, reminiscent of one of Dante's less happy visions. Frankly, I was scared pink.

To add to the macabre scene, a strange contraption squatted in the middle of the chamber. As I approached slowly through the mist, I could make out a large drum sitting over a crevice in the floor from which issued a steady stream of steam. Attached to the top of the drum were several pipes connected to a long copper coil leading to a vat. Along the wall nearby stood a row of gasoline barrels; by the smell, I judged they must have contained mash. I had stumbled on Jeb's famous distillery, which everyone knows exists but no one knows where. What a perfect set-up. Since he uses the heat of the natural steam from the ground, the still does not require much attention and can be left for long periods of time. And the place is beautifully hidden.

Incidentally, this still is, of course, the key operation in Jeb's moonshine activities. That still the cops confiscated in the coulee north of the town was just an ancillary contrivance for emergencies. Although Jeb and I are good friends, I have never let him tell me where his stills are hidden, although he has offered to do so. I have always felt, rightly or wrongly, that as a lawyer, and thereby an officer of the court, I did not want to know their location so I would not be a party to an illegal activity.

All of this flashed through my mind as I followed Roscoe to a corner of the cavern. He was whining down a hole in the floor. I lay on my stomach and peered down, but could see nothing.

"Jeb, are you there?" I hollered. Roscoe whimpered nervously.

There was a long pause and I called again. Then I heard Jeb's voice echoing feebly up the well. "Yeah, I'm here." Roscoe barked excitedly and I told him to shut up.

"Are you all right, Jeb?"

"Yeah, I'm okay."

"Any bones broken? Are you injured in any way?"

"No, I'm fine. Who is it?"

"George," I shouted. "Roscoe brought me."

"Good. Just get me to hell out of here." His voice sounded stronger and I breathed a sigh of relief.

"How?" I called.

"Rope in my car. Down the valley." His voice came echoing up out of the darkness.

"I saw it. How deep is the hole you're in?"

"Dunno. About forty feet, I reckon."

"Okay, I'll be back. Don't go away," I added stupidly.

"I ain't going nowhere," replied Jeb, with a chuckle which reverberated up the shaft.

I hurried out of the cave down to Jeb's old Essex and found several lengths of rope in the back seat. I tied them securely together and returned to the cave praying they would be long enough. "Here comes the rope," I called, playing it out down the hole. "Holler when it reaches you." I held my breath until I heard him call, "I've got it." I still had several feet left.

"Tie it around your chest," I shouted, "and I'll pull you out."

"No," called Jeb, "tie it to something and I'll pull myself out."

I tied the end of the rope to a large stalagmite protruding from the floor of the cave and told Jeb it was ready to go. The rope went taut; I could hear him huffing and puffing down the hole. After several minutes the rope went slack. "I can't make it," called Jeb. "Too weak."

"Then tie the rope around you and I'll pull you up."

After Jeb gave me the signal, I started trying to drag him up. I put the rope over my shoulder and hauled at it away from the hole. It soon became apparent that this was going to be a difficult job. The problem was that Jeb weighs more than I do, and with the friction of the rope over the edge of the hole I wasn't making much progress. My feet finally slipped on the damp floor; I went slithering back across the floor almost into the hole.

After a few minutes, Jeb's muffled voice came up the shaft. "What happened?"

"You're too heavy for me. I can't lift you. There's a better chance of you pulling me in than me pulling you out. Have you got a block and tackle?"

"No."

I racked my brains. The hole was too deep for me to improvise a ladder, and I wasn't sure if Jeb was in any shape to climb up anyhow. Roscoe whined and looked up into my eyes. It would be a long way to go to try to get help and I was reluctant to leave Jeb any longer in the hole. Furthermore, I wasn't sure if I could find the cave again.

"Jeb," I hollered, "shall I go for help?"

"No. We'll figger out something."

"Like what?"

"How about a counterweight? Anything you can use?"

Why hadn't I thought of that? I looked around the cavern. The only thing that looked useful was an old ten-gallon cask standing against the wall. It gurgled when I shook it, probably hooch, and weighed about a hundred pounds. A metal band around its middle had a loop which could be attached to the rope. I returned to the hole and told Jeb about the cask. "How wide is the shaft halfway up?" I asked. "It's only about six feet across up here. You've got to be able to get past the barrel as you come up and it goes down."

"Try it. What have we got to lose?"

We had a lot to lose. If the rope broke, the barrel would land on Jeb and crush him. If the shaft wasn't wide enough, Jeb and the cask could get wedged in it. I rolled the heavy cask to the edge of the hole. I looped the rope around the stalagmite and tied the end to the cask. The stalagmite seemed as solid as a cement pillar.

"Are you ready, Jeb?"

"Fire away," said Jeb.

I pushed the cask into the hole and it dangled on the end of the rope as the rope tightened. I heard Jeb give a big "Woof" as the weight of the keg jerked him off his feet. Much to my relief the rope and the stalagmite held securely.

"Everything all right, Jeb?"

"Yes," grunted Jeb faintly.

"Now I'm going to pull you up bit by bit. Watch for the cask as it comes down."

I heaved on the rope and moved it a few inches. Even with the cask as a counterweight it was tough going. I pulled and strained, gaining a few inches at a time. It was exhausting, nerve-wracking work; I puffed and panted, inching the keg downward and Jeb upward. When Jeb got to the halfway mark the cask was apparently coming right down on his head, although it was too dark for me to see anything in the hole. He had to do quite a bit of manoeuvering and swearing in the narrow shaft to get by. Finally, inch by inch, he squeezed past. Once that critical stage had been passed, things went a little easier.

Then Jeb's head appeared in the opening. The cask reached the bottom before Jeb was completely to the top of the hole, and the last few feet were the most difficult. Jeb got his hands over the edge; with that help, I was able to flop him over the lip onto the floor of the cave. We both lay there several minutes, panting and exhausted. Roscoe danced around barking ecstatically.

Jeb was a mess. His face was gaunt and haggard; he was covered with mud and dirt from head to foot. In the eerie light of the cavern, he looked like an earth gnome from the underworld. When we had stopped panting, I untied the rope around his chest, and we staggered over to sit on a couple of packing boxes.

"I thought I was a goner," gasped Jeb. "How'd you get here?"

"Roscoe brought me." I briefly described Roscoe's remarkable performance. Jeb rubbed Roscoe's ears and the dog whimpered happily. "This is the second time he saved my life. See that scar on his face? He got that from a grizzly bear up north of Hinton. Gave me time to get away."

"What happened here, Jeb?"

"The floor of the cave just gave way and there I was."

"You weren't hurt?"

"I was shook up some. Landed on a pile of mud and stuff. Didn't even break the bottle I was holding. Been nipping on it ever since. It's been dry for some time though."

"How long have you been down there?"

"I don't know. What day is it?"

"Tuesday afternoon."

"I been there since Friday. I'd about given up hope. There was no way out below and the walls of the chimney are as hard and slick as glass."

"Was Roscoe here when you went down?"

"Yeah. In the cave but not beside me, so he didn't fall in. He whined around and I told him to get help. Didn't think he would. He came back a couple of times. Wonder where all he went."

I learned later some of the travels undertaken by this amazing dog. He had turned up at a ranch some five miles away and had been run off the place after a fierce battle with the resident dogs. He visited a small homestead and got chased away by the farmer. He had put on the performance, which had stopped me on the road, for at least three other cars without success. One fellow, thinking the dog was rabid, had taken a shot at him with a handgun, but fortunately missed.

"I'm going to have to get a block and tackle and pull up that keg of booze," said Jeb ruefully. "Here, let's celebrate." He wobbled over to a bottle by the still and poured us each a tin cup full of liquor. He also poured Roscoe one and set it on the ground.

"Does Roscoe drink that stuff?"

"Sure does. Loves it. He's as much a souse as I am. Ain't you, Roscoe?" Roscoe smiled happily and wagged his entire rear end.

The three of us drank gratefully.

"I guess you don't need to tell nobody about what happened, or about this place, huh?" said Jeb waving his hand at the still.

"Whatever you say, Jeb."

Roscoe finished his drink and wagged his tail for more. The liquor felt good; if I'd had a tail I'd have wagged it too.

"I guess you saved my life," said Jeb diffidently. "Thanks." He held out his hand and we shook.

"Don't thank me. Thank Roscoe."

When Roscoe heard me speak his name, he stalked over to me and put his head into my hand and licked my wrist.

"I'll be damned. Ain't never seen him do that with nobody before," said Jeb.

So that's how Roscoe and I established our present relationship. And I am mighty proud and honoured that Roscoe regards me as a friend.

Chapter Eighteen

POISONED RELATIONS

MANY OF GEORGE INGRAHAM's court cases were, of course, routine and dull; some were highly comedic, as befitted Blossom's penchant for the bizarre; but one case had overtones of tragedy. This latter case involved Jenny and Johnny Sweetgrass when they reappeared on the scene in Blossom.

Jenny stayed only a short time in Medicine Hat before returning to Calgary where she got a job as a waitress in the Sunshine Cafe on the presentation of Wong's letter. Shortly thereafter, a contrite and chastened Johnny returned to Jenny; he also got a job in the cafe, as a dishwasher. The two of them were getting by fairly well until Jenny became pregnant.

Meanwhile, Mr. Zarda, whose health was none too good, had been trying to run the farm with the help of an indolent hired hand who finally got so fed up with the irascible old man that he quit. Nobody else would take the job which left Zarda entirely on his own. His wife had died of cancer two years previously, not long after Jenny had eloped; many people in the district felt that Zarda's stubborn refusal to permit her to obtain medical attention, on religious grounds, had hastened her demise.

Fred Peters, prodded by his wife Audrey, undertook to try to work out a reconciliation between Zarda and the young couple, which seemed to be the only solution to both their problems. Fred drove out to the farm for a talk with Mr. Zarda, where he was subjected to a rambling diatribe on economics, the stupidity of governments, the laziness of hired hands, the perfidy of Indians and filial ingratitude. When Fred first raised the suggestion that Jenny and Johnny be permitted to return to the farm, the old man nearly hit the roof. Fred retained his composure and kept quietly trying to get Zarda to change his mind. Fred found that he didn't get anywhere appealing to Zarda's conscience or paternal responsibilities. What finally won the day was the practical approach on how Zarda was going to survive on the farm by himself. Fred left with the grudging agreement that Jenny and Johnny could return. Fred was by no means sanguine that things would work out satisfactorily, but felt it was worth a try.

Fred communicated with Jenny and Johnny and later drove to Calgary to return with them and their scanty belongings. The two young people accepted the proposition with considerable reluctance, but they really had no practical alternative. The household settled into a regimen much like an armed camp, but it did hang together. Jenny ran the household and Johnny worked on the farm to Zarda's carping instructions.

Mr. Zarda's health continued to deteriorate until he finally died. The post-mortem finding was that he had died of lead poisoning. The police undertook an investigation which culminated in Johnny being charged with murder.

The town was deeply shocked. No crocodile tears were shed for Mr. Zarda – the consensus being that his departure was good riddance. However, the moral dilemma of balancing wrong against justification kept the rumour and gossip mills bubbling and seething all during the pre-trial period. There seemed no doubt that most of the sympathy of the town rested with Johnny.

As the date of the trial approached, Jenny and her baby moved into town to stay with Fred and Audrey Peters, who did their best to keep her spirits up. George Ingraham accepted the role of defence attorney; Cyril Thorndyke acted for the prosecution. The case was heard by Judge Broome in the courtroom of the Embassy.

Cyril, in his opening remarks, outlined the case against Johnny, which certainly sounded pretty damning. He said he would show by the coroner's report that there was no doubt that Mr. Zarda had died of lead poisoning; that a bottle of lead salts had been found in the Zarda barn bearing the fingerprints of the defendant;

that there was animosity between Mr. Zarda and the defendant; and that the defendant had threatened Mr. Zarda's life. He pointed out that, whereas three adults and a baby lived on the farm, only one of them, Mr. Zarda, had been poisoned, which ruled out accidental ingestion. He emphasized that, although the evidence was circumstantial, no one other than the defendant had the motive, opportunity and means to have committed the crime.

George did not present an outline of the defence beyond emphasizing and re-emphasizing, that in a case relying upon circumstantial evidence, the prosecution must prove beyond a shadow of a doubt that no other explanation than that put forward was possible. He said he would raise such doubts. As far as Judge Broome was concerned, this peroration must have been a case of George teaching his grandmother to suck eggs.

The first witness called by the prosecution was the coroner, Dr. Strickland, a tall, thin man with a shock of white hair, an acidulous mouth and a clipped, precise manner of speech. He indicated that the deceased had died of chronic lead poisoning, giving medical and scientific evidence in support of his findings.

George began his cross-examination rather cautiously. "Dr. Strickland, I do not question your diagnosis that Mr. Zarda died of lead poisoning. But it is my understanding that poisoning by lead over a considerable period of time is an insidious disease wherein a small amount of the chemical may be ingested or inhaled until it reaches toxic levels."

"That is correct."

"The lead may come from a variety of sources, apparently innocuous, such as paints, dusts, sprays, ceramic vessels and lead pipes. Is that correct?"

"Yes, sir."

"Have you explored these possibilities?"

"Yes, sir. The few water pipes in the household are of cast iron. Furthermore, the important fact to be kept in mind is that all members of the family used the same water and utensils, yet only Mr. Zarda developed plumbism."

"You have examined the other members of the household for lead poisoning?"

"Yes, sir. They show no evidence of such toxicity."

"I understand that Mrs. Zarda, wife of the deceased, died some two years ago, presumably of cancer. Could her death have been caused by lead poisoning?"

"No, sir. I have examined the autopsy report and other relative documents, and there is no doubt that Mrs. Zarda died of cancer."

"Would it not have been possible that Mrs. Zarda suffered from lead poisoning, the symptoms of which were obscured by the cancer?"

"No, sir. Some of the symptoms of lead poisoning, such as the black line along the gingival margin, would be readily apparent."

"Could not such evidence have been missed in view of the preoccupation of the examiner with the cancer syndrome?"

"It is very unlikely. But no human action is infallible."

"Thank you. Now let us return to other possible sources of accidental contamination, such as paints, dusts, sprays, fumes, and so forth."

"We found no such source which could be implicated."

"There have even been, I understand, poisonings from deposits of lead in the caecum, arising from shotgun pellets in birds which had been eaten."

"I am familiar with such cases. No such deposits were found."

"There have also been poisonings arising from distillation of home-brew in stills containing lead, such as car radiators."

"That is true. We found no such device."

"Since you searched so diligently for other sources of contamination, you must have been dissatisfied with the basis of the prosecution."

"We undertook to rule out any possible adventitious contamination."

"The fact that you found none does not eliminate the possibility that it exists, however."

"No."

"Thank you." George turned to the judge. "That concludes my questioning at the present time, m'lord, although I may wish to recall Dr. Strickland to the stand later."

Cyril Thorndyke next called forward two witnesses, a police officer who reported finding a bottle of lead acetate in the Zarda barn, and a fingerprint expert who testified that Johnny's fingerprints had been identified on the bottle. George did not question either witness.

Cyril then called to the stand Homer Patterson, a neighbour of the Zardas. Homer was a scrawny man in his fifties with a knobby, bald head and teeth blackened by constant use of chewing tobacco. His shiny black suit of outmoded style might have been purchased for his wedding thirty years ago, when he weighed twenty pounds heavier. He did not appear to be at all intimidated by the situation in which he found himself; he spoke in a forceful, rasping voice.

When Homer had been sworn in, Cyril began his questioning. "Mr. Patterson, where do you reside?"

"On a farm six miles out."

"Where is your farm with respect to that of the late Mr. Zarda?"

"Right next to it."

"So you knew Mr. Zarda for many years?"

"Yes."

"How did you get along with Mr. Zarda?"

"Not very good."

"Why not?"

" 'Cause he was a cantankerous old bastard who didn't get along with nobody."

"Did you, over the years, have a number of acrimonious exchanges with him?"

"How's that?"

"Did you have rows with him?"

"Yeah, I sure did. He wasn't too bad up until his wife died, but after that he got meaner than ever as he got sicker – almost crazy-like. Everytime we met, he had his tail in a knot about something – fences, or weeds or irrigation ditches or something. If he didn't have nothing else to fuss about, he set about trying to save my soul. So I kept away from him as much as possible."

"Is it fair to say that you detested Mr. Zarda?"

"Well, I don't know about that. I didn't like him." Homer leaned forward with his jaw outthrust. "But that don't mean that I killed him."

Cyril was somewhat taken aback by this response. He held up his hand. "No one is suggesting for a moment that you did, Mr. Patterson. But you have indicated that Mr. Zarda didn't get along with you or anybody else. How did he get along with Johnny Sweetgrass, his son-in-law, and defendant in this case?"

"I must object, m'lord," interposed George.

"Sustained," said the judge.

"Do you know Johnny Sweetgrass well?" asked Cyril.

"Yes. Since he moved onto the Zarda farm next door I've got to know him real well. He's a good, hard-working boy and Zarda treated him very bad. Very unfair. Johnny often came over in the evening, particularly when the situation got unbearable-like, and we'd sit around and chew the rag and have a drink together. That's another thing about Zarda – he was death on booze."

"So you've had a number of discussions with the defendant?"

"Yes. I just said so, didn't I?"

"Did you discuss the situation in the Zarda household and his relationship with Mr. Zarda?"

"Well, uh, yes."

"What were the bones of contention between Mr. Zarda and the defendant?"

Homer paused for a moment. "Well, them things are kind of private and confidential." He turned to the judge. "Do I have to tell them things, sir?"

"Yes, you do," said Judge Broome. "Just what was said, not your interpretation of the situation or of the matters discussed."

"Well, alright, if I have to," said Homer reluctantly. "For one thing, Zarda never forgave Johnny for marrying his daughter, 'cause he was an Indian. Zarda never let up on Johnny for being an Indian and kept making snide remarks about it – as if Johnny could do anything about it. Another thing was that Johnny is a Catholic and Zarda kept trying to convert him to his religion. Johnny kept quiet most of the time and didn't say nothing, but once in a while Zarda would get under his skin and Johnny would blow up and they'd have a big row. Then he'd come over to see me to let off steam."

"Why didn't Johnny leave, if things were so intolerable?"

"He did a couple of times, but he came back because of his kid. He didn't have no place to take his wife and kid and didn't have no way of making a living, so he was stuck with Zarda if he wanted to keep his family together. He just tried to put up with things, but it wasn't easy."

"Why did Mr. Zarda permit Johnny and his family to remain on his farm if he found their presence so disquieting?"

"Well, he needed Jenny to run the house and to look after him as he got sicker, and he needed Johnny to run the farm. And another thing, the old man was just crazy about his little grandson. He just loved the kid, and would play with him and talk to him for hours. That kind of caused some trouble too, 'cause Zarda was sort of jealous of Johnny about the kid. Funny, huh?"

"The defendant told you these things?"

"Yes."

"What else did he tell you relative to his relations with Mr. Zarda?"

"Johnny worked awful hard on the farm, but everything he did Zarda found fault with it and kept hinting that he was a good-for-nothing Indian."

"The defendant resented this abuse?"

"Of course. Wouldn't you?"

"Would you say that the defendant hated Mr. Zarda?"

"Objection, m'lord," said George.

"Sustained," ruled the judge.

"Did the defendant ever say to you that he hated Mr. Zarda?" asked Cyril.

"Not that I can recall. Not in so many words."

"Did the defendant ever say to you that he intended to kill Mr. Zarda?"

"Well, uh, yes, he did," admitted Homer. "But he didn't mean it. He was just letting off steam. He was mad 'cause he'd asked the old man for some money and he refused because he said Johnny would just use it to buy booze and get drunk. You see, Zarda would give money to Jenny for herself and the kid, but he wouldn't give Johnny any wages. That wasn't fair and Johnny got mad, but he didn't really mean it."

"Never mind your interpretations. Just answer my question. Did the defendant ever say that he intended to kill Mr. Zarda?"

"Yes, he did. But he didn't mean it."

"What were his exact words?"

"Uh, uh. He said, 'Someday I'll kill the old son of a bitch.' But he didn't mean it."

"But he did say it."

"Yes."

"Thank you. Your witness, counsellor." Cyril bowed to George.

George rose to his feet. "Now, Mr. Patterson, further to your conversations with the defendant, did you believe that the defendant was serious in his comments about killing Mr. Zarda?"

"Objection, m'lord," said Cyril.

"Sustained," said the judge.

"But his comments were made in a moment of exasperation and frustration, were they not?"

"That's right."

"It was not a serious, calculated threat?"

"No."

"In your discussions with Mr. Sweetgrass, did he ever express sympathy for Mr. Zarda?"

"Yeah. He felt sorry for him being sick all the time and thought that was why he was so ornery."

"So, instead of expressing hatred for Mr. Zarda, he expressed some affection for him?"

"Well, uh, I wouldn't go that far, to be truthful, but he did say he was sorry for him being so sick."

"When did Mr. Zarda begin to fail in health?"

"It was after his wife died, about two years ago, that he started to go downhill. He was very upset by his wife's death and because Jenny had run off with Johnny. He disowned Jenny and wouldn't have nothing to do with her."

"But he did relent in his attitude and accepted them into his home."

"Yeah, when Jenny got in the family way and they didn't have no place to go, he took them in."

"Then he must have had some deep affection for them which he hid behind a cantankerous façade?"

"No, not really, I'm afraid, to be very honest."

"Did Mr. Zarda ever go to a doctor about his ill health?"

"No. He didn't believe in doctors. Part of his religion. Jenny and Johnny tried to get him to go, and so did I, but he wouldn't. He said it was the will of the Lord. He prayed a lot, but it didn't do no good. Praying is okay for things you don't really need. He should have went to a doctor."

"You said Johnny tried to get him to go to see a doctor?"

"Yeah. Him and Jenny both, but the old man was as stubborn as a mule."

"It would seem unlikely that Johnny would do that if he were administering poison to Mr. Zarda, would it not?"

"I must object, m'lord," interrupted Cyril. "The question calls for a conclusion by the witness."

"The objection is sustained."

"Thank you, Mr. Patterson. That is all, m'lord," concluded George.

After Mr. Patterson had been dismissed, Cyril indicated that he had no further witnesses to introduce. George then called on Johnny to take the stand. Johnny was a good-looking young man with typical Indian features of high cheekbones and straight black hair; he was dressed in blue denims and a white silk shirt with a yellow kerchief at the neck. His manner was subdued, but by no means cowed; he held his head proudly as he gazed at the court.

When the swearing-in procedure had been completed, George began his questioning in a quiet voice. "Johnny, did you kill Mr. Zarda?"

"No."

"Did you at any time give Mr. Zarda any poison?"

"No."

"The prosecution has entered into evidence a bottle of lead acetate, called Sugar of Lead, which was found on a shelf in the barn and which carries your fingerprints. How do you account for those fingerprints?"

"I guess I picked it up and moved it. I don't remember."

"Did you ever remove any material from the bottle?"

"No."

"What was your attitude towards Mr. Zarda? Did you feel sorry for him?"

"Yes. He was old man, very sick."

"But sometimes Mr. Zarda could be very irritating, I gather?"

"Yes. He was mean. Talk a lot."

"What was your reaction? What would you do?"

"Most time I keep quiet. Not talk. Sometimes he make me mad and I holler at him. Then we have a fight."

"What was it about you that he resented? Was it because you are an Indian and a Catholic?"

"Yes. He was mad because Jenny marry an Indian."

"But you are part white, are you not?"

"Yes. My grandfather white. I'm proud of Indian blood. Not proud of white blood."

"I can't say I can fault you on either count. Were you satisfied with the arrangement whereby you and your family lived on the farm in exchange for your work?"

"Yes, pretty good saw-off. But he should have paid me some."

"So, as I understand it, you were reasonably satisfied with the arrangement and were prepared to accept philosophically his ill temper because he was old and sick, although he did sometimes provoke you into an argument. Is that right?"

"Yes."

"Did you ever say to Mr. Patterson that you would kill Mr. Zarda?"

"Yes. One time. Just shooting mouth off."

"So you did not mean it, literally?"

"No. Just talking big. What Mr. Patterson call letting off steam."

"Thank you. You may enquire, Mr. Thorndyke."

Cyril rose to his feet and went up and down on his toes a few times before beginning his questioning. "Mr. Sweetgrass, you said you are proud to be an Indian?"

"Yes."

"A worthy and appropriate attitude. But you are not proud of your white blood. Why is that?"

"White man not respect Indian."

"Therefore, you would resent deeply and bitterly Mr. Zarda's denigration of you as an Indian?"

Johnny looked puzzled. "I don't understand."

"Were you mad at Mr. Zarda when he ran you down as an Indian?"

"Yes."

"You disliked Mr. Zarda intensely?"

"Yes, not like him."

"In other words you hated him."

"Not hate him, but not like him."

"What's the difference between hate and dislike intensely?"

"If you hate someone, you want bad things to happen to him; if you not like, you don't care – just shrug."

Cyril became somewhat more forceful. "Come, come, Mr. Sweetgrass, you would have us believe that Mr. Zarda could show contempt for you – a proud Indian – about your heritage, could run down your religion, could refuse you just wages for your work, could belittle your efforts on the farm, and you would not hate him?"

"Not hate. Not like."

"You did threaten to kill him, did you not?"

"Not threaten him. I blow off steam to Mr. Patterson. That's all."

"You did have rows with Mr. Zarda where you shouted and hollered at one another?"

"Sometimes. Not very often."

"In view of your threat on Mr. Zarda's life, your deep and understandable dislike for him, if not hate, your shouting altercations, is it not conceivable that in the heat of the moment you would kill Mr. Zarda? I submit to you that that was indeed what happened."

George rose quickly to his feet. "I would point out, m'lord, that the allegation against Mr. Sweetgrass is not based upon a 'heat of the moment' episode, but upon a poisoning over a considerable period of time."

"The heat of the moment could have triggered such a plan," replied Cyril.

"A fatuous contention. With respect," said George contemptuously.

Cyril glared at George before turning back to Johnny. "Mr. Sweetgrass, you would be aware that your wife, as next of kin, would inherit her father's farm which would leave you sitting pretty, would you not?"

"I not understand those things."

"I find that difficult to believe." Johnny just shrugged his shoulders. Cyril shuffled through some papers in front of him. "Now, Mr. Sweetgrass, a bottle of Sugar of Lead, bearing your fingerprints was found in the Zarda barn. I understand that solutions of lead acetate or preparations such as Goulard's Extract and Goulard's Solution, containing lead acetate, are frequently used to treat bruises, strained tendons and superficial inflammatory conditions in livestock, so I presume you are familiar with the chemical?"

"Yes, I seen it used on horses for sore legs."

"You are therefore aware of the poisonous nature of Sugar of Lead?"

"I guess so. Got skull on label."

"So you would be aware that if a small amount were administered over a long period of time, the effect would be to produce death without probability of detection?"

"I not think about it."

"But you were aware that Sugar of Lead was poisonous?"

"Yes."

"That is all, m'lord." Cyril seated himself with an air of satisfaction.

In response to questions by the judge, Cyril and George indicated that they had no further presentations to make. The judge thereupon adjourned the hearings until ten o'clock the following morning and instructed Cyril to be ready to present his summation at that time.

When court had adjourned, George met with Johnny in a small consulting room near the courtroom. Johnny was looking dejected and discouraged.

"You did very well on the stand, Johnny," said George, trying to cheer him up.

Johnny slouched in his chair. "Won't do no good. They going to hang me. No way Indian get justice in white man's court."

"I assure you that's not true, Johnny. You will get the same treatment as any white man would get. Judge Broome is a very fair and just man."

"That Mr. Thorndyke, he really hate me."

"No, he doesn't. He's just doing his job. He's supposed to bring out the evidence against you. It's my job to bring out the evidence in your favour, which I shall do tomorrow morning. The prosecution must prove its case beyond a shadow of a doubt and I am sure I can raise sufficient doubts. But I would like to do more than that and get you cleared of the charge, so the stigma will not haunt you the rest of your life."

"You don't think I done it, do you?" asked Johnny, with a searching look into George's eyes.

"No, I don't, Johnny. And I have the feeling that I'm missing something obvious somewhere along the line. Lead poisoning is such an insidious thing that it could arise from any one of a multitude of sources, though I must say Dr. Strickland was very efficient in ruling out all those I could think of." George paused for a moment. "Did Mr. Zarda have a favorite cup or mug or jug that he used all the time?"

"No."

"Well, let's go through the daily regimen on the farm once again, Johnny. I know we've done it before, but let's try it again. The problem is that Zarda apparently did everything the same as everyone else in the household – same food, same drink, same utensils, same routine. We've got to find something he did differently from the rest of you where he could have picked up that lead."

"We all do same things."

"Did he chew tobacco or smoke?"

"No."

"Is it possible he had a whisky still and you didn't know it."

"No, he didn't drink whisky. Said booze was instrument of the devil. If he'd had a still, I'd of knowed."

"Well, let's start a usual day. Who got up first?"

"He did. Even when he very sick. He go to kitchen, get

things started and then bang on my door. He always get up first, so he could say I'm lazy."

"What did he do when he got up? Wash his teeth?"

Johnny laughed. "Naw, he never wash his teeth in his life. First thing, he pump water and drink two glasses of water. Said best way to start day. Health thing – wash out stomach. Then he make fire, put water on for coffee, make porridge and call me, 'Get up, lazy Indian.' "

"What did you have for breakfast?"

"Porridge, eggs, bread – sometimes meat and potatoes."

"You all ate the same things on the same kind of dishes?"

"Yes."

"Then after breakfast you went about your respective chores. What did you do and what did he do?" George paused for a moment with his mouth hanging open. "Hey, wait a minute." He sat for a further period of time in deep thought. Then he leaped to his feet and dashed out the door, leaving a surprised and startled Johnny.

The next morning, the opening of court was delayed several minutes, much to Cyril's annoyance. He shuffled his papers and glanced ostentatiously from time to time at his watch. George finally entered hurriedly, carrying some documents. The clerk reported to the judge that the lawyers were in place and Judge Broome entered with a frigid look in George's direction.

As soon as the judge was seated, George rose. "M'lord, I must crave the indulgence of the court on a most important matter."

"Yes, Mr. Ingraham, what is it?" growled the judge in obvious ill humour.

"I must petition the court for permission to present some additional evidence which has come to my attention since our adjournment yesterday."

Cyril leaped to his feet. "I must object, m'lord. This is most irregular. The defence had completed its submission and I have already prepared my summation based on that evidence."

"I realize that my proposal is irregular, m'lord, but I give you my assurance that this evidence is crucial to the proper resolution of this case. I must emphasize, m'lord, that a man's life hangs in the balance here, and every effort must be made to make certain that justice is obtained."

"You assure us that this evidence was not known to you yesterday?" asked the judge.

"That is correct, m'lord. Indeed, some of the vital information was not made known to me until this morning, a few minutes ago – which is why I was slightly late entering court, for which I apologize."

"I accept the proposition that in a situation where a man's life is in jeopardy, every opportunity must be provided for his protection. On your assurance that the evidence is new and was unknown to you yesterday and that the information is crucial to the proper resolution of this case, I would be inclined to permit its presentation at this time. Do you object, Mr. Thorndyke?"

"I find the situation annoying and disconcerting," replied Cyril petulantly, "but in view of the assurances of my learned friend, I am prepared to go along with it."

"Thank you, gentlemen," said George with a sigh of relief. "I wish to call one new witness and to recall one previous witness. I also crave the indulgence of my esteemed colleague even further in requesting that he withhold cross-examination until both witnesses have been heard. The reason for this request is to enable me to connect up and correlate certain apparently disparate pieces of information."

"I have gone part way, so I might as well humour my friend completely in his manoeuvers," said Cyril ungraciously.

"Very well," said the judge. "Mr. Ingraham, you may proceed."

"Thank you, m'lord. The new witness I wish to present is Jenny Sweetgrass, wife of the accused. I should add, m'lord, that the information is so recent that I have not had an opportunity to inform the witness of this possibility nor to brief her on the tenor of my inquiries."

"You realize, Mr. Ingraham," said the judge, "that a wife cannot be required to testify against her husband, but if she is placed on the stand by the defence, she will be subject to cross-examination."

"I am aware of that, m'lord."

George walked across the courtroom to escort Jenny to the witness stand. Jenny looked appalled and frightened at this sudden development. She handed her baby to Audrey Peters beside her and made her way to the floor of the courtroom. George placed a hand under her arm as they walked forward, whispering in her ear, "You've nothing to be afraid of, Jenny. Just answer the questions I shall ask you." She responded to the swearing-in procedure in a tiny, nervous voice.

"Now, Jenny," George began, "you needn't be apprehensive. I have just a few questions to ask you. Please tell us, when your mother was alive and you were living at home, who in the household got up first in the morning?"

"Mamma did."

"What did she do when she first got up?"

"She started the breakfast, and then called Poppa and me."

"What was the very first thing she did when she got up?"

"Well she, uh, uh, went out to the privy."

"And after that?"

"She washed her hands and face."

"She pumped water out of the hand pump in the kitchen and washed herself?"

"Yes."

"Then she continued making breakfast and called you and your father?"

"Yes."

"What was the first thing your father did when he came into the kitchen?"

"In the kitchen? He always drank two glasses of water and then went out to the privy."

"Now, when you and your husband moved back to the farm, who got up first in the morning?"

"Poppa."

"Did he continue his custom of drinking two glasses of water as soon as he entered the kitchen?"

"Yes. He said it was good for him."

"Thank you, Jenny. That is all. You may return to your seat."

A puzzled Jenny returned to her place beside Audrey Peters. Audrey handed the baby to Jenny and patted her on the shoulder, whispering some words of encouragement in her ear.

George addressed himself to the bench. "M'lord, before calling my next witness, I wish to present a brief preamble in order to get the time factors clearly before us, so that the evidence presented by the witness can be appreciated.

"As your Lordship is no doubt aware, a farm family tends to develop a routine which, through custom, becomes quite rigidly adhered to. In the twenty or so years during which the Zardas lived on the farm, it was the custom in the household that Mrs. Zarda rose first in the morning and pumped water from the hand pump in the kitchen in order to perform her ablutions. She then proceeded to begin breakfast before calling the others.

"Approximately two and a half years ago, Jenny eloped with Johnny Sweetgrass, which led to an estrangement with her father. No doubt the morning routine on the farm continued as before, although Mr. Zarda may have taken to rising first as Mrs. Zarda became increasingly ill. When Mrs. Zarda died of cancer two years ago, the rift between Jenny and her father was healed and she and her husband moved back to the farm. Her baby was born shortly thereafter. As you have heard, Mr. Zarda rose first in the morning ing and continued a routine of drinking two glasses of water before beginning the preparation of breakfast and calling the others.

"Now, m'lord, I would like to recall Dr. Strickland to the stand."

When Dr. Strickland had taken his place in the witness box, the judge spoke to him. "Dr. Strickland, you are still under oath." He turned to George. "You may proceed, Mr. Ingraham."

"Before beginning with my questioning," said George, "I must introduce an exhibit." George made a signal to a policeman at the side door, who thereupon pushed into the courtroom a trolley bearing an old hand-operated water pump.

The crowd whispered and shuffled as they craned their necks to get a look at this unexpected piece of evidence; they continued their whispered speculations until Judge Broome banged his gavel for silence.

Cyril rose to his feet. "M'lord," he declaimed, "I must protest this dramatic grandstanding by my learned friend. This exhibit could have been introduced earlier."

"Well, it's here now, so let's go along with it," growled the judge.

George turned to the witness box. "Dr. Strickland, would you kindly identify this exhibit please."

"It is the hand pump from the Zarda kitchen. I went with you last evening to the Zarda farm and removed this pump."

"Dr. Strickland, before removing the pump from the house, did you run certain tests on the water from it?"

"Yes, I did."

"Would you explain to the court the nature of those tests?"

"The pump had not been touched for two days, because Mrs. Sweetgrass is residing with friends in the town during the course of this trial. At your suggestion, I carefully pumped about two tumblers of water from the pump."

"Did you run some chemical tests on that water?"

"Yes, I did. The water contained 1.25 milligrams percent of lead for a total of approximately 3 milligrams in the two tumblerfuls."

"Would that be sufficient, if taken daily over a considerable period of time, to produce lead poisoning?"

"Yes, it would. Definitely."

"Did you run further tests on the water from the pump?"

"Yes, I did. After pumping the residual water from the pump, I pumped further water and tested it. There was no detectable lead in the water."

"How do you account for this difference between the residual water and the fresh water?"

"When the pump is left overnight, a certain amount of water remains in a chamber within the pump as a primer. I removed and examined that chamber. It is lead-lined to make it watertight. Therefore, water left sitting in that chamber overnight would absorb a significant amount of lead, while water passing through it thereafter would not. Thus, a person drinking the residual water would receive a toxic dose of lead, while others during the course of the day would not."

George turned to the judge. "M'lord, you have heard evidence that it was Mr. Zarda's custom to drink two glasses of water from that pump first thing in the morning, thereby imbibing a toxic quantity of lead, while others of the household drinking from the same pump later on were not poisoned. Dr. Strickland has provided the explanation for this paradox.

"Your Lordship, I respectfully suggest that the charge against Mr. Sweetgrass be withdrawn." George seated himself with a flourish of his robes.

The judge looked towards Cyril. "What do you say, Mr. Thorndyke?"

"I happily concur, Your Lordship," said Cyril. He bowed gravely to George. "And may I congratulate my esteemed colleague on his acumen which has led to this happy denouement, and which has saved this court from the ugly possibility of a grave miscarriage of justice."

"I share your sentiments, Counsellor," said the judge. He turned his eyes to Johnny. "Mr. Sweetgrass, the charge against you has been withdrawn. You are free to go."

Jenny let out a squeal, and, with her baby in her arms, ran across the room to Johnny where the three of them embraced, laughing and crying.

There wasn't a dry eye in the room.

Chapter Nineteen

SERENADE

ONE EVENING IN LATE SEPTEMBER, I was fortifying myself at Wong Toy's restaurant with a cup of coffee before going back to my chilly room at the Palaza Hotel. It was nearly midnight and Wong and I had the restaurant to ourselves. I always enjoyed talking to Wong as he was a delightful chap with a nice sense of humour. He wasn't exactly a gourmet cook, but since his only competition was the Buffalo Grill in the Palaza Hotel – where the cooking was terrible – he had a loyal clientele which made his place the principal social hangout of the town.

Wong was fussing around getting ready to close up when George Ingraham and Jeb Wilson came tramping in. They had been out duck hunting all day and the two of them had obviously taken on a snootful of Jeb's famous moonshine. Jeb was always in a partially looped state, but George as a rule didn't drink very much.

"I hope you two weren't in the condition you are now when you were hunting, or it's a wonder you didn't shoot each other," I said reprovingly. There is an unwritten law amongst hunters that nobody drinks during a shoot.

"Certainly not," said George, ordering coffee by holding up two fingers to Wong. "We just took enough to keep the chill off, but after the evening flight we sort of got into the sauce. Come to think of it, I believe I feel a severe chill coming on again. Don't you, Jeb?"

"Yeah," grinned Jeb. "I got a real bad chill. Brrr." He

shivered in an exaggerated fashion, rubbing his hands together briskly.

"For medicinal purposes only, I prescribe a tot of Dr. Wilson's magic elixir," said George. He rummaged around in the back of his hunting jacket and brought out an unlabelled bottle which he set on the counter. "Jeb drew off a new batch yesterday; there it is in all its puissant beauty." He held his hands over the bottle in a gesture of blessing.

"No, no," cried Wong in alarm. "Mountie go by. See bottle and stick me in hoosegow. You come." He hurried to the door, locked it and turned the lights out. "You come," he repeated, leading us out to his immaculate kitchen. He cleared off a table and set three chairs around it. "Now, okay," he explained with a cheerful grin. "Plivate party."

"Hey, this is real cozy," said George, setting the bottle in the middle of the table. The big old coal stove sent out a cheerful warmth which felt good on a chilly night. Wong brought an armful of assorted soft drinks and set out three glasses. "Hey, you only brought three glasses," said George. "Aren't you going to join us, Wong? Come on, chum, you're a prime and amiable candidate to become a member of our fraternity of happy inebriates."

"Sure, Wong," said Jeb, "I can say in all modesty that my version of usquebaugh has it all over sam suey."

"Okay," said Wong. "Work all done. Now have good time." He placed another glass on the table.

George poured a generous portion of Jeb's liquor into the glasses, and we each selected a diluent from the array of pop bottles. George lifted his glass. "Here's to us; good people are scarce." The three of us raised our glasses and joined in the toast. Even well-diluted, Jeb's brew burned all the way down.

George and Jeb began a confused account of their hunt that day which apparently had been highly successful. George was always a great talker and a gifted raconteur. Jeb, on the other hand, was usually a rather taciturn individual, although given to quoting salty Western maxims, some of which were common parlance in the district but many of which were, as far as I know, original aphorisms of his own. However, on this occasion Jeb was in just the right stage of inebriety to be loquacious. The discussion about their day of hunting led to the recounting of other hunting tales. Jeb told us a hilarious story about a rancher up the Cariboo Trail near the 70 Mile House who was out hunting with an old muzzleloader and got so excited he shot away his ramrod. George recounted a case where he had defended a client who had shot a prize bull, thinking it was an elk. I told them about the time I had shot at a grouse on the wing, missed and killed a crow sitting in a tree. From time to time, we replenished our glasses with liberal dollops of Jeb's moonshine whisky. I have a low tolerance for alcohol, and although I had started well behind the other two, I caught up to them in short order. Jeb was accustomed to carrying a heavy load so seemed little different from his normal state; George betrayed his condition by an exaggerated precision of movement, an excited glitter in his eyes and a tendency to "sh" his esses when he talked. Wong's smile got wider and wider, until his almond eyes practically disappeared.

Without any warning, Jeb stood up suddenly and launched off on a rendition of *Casey at the Bat*, complete with demonstrations of batting and pitching and with explanatory interpolations. At Jeb's direction, the rest of us, including Wong, provided the crowd noises at appropriate places in the story. Where he had learned the piece, I haven't the faintest idea. We gave him a big hand when he finished. Jeb bowed and shook his hands over his head. Not to be outdone, I got on my feet to recite my ribald version of *The Stag at Eve* which I had learned in high school. George then got up and declaimed a piece of poetry entirely in Latin which he said was written by Virgil. Since none of the rest of us understood a word he said, our reaction was rather restrained. George was somewhat miffed at our lack of response. We all had another drink.

At this point Wong got to his feet, lifted his glass, and began a lengthy dissertation which he presented with eloquence and fervour – entirely in Chinese. We were fascinated. We nodded solemnly from time to time to show we were in complete agreement. When he laughed cheerily, we joined him, gauging the degree of our response by the level of his merriment; when he spoke with great seriousness and pounded the table, we frowned and shook our heads sadly at the gravity of the situation. When he finished his discourse, we cheered and clapped. Wong shook his hands over his head in imitation of Jeb and did a little dance.

"It was a hell of a lot better than Vergil," I said to George.

"I regretfully agree," said George.

George suddenly sat up straight, glanced at his watch, and held up his hands in horror. "Great balls of fire," he cried. "I just remembered I was supposed to take Mamie over to the Peters' place tonight. She'll kill me."

"Angly woman heap bad medicine," said Wong.

"What do you mean, 'heap bad medicine' – that's Indian language," said George. "That's no way for a Chinaman to talk. Yellow man speak with a forked tongue."

"Me learn that from Chief Eagle," explained Wong. Chief Eagle was an Indian who came to town quite frequently and hung around the restaurant.

"Anyhow, he's sure as hell right," said George. "Boy, oh boy, will I be in the doghouse tomorrow!"

"The only way for a married man not to get in the doghouse," said Jeb ponderously, "is not to marry a lady dog to start with." He paused. "I guess that goes for single men too."

"Man who kick lady dog get bit," said Wong.

"Did Confucius say that?" I asked.

"No. Wong say that," replied Wong proudly.

"Wong, you have the happy faculty of getting to the nub of things with a statement that is cogent and pithy," said George.

"Yes, velly pithy," said Wong. "Go pithy now." And he went out the back door.

"Our rapport with the mysterious East seems to have come unstuck somehow," said George, looking at the door with puzzled eyes. "Oh well, it's too late to do anything about Mamie now, so let's make a night of it. Here's to doghouses and the poor benighted males who inhabit them." He held up his glass.

"That brings to mind a significant question," I said. "When are you going to marry Mamie and let her make an honest man of you?"

To my surprise George didn't respond with his usual offhand dismissal of the subject. "I've thought about it," he said slowly.

He mused for a few moments, then banged his glass down on the table. "Nope, can't afford it right now."

"If everyone waited till they could afford to get married, the race would die out," I stated. "Anyhow, certainly you can afford to get married. In your program to get established in the community, you have made giant strides in the short time you have been here." I held up my hand and counted on my fingers. "You are President of the Board of Trade; you are the star of the baseball team; your handling of the 'Venetian Affair' has won you the reputation of a legal wizard; you are responsible for the building of the Embassy. You –"

"I'm just a run-of-the-mill genius," interrupted George with a gesture of modesty.

I continued enumerating on my fingers. "You've been accepted by such diverse characters as Mrs. Frobisher and Flossy Macabee. You've even received the stamp of approval from Roscoe, and that's got to be the acid test with a low pH. While I hate to introduce a crass factor into romance, there's only one step remaining to integrate you fully into the community. You know what it is?"

"I can guess," growled George.

"Marry a local girl." I leaned back with an air of dignified authority which was negated to some extent by dropping my glass in my lap. I poured myself another drink.

"Mamie is a beautiful and lovely gal," contributed Jeb. "You'd be lucky."

George scratched his chin. "You're right. But I dunno." He turned to Wong, who had returned from his trip outside. "What do you think, Wong. Are you married?"

"Yep. Me here, wife in China. Work velly good."

"A splendid arrangement," nodded George. "I predict a long and felicitous nuptiality."

"Don't change the subject," I admonished. George was in such a receptive frame of mind, I had no intention of letting him off the hook.

George gnawed at his lower lip. "I admit, that, like all males, I have given some philosophical consideration to the proposition of marriage but I have been offput by the malefic characteristics of many women. Some are asps who practice asperity; some are bitches who practice femininity. But –" he held up his hand, "there is a very small group who are angels. I always said I wouldn't marry until I found an angel. Mind you, I hasten to add, I never said I would marry if I found one, but I wouldn't if I didn't. Did that come out right?"

"Legal nit-picking," I snorted.

"Anyhow," continued George, "my present dilemma is that, by all evidence, tests and corroborative data, Mamie is an angel – and beautiful to boot. I'm hoist with my own petard."

"You are indeed," I agreed. "Incidentally, I don't want to tell tales out of school, but I've noticed that Corporal Rankin has been hanging around Mamie quite a bit lately, and he's a handsome young fellow who would be a tough competition for a bony scarecrow like you. You've been mighty careless about this courtship, I must say. As a lover, you've got to be the Great Canadian Dingbat. If you wait any longer, you may be too late." This was a lie, but then all's fair in love and war, I told myself. "You've said you wouldn't marry until you found one of the rare species of feminine angels. You've admitted that Mamie is an angel, and beautiful to boot. What are you waiting for?"

George looked startled. "What indeed?" he said banging his fist on the table.

"The time to shoot bears is when there's bears around," said Jeb, also banging his fist on the table.

"Let's go and propose right now," I pressed. "Jeb and I will come along to support you. Let's strike while the fat is in the fire."

"Good idea," said George, banging the table again. "We'll do it!"

Wong unlocked the door to let us out and wished us good luck in our mission. The three of us set off somewhat unsteadily to propose to Mamie on George's behalf. It was a crisp, sparkling night with a full moon bright enough to read by. Quite frankly, the rest of the evening is something of a blur to me. We woke up next morning in bunks in Jeb's old shack with three of the worst hangovers this tired old world has ever seen. Putting together my own fuzzy recollections with those of my colleagues, what happened was as follows.

We went out to the Sutherland home and took up a position beneath an upstairs window which George said he thought belonged to Mamie's bedroom. I hoped he was right because Mamie's father, Duncan, was a dour Scot with about as much sense of humour as a hitching post. I sure didn't want to tangle with him. Mamie got all her charm and ebullience from her Irish mother. Mal Morgan lived next door to the Sutherlands, so his house was at our backs.

We held a powwow about what we should do next. After a good deal of discussion, we launched off on a rendition of "I Love You Truly." I have a voice like an asthmatic crow, but when I'm in my cups I think I can sing harmony. George's voice was nearly as bad as mine – sort of a croupy growl. I presume he thought he was singing bass. Surprisingly enough, Jeb turned out to have a beautiful voice – a high, lyric Irish tenor. He carried us through to what we fancied was a soulful dramatic finale. When we finished, we waited expectantly for some appreciative and romantic reaction from Mamie. None was forthcoming.

I got tired of waiting and decided to toss a pebble at the window. Jeb claimed later that my pebble was as big as a baseball Maybe it was, because it went right through the upper part of the window with a crash. That got some action. There was a flutter of white and we could dimly see Mamie's startled face. She raised the lower window and crouched down so that just her face was visible over the window sill. She looked beautiful with her hair hanging loosely down to her shoulders. The moon was at our backs, so we could see her clearly.

"What on earth's going on down there?" she whispered.

"We're serenading you," I explained.

"Well, that's very nice of you, I'm sure. But why didn't you all sing the same song?"

"We did," I protested. "We were singing harmony."

"Oh, sorry," said Mamie chuckling. "Who threw the rock through my window?"

"Merv did," said George promptly – the big blabbermouth.

"Why?"

"I wanted to get your attention," I explained.

"Well, you certainly succeeded," said Mamie with a bubbling laugh. "Wasn't there a more subtle method you could have used?"

"Couldn't think of one offhand."

"Tell me, boys," said Mamie. "This is just a wild guess, but by any chance have you been drinking?"

There was a long pause. "To be perfectly honest," said George finally, "and I am always perfectly honest when there is no alternative, we have hoisted a few, I admit. But it was just a few, wasn't it fellows?"

"Oh yes, just a few," said Jeb and I hastily.

Mamie giggled. "I kind of suspect it was quite a few. Well boys, thanks very much for the lovely serenade. Now you'd better get along home before you wake up all the neighbours. Good night."

"No, no, Mamie," I interposed hastily. "Don't go. We came to seek your hand in marriage."

"Also the rest of you too," added Jeb practically.

Mamie laughed. "This is very flattering, but I can't very well marry all three of you. Merv, do you really want to marry me?"

"Madame, my heart is at your disposal," I said grandly. I bowed deeply.

"How about you, Jeb?" asked Mamie.

"I would be delighted ma'am," said Jeb. "But I would advise you against it. I ain't no bargain."

"Now just a minute you two," interrupted George. "You were supposed to support me – not make a pitch on your own behalf. That's what I get for getting involved with a couple of drunken bums."

"I resent that," I said huffily. "I may be drunk, but I'm no bum."

"I resent it too," said Jeb. "I may be a bum, but I'm not drunk."

"For Pete's sake, Mamie," said Mal Morgan's voice behind us, "say you'll marry one of those bums, so we can all get back to sleep." We turned around. Mal's round, fat face was dimly visible at an upstairs window.

"Hi, Mal," said Mamie. "Which one of them do you think I ought to marry?"

"It don't look like there's a hell of a lot of choice. Just go eeny-meeny-miny-mo," said Mal. "I just wish I was twenty years younger myself, by gad, and I'd be in the line-up too."

"This has to be the craziest marriage proposal of all time," laughed Mamie.

"Any proposal of marriage is crazy," observed Mal.

"Don't knock it, Mal," said Mamie happily. "It isn't every night a girl gets three-and-a-half marriage proposals."

The more I thought about it, the more I realized that George was absolutely right – Mamie was an angel. Not many girls would put up with being awakened in the middle of the night by a rock thrown through her window without getting mad about it. On the contrary, she was apparently enjoying the whole silly situation.

"Mamie," I said. "George says you are an angel and I agree with him a hundred percent."

"George," said Mamie in a surprised voice. "Did you really say I am an angel?"

George sort of shuffled his feet. "Well yes, I did."

"You never told me."

"I just never got around to it, I guess. Damn it, things aren't working out at all the way they were supposed to. I came here to propose to you and my so-called friends were going to help. I guess it was all a mistake." George sounded disgruntled. "I guess we'd better leave."

"Did you really and truly come here to propose to me?" asked Mamie.

"Yes, I did."

"Then why don't you?"

"I thought I had already done so."

"Not really. Everybody else did."

"Well, uh, will you marry me, Mamie?"

"Why should I?"

"What do you mean, 'Why should I?' That's a silly question if I ever heard one."

"Tell her you love her, you stupid oaf," I whispered fiercely.

"Oh hell, Mamie," said George in an exasperated voice, "how

can I tell you I love you, surrounded by a Greek chorus of two drunks and a nosy neighbour."

"Go ahead and try, George boy," encouraged Mal.

"Yeah, go ahead," I urged, poking him with my elbow.

"I'm waiting, George," said Mamie quietly.

George gulped and spluttered. His usual poise was completely shattered. Finally he blurted, "I love you, Mamie. Will you marry me?"

"I love you too, George," said Mamie gently. "Yes, I'll marry you. And now . . . good night." She blew him a kiss and disappeared from the window.

Jeb and I let out a war whoop. "We did it," I shouted. "Congratulations, old pal." We pounded George on the back; we shook his hand; we danced around him; we sang bits of the wedding march.

"Congratulations, George," hollered Mal from the window. "It was touch and go there for awhile, but you came through noble. And now you idiots buzz off so us law-abiding citizens can get some sleep."

"Good night, Mal," we shouted back.

We linked arms and walked happily up the street singing, "Those Wedding Bells are Breaking Up That Old Gang of Mine." In three-part harmony too.

ABOUT THE AUTHOR

Dr. Mervyn J. Huston has a long and distinguished career as a scientist and an educator. He was for thirty-two years Dean of the Faculty of Pharmacy and Pharmaceutical Sciences at the University of Alberta before retiring as Professor Emeritus in 1978. He was born in Ashcroft, British Columbia, in 1912, and took his early education there and in Kamloops. He was awarded the B.Sc. (Pharmacy) in 1937, and the M.Sc. (Biochemistry) in 1941, by the University of Alberta, and the Ph.D. (Pharmacology) in 1944 by the University of Washington. He has been active in professional affairs including: President of the Canadian Pharmaceutical Association; President of the Canadian Foundation for the Advancement of Pharmacy; Canadian delegate to the Council of the Federation International Pharmaceutique; and, for fifteen years, Editor of the Canadian Journal of Pharmaceutical Sciences. He was awarded the Centennial Medal in 1968, the Dr. E.R. Squibb Award in Pharmacy, Biochemistry and Public Health in 1971, and the Alberta Achievement Award in 1971. He has published four textbooks and over a hundred scientific and professional papers.

There is another side to this distinguished academic. He financed his university education playing saxophone in dance bands and bassoon in the Edmonton Symphony Orchestra, and once rode a bucking cayuse (for a short time) in a rodeo. He has established himself as one of Canada's favorite humorists by the publication of the bestselling *The Great Canadian Lover*, (Hurtig 1969), *Toasts to the Bride*, (Hurtig 1969), and *Canada Eh to Zed*, (Hurtig 1973). He draws on his experience as an avid golf duffer in the editing of *Great Golf Humour*, (Hurtig 1977). He has now followed up his golfing enthusiasm with another milestone, *Golf and Murphy's Law*, (Hurtig 1981).

With *Gophers Don't Pay Taxes*, (Tree Frog Press 1981), he sees the realization of his favorite book. The creation of the Blossom stories has been his overriding passion for the past decade.